D1025293

PORTOBELLO

**Center Point
Large Print**

**This Large Print Book carries the
Seal of Approval of N.A.V.H.**

Ruth Rendell

PORTOBELLO

CENTER POINT PUBLISHING
THORNDIKE, MAINE

This Center Point Large Print edition
is published in the year 2010 by arrangement with
Scribner, a division of Simon & Schuster, Inc.

The text of this Large Print edition is unabridged.
In other aspects, this book may vary
from the original edition.
Printed in the United States of America
on permanent paper.
Set in 16-point Times New Roman type.

ISBN: 978-1-60285-883-1

Library of Congress Cataloging-in-Publication Data

Rendell, Ruth, 1930-
  Portobello / Ruth Rendell. — Center Point large print ed.
    p. cm.
  ISBN 978-1-60285-883-1 (library binding : alk. paper)
  1. Notting Hill (London, England)—Fiction. 2. Psychological fiction.
  3. Large type books. I. Title.
PR6068.E63P67 2010
823'.914—dc22
                                                          2010021035

For Doreen and Les Massey with love

1

IT IS CALLED the Portobello Road because a long time ago a sea captain called Robert Jenkins stood in front of a committee of the House of Commons and held up his amputated ear. Spanish coast guards, he said, had boarded his ship in the Caribbean, cut off his ear, pillaged the vessel, then set it adrift. Public opinion had already been aroused by other Spanish outrages, and the Jenkins episode was the last straw to those elements in Parliament which opposed Walpole's government. They demanded British vengeance and so began the War of Jenkins's Ear.

In the following year, 1739, Admiral Vernon captured the city of Puerto Bello in the Caribbean. It was one of those successes that are popular with patriotic Englishmen, though many hardly knew what the point of it was. In the words of a poet writing about another battle and another war: "That I cannot tell, said he, but 'twas a famous victory." Vernon's triumph put Puerto Bello on the map and gave rise to a number of commemorative names. Notting Hill and Kensal were open country then where sheep and cattle grazed, and one landowner called his fields Portobello Farm. In time the lane that led to it became the Portobello Road. But for Jenkins's ear it would have been called something else.

Street markets abounded in the area, in Kenley Street, Sirdar Road, Norland Road, Crescent Street, and Golborne Road. The one to survive was the Portobello, and from 1927 onwards a daily market was held there from eight in the morning to eight in the evening and 8 a.m. till 9 p.m. on Saturdays. It still is, and in a much reduced state on Sundays too. The street is long, like a centipede snaking up from Pembridge Road in the south to Kensal Town in the north, its legs splaying out all the way and almost reaching the Great Western main line and the Grand Union Canal. Shops line it and spill into the legs, which are its side streets. Stalls fill most of the centre, for though traffic crosses it and some cars crawl patiently along it among the people, few use it as a thoroughfare. The Portobello has a rich personality, vibrant, brilliant in colour, noisy, with graffiti that approach art, bizarre and splendid. An indefinable edge to it adds a spice of danger. There is nothing safe about the Portobello, nothing suburban. It is as far from an average shopping street as can be imagined. Those who love and those who barely know it have called it the world's finest street market.

You can buy anything there. Everything on earth is on sale: furniture, antiques, clothes, bedding, hardware, music, food and food and more food. Vegetables and fruit, meat and fish, and cheese and chocolate. The stalls sell jewellery, hats, masks, prints, postcards old and new, shawls and scarves, shoes and boots, pots and pans, flowers real and artificial, furs and fake furs, lamps and musical instruments. You can buy a harp there or a birdcage, a stuffed bear or a wedding dress, or the latest bestseller. If you want to eat your lunch in the street, you can buy paella or pancakes, piping hot from a stall. But no live animals or birds are for sale.

Cheap books in excellent condition are on sale in the Oxfam shop. A little way up the road is the Spanish deli which sells, mysteriously, along with all its groceries, fine earthenware pots and bowls and dishes. There is a minimarket in most of the centipede's legs and at Portobello Green a covered market under a peaked tent like a poor man's Sydney Opera House. In Tavistock Road the house fronts are painted red and green and yellow and gray.

The moment you turn out of Pembridge Road or Westbourne Grove or Chepstow Villas and set foot in the market, you feel a touch of excitement, an indrawing of breath, a pinch in the heart. And once you have been, you have to go again. Thousands of visitors wander up and down it on Saturdays. It has caught them in the way a beauty spot can catch you and it pulls you back. Its thread attaches itself to you and a twitch on it summons you to return.

9

• • •

QUITE A LONG way up the Portobello Road, a glossy arcade now leads visitors into the hinterland. There is a children's clothes shop, for the children of the wealthy who go to select private schools, a shop that sells handmade soaps, pink and green and brown and highly scented, another where you can buy jerseys and T-shirts but exclusively cashmere, and a place that calls itself a studio, which offers for sale small watercolours and even smaller marble obelisks. It was here, long before the arcade came into being, that Arnold Wren had his gallery. He never called it that but preferred the humbler designation *shop.*

Stalls filled the pavement outside. Mostly fruit and vegetables up here. When Arnold's son, Eugene, was a little boy, the vegetables and fruit were of a kind that had been sold in English markets for generations. Eugene's grandmother could remember when the first tomato appeared, and he, now a man of fifty, saw the first avocado appear on old Mr. Gibson's stall. The boy's mother didn't like the taste, she said she might as well be eating green soap.

Arnold sold paintings and prints, and small pieces of sculpture. In rooms at the back of the shop stacks of paintings occupied most of the available space. He made enough money to keep himself, his wife, and his only son in comfort in their unprepossessing but quite comfortable

10

house in Chesterton Road. Then, one day when the boy was in his teens, his father took his family on holiday to Vienna. There, in an exhibition, Arnold saw paintings by the Swiss symbolist Arnold Böcklin on loan from various European galleries. The Christian name struck him because it was the same as his own. Arnold Wren never forgot the paintings; they haunted his dreams and later on he could have described some of Böcklin's works in the greatest detail entirely from memory, *The Isle of the Dead*, the frightening self-portrait with the skeleton's hand on Böcklin's shoulder, the *Centaurs Fighting*.

He had forgotten where most of the paintings in the rooms behind the shop came from. Some had been inherited from his father. Others were sold to him for shillings rather than pounds by people clearing out their attics. There were thousands of attics in old Notting Hill. But looking through the paintings one day, wondering if this one or that one was worth keeping at all, he came upon a picture that reminded him of Vienna. It wasn't at all like *The Isle of the Dead* or *The Centaur at the Forge*, but it had the scent of Böcklin about it, which made him catch his breath.

It was a painting of a mermaid swimming inside a glass vase with a narrow neck, trying perhaps—from the expression on her face of fear and desperation—to climb out of the water and

11

the vase. All was glaucous green but for her rosy flesh and her long golden hair. Arnold Wren called the picture *Undine in a Goldfish Bowl* and showed it to an expert without telling him what he suspected. The expert said, "Well, Mr. Wren, I am ninety-nine percent certain this is by Arnold Böcklin."

Arnold was an honest man and he said to the potential purchaser of the painting, "I'm ninety-nine percent sure this is a Böcklin," but Morris Stemmer, rich and arrogant, fancied himself an expert and was a hundred percent sure. He paid Arnold the sort of sum usually said to be "beyond one's wildest dreams." This enabled Arnold to buy a house in Chepstow Villas, a Jaguar, and to go farther afield than Vienna on his holidays. His was a Portobello Road success story while old Mr. Gibson was a failure. Or so it appeared on the surface.

When his father died, Eugene Wren moved the business to premises in upmarket Kensington Church Street and referred to it as "the gallery." The name in gilded letters on a dark green background was EUGENE WREN, FINE ART and, partly through luck and partly due to Eugene's flair for spotting new young artists and what from times past was about to become fashionable, made him a great deal of money.

Without being a thief himself, Albert Gibson the stallholder married into a family of thieves.

His only son, Gilbert, had been in and out of prison more times than his wife, Ivy, cared to count. That, she told her relatives, was why they had no children. Gib was never home for long enough. She was living in Blagrove Road when they built the Westway, which cut the street in two and turned 2 Blagrove Villas into a detached house. The Aclam Road minimarket separated it from the overhead road and the train line, and the Portobello Road was a stone's throw away if you were a marksman with a strong arm and a steady eye.

2

JOEL ROSEMAN NEVER walked with a purpose, a destination. He wasn't going anywhere but mostly round in a sort of circle from his flat in a mansion block at the eastern end of Notting Hill Gate and back again. Once, when he first tried it, he had attempted going out in the late afternoon, but it was March and still broad daylight. Next time he went out after dark and that was better. Sometimes he walked clockwise into Bayswater, down to the Bayswater Road and home again, sometimes widdershins, in a loop up to Campden Hill and back to the high street. Mostly he wandered aimlessly.

For a long time now he had found life better in darkness. That was why he dreaded the summer,

13

when it wouldn't start getting dark till ten. But now it was April and exceptionally warm, light too in the evenings but dusk coming at seven. He wore sunglasses, a special pair in which the lenses were darker than usual. At home he had several pairs of sunglasses but none with lenses as black and smoky as these.

The allowance Pa had paid into his account regularly on the tenth of the month had just come in on the previous day. Joel brooded on Pa as he walked along, wondering in despair what made him tick, why he was so cruel, and how it was possible that a man whose child had drowned could have that picture hanging up in his house. He stopped thinking about it when he found a cash dispenser in a bank wall at the bottom of Pembridge Road. The sunglasses had to come off briefly while he drew out 140 pounds. It came in twenty- and ten- and five-pound notes. Carefully looking over his shoulder (as the bank said you should) he put twenty-five pounds into the pocket of his jeans and the rest into an envelope. This went into an inside breast pocket of his rain-proof jacket. There was no sign of rain, but Joel possessed few clothes and this jacket had happened to be hanging up, in the dark, just inside his front door.

He was taking these precautions with his money because he intended walking up the Portobello Road. It would be his first visit. He put his sunglasses on again and the world went dark and rather foggy. When she was young, his mother had lived in Notting Hill, and she had told him—she went on speaking to him when Pa did not—that if your house was burgled and your silver stolen, the police would advise you to go look for it on the stalls in the Portobello Road, where you were likely to find it up for sale. This had made Joel think that the market was a dangerous place, somewhere to be careful, but he had decided that the stallholders would be packing up by seven thirty. He was surprised to see that this was not so. The place was blazing with light and colour, packed with jostling people, voices and music, a flourishing trade still going on. When the natural light was dying, they had to make up for it artificially. They never thought what it was like for people of his sort. He blinked behind his glasses. According to his mother, Pa called him a mole and sometimes an earthworm.

No one took any notice of him. He walked up the western side, past knitwear shops and blanket shops and print and china shops. It surprised him to see any shops at all because he had expected only stalls. These were there in abundance, shops on the left, stalls on the right, and people, hundreds of people, walking, dawdling, strolling between them and up the roadway itself. All the people looked busy and happy. Joel could always spot happiness, he was an expert at noticing it, perhaps because in everyone he personally knew it was absent. On the other side of the road crowds were going home, heading southwards for the tube and the buses. They looked happy too and, the ones carrying bags and packages, satisfied or excited. He went on, not stopping, not considering buying anything. He never needed anything except food and not much of that. He shopped for nothing else. The special sunglasses were his last buy and he had had them for two years.

By the time he had been walking fairly steadily for twenty minutes, he came to the pub Ma had mentioned called the Earl of Lonsdale. He crossed the road and turned down Westbourne Grove. No one had looked menacingly at him while he was in the market, and he was beginning to think reports of the place had been exaggerated. But it was still a relief to find himself among the genteel boutiques and soon the gracious houses of this corner of Notting Hill. He had begun to feel a little tired. Well, they told him he had a heart problem. Young as he was, he had a bad heart.

It was quiet. The poor live among strident voices, clatter, crashes, deafening music, barking dogs, shrieking children, but places inhabited by the rich are always silent. Tall trees, burgeoning into spring leaf, line their streets and their gardens bloom with appropriate flowers all the year round. Joel was reminded by the silence, if by nothing else, of Hampstead Garden Suburb, where Pa and Ma had a big, low-roofed house squatting in landscaped grounds. Around here wasn't much like that, but the peace and quiet were the same, yet somehow uneasy, almost uncanny.

No one was about but for two men, not much more than boys, loitering on an opposite corner. They wore jackets or coats with hoods pulled down over their eyes, and Joel had learnt from newspapers he occasionally saw that hoods meant their wearers were up to no good. They looked at him and he looked at them, and he told himself that they would do nothing to him because they could see he was young and tall and they didn't know that his pockets were full of money. He looked poor in his old clothes, his ragged jeans and that jacket with one sleeve torn and the other stained.

He had once read somewhere about the assassination of the Empress Elisabeth of Austria, how she had been walking onto a boat, which was to take her across Lake Geneva, when she had felt someone jostle her and she received a mild enough blow in the chest. Only when she was in her stateroom, some minutes later, was it realised she had been stabbed and was about to die. This was how Joel thought afterwards of what happened to him on the corner of Pembridge Crescent and Chepstow Road. He had been struck not in the chest, but on the left shoulder and from the back. He felt the pain grip him with iron claws down his upper left arm.

Perhaps he cried out. He never knew. He fell or sank or plunged to the ground. But he must have leant backwards at some point for his head struck against the bell push in a plastered brick pillar, which was one of the gateposts of the house on the corner. Had someone assaulted him, as someone had assaulted the Empress Elisabeth? He forgot that he had a bad heart, he forgot everything as he lost consciousness.

THE TWO BOYS in the hoods crossed the street and stared fearfully at this shabby, long-haired man who lay spread-eagled on the pavement. They thought he was dead. The front door of the house behind those pillars opened. They ran.

If Joel had fallen forwards, his mother told him, no one and nothing would have pressed that bell. He would have died. What she didn't tell him, until a lot later and she was in a temper, was that his father had said it was a pity he hadn't. As it was, the occupants of the house had come out to see why their chimes were ringing and ringing. They found him slumped against the pillar and called an ambulance.

3

JUST FIFTY YEARS old, single still but not unattached, Eugene Wren was a tall, handsome man who would have looked young for his age but for his white hair. It was thick hair, a glossy thatch, but there was no doubt that it aged him. He minded this but he was careful not to let it show that he minded, just as, though he chose his clothes with care and wore them with appropriateness, he gave the impression of being indifferent to his appearance. Only his girlfriend knew that his sight wasn't perfect but that he wore contact lenses.

He was secretive. Why? Who can tell why we are the way we are? Psychiatrists can. Innumerable books have been written tracing our faults and foibles, fantasies, criminal tendencies, sexual tastes, inhibitions, and other peculiarities back to events in our childhoods. Eugene had read a good many of them without being any the wiser. He could have understood his secretiveness if when owning up to something as a child he had been punished, but his parents had unvaryingly been loving, easygoing, and kind. In fact, he was encouraged to be open. It made no difference. He kept hold of his secrets. Like his mind, his house in Chepstow Villas held many secret drawers and locked boxes.

One of his secrets was his addictive personality. He had been a heavy drinker and had never given up drink but, by an almost superhuman effort, cut down to a reasonable couple of glasses of wine a day. That was before he met Ella, so he was able to keep his onetime alcoholism a secret from her. The breakup with his previous girlfriend, a long-term partner of several years, had happened because she found the bottle of vodka he kept in the bottom of a wardrobe he thought he had locked. His smoking was impossible to hide. But as he had with his drinking habit, he eventually conquered it. Several attempts were made at giving up, the last and successful one helped by nicotine patches and hypnotism. It had been horrible for Eugene to reveal his weakness to Ella, not least of it the disclosing that he had a weakness. But when it was over, he was quite proud of himself and Ella was proud.

"You can't really continue to smoke when you are going about with a doctor of medicine," he said to her with a light laugh.

For a while he was without an addiction, but not for long.

He hoped he wouldn't put on weight, though he didn't say this to Ella, and when he did put it on, he did his best to keep it secret. The difficulty was that he tended to eat between meals. Once he would have had a cigarette.

Eugene called his habit snacking and Ella called

it grazing. To combat it he tried eating Polo mints, but he didn't really like the taste of mint, and besides, Polos had sugar in them. Considering how he fulminated against gum-chewing, especially against those who spat out their gum on the pavement, he couldn't take it up himself. Well, he could, but it would have to be done in secret and that would be just one more secret. He was anxious not to succumb to deception with Ella. No doubt he would soon propose to Ella and they would live happily ever after, something he sincerely wished and thought likely. Then he had what he called the fat-bridegroom dream. He was standing at the altar in a morning suit, marrying Ella, and when he looked down to take the ring out of his pocket, all he saw was his huge paunch. He said nothing of this to Ella but pretended to be indifferent to weight or girth.

IT WAS A Saturday morning and he was on his way to the shops. It would be a long walk, some of it perhaps not a walk but a taxi ride. What he sought wasn't readily obtainable even in the sort of shops whose business (he thought) was to sell it. On occasion it was a weary quest he undertook. Although it had been going on for no more than six weeks, sometimes he found it hard to remember what he had done with his time before that day he went into the pharmacy at the top of the Portobello Road.

But spring had come, the day was fine, and his scales had just informed him he had lost two pounds. Think of the positive things, he told himself, think what a harmless indulgence this is, then, glancing down at the pavement, he saw the sprawl of litter. A tumble of fish and chips remains, part but not all of a bright blue polystyrene container, a can that had once held Red Bull, and some fragments of a meat pie. Eugene recoiled from this rubbish but braced himself to remove it. The plastic carrier he always took with him on a shopping expedition (in the interest of saving the planet) he took out of his pocket, and covering his fingers with a tissue, he picked up and deposited inside it the remains of some lowlife's supper. Underneath it—or, rather, behind it, up against a garden wall, pillar, and hedge—was an unsealed and bulging envelope. When he picked it up, he could see that inside were five or six twenty-pound notes, a ten, and a five.

Without counting the notes, he put the envelope into his pocket before dropping the plastic bag into the next waste bin he passed. Ahead of him he could see in the distance the swarms of people, mostly young, heading for the Portobello Road market. It was always the same on Saturdays. They poured off the buses and out of Notting Hill tube station and charged along, talking and laughing at the top of their voices, in their weekly quest for bargains and the companionship of their fellow shoppers.

As soon as he had the chance, Eugene turned left to avoid them. Not that he disliked the Portobello Road, but he preferred it on Sundays when it was half-empty and you could see its buildings and feel its charm. On weekdays he only went there now for one purpose, and he had been up to the pharmacy in Golborne Road on the previous Tuesday. Today one of the other selected shops he patronised must be visited. So now to the serious business of the morning.

What would they think he was in need of and was off to buy, those shoppers heading for the market whose indifferent gaze rested briefly on him before passing on? If they thought about it at all, they would assume that a man seeking an addictive substance would look for alcohol, tobacco, cocaine, heroin, amphetamines, ecstasy, crack, or, at the very least, marijuana. Eugene allowed himself to feel vaguely glad that it was none of these he sought.

It had begun when he decided he must find some way to curb his appetite. Some kind of slimming pills, he had vaguely thought. But when first he turned out of the Portobello Road in the direction of the illuminated green cross outside the Golborne Pharmacy, it wasn't with slimming or appetite suppression in mind but in search of a plug-in mosquito repellent for the summer ahead.

Though it was early March, on the previous night his sleep had been disturbed by the whine of a mosquito in his bedroom, and he had spent a frustrating quarter of an hour flapping about with a towel before squashing the thing. Paying for the device, he noticed a row of packets of sugar-free sweets absurdly named Lemfresh, Strawpink, and Chocorange on the counter by the till. Probably they tasted disgusting. But he picked up a Chocorange and read the label on it: sugar-free, healthy, tooth-friendly, it said, only four calories per pastille. Suppose they didn't taste too bad. He could eat one halfway between breakfast and lunch, and one between lunch and dinner or maybe two. He could give it a try. They had no sugar in them and few calories.

He took two packets, one Chocorange and one Strawpink. It was four o'clock and hunger was beginning to bite. Like every container these days, the Chocorange pack was hard to open, but he got there. It held perhaps a dozen dark brown lozenges. Tentatively, Eugene put one in his mouth and was pleasantly surprised by the taste. A rich chocolate flavour with a hint of sharp citrus. Delicious, really. And no bitter aftertaste, which used to be the case with sugar substitutes. He took another to confirm his judgment, trying a Strawpink this time. Nice enough, with an authentic flavour of strawberries but a bit insipid, not a patch on Chocorange.

Why not keep some of these by him so that he could help himself to one or two instead of snacking? Money didn't worry him, but if it had, these were cheap enough for anyone to afford: seventy-five pence a packet. And he knew where to find them. Golborne Road was ten minutes' walk away from his house. It looked as if he had found the solution. No voice inside his head said, "Don't go there." No small cautionary thought came to him, telling him to remember the cigarettes, climbing from five to forty a day, or the drinking, which started with two glasses of wine and mounted to a bottle of vodka plus wine, and now was only shakily reduced to two glasses once more. Don't go there was unspoken or went unheard.

Should he tell Ella? Sucking a Chocorange, he had asked himself that on the way home from the pharmacy. Of course. He must. She would be pleased that he had found such a simple solution. On the other hand, perhaps he wouldn't tell her. She, after all, was a doctor and one who often said how much she disapproved of additives, E numbers, and the various inadequately tested chemicals that found their way into food today. The Chocorange packet carried a daunting list of the chemicals in it. She might try to stop him. She might tell him it was healthier to have an expanding waistline than fill up his body with junk.

"We're not talking about obesity," she had said the other day apropos of something else. "Being a little overweight won't do you any harm." After all, she was a little overweight herself, though he loved her the way she was.

But it should remain his secret. After all, he was a secretive man and there was no use in pretending otherwise. Not to himself. He might pretend to others, but was that not the essence of secretiveness?

SIX WEEKS HAD passed since that day, which had also been fine and sunny, much like this one, only today was hotter than had been expected for April, but that, of course, was global warming. It was hard not to be glad of its side effects, warmth and perpetual sunshine. The trees were in the sort of full leaf usual three weeks later, the cherry blossom was past and the lilac out. The gardens of this part of west London had the exaggerated look of a seedsman's catalog illustrations, banks of pink and white blossom above cushions of purple and rose, all overhung by frondy branches of lemony green and a rich dark emerald. Six weeks. In those weeks he had consumed a large number of packets of Chocorange, and now he was on his way to replenish his stocks. In them too he had lost weight.

Visiting pharmacists was what this now regular Saturday-morning quest of his was all about.

One of these was in sight, in a parade of shops on the other side of Notting Hill Gate; he couldn't bring himself to call in there. He had visited it last Saturday and the pharmacist would remember such a recent purchase and, worse, make some comment such as "You're really fond of these things, aren't you?" or, most horrible and shame-making because almost true, "You must have your fix, mustn't you?"

He began to walk down Kensington Church Street, where there were no pharmacists but only antique dealers, picture galleries, and purveyors of eighteenth-century furniture. About to pass Eugene Wren, Fine Art, in accordance with his nature, rather in the way he wished for no comments on his behaviour from pharmacists, he kept his eyes averted as if fascinated by the sight on the opposite side of the street of a young man emerging from the florists under an enormous bouquet of flowers. It wasn't that he doubted all was well inside the shop but, rather, that he wanted to go about his Saturday business unobserved. Dorinda Clements, in charge in his absence, was entirely reliable. He sometimes made jokes with valued customers, for instance, that she was "management incarnate" and that he trusted her more than he trusted himself. But he didn't want her knowing his private business.

The only regular stockists of what he sought were the pharmacy and cosmetics chain Elixir.

They had become his default store and, like Dorinda, unfailingly reliable, but again their assistants were human, had eyes and memories, and were also capable of remarking on his frequent visits. How satisfactory it would be when you could do all your shopping without benefit of other human beings and, as you already could in some supermarkets, put your credit card into a machine, key in various numbers, and—hey, presto!—you had paid for your goods. You had kept your secrets. Better not go to Elixir today, then, though he could see the branch he most often used ahead of him in Kensington High Street. That was the one where, a few weeks back, he had bought his second packet of Chocorange, replacement for the one from Golborne Road. As he had intended it should, Chocorange had admirably fulfilled its purpose. As a between-meals snack it worked, deadening his hunger and staving off grazing; the result had been that he had lost those two pounds he had gained and then one more. If it had a drawback, this was, paradoxically, that it tasted too delicious. Eugene had never got over how something synthetic and harmless could taste so good. The result was that instead of one or two eaten in the morning, he tended to take three or four, and in the late afternoon, once he had started, he found it hard to stop. Sometimes, between three and reaching home at six, he ate half a packet. Still, it worked and that was the main thing. The unfortunate thing was that not all pharmacists stocked them, and those that did tended to run out.

He would try a place farther along towards Knightsbridge. This was a small shop called Bolus, run by a stout Asian man with a chilly manner. That suited Eugene. He went in and picked up two packets of tissues and a tube of toothpaste before raising his eyes to the section on the counter where Mr. Prasad presided. The brown-and-orange design on the small packets always leapt to Eugene's eyes before any other colours—you might have said that in this situation there were no other colours—but their absence was as immediately noticeable. The red and pink of strawberry flavour were present, the green of mint, but not a single pack of Chocorange. Mr. Prasad had sold out. Eugene might have admitted to himself, but did not, that this was largely due to his own excessive buying. After all, the inhabitants of this part of west London, though no strangers to addiction in various forms, weren't prone to spend their leisure time seeking sugar-free sweets.

Eugene was paying for his tissues and his toothpaste when Mr. Prasad said in what sounded like sarcastic tones, "Your favourites will be in by the end of the week."

The unexpectedness of this assault as well as its content brought the blood rushing into

Eugene's cheeks. He muttered, "Er, yes, thanks."

"Would you like me to put in a double order next time?"

"Oh, no, thank you. Really, that won't be necessary."

He wanted to flee but he made himself saunter out of the shop. He would never go in there again. That went without saying. This subtraction reduced the possible Chocorange outlets to ten. Yet, why couldn't he have looked the man in the eye, laughed lightly, and said, yes, he'd like some ordered specially for him? He was more or less hooked on the things, as Mr. Prasad doubtless knew, ha-ha. They were so tasty. Why couldn't he say all that? He doubted if he could actually utter the word *tasty,* just as he couldn't say *toilet* or *kinky.*

He began to recognise he would have to go farther afield, perhaps to the outer suburbs. Of course, as always happened in these circumstances, he began to experience a craving for a Chocorange, the smooth oval shape of it, the rich creamy flavour of milk chocolate, and the sharp sweetness of citrus. There was nothing for it now but Elixir. They always had Chocorange in stock; indeed, in stock in reassuringly large quantities. His most recent visit to one of their branches had been to the store in Marylebone High Street and before that to New Oxford Street. It must be at least a fortnight since he had used the branch in Paddington Station. Enough walking had been done for one day and Eugene hailed a taxi.

He didn't ask the taxi driver to take him to Paddington Station; not, that is, through the glazed-in approach area in front of the entrance where Isambard Kingdom Brunel, architect of the Great Western Railway, sits on his plinth. That would have led to the driver asking him what time his train was, whether he wanted him to take this route or that, and what was his destination. Better ask the man to set him down in one of the streets that run from Sussex Gardens to Praed Street and leave him to make his own way to the station. He had tried to remember street names but only came up with Spring Street. That would do.

The first thing he noticed—the first thing he always noticed—was the illuminated sign with the green cross on it that hangs above pharmacies. There it was, halfway up little Spring Street, a small shop like Mr. Prasad's between a bank and an estate agent. Eugene felt that catch of breath and lifting of the heart most people would associate with the sight of the person one is in love with. He used to feel it at first sight of Ella; now it was for a purveyor of sugar-free sweets. Don't think of it like that, he told himself, don't be silly. The pharmacist this time was a woman, also Asian, wearing a sari, beautiful, calm, with downcast eyes. But he didn't look at her. The moment he entered her shop a plethora of Chocorange, radiant in their orange-and-brown wrappings, seemed to leap up and meet his eyes, to jostle for his attention. This was a treasure to add to his list, a number eleven to oust Prasad's Bolus forever. Without bothering to stock up on more tissues and toothpaste, he went up to the counter, picked out three packets of Chocorange, and laid them in front of the deferential shop-keeper. She smiled at him, but courteously, without a hint of cunning or amusement, and rang up the sum of two pounds twenty-five.

NOW FREE TO make his other purchases, Eugene took a bus back to Notting Hill, where he bought the ingredients for the dinner he intended to cook for Ella that evening and dropped into one of the bags the envelope he had picked up earlier. Walking home with his two fairly heavy bags and sucking his second Chocorange of the morning, he wondered if tonight would be a good time to ask Ella to marry him, whether it might not be better to put it off for a further week or two. After all, their present arrangement worked pleasantly. There were none of the problems of living under the same roof but plenty of lovely sex two or three times a week. He checked these thoughts, while telling himself that all men thought along these lines. He loved Ella. If she wasn't quite the only woman he had ever loved, he loved her best.

He could hardly imagine being parted from her.

But he was secretive. Should someone who treasured his privacy so much marry at all? Still, he had more or less been living with Ella, at least at the weekends and on holidays, for three years now. She hadn't probed into his secret life. But another problem was this habit of his. Even as things were, there were difficulties. Once or twice she had caught him out and he had had to say he had a sore throat and was "just giving these things a go." Worst, he had been obliged to offer her one, which she had taken and liked. When he got married, he would have to give up. He knew he must give up anyway and to some extent longed to give up, but, like St. Augustine and sex, he asked to be released from his habit but not yet. After all, as he told himself every day, several times a day, it was harmless. He enjoyed it so much. And it stopped him from eating calorific food. Once, when he was cooking as he intended to cook this evening, he would have picked at and tasted the ingredients. Tasted again during the process and before he served the food. Now two Chocoranges would see him through.

At home he unpacked the groceries first. The Chocorange were in his shoulder bag, and there also was the envelope containing the five-, ten-, and twenty-pound notes and the pound note he had found on the corner of the street. Sucking his third Chocorange of the day, he counted the notes. Some drug dealer's haul, he thought vaguely, but perhaps not. Eugene wasn't indifferent to other people's feelings, especially in the matter of money, and it might be, though he couldn't as yet see how, that these were someone's legitimate earnings that he had dropped—while being attacked? Such things happened and more often than ever these days. The obvious thing was to take the money to the police station in Ladbroke Grove. But he had another idea.

He sat down at his desk and wrote, *Found in Chepstow Villas a sum of money between eighty and a hundred and sixty pounds. Anyone who has lost such a sum should apply to the phone number below.* He transferred this to his computer in various sizes and styles of type and printed it out. He would attach it to one of the lampposts as his neighbors attached appeals for lost cats. Armed with Sellotape and Blu Tack, he went outside into the street with his sheet of paper and looked for a suitable lamppost. For the past week such an appeal had been fastened to the post outside number 62 and it was still there, though the missing animal, a spiteful Persian kitten called Bathsheba, had returned home two days before. Eugene peeled off the notice and put up his own in its stead.

He thought about it while he was cooking

Ella's dinner. The applicant had only a telephone number. But he had no intention of handing over the money on a phone call alone. Whoever applied must be invited here and then asked to name precisely the sum he had lost. Not 80 or 160 pounds but somewhere in between. No one could get it right except by the most enormous coincidence or by being the true loser of the money.

The phone call was really something to look forward to. He would tell Ella all about it later. Absently, he helped himself to another Chocorange.

4

YOU COULDN'T WALK down any of these posh streets without coming on a notice appealing for a lost cat. Always on the lookout for moneymaking scams, Lance thought it might be a good idea to find one of them and take it as a what-you-call-it, a hostage. You could ask a big ransom. Those crazy cat owners would pay anything you cared to name. The difficulty, of course, was to catch a cat. One of them, a stripy chestnut and dark brown job, had just come out from a bank of greenery and flowers and sat down on the wall opposite the lamp standard on which a member of its tribe was posted as missing. It began to wash its face.

Grab it, thought Lance. No, maybe go and get a sack or bag from somewhere first. He put up one hand, then the other, to see how easy grabbing it might be. The cat was a lot faster than he. Quick as a flash, its paw shot out and scratched him right across his four fingers and the back of his wrist. With a curse, Lance put his bleeding hand up to his mouth and stepped back. The cat had gone.

Kidnapping a cat was obviously a tougher task than he had supposed. He turned to read the notice on the lamp standard. It would be just his luck if the missing animal turned out to be that stripy thing, which looked valuable but had now disappeared. But the print on the sheet of paper wasn't about a cat at all. Found, Lance read, found in Pembridge Crescent, a sum of money between 80 and 160 pounds. Anyone who had lost such a sum should apply to the phone number below. That was a funny way of putting it. Was it 80 or 160 and what was the point of putting the two amounts? It took Lance a few moments to understand, and when he did, it made him angry. Trying to catch people out, that's what it was. The person who stuck that up there wanted to have a good laugh when the caller said 100 pounds and it was really 120 or 90 or whatever. Lance felt like tearing the notice down and stamping on it. He didn't. A woman would have written that, he was sure of it. He'd remember that number all right, it was the same code as his ex-girlfriend's and the four digits were those of his birthday, 2787. Phoning would do no harm. But think about it first. Think carefully.

He might even ask Uncle Gib. He hated Uncle Gib and his religion and his horrible house, but still he had to admit that the old man was clever. Not cleverer than him, of course, but clever in a different way.

GILBERT GIBSON HAD put down a deposit on the house in the days when he was a burglar. Prison was an occupational hazard in his job, and all in all he must have spent about twenty years inside. While he was away, his wife, Ivy, went to work in the Chevelure hair-products factory to pay the mortgage and had just handed over the final installment when she dropped dead of a brain haemorrhage. Her death coincided with Gilbert's exit from his fourth imprisonment. It would be his last. While inside this time his cellmate had been the assistant shepherd at the Church of the Children of Zebulun, and the result of their frequent talks and Reuben Perkins's proselytising was that Gilbert got religion. This meant no more breaking of the eighth commandment. It also meant clothing the naked and giving shelter to those without a roof over their head.

Uncle Gib, as he was known to everyone in

the family, knew no one who was naked. However, his own nephew—in fact, his late wife's great-nephew—was without a home. When Lance Platt's parents threw him out and the girlfriend he moved in with got her brother to deal with him after he blacked her eye and knocked out one of her teeth, Uncle Gib took him in. Lance didn't want to live with Uncle Gib. It wasn't that he was fastidious or ambitious—he was in no position to be either—but even his parents' flat was moderately clean, had central heating, and quite a nice bathroom. The girlfriend's place had been newly decorated by the council before she moved in with her baby. She had a microwave and an espresso coffeemaker, and a huge flat-screen TV on which you could get about five hundred channels. Her flat in Talbot Road was always clean and gleaming and had a balcony that caught the afternoon sun. Uncle Gib's house, on the other hand, standing in Blagrove Road right up against the Westway and the train line, was decorated now about as it had been when he put down that deposit on it in 1965. What had changed was the immediate neighbourhood, now packed with social housing, blocks and blocks of flats, rows and rows of little houses. Lance knew this because Uncle Gib often boasted about the unchanged condition of his home and the virtues of his wife.

"My poor dear wife, your auntie Ivy, she

couldn't afford the paint, let alone what you might call structural alterations. Everything she earned went into paying off the mortgage. A saint she was. They don't make them like that no more."

The saint had nailed up the bathroom door when only a rusty trickle was coming out of the cold tap and the old geyser broke. The prevailing view of Uncle Gib and Auntie Ivy was that when you had a kitchen sink and an outside toilet, you didn't need a bathroom. One icy morning in early spring when Lance opened the toilet door, he saw a rat scuttle away behind a rag-wrapped pipe. He reported this to Uncle Gib who merely looked up from his scrambled egg and slice of black pudding and said, "Don't let the folks next door hear you or they'll all want one."

When he had got over laughing at his own joke, he added, "Beggars can't be choosers."

Lance was a beggar and he couldn't be a chooser. He lived on the benefit, and Westminster City Council paid his rent to Uncle Gib. The council had been told he had the whole first floor, but this was a joke, considering Uncle Gib had the main bedroom, the box room was unusable on account of a leak in the roof over the window where water came in every time it rained, and the bathroom was boarded up. The second floor was never used or even visited. A rope had been tied across the bottom stair with a card hanging on it which said No Entry like on a one-way street. Lance and Uncle Gib lived in the quite large kitchen and a kind of cavern with a stone floor and a sink the old man called the scullery. The front room and "dining" room were never used, though they were furnished with hand-downs inherited by Auntie Ivy when her own parents died in the seventies. These rooms, according to Uncle Gib, were to be kept "looking nice" for when he put the house on the market and prospective vendors came to view it.

When he wasn't writing tracts for the Church of the Children of Zebulun or being an Agony Uncle, answering *The Zebulun* magazine's readers' queries, Uncle Gib spent his time leafing through the glossy brochures estate agents put through his letter box almost every day. The neighbourhood was "coming up" and houses soaring in price into the four- and five-hundred-thousand bracket and beyond. Only after considerable refurbishment, of course, a requirement that Uncle Gib ignored while reiterating the enormous advantage of the house's being made detached by the construction of the flyover. His laptop in front of him, he sat at the kitchen table drinking cup after cup of dark brown tea and chain-smoking. Another thing Lance hated about the house was the all-pervading stink of cigarettes.

"There's a poky little place here," said Uncle

Gib, "only two bedrooms, no garden, what they call a patio, which means a backyard, no scullery, couple of streets away in Elkstone Road. What d'you think they're asking?"

"I don't know," said Lance. "Might be five fucking million for all I know."

"Don't you use that language here. This is a godly house. Of course it's not five million. Have a bit of sense. Be your age. Four hundred and fifty thousand, that's what."

Lance tried to get his own back by making a fan out of one of the brochures and waving it briskly to clear the air.

"You don't like my fags, the remedy's in your own hands. You don't have to stay here. I don't want you. You'll have to go when I sell the house." Uncle Gib pointed a nicotine-stained finger at him. "I'll tell you something. Our Lord would have smoked if there'd been any tobacco about in the land of Galilee. He drank, didn't he? It wouldn't just have been water into wine at the marriage at Cana, it'd have been Marlboro Lights for all the guests."

But in need of fresh air, Lance had gone out into the garden, a small, trapezium-shaped plot where nature prevailed untouched and where grass, nettles and thistles, dock and the occasional large, speckled fungus, grew unchecked. A shed in the far corner, its roof long caved in, served as a winter store place for Uncle Gib's

41

garden furniture, an iron table he had stolen from a pub and two kitchen chairs, one of them with a leg missing. Lance sat down on the intact chair—the other one had to be propped up with bricks—and began thinking carefully. She'd want to see him, whoever she was, she wouldn't just be content with his talking on the phone. Maybe she wouldn't even ask him for the right number between 80 and 160. He'd have to go to her place and have her question him. He went back into the house to consult Uncle Gib.

The old man had opened his laptop and was answering his letters. Immensely proud of his role as amateur psychologist and adviser, Uncle Gib never minded other people reading what he had written, though criticism wasn't allowed. Over his shoulder, Lance read: *What you are doing, cohabiting with a man outside wedlock, is morally wrong and against God's law and you know it. Now, after nine years of sin, you say you have met another man and think of leaving your paramour. Leave him you must if he refuses to marry you. As for the other man, you can never enjoy the glory of God's love if you persist in seeing him.* . . . Lance couldn't help admiring Uncle Gib's command of language, not to mention being able to spell all those words. He waited until Uncle Gib had finished the letter.

"I want to ask you something."

"Can't you see I'm working? You don't know

what that is, though, do you? Not just ordinary work either, God's work. Showing this bunch of sinners the error of their ways." Uncle Gib's tone changed from droning piety to an aggressive bark. "What is it, then? Come on, don't beat about the bush."

Lance told him.

"She's got your measure all right, hasn't she? You and them as are like you. Want me to break the commandment, do you, teach you how to thieve, teach you the tricks of the trade?"

"I'm only asking what you think I ought to do."

Uncle Gib was a tall, thin man whom prosecuting counsel had once described as looking like the famous statue of Voltaire. "The resemblance is purely physical, my lord," he said to the judge, and was reprimanded for irrelevance, misguided wit, and trying to be clever. True, his piercing eyes, cadaverous face, and emaciated body gave Uncle Gib an intellectual look. He had good white teeth, which had miraculously survived years of prison food and only sporadic cleaning. These he bared now in what might have been a smile but was probably a snarl.

"You've lost a sum of money in Pembridge Crescent, have you? You was strolling down there with a hundred-plus in your pocket when the wind blew, all them notes flew out and settled in a little pile on the pavement, and you never noticed. Give me a break."

43

"You reckon it's all notes, do you? That means it's got to be a round figure, not like eighty pounds forty-two or something. And it's more than a hundred or else she wouldn't have put the what-you-call-it, the high number, right up there—I mean like a hundred and sixty. Maybe it's halfway, like"—Lance had to work it out—"like a hundred and forty." That wasn't right. He tried again. "A hundred and twenty. Or it could be a hundred and twenty-five." He looked help-lessly at Uncle Gib.

The Voltaire look-alike said, "You're doing fine. Keep at it. Only don't you forget all the time you're diving deeper and deeper into sin."

"Why d'you reckon she's doing this? Why not just keep the money?" Lance found it hard to imagine anyone who wasn't in need of a hundred pounds. "I mean, she's playing some game, isn't she?"

"Suppose she's just an honest woman? Didn't think of that, did you? No, you wouldn't."

"Why don't you fuck off?" Lance said, making a quick exit, though not so quick as to avoid hearing Uncle Gib's bitter reprimands for his language and threats of unquenchable fire coming down from heaven.

HIS LATEST MOBILE had ceased to work after its owner had had a bar put on it. This hadn't hap-pened until five days had passed after Lance stole it from the backseat of a car. No doubt its owner hadn't noticed its absence. People had too much money for their own good. Anyone who left a mobile inside an unlocked car deserved all he got. Lance threw the mobile away before someone told him all it needed was a new Sim card, and now he was obliged to use Uncle Gib's phone. It was a wonder the old man had one at all. No doubt it had been Auntie Ivy's decision and she had the phone installed during one of his long periods as a guest of Her Majesty's government.

Lance dialled the code, which was shared by his ex-girlfriend, though, as is the way with exchange codes, in a considerably less upmarket neighbourhood. The first time he tried he got the engaged signal; the second time, much later, a woman answered. Just as he thought.

"It's about the paper you put up in the street."

"I'm sorry?"

"Up on the pole. The one about the money you found."

"I'm afraid you've lost me. Gene! It must be for you, Gene."

Another woman, thought Lance. Probably a couple of lesbians. But it was a man's voice. "Eugene Wren. What can I do for you?"

Lance repeated what he'd said.

"Ah. You lost some money, did you?"

"Yeah. That's right."

"I'm not going to ask you how much it was. Not now. Perhaps you'll do me the courtesy of coming here and we'll have a chat about it. When would suit you? Tomorrow evening about six thirty?"

Lance agreed. The rest of the empty day stretched before him. He would have liked to go out somewhere for the evening, pub first, then maybe a club up West. He'd never been to a club, he couldn't afford it, he couldn't afford anything. His benefit was basic. He was a "Jobseeker," but he didn't know what to say at interviews, he just sat there in hopeless silence. No one wanted to employ him, and now he had given up trying, though poverty was a perpetual trial to him. Everything he received went on food to supplement the small amounts Uncle Gib made available to him. If you were rationed to an egg a day, two slices of black pudding or luncheon meat, four slices of bread, a bun, and a small wedge of processed cheese, you needed a good deal extra. When he complained, Uncle Gib said that was all he had and people ate too much. God would have vengeance on them for not thinking of the starving millions in Africa. Lance bought tins of baked beans and tins of sliced peaches, pork pies and sausages, king-size bags of crisps and chocolate bars, and the biggest loaves of sliced white bread he could find. He also bought quite a lot of booze, Bacardi breezers, bottles of cider, and the cheapest gin as well as wine from Kurdistan and Bulgaria. All his benefit was gone and he remained stick-thin.

He had no faith in securing this "found" sum of money for himself but he'd get a look at the place where this Eugene Wren lived, he'd have an idea of the house and its contents. Remembering some of the things Uncle Gib had said years ago in his unregenerate days when Lance was a child, he thought of the term *casing the joint,* and he thought of observing entrances and exits, ways of getting in and out. And of course, he might get the money as well.

5

IN THE HOSPITAL, when he regained consciousness, they told him he had had a heart attack and requested his consent to the operation he should have had a year or two before. Joel asked to have it done privately, knowing Pa would pay. Pa would pay anything to keep him out of his way; out, preferably, of Hampstead Garden Suburb and its environs, out of the whole of north London. The operation was performed with the frightening (if he had known about it beforehand) splitting of his breastbone and lifting out of his heart—and something else.

His surgeon told him afterwards, "We nearly lost you. Don't know why. You seemed OK, thriving no less, and then you arrested. Of course we brought you back. Don't suppose you remember anything about it, do you?"

Joel said he didn't. What had happened to him he intended to tell no one—not yet, at any rate. If he really tried, it might go away. Concentrate instead on trying to remember exactly what had happened before he passed out and fell over in the street. His mother came to see him, unknown to Pa, and he told her where he had had his heart attack.

"I think I'd drawn some money out of the hole in the wall," he said to her. "I think it was a hundred and forty quid, but there was only twenty-five in my pocket. It's in the drawer in that cabinet now."

"You were never any good with money, Joel," said his mother mournfully.

"Someone might have handed it in to the police. It's worth asking."

His mother looked doubtful. She said she would enquire, then said she wondered if it was "all those drugs" he had taken in time gone by that caused his "little heart problem." Joel said he'd gone into rehab, hadn't he, he'd got cured, and then he lay down and pulled the sheet over his head. It was too light in his room. He had asked them for dark blinds and preferably dark curtains too, but they said the ones at his window, pale blue and translucent, were the best they could do. He had read in a travel supplement about a place in the north of Sweden called Kiruna. It was inside the arctic circle, and at midsummer when daylight endured all night, the Ferrum Hotel put up pitch-black blinds at their windows to give guests a dark night. At midwinter it stayed dark night and day. Joel liked the thought of Kiruna. It was just the place for him.

AN ONLY CHILD for a long time, he had had an imaginary friend from the time he was seven until he was ten. The friend was a boy of his own age he didn't just pretend-talk to or imagine he was talked back to; he actually saw him. Not as clearly as he saw his schoolfellows, but enough to describe him if someone asked. No one ever did ask because he told no one, but if he had, he would have said that the friend he called Jasper, because Jasper called himself that, was fair-haired with blue eyes and had an expression of great sympathy and understanding.

No one at school was as nice as Jasper or as good a companion. Most of them ignored Joel or else mildly bullied him. Until, that is, he grew too tall for them to dare do too much to him. By that time Jasper had slowly faded away, the golden hair and blue eyes losing their colour, the features blurring, until he became a shadow falling sometimes across a patch of sunlight, then disappearing altogether. Joel had been saddened

49

by his loss, which was not to say he was made happy by his return. Lying in his hospital bed, he closed his eyes and put his hands over them so as not to see the figure in the chair.

The real figure in the chair later that day when the bright sunlight had faded was Ma. She hadn't been to the police. She had gone to Pembridge Crescent to see where his heart attack had happened, notably to find the bell in the gatepost her son had fallen against. When she found what she thought was the right one, she rang the bell. The people who lived there were "absolutely charming," couldn't have been nicer. Of course she had thanked them for saving Joel's life, and they were "most anxious" to know how he got on.

Joel asked, emerging, "How about the money, Ma?"

"Well, such a funny thing, dear. There was this notice on a lamppost saying someone had found it. You were quite right about the amount. That really was clever of you after all you've been through. I wrote down the number you're to phone. Would you like me to do that for you?"

"I'll do it," said Joel.

"All right, if you're sure."

"I nearly died, you know. They said they nearly lost me."

"I know, dear. You told me." It was plain she didn't believe him. "I want to talk to you about coming out. You're going to need someone to

50

look after you for a while. Your father won't have you in the house. He's very hard but that's the way he is. Well, you know how he is, he doesn't change. He says he'll pay for a live-in nurse. Would you like that? I can come over every day of course."

"You'll be in deep shit with the old bugger," said Joel, and he pulled the sheet over his head.

Once more under the blanket, in the stuffy semidark, he was aware of his mother sighing and at last stealing quietly away. Would his father have been sorry if he'd died? Joel doubted it. Pa would remember to his dying day what had happened to Amy. He would never forget and never forgive. Amy had been as much Ma's child as his, and if Ma hadn't forgotten, she had got used to it, she had forgiven Joel. She knew he hadn't meant to do what he did or, rather, left undone. Pa would never understand that, and so he would pay out any amount of money to keep his son out of his sight forever.

"I HOPE YOU know what you're doing, Gene," said Ella Cotswold. "Inviting this person into your home, I mean. Why couldn't you simply ask him to—well, name the sum, and if he got it wrong, that would be the end of it, wouldn't it?"

"And if he got it right, he'd have to come here anyway. You don't suppose I'm going to send it to him by telegraphic transfer, do you?"

"But, darling, if he gets it wrong, and he probably will, he may get angry and—well, do something nasty."

"Nonsense, Ella," said Eugene robustly. "I'm curious. I want to see this chap. He sounded a bit of a wimp."

"I sincerely hope he is."

They were going out to dinner at a newly opened restaurant in Kensington Park Road. While Ella applied lipstick and contemplated her reflection in one of his beautiful gilt-framed mirrors (he called them looking glasses), Eugene nipped into the kitchen and took from a secret drawer two Chocorange sweets, which he slipped into his jacket pocket. The secret drawer had no handle and looked like part of the decorative frieze that ran along under the worktops. He noted that he still had three packets left, so perhaps he should take a third sweet with him to be on the safe side. No, two in his pocket and one to suck now should be enough.

Ella had an acute sense of smell and detected it on his breath but supposed he had helped himself to a chocolate while in the kitchen. He knew she never ate chocolates, but he might have offered her one just the same. She was small and slightly plump, with a pretty face and dark brown, curly hair, proud of her full bosom and showing it off whenever she could while remaining decent. Her fortieth birthday would come before the end of the year, and she looked forward to it with dread. As a busy GP with a full life, a devoted lover, a passion for opera, and a great reader, she realised how foolish this was. Forty was nothing these days, forty was young. Yet those months stretched before her like a sunny plain at the end of which a sheer cliff face dropped down into an abyss.

The abyss could be avoided and the sunshine made permanent if Eugene would ask her to marry him. She imagined walking into the medical centre and showing her engagement ring to her three partners, the medical secretary, and the practice nurse. Maybe she could have a baby. She wouldn't attempt that without being married, but if only he would ask her—the whole world would change. She had even thought of asking him. But you couldn't do that if you were an ordinary sort of doctor in a busy practice and he was a rich man. He smiled at her and, when he had helped her into her coat, gave her a chocolaty kiss on the lips. It was quite hurtful, she thought, not being offered a chocolate even though he knew she wouldn't have taken one.

"By the way, Gene," she said when they were in the restaurant, "how much did you find?"

"How much did I . . . ? Oh, the money I found in the street? A hundred and fifteen pounds."

"And you've only had one response in how long?"

"About two weeks, my darling."

"What will you do if this chap doesn't get it right?"

"Take it to the police, I suppose."

That would be a bit awkward after so long. But there was no point in thinking about it yet. Eugene looked fondly at Ella. How pretty she was and how nice. He would miss her terribly if she weren't around, though there was no prospect of that. This evening, in this charming restaurant with its delicious food, its candle on the table and its gazanias in a silver vase, would be a good time and a good place to ask her to marry him. Maybe when they were having their dessert wine and their double espressos . . .

But the time passed and he didn't ask her. Candlelight there might be and gazanias, but a restaurant wasn't quite the place. It must be at home when they were quite alone. It might also be a good thing to give up this habit of his. It shouldn't be too difficult, for there was no question of its being an addiction like drink or drugs. But give it up he must, simply by the expedient of buying no more. Possibly it would take him a week or two, so there would be no proposal of marriage that evening.

Perhaps she had expected it. He couldn't tell whether that was the case or she was just tired. Whatever it was, she said she'd like to go home to her own flat, and he put her into a taxi for that rather less salubrious northwestern edge of Notting Hill beyond the Portobello Road. An early night for him also, then. He would propose soon; there was no doubt he loved her. Next time they met, perhaps, or in a week's time. By then the habit he had mysteriously got into would be behind him. She would certainly say yes, they would fix a wedding date, and she would move in. That was what he wanted, wasn't it?

It was not yet quite ten thirty but he fell asleep quickly and therefore was awake at six, scarcely able to believe his ears when the phone rang at ten past. That no one should phone anyone after nine in the evening was a principle of Eugene's, and certainly not before nine in the morning. His "Hello" was icy.

A man's voice, educated, not unlike his own but younger, said, "I've only just seen your notice. Well, I didn't see it. Someone told me about it. My mother, actually."

"Do you know what time it is?"

Instead of taking this question as rhetorical, the caller said, "No, I don't. Quite early, I should think."

"What is it you want?"

"I think you've got my hundred and fifteen pounds."

"Ah, yes." Eugene tried to consider. "You did say a hundred and fifteen?"

"Yes. It's mine."

Eugene wasn't yet fully awake. Still, it was apparent this was the rightful owner of the money. What was he going to do about the other chap, he thought fuzzily, the one who was coming today? "Perhaps you'd like to come here and collect it?"

"I can't do that." The voice might be educated, but it was odd for all that, vague somehow, in no hurry. "I'm in hospital, had a heart operation." This perhaps accounted for the oddity. "I'm going to be in here quite a bit longer. Could you send it?"

"I suppose so," Eugene said ungraciously and with a sigh. "Who are you and where do you live—when you're not in hospital, so to speak."

"But I am in hospital. Look, I'm called Joel Roseman and I live in Ludlow Mansions, Moscow Road. That's West Eleven. But I don't see why you can't send it to the hospital. It's the Welbeck Nightingale Heart Hospital, only it's not in Welbeck Street, it's in Shepherd's Bush. The McCluskie Wing. Have you got that? A cheque would be safer than sending cash."

What a time to phone! And from a hospital bed! Surely a private clinic by the sound of it, so this Joel Roseman could hardly be in need of the money. Eugene began to feel uncomfortable, and the hot, verbena-scented bath he took didn't much improve matters. He should have got the name and phone number of the man who was coming at six thirty today so that he could put him off. How could he have failed to do that? In his blue silk dressing gown he sat up in a pink velvet armchair, thinking about it. Looking at the nice Cotman on the opposite wall usually calmed him down, but not this morning. He went downstairs, which he seldom did before he was dressed, and in the drawing room, from the fifth drawer down in a tallboy of tiny drawers, opened a fresh pack of Chocorange, put one in his mouth and another in his dressing-gown pocket. "Tooth-friendly," it said on the packet so that was all right. Still, it was the first time he had sucked one of the things before 10 a.m. Another thin end of the wedge. He would just have to go through with it, see this chap and tell him he was too late. Awkward but inevitable. And those things had better be rationed from now on, one more after lunch, two in the afternoon, and maybe one before Ella arrived.

But, no, not rationed. Given up. He would buy no more.

SUPPOSE THE NAMELESS man, his first caller, happened by chance to fix on the right sum? It would be a remarkable coincidence, Eugene thought, but not impossible. He might, for instance, calculate that in naming 80 pounds and 160 pounds as the lower and upper limits he, Eugene, would have avoided the sum arrived at by adding 40 to the lower and subtracting 40 from the upper. So why not take this figure, which was of course 120, and take away 5 from it? Put like that it seemed not impossible at all to reach this conclusion, hardly a coincidence. Anyone of moderate intelligence could reach it, choosing only between 5 pounds added to 120 and 5 pounds subtracted from 120.

The only thing to do, then, would be to send a cheque for 115 pounds to Joel Roseman at the Welbeck Nightingale Clinic or the Bayswater address and hand over another cheque for 115 pounds to the man who was coming at six thirty. He could afford it, he would hardly notice it, but still he had begun to wonder why he hadn't gone to the police in the first place. Leaving Dorinda to close up the gallery, he left in a taxi for Moscow Road. There was no point in going there, Joel Roseman must still be in hospital, but he was curious about this man who had had a heart attack in the street not far from his own house. Ludlow Mansions turned out to be what he expected, Edwardian redbrick with the usual turrets and cupolas protruding from its slate roof, stone steps going up to double doors, and inside a gloomy hall with a porter sitting behind a desk. Eugene thought of asking him for Mr. Roseman and perhaps being told that he hadn't been in hospital at all but was away on holiday or even up in his flat, but he decided against it.

Another taxi took him to Spring Street. Eugene got there just as the woman in the sari was turning the sign on the door from Open to Closed. It was a sign. The fates or his guardian angel were helping him to give up. From the window he could see the packets of Chocorange and Strawpink ranked neatly alongside throat pastilles and indelicately close to condoms. He turned away. Stopping cold turkey was the only way, and though already craving a Chocorange, he congratulated himself on his strength of mind. But *cold turkey* was an unfortunate expression, associated with hard drugs, and he wished he hadn't used it even in his thoughts.

A taxi with its orange light on arrived just as he was back on the pavement. Sometimes he thought London taxi drivers ought to give him points for being a frequent fare like a frequent flier. By this time he would be up for a free round-the-world trip. Home now and prepare for the arrival of the nameless man.

6

ALTHOUGH THE FRONT room of Uncle Gib's house was kept "looking nice" and therefore its door never opened, the exception was when he held a prayer meeting. In preparing for selected guests from the Church of the Children of Zebulun, he went so far as to fill twelve small glasses (of assorted shapes and patterns) with orange squash, but not so far as to clean the room. Fortunately, most of the visitors to the house in Blagrove Road spent their time on their knees, for if anyone sat down on the horsehair sofa or one of the chairs, clouds of suffocating dust puffed out of the upholstery.

Normally calm and laid-back, Uncle Gib became rather nervous on prayer-meeting evenings and got through at least ten cigarettes in the preceding two or three hours. He was anxious to be rid of Lance before the first Child of Zebulun arrived. His own past was no longer of importance. Several years before, he had repented in front of the whole congregation, been named and shamed, called a lost sheep, bleating and wretched, at last been forgiven, and received into the fold. Now, thanks to the infinite mercy of God, he was an elder. Things were different for Lance, unregenerate shoplifter, mugger, mobile-phone thief, and batterer of the woman he had lived in sin with, taker of the Lord's name in vain, and a no-good son to his parents. When you came to think of it—and Uncle Gib did often think of it—there was no commandment Lance did not regularly flout, except the one about not making a graven image. Nor, as far as Uncle Gib knew, had he yet killed anybody.

Lance must be well out of the place before six when the prayer meeting was due to start. Earlier in the day he had announced his intention of leaving the house at "around six" and "going to see a bloke about a job." Uncle Gib didn't believe in the job or in any job connected with Lance, but he felt his usual satirical rejoinder might be out of place. Lance might change his mind and stay at home. At twenty to six Uncle Gib had his eye on the minute hand of Auntie Ivy's family grandfather clock and was already beginning a nervous pacing. Lance had been up in his bedroom, sitting on the bed thinking about the money in no very systematic way, and concluding that the sum might be 90 pounds or 155 and he was just going to have to guess. Gradually, his thoughts turned, as they often did, to Gemma, the girl whose eye he had blacked and tooth he had knocked out. He missed her and not just her TV set and her microwave. The walk to Chepstow Villas would take him very near her flat in Talbot Road. She might come out onto her balcony to hang out her washing. Or she might be parking the baby buggy or, since it was warm and sunny, just sitting in one of the chairs opposite the one he used to sit in. After a moment or two, brooding on what he had lost, he went to the top of the stairs and traipsed slowly down them.

From there, he could see Uncle Gib just inside the open front-room door, pacing up and down, a cigarette hanging from his lower lip. This cheered Lance up. Even if he stopped for as much as five minutes under Gemma's windows, it still wouldn't take him more than twenty minutes to get to Chepstow Villas. If he was late, the guy would just have to wait. Better to get his own back on Uncle Gib for all those starvation-level meals and the rat in the toilet and his poxy bedroom and the smoke. He went back upstairs and watched the minute hand moving sluggishly towards six o'clock on the imitation Rolex he had stolen from a man he mugged for his mobile.

The grandfather clock chimed, and when the sixth stroke died away, Uncle Gib called out, "Come on, you. Time you was on your way."

Lance winced at that *you*. This was the way Gemma had sometimes addressed him, but with a loving or sexy note in her voice: "Come on, you" when she was in bed waiting for him, for instance. Uncle Gib just sounded nasty. "I'm on my way," Lance called out. "No need to lose your cool." As he spoke, the letter box on the front door clattered. There was no bell.

A deep voice said, "God bless you, Brother Gilbert," and heavy footsteps sounded, making their way into the front room.

Lance started laughing. He couldn't help himself. Slowly he got up off the bed, crossed the landing, and paused at the top of the stairs. Once more, the letter box clattered. Lance descended two stairs as Uncle Gib came out of the front room to answer the door and, looking up, shook his fist at him. Another Child of Zebulun was admitted, this time an old one with a white beard. Lance would have liked to say, "Hi, Santa, how're you doin'?" to him but didn't dare. He might come back to find the front door bolted on the inside.

His mood more cocky than it had been for days, he walked quite jauntily along Raddington Road and into the Portobello. The block of the Royal Borough of Kensington and Chelsea social housing where Gemma lived was a little way south of here. Lance walked under the Westway and the train bridge, down Westbourne Park Road and Powis Mews. In Talbot Road he skirted the yellow-painted concrete wall, thickly defaced with red and blue graffiti, and, superstitiously, stopped himself from looking up until he was directly under her balcony. If he didn't look, she might be there. He closed his eyes, then opened them. The washing was on the line, including a T-shirt with pink roses on it—painfully familiar to Lance—the buggy was there and the chairs, but no Gemma. Lance experienced such a wave of nostalgia and longing at the sight of that T-shirt that he had to hold on to the concrete gatepost. Tears came into his eyes. He rubbed them away with his fists and walked on down Leamington Road. Depression had returned and settled on him like a heavy black bag strapped on his shoulders.

• • •

THE HOUSE IN Chepstow Villas was semi-detached, a white stucco Georgian house, as estate agents would have described it, of three floors and a basement. Behind the wall and the gateposts with lions' heads on top of them was a large front garden full of flowering shrubs, some in full bloom. A flight of six stone steps ascended to the front door. Lance noted that to the left of the garage was a side gate, perhaps six feet high. He would note more of that sort of thing later.

The old guy who opened the front door was tallish and thinnish, but nowhere near as thin as Lance. Gemma said no one was. He had white hair and lots of it. Saying, "Pleased to meet you," in response to his "Eugene Wren. How do you do?" Lance thought how unfair it was, what a sign of filthy class differences, that this old fellow was wearing a brown suede jacket that must have come from one of those places in Bond Street and a real Rolex. When he got inside the house, into a sort of front room only it wasn't at the front, the unfairness of it was almost too much for him.

He had never seen anywhere like it. He didn't know places like this existed except on TV, and those he'd never really believed in. When he'd seen them on Gemma's super-TV, he and she sitting side by side on her settee, she'd said to him, "There's no places really like that. They make them look that way to get you to watch." And he'd said, "You don't reckon those Beckhams or Elton John have stuff like that in their places?" "Well, they're billionaires, aren't they?" she'd said. "They don't count."

So was this guy a billionaire? The room dazzled Lance, the pictures, the furniture, the jugs and pots and statue things, the curtains, yards and yards of them trailing on the carpet, the satin cushions coloured like jewels, the little tables, the clocks, the books done in leather and gold, the crystal that a sunbeam turned to diamonds. He stood and stared, feeling a fool, wishing he hadn't come—then glad he'd come, determined to make the most of it.

"Do sit down," said Eugene Wren. "May I know your name?"

Lance sat. He lived in a world where no one used surnames. "Lance," he said, and when the guy looked puzzled, "Lance Platt."

Lance was no longer staring but looking about him. Those were French windows the sunbeam came through, ordinary glass windows without bars. Outside, the garden had a high wall round it, all overgrown with ivy and stuff, but there was a side gate, wasn't there?

"Now," said Eugene Wren, "I have a sum of money here for you. All you have to do is tell me the amount you lost."

What with his disappointment over Gemma

and the shock of this place, Lance had forgotten about the money. "Ninety-five."

The old guy smiled. "Ah, then I'm afraid the sum I found in the street wasn't yours. Pity."

Lance didn't know what to say. He didn't much care. Ninety-five pounds or whatever it really was would be nothing to the rich pickings in this place. He got up. "I'll be going then."

Having nothing more to say, he said nothing, until out in the hall again. "Cheers." In passing he had observed the burglar alarm on the wall, the bolts on the front door. It closed when he was halfway down the path. The whole visit had lasted no more than six minutes.

Bars at the ground-floor front windows, he noted, and also at the basement window down a flight of iron steps. That side gate presented no problem. There would be other ground-floor windows at the back, most likely not barred. I wonder if he lives alone. No sign of a woman, but what sign would there be? He, Lance, would have to keep some sort of watch on the place, something more easily done from a car or van. Now who did he know who would let him have a loan of a van? Gemma's brother? You must be joking, Lance thought, as he walked back in the direction of her flat.

She was there! She was standing on the balcony up against the railing, holding her baby in her arms. Lance wasn't the first man to be moved by the sight of the woman he loved holding her child close against her heart. He let out a low cry of anguish. Gemma heard him and looked down, retreating immediately into the flat and slamming the glass door behind her.

WELL, THAT HADN'T been so bad, Eugene reflected. A non-descript sort of young man, all skin and bone, fairish, potato-faced—but what did it matter? He sat down to wait for Ella, then, seeing there was still half an hour to go before she was expected, pulled open the drawer in the carved black oak table (Danish, circa 1790), a heavy drawer invisible when closed, and contemplated the three Chocorange sweets remaining in the last packet inside it. They were the last he would ever have, or would he perhaps not have them at all? Was the strength of mind he had earlier been so proud of strong enough to help him throw them in the waste bin?

As often happened when thinking about his habit, he made fresh discoveries about himself and about his addiction. Today's was that no matter how many of the things he ate in quick succession, he never got tired of them. He always wanted another one. And that wasn't true of all addictive substances. Take drink, for instance. If you drank too much, you either passed out or were sick. Too many cigarettes made you nauseated or start coughing. As for those joints, two had been enough to make him float while things happened in his head that caused him to fear for his sanity. There was nothing like that with Chocorange. He just wanted more and more. Therefore he must stop. What he would do was throw away two of them and suck the third.

The last one, the last of all, he conveyed slowly to his mouth, then took the remaining two to the kitchen and dropped them, not directly into the bin, but into a plastic bag containing the outside leaves of a lettuce, several tea bags, and some pâté past its sell-by date. Disposing of the sweets like this among damp, unsavoury rubbish would be a sure way of stopping him from retrieving them later. He tied the handles of the plastic bag together and dropped it into the bin.

Buy no more. It would be hard but he knew that already. Out of nowhere came a memory of running down supplies once before, of being alone here after all the shops were shut. A frantic search had begun, looking in all the unlikely places until—wonderful discovery, better than the first drink of the evening, almost better than sex—he had found an unopened packet in the bottom of the plastic bag he kept by him for taking to the shops. It was untouched, still sheathed in that ridiculous cellophane stuff which took such efforts, such tearing and biting, to rip off.

He heard Ella's key in the lock and made himself swallow the last sliver of Chocorange. The very last he would ever taste. In a few weeks' time it would be no more than a memory and, he hoped, a source of wonder that he had ever approached being hooked on a sweet. Ella was looking pretty in a pink suit with a sort of frill round the neck, which seemed to be the fashion. Pink suited her. She put her arms round his neck and kissed him.

"You've been eating chocolate again, Gene."

"My weakness."

"Yes, well, I'm as bad. And I had far too much lunch. How did you get on with your caller?"

He told her.

"You haven't sent that cheque to Mr. Roseman yet, have you? Because if not, I've got to go over to the Welbeck Nightingale in Shepherd's Bush sometime tomorrow. A patient of mine is in there. Would you like me to take the cheque and give it to him? The post is so unreliable."

LANCE WASTED NO time. Having racked his brains for hours the previous evening, he could think of no one he knew who would lend him a car or van, so he began his campaign by going back to Chepstow Villas on foot. It was a bright sunny morning. The house opposite was clearly empty, no curtains or blinds at the windows, the front lawn uncut, and a Sold notice planted just inside the gate. Lance looked all round to check no one was about. He slipped through the gateway of the empty house and squatted down behind a wall of solid stucco up to a height of about two feet with a row of small pillars and a coping on top of it. Squatting is uncomfortable after about five minutes. So Lance sat on the ground, which, fortunately, was bone-dry, after an April of lower rainfall than any other since records began. It was just after eight thirty.

He was soon cursing the kind of people who don't need to leave for work until nine thirty or ten. What did that rich guy do for a living? Never having worked himself, Lance knew little about other people's jobs. In a bank, he thought vaguely, or was the guy something called a stockbroker? He had no idea what this might be. Maybe the man didn't work at all. Maybe he stayed in all day. Lance was deciding this must be true, that the guy stopped in to guard all that stuff he'd got in the house, when the front door opened and the white-haired man emerged. He was dressed today in a dark suit, white shirt, and a gray tie with some sort of pattern on it in purple. Lance thought the bag he was carrying was called a briefcase. And now he was in a dilemma. Should he follow him to find out where he went or take advantage of his absence to get round the back of the house? The latter option. White Hair wouldn't be carrying that case thing if he were just going down to the shops.

First, though, Lance tried ringing the doorbell. There might be a woman in there. Just because he hadn't seen a woman the evening before didn't mean the guy hadn't a wife or a girlfriend on the premises. He rang again, waited, listened at the letter box for a movement from inside. There was nothing. At the side of the house, the detached side, was a small, barred window. He hoisted himself up, peered between the bars. He could see the hallway he had passed through on his extremely short visit. No one there, no movement. He tried the side gate. It had no latch but a handle that turned, and it was a solid gate, made from some sort of hardwood. Of course it was locked or bolted on the other side. There was no way he could get over it without a pair of steps.

Lance walked down Chepstow Villas into Pembridge Villas, where he soon turned right from where he calculated which garden of these houses backed onto the guy's place. A woman was staring at him out of a ground-floor window. He carried on walking until he came to the next cross street. A house about halfway down was being renovated. Scaffolding covered the front of it and a sign in the front garden said WILLIAMS AND DHALIWAL, SPECIALISTS IN ELEGANT RESTORATION. However, Williams and Dhaliwal weren't working today, though they had left a good deal of their equipment about, including a pair of aluminium steps resting against the lowest bar of the scaffold.

People who see a man carrying a pair of steps don't assume he has stolen them. They suppose he is on his way to a building job. Without more thought, Lance picked up the steps, which were light, rested them on his shoulders, and set off back to old White Hair's. He put the steps up against the side gate, climbed up them, pulled them up after him, and dropped down on the other side. Silence. No shocked yells. No cries of "What do you think you are doing?"

As he had thought, the windows at the rear weren't barred. No doubt White Hair thought that no one could get into that garden from the back, and maybe he was right. The high walls surrounding it were covered in creepers, which looked to Lance like the prickly kind you couldn't climb up. Only a cat could climb them, and one had, the stripy devil that had raked its claws across his fingers. From among the thorny leaves it stared malevolently at Lance, unblinking and perfectly still. Never mind. He wasn't going to climb any walls. Some awareness of danger kept him from going boldly up to the French windows. It was as well for him it did, for as he crept up to a small sash window to take a look inside, a roar, a crescendo of sound, held him frozen there on the paving. A vacuum cleaner. It was a Hoover starting up. Without going any closer, he could see a woman plying this machine up and down a carpet, like someone mowing a lawn.

This woman must have arrived while he was walking round the block looking for a way in. She had her back to him now but was about to turn round. He ducked down and went back on all fours the way he had come. How long would she be in there? Hours? With no ground-floor windows on this side of the house there was no possibility of her seeing him unless she came out into the garden. He undid the bolts on the side gate and turned the key, listening all the time to the rise and fall of the Hoover's bray. What to do with the steps? If he took them with him, where could he dump them? By this time he had moved them out into the front garden and locked the gate behind him. He was scared to take them back to where he had found them. In the end he slipped the key into his pocket and left the steps behind, leaning up against the house wall.

He'd go back again next day. After eight forty-five when the old guy went out and before nine thirty when that woman came in. The chances were no one would notice the gate was unbolted or that the key was missing.

7

THE PRIVATE WING was newly built, but that part of the hospital Ella had come from had changed little from the old workhouse it had once been. Her patient had been in a mixed ward, shared by old men and old women, and hated by both. That sharing at any rate would not have been allowed in Victorian England when this place was built. She went up to the streamlined green glass desk to ask for Joel Roseman, fulminating inwardly against the government (or maybe the primary care trust) and its promises to put an end to this state of affairs, and was told he was in room 5. She found him not in bed but asleep in an armchair. Ella saw a man in his thirties, dark-haired, rather good-looking, dressed in jeans and a T-shirt with a blanket over his knees. The room was warm and the windows were shut.

Ella sat down in the other chair, the one on the opposite side of the bed. He woke, as she knew he would, but instead of taking her for yet another therapist come to manipulate him, he started and then stared.

Ella got up and held out her hand. "How do you do? I'm Ella Cotswold, Dr. Cotswold, but I'm not here professionally. I've brought you a cheque for the money you lost."

He blinked and, seeming to shrink away from

74

the brightness of the window, put out his hand and took the envelope. "That's very kind of you. I thought for a moment you were—well, someone else."

"How are you?"

"I'm sort of OK," said Joel Roseman. "Only it's too bright in here for me. Just a moment." He reached for the drawer in a bedside cabinet and took out a pair of large, black sunglasses. They obscured a good deal of his face. "I'd like to go home soon."

"You must be looking forward to that."

He was silent, opening the envelope, contemplating the cheque. "This signature, that's the man I spoke to on the phone? Is he a friend of yours?"

Ella nodded. She wished she could say Eugene was her fiancé but she couldn't. Not yet. "You've someone to look after you when you get home?" she asked in doctor mode.

"My mother will come over sometimes." He moistened his lips, leant towards her across the bed. The black glasses turned his face into a mask. "My father doesn't have anything to do with me. We don't speak. Well, he doesn't speak to me." The voice changed and became a child's, confiding, innocent, naive. "He pays, though. He pays for everything. They'd call me a remittance man, wouldn't they?"

"Perhaps. I don't know."

"Are you a GP?" When she nodded again, he said, "I haven't got a doctor. I mean, I'm not on a doctor's list. Of course, I've got doctors in here, lots of them. Do you take private patients?"

Ella tried not to let her astonishment show. "I have two or three friends who come to me privately."

"When I get out of here, could I be your private patient? My pa will pay, there won't be any difficulty about that."

Nonplussed, she said, "You don't know me, Mr. Roseman. Perhaps you should wait until you get home before you make decisions like that. I'll give you my card and you can phone me if you want to."

Joel Roseman took a long time reading the card. He took his sunglasses off, put them on again, turning the card over, rereading it. He put it in his jeans pocket, handling it more carefully than he had the cheque. "I won't tell you what's wrong with me now if you don't mind. That can keep till I'm your patient. You'll think it strange, I know you will, but it's all absolutely true."

She got up, sure she would never see him again. "Good-bye. I hope all goes well for you."

"I'll tell you when next we meet."

GOING INTO A Tesco Express in Kensington High Street for a pint of semiskimmed milk, he had come upon a metal rack in front of the counter crammed full of packets of Chocorange and Strawpink. He stood in front of them, contemplating them sadly. It was too late. Tesco of all places, Tesco, which he had always affected to despise! How happy this discovery would have made him a week ago. This meant it wasn't only in this Express but surely in all, in all the main stores too and the Metros, including the one in the Portobello Road, a stone's throw away. And such an impersonal place too, five bored-looking, mechanical youngsters lined up behind the checkout, indifferent to what customers bought or didn't buy. He took a packet off the shelf, put it into his basket, then put it back again. Quickly he turned away and took his milk up to the checkout.

Once out of the shop, he began to regret not taking the Chocorange with him. Surely he could have taken one packet, made it last two days or three. It was harmless, after all. He wasn't talking about crack cocaine, for God's sake. But he didn't go back to the Tesco Express. He comforted himself with self-congratulation. It was three days now that he had been without a Chocorange and it had been bearable. A lot was to be said for not having the things in the house, for he knew that, even if he had put a packet on top of a cupboard he would need a ladder to reach, he would have fetched that ladder and climbed it. Best not to put temptation in his way, and this thought brought him a kind of euphoria that lasted for most of the afternoon, enduring even when the man who came in regularly to walk up to the Rothko, eye it, finger its frame, but postpone any decision he might make about it, returned for the last time to say he had definitely decided against it.

Dorinda was wrathful. "These people have the most colossal nerve. And there's absolutely nothing one can do."

"Nothing at all," said Eugene. "It's time we changed the window. We could try some of those minor Pre-Raphaelites. Well, maybe two. The girl walking with her baby in the woods, I think, and the woman waiting for the lifeboat to come back. Oh, and that famille noire vase. Jackie can do it."

Look at the upside of your self-denial, he told himself. There will be no more pretending you've a sore throat or you've been eating a chocolate. No more removing the thing from your mouth in a tissue when a potential customer comes in. The days of never passing a pharmacy without wondering if they stock the things, those are gone. Secrecy is past. A small voice somewhere inside him said, "But you like secrecy, it's what you do."

Now, for instance, as he chose two paintings among the Pre-Raphaelites, taking a long time over whether he preferred the girl and her baby or the wounded soldier and his wife, he told himself that at least he no longer had to fear Jackie's observant eye when she spotted the telltale bulge in his cheek. He carried the painting into the window, moved the Chinese vase a little off-centre, and sent her to find a length of yellow damask to drape an easel.

The craving had suddenly become bad. He took a deep breath, which made Jackie turn to look at him. "Are you OK, Eugene?"

"I'm fine."

Leaving her to finish, he went into the little kitchen at the back of the gallery and filled a glass with water from the tap. Water sometimes helped, but not this time. There was nothing to be done but bear it. He walked home, telling himself that he had been shut into a prison but that he had opened a door to his cell by willpower. He should be proud of himself. He had said no and walked past those shops. He had put his hands in his pockets, turned his head away, and walked past. Perhaps he should tell Ella. He could tell her now he had given up. But wouldn't it be better and wiser to keep his addiction and his conquest of it a secret?

Once in the house, he thought how only a few days before he would have put six packets into the secret drawer in the kitchen, four into the carved drawer in the black oak table, and the rest into various pockets in his coats and jackets, keeping one out for dipping into during the evening. No longer. The feeling of deprivation was profound, a sensation of emptiness and that nothing he might do could be of any value. A vast interminable evening stretched ahead of him, unrelieved by a secret helping himself to a Chocorange while Ella was in the kitchen or having a bath.

The doorbell rang.

He wasn't expecting anyone, and for a brief moment his thoughts went to the young man without a name who had tried to claim the 115 pounds. But why should he come back? Eugene went to the door.

A man in an orange Day-Glo anorak over dirty jeans stood on the step, his face convulsed with anger. In his left hand he was carrying a lightweight aluminium stepladder. "I could have the law on you," he shouted when Eugene opened the door. "You're lucky I haven't got on to the police already."

"I have no idea what you're talking about."

"You didn't borrow my steps from my building site in Pembridge Crescent? Oh, no. You didn't have the bloody nerve to leave them stuck up against your house. You don't know a fucking thing about it, do you?"

"Well, no, I don't. I've never seen that—that ladder before."

The builder flapped his right hand in a gesture

of despair, said, "Bloody toffee-nosed creep," and retreated down the steps, carrying his stepladder. When he was out of sight, Eugene went up to the side gate where the steps had apparently been. If they had been there earlier, he wasn't much surprised that he hadn't noticed them. He wasn't particularly observant of domestic detail and usually attributed this deficiency, if deficiency it was, to his mind being on higher things. He felt the side gate and noted that it was locked. Was it possible that Carli, his cleaner, had helped herself to the stepladder and left it there? It seemed unlikely and unwise to ask her. She might take offence and leave, and then where would he be?

He couldn't have a Chocorange, so he decided to calm his disturbed nerves with a drink. It surely proved his addiction wasn't as intense as he had feared. A real addict would need his fix more than any possible substitute. A large gin with a little drop of tonic worked wonders. He reclined on the raspberry-coloured chaise longue, admiring his surroundings. His beautiful furniture, exquisite porcelain and glass, and his carefully chosen, extravagantly draped curtains always calmed him and put him in a good mood.

He sighed and thought of Ella, who would be along when her evening surgery ended in ten minutes' time. Tonight he would take her somewhere especially nice for dinner, but, before that, over another gin for himself and a dry sherry for her—but, no, it should be champagne. He went off to the kitchen to put a bottle of Moët on ice. Before that, as the soft late-spring dusk began to close in, he would propose. Her perpetual presence in his house would be the best inhibitor of his dependency he could think of. He had given up, he told himself. It was over, and now was the time to make this major change in his life. The sight of her lovely face daily across the breakfast table and nightly at drinks time would keep him on the straight and narrow. . . . Keep him? There was no question of his lapsing. Not now. He had got over the first day, the second, and the third. Those were the first steps that counted.

She arrived a little sooner than he expected, looking almost prettier than he remembered. She should always wear dresses, he thought, dresses of floral silk with that crossover neckline effect, so flattering and sexy on a woman with a large bosom. He hadn't got a ring but they could buy one together tomorrow and no expense should be spared.

"My darling, champagne for us this evening. Will that be nice?"

"Lovely," said Ella. "But I have to tell you about Mr. Roseman and the cheque first."

"Oh, no, please, spare me. I'm sure you did it all perfectly. You always do everything perfectly."

Ella laughed. "Just as you like. Why the champagne?"

But Eugene had gone outside to fetch it. She wouldn't have told him very much, anyway, she thought. Nothing about that strange stuff Roseman had hinted at. Soon, if he carried out his promise—threat?—of becoming her private patient, she wouldn't be able to reveal anything of what he said to anyone else. Eugene came back with the champagne and two cut-glass flutes on a black japanned tray. The wine was poured, he raised his glass to hers, and the flutes touched with a delicate ring.

"Going down on one knee is a bit absurd, Ella, wouldn't you agree?"

Awestricken, she whispered what she had murmured to Joel Roseman, "I don't know."

"Still, I'll try it." Eugene knelt down, surprising himself by the ease with which he did this and with no creaking of joints. "I want you for my wife more than anything in the world. Will you marry me, Ella? Say you'll marry me."

She nodded. "Yes, oh, yes."

IN THE MIDDLE of the night Eugene got up to fetch himself a glass of water. Ella was fast asleep, a half smile on her lips, one white arm lying outside the barely whiter quilt. He had drunk rather a lot the evening before but refused to fill his tooth glass from the cold tap in the en suite bathroom. All his life he had been told, first by his mother, then by various women including Ella, that it was unwise to drink from any but the mains tap in the kitchen. Upstairs, water had stood too long in a storage tank where bacteria would abound. So he went downstairs and drank two glassfuls straight down, filled another glass, and, at the top of the stairs, used the toilet (which he would never have called a toilet) in the other bathroom so as not to wake Ella with the sound of the flush.

The craving for a Chocorange had started from the moment he woke up, but it had been mild at first, controllable. Now, with his thirst quenched, it began to rage. He reminded himself that he had none in the house. There ought to be a version of the nicotine patch for those giving up sugar-free sweets. Some sort of throat pastille? The irony didn't escape him. You began on sugar-free sweets to avoid sugar with its weight-adding potential and had recourse to sugar to avoid an addictive substitute. Suppose that somewhere in the house there was just one left? He opened the door of the little wall cupboard and found only a lone tin of Fisherman's Friend. That was no good, he couldn't stand the taste of liquorice. Four drawers underneath seemed only to hold the usual accumulation of bathroom rubbish, scattered cotton buds, hairclips and a pot of lip gloss left behind by a onetime girlfriend, used and unused tissues, combs with missing teeth, half-used tubes of hair gel, and several toothbrushes, their bristles worn down and clogged with toothpaste. Except the lowest drawer. He opened that one and checked the cry of surprise and joy he would have uttered if Ella hadn't been in the house.

In the bottom drawer lay one Chocorange packet. Don't touch it, he said to himself, leave it. He picked it up but knew before he opened it that it was empty. Downstairs in the coat cupboard in the hall, in the pocket of a coat or jacket, one might remain. It had happened before when he ran out. Despising himself, he went down to look, and after grubbing about in pockets had failed, on the floor of the cupboard he found a single dusty Chocorange lying in the far corner behind an umbrella.

But instead of eating it, he saved it. It would keep till the morning, and then he would have it after Ella had left for the medical centre. It would be something to look forward to. He put it into the pocket of his dressing gown and returned upstairs. Worn-out by his struggles, he crept quietly back into bed in the predawn dusk and, lying close beside Ella, one arm round her waist, fell asleep at once.

Perhaps it was just as well, he told himself in the morning, that the sweet had disappeared. He could have sworn he had put it in his dressing-gown pocket, but it must have fallen out or he had forgotten and put it somewhere else. Eating it would have been a terrible mistake, taking him back four days and undoing all the firmness he had achieved and all the conquering of a foolish habit he had done. Better this way. And he did feel he was getting somewhere at last. The temptation was easing, the craving less. It filled him with jubilation.

Later, at the gallery, he announced his engagement to Dorinda and Jackie, kissed them both, and promised champagne to come. No, they hadn't yet fixed a date for the wedding, but it would likely be October. He took Ella out to lunch at the Ivy and afterwards, at a jeweller's in Bond Street, spent an awesome (her word) amount of money on an engagement ring with a large and perfect solitaire diamond set in platinum.

JON HENLEY, THE *Guardian* columnist, had written a piece about Uncle Gib in his daily diary. One of the Children of Zebulun brought the paper round for him to see. It quoted his Agony Uncle replies in the magazine and had a lot of praise for their out-and-out condemnation of pre- and extramarital sex. Uncle Gib was over the moon, though he attributed the comments to God's efforts rather than Henley's and kept saying how his strict morality had at last been recognised. But Lance wasn't so sure. He couldn't have explained why, but it looked to him as if the diarist was mocking Uncle Gib, sending him up, and didn't really think the way he answered young couples' letters was the right thing to do but was—well, something to laugh at.

But it made Uncle Gib stricter than ever. He gave Lance a lot of pain by referring more and more often to Gemma and to Lance's wickedness in hitting her, which Uncle Gib said would never have happened if the two of them hadn't lived in sin. As if married people never fought. He said he might write to Jon Henley and tell him this was living proof of what immorality led to. And when Lance tried asking him about receivers of stolen goods, just a name or just a street number, just a hint, Uncle Gib said not to be surprised if he came home one night and found the locks had been changed.

The result of all this was that Lance didn't go back to White Hair's place for several days. He went to Gemma's, though. The weather had changed and grown cold, as unseasonably cold as the previous weeks had been unusually hot. She wasn't to be seen on the balcony with her baby and certainly not sitting in one of the cane chairs. The third time he went, a man was up there, a young, olive-skinned, and good-looking man with a moustache, doing something to the railing with a screwdriver. Just some workman, a council bloke, Lance thought, sent round to do a bit of maintenance. But he went away with an uneasy feeling. A council workman might look the same as a new boyfriend, and a new boyfriend might mend a railing. Why not? When he'd lived there, he'd often done little jobs for Gemma. Thinking like that brought back his depression, and he had to spend money he couldn't afford on a couple of Bacardi Breezers. Next morning, avoiding her flat, he went round to Chepstow Villas.

He arrived outside the house just as White Hair was coming down the steps, briefcase in hand, and had no time to hide himself. But the guy didn't recognise him because he didn't notice him. People like the guy didn't even see people like him except after dark when they thought people like him were going to mug them. He watched White Hair go off up the road towards the bus or the tube or whatever work he did. Then, turning back, he saw the steps had gone, but he didn't wonder where they had gone or how they had got there. He wasn't bothered. He had the key to the side gate with him, though he feared that by now the guy would have seen that the gate wasn't bolted. But he hadn't seen. Or if he had, he'd done nothing about it. Lance unlocked the gate and let himself into the garden.

That window, the one on the right-hand side of the French windows, was the focal point of his study. It consisted of sixteen rectangular panes. He could break one of the panes, but that would do no good as this was a sash window without a handle and probably fitted with pegs, one on each side, which constituted window locks. Even if the sash was raised, it would rise no higher than six inches because of the locks. You couldn't get skinnier than him but even he couldn't have squeezed through a six-inch gap. How about the French windows then? There were four of them and he could tell from their handles that all were openable. His mind went back to the only occasion he had been in that room. No bolts on those windows, he remembered, keys in the locks but no bolts. If he had a stick or, preferably, an electric screwdriver, could he push one of those keys through from outside? The key would drop to the ground, and then, using something thin and flat, say one of those nail files Gemma used, perhaps he could ease the key under the door and carefully tease it . . .

The sound of a door slamming, the front door surely, sent him retreating to the cover of a dense, dark green bush with flat, white bracts of flowers. Veiled in leaves, he could see into the room without being seen. The woman he had seen earlier in the week plying the vacuum cleaner had come in, and now she dropped the two bags she was carrying with a grunt and collapsed into an armchair. Lance didn't stay to see what happened next. He let himself out the side gate, locked it after him, and put the key into his jeans pocket.

It was crazy, it was only tormenting himself, he knew all that, but still instead of going back the way he had come, he took the small diversion that led him along Talbot Road. No one was on Gemma's balcony. No washing hung there and the chairs had been taken indoors. But as Lance leant against the custard-coloured wall with its red-and-blue hieroglyphics and stared upwards, he fancied he saw a movement behind the glass door. He thought he could make out two heads, and though he could see no more than blurred outlines, he was quite sure neither of them was the baby's. Once or twice he had heard Uncle Gib use the expression *a heavy heart,* and now, for the first time, he knew what it meant. His heart was heavy. It felt like a stone hanging inside his chest and his muscles and his collar-bone weren't strong enough to hold it up. He would have liked to let it sink him, to lie down on the pavement and give himself up to his grief.

But he plodded on his way, hunched inside his hoodie. Why had he punched Gemma? It all came back to that, that was what set it going. He wasn't the sort of bloke to smack a girl around, or he thought he wasn't. But that time . . . She had told him he ought to get a job, any job, it didn't matter much what, so long as he could stop being a Jobseeker. Not all those employers he had interviews with could have rejected him, he must be setting out to make himself unemployable on purpose. As for her, once the baby was at school, she'd get work, she'd be along at the Job Centre the first day she'd dropped him off at primary school. As things were, she didn't want Lance under her feet all day and every day. It wasn't as if he'd babysit for her while she went to the gym or had a coffee with one of her girlfriends. All he'd do, she said, was sit about with the telly on like the lazy layabout he was. When she said those words, he saw red and punched her.

At first he thought he'd broken her jaw, but it wasn't as bad as that. Her eye went dark red, and when she'd sworn at him, she put her hand up to her mouth, then held it out to him to show the bloody tooth he'd knocked out. He was sorry at once, he said he didn't know what came over him and he'd never do it again.

"Too right you won't," she said. "You won't get the bloody chance. If you're not out of my house in fifteen fucking minutes I'm getting Dwayne round here to put you out."

Dwayne was her brother, an amateur heavyweight boxer and rumoured to be a bare-knuckle fighter as well. Lance had got out, though not before Dwayne had roughed him up a bit, and eventually he had ended up with Uncle Gib. But

91

the regrets never ended. The funny thing was he hadn't lost his temper a single time, not once, since then. He'd been a different man.

IN THE EVENINGS they sat in front of Auntie Ivy's black-and-white television set. Lance found the telly soothing, it didn't much matter to him what was on, though he drew the line—when he was in a position to draw the line—at documentaries. They reminded him of school. The great drawback to watching was Uncle Gib. He chain-smoked. He talked through every programme, especially the sexy ones, and they were mostly sexy or violent or both. Uncle Gib called everything disgusting or ungodly and, puffing away, said it was liable to bring fire from heaven down on Channel Four and he was particularly incensed by what Lance liked best, girls with not many clothes on. The two of them sat on Auntie Ivy's sagging mock-leather sofa, its seat cushions cracked and wrinkled like Uncle Gib's face, while Lance stared in silence and Uncle Gib fidgeted about, sometimes shaking his fist at the screen and shouting, "Harlot!" or "You wait till the Day of Judgment."

Lance's favourite sitcom had just begun when the letter box rattled. Uncle Gib went off to answer it. It was his house, as he often said, and he wasn't having Lance answering his door. Lance was watching the female lead, a beautiful girl mysteriously wearing a bikini in the living room in the depths of winter, trying to persuade her dad to let her boyfriend stay the night, when Uncle Gib came back with two men, one of whom Lance recognised at once as the guy with the moustache he had seen on Gemma's balcony. The other man had a red face and quite a belly on him, though he was young, no more than twenty-something.

"Ian," said the big man. "Ian Pollitt. This here's Feisal Smith, but you can call him Fize."

Lance got up. "What d'you want?"

"My mate and me, we've come here to tell you," said Ian Pollitt, staring at Lance the way a policeman might.

This seemed to be the signal for Uncle Gib to switch off the telly. He turned back to Lance, said, "I don't know what this is about but don't think I'm going. This is my house and I'm staying to hear what he's got to say."

"Suit yourself," said Fize. "I'm not bothered." It was the first time he had spoken. He had a funny accent, not like the Indians but not English either.

"Sit down," said Uncle Gib with the nearest to graciousness he ever got. "Make yourselves at home." His cloudy, old eyes were glittering with malice. "Any friends of my nephew's are friends of mine." He poked two cigarettes out of the packet. "Want a ciggie?"

Ian Pollitt took no notice. Fize shook his head. From his jeans pocket Fize fetched something in a small plastic bag. "You know what this is?"

Lance did. He had seen it before, though in a bloodstained condition. It was Gemma's tooth. Dry-mouthed, he nodded. Uncle Gib looked at the tooth, did a double take, and jumped to his feet, throwing up his hands. Fize watched him, apparently with sympathy, and at last Fize sat down, patting the seat beside him and smiling quite pleasantly.

"It's like this," Fize said when Uncle Gib had joined him, looking up at Lance, "Gemma's a very good-looking girl, as you know. Now she's got a horrendous great gap in her mouth, thanks to you. You'd agree with that, wouldn't you?"

"Don't matter whether he does or not," said Pollitt.

Again Lance nodded. Uncle Gib said, "He'll agree all right. He knows what he's done."

"Now, Gemma's been to the dentist and he says she needs an implant, that's what he called it, an implant, and that don't come cheap. Now Gemma's a single parent and she don't have that kind of money."

"What kind of money?" Uncle Gib was relishing this. Lance could see he had difficulty in suppressing his laughter.

Pollitt said, "The dentist said he'd do it as economical as what he could, but it'll still be a grand. One K, if you get my meaning."

94

Lance found his voice with difficulty. "A thousand pounds?"

"Right. You got it."

"But I haven't got it. Where am I to get a thousand pounds? I'm signing on."

"You should have thought of that before you smacked a young lady in the mouth."

"Me and Gemma," said Fize, "we're not unreasonable, we'll give you till Saturday."

Pollitt intervened again. "Next Saturday, that's May twenty-six. By midnight, mind. That's the deadline. You can bring it round to her place, you know where it is."

Lance nodded, dry-mouthed.

"Don't think her and Fize haven't seen you stalking her, hanging about outside at all hours."

"I haven't got no money," said Lance.

"Get it off this gentleman then," said Fize politely. "He's a property owner, isn't he? He's got to be loaded."

"He knows better than that," said Uncle Gib. "What, me lend a thousand quid to a fellow who's only my dear late wife's great-nephew? I should coco."

BUT ALL THIS talk of money stayed in Uncle Gib's mind. He was a property owner but he wasn't making prudent use of his property. As a religious man dedicated to God's work, he attributed this to his innocence and lack of worldliness. But next day, when Lance was out, he went up to the top of the first flight and untied the rope that cut off access to the second floor. That faculty which, in most people, detects dirt and disorder had been left out of Uncle Gib's makeup. Up in the three rooms on the attic floor he noticed nothing of the cobwebs and the grime, nor did the lack of bathroom facilities or even running water strike him. There was no furniture, of course, and some idea retained from one of the short periods in his middle years when he hadn't been inside told him that the law wouldn't let you evict a tenant from unfurnished accommodation. Still, that was easily solved. Take that good table from Lance's room, a couple of chairs from the dining room, and pick up a mattress from somewhere. A bed wasn't needed, a mattress on the floor would do perfectly well.

No need to think twice. Uncle Gib sat down at the table in the kitchen to compose his advertisement. Lately he'd seen quite a bit on the TV about young people not being able to get on the property ladder, and seeing the prices of those places he studied in estate agents' brochures, he wasn't surprised. He'd be doing a service to humanity, showing love for his neighbour by offering accommodation to rent. So how much to ask? Rented property advertised by some of those agents was fetching four and five hundred pounds a week. Uncle Gib was a realist, and though he had an inflated idea of the value and desirability of his home, he understood three rooms in it weren't in this league.

Using the reverse side of the No Entry card (waste not, want not) he wrote: *To let: self-contained furnished flat in fashionable movie-featured Notting Hill. £150 per week.* He added the address and phone number. When it was done to his satisfaction, he took it down to the newsagent in Powis Terrace and paid—through the nose, in his opinion—to have it put in the window.

Every other shop these days had been turned into an estate agent. He passed five on his way to the Portobello Road, except that he didn't pass them but stopped in front of each, noting to his satisfaction how houses no bigger or better than his own were commanding prices of seven and eight hundred thousand pounds. More than that if, like his own, they were detached. His would soon be in the million league.

In the window of the Earl of Lonsdale he saw a notice offering a trading site to let outside. Such signs weren't uncommon, and every time Uncle Gib saw one, he thought of the stall his father had had here and from which he sold fruit and vegetables and in the winter roasted chestnuts; thought too how maybe he could take that site and keep a stall of his own. But perhaps not, perhaps it was too late. No, he would become a landlord instead and maybe a millionaire, even if a homeless one.

He went into his favourite delicatessen and bought black pudding, salami, a piece of cheddar, half a dozen large eggs for himself and the same number of small ones for Lance, and a bottle of orange squash. It never did to economise on food.

8

ELLA SHOWED HER engagement ring to Dr. Carter, Dr. Endymion, Dr. Mukerjee, and the practice nurse, Martha Wilcox. Aware from the appearance of the ring that Ella's fiancé must be a rich man, Malina Mukerjee expressed the hope that this didn't mean Ella would be giving up work, did it? Ella assured them all that she wouldn't. She was sitting behind the desk in her room, called a *doctor's office,* American fashion, preparing for the arrival of her first patient, a mother of four, all of whom she had brought with her, when her phone rang.

It was Joel Roseman. "I do want to be your private patient," he said without preamble, "and I'd like to start today. What do I have to do?"

"Mr. Roseman, I have patients waiting. May I call you back?"

He sounded disappointed, like a child whose mother is busy. Ella opened the office door and let in Mrs. Khan, her two daughters and her twin sons, all of whom vied for the job of interpreter, their mother having not a word of English. It was almost midday before the departure of Ella's last patient, a woman with nothing wrong with her but complaining loudly about a rumour that all prescriptions in future were to cost a pound each.

Joel Roseman picked up his phone on the first ring. He sounded as if he had been sitting by it for the past three hours. "I haven't been out yet. Could you come to me? Would you do that?"

All of them in the practice made house calls occasionally. Besides, if he was to be a private patient, Ella felt she could hardly refuse him. Moscow Road was at the other end of Notting Hill, and she was about to say she couldn't manage it today when she realised she could. She easily could. The euphoria brought about by her engagement was enduring, filling her with energy and a desire to move about, be out in the fresh air, enjoy life. Sunshine had come back, if intermittently, and she would walk. Walking would help her reduce to the size 12 she hoped to be for her wedding dress.

"Two o'clock this afternoon, Mr. Roseman?"

"That will be lovely." *Lovely,* the little boy's word. "Please call me Joel."

A mansion block, redbrick, with gables and turrets and things she thought were called cupolas. Ten stone steps up to glass doors with art nouveau panes and ironwork. A porter sitting at a desk behind glass directed her to the lift down a narrow, green-painted passage, but the lift itself was a rather luxurious carpet-lined box with gilt-framed mirrors on two walls. Joel Roseman opened his door before she got there. He looked frail, thinner than she remembered, and though he wore jeans and a sweater, he had a dressing gown over them. But no sunglasses today.

No doubt this was because the place was dark. Almost her first thought was that the flat, which seemed large for one person, was the kind of place she would have expected an old lady to live in, not a young man. And that, he told her, as she tried not to show her incredulity at the stuffy darkness, the cumbersome Victorian furniture, the drab, shabby covers and curtains, was exactly what it had been. Old Mrs. Compton-Webb, ninety-six, had died there, her body discovered by a great-grandson a week later.

"Pa bought the place lock, stock, and barrel. Isn't that what they say? All the furniture and those carpets, the lot. Everything dark red and dark brown and mud. I expect it was done on purpose, to punish me. He was wrong there because it suits me. I like the dark."

Doors were open and she could see into darkened caverns where carved cabinets, marble-topped tables, and thickly padded chairs, all crowded together, loomed in the dimness. The curtains, of mud-coloured or oxblood plush, were thick enough to exclude all external light. Not even bright cracks of it showed round their borders. The atmosphere was stuffy and musty, and it seemed to Ella that the suffocating silence was unnatural in the heart of busy Notting Hill. It was a relief to be taken into a sitting room where there was a little more light, the fawn, red-figured velvet curtains held back by loops of brown braid, and the blinds behind them raised perhaps six inches. For her benefit? The furniture here was brown velvet, the carpet the kind that is called a Turkey, not Turkish, crimson patterned with brown and black squares and triangles. On a console table, a bronze bust of one of the Caesars was reflected in the mirror behind it and again and again infinitely in another mirror hung opposite. Ella found herself staring in horrified fascination at these endlessly repeated gaunt profiles and bald heads.

"I'm always meaning to make some changes," Joel said in the kind of hopeless voice people use when it is clear they will do nothing. "I could afford it. Pa gives me loads of money, but I never get around to it. Would you like something to drink?"

She thought he meant tea or coffee. He came back with two glasses of water. She noticed that he walked slowly and his hand trembled when he set her glass down. "What do I have to do now?"

"To be my private patient? Nothing. Or, rather, you've done it and here I am."

"So now you ask me what seems to be the trouble?"

She smiled. "Something like that."

"Well, you will believe me, won't you? You won't say it's all in my head or I'm making it up, you won't say that?"

"Why don't you tell me what's wrong?"

He was silent. She looked at him properly for the first time, saw a pale, fine-featured face, dull eyes, dark hair falling forward over his forehead. He drank some water, spoke in a low voice she had difficulty hearing. "When I was in hospital, I had a near-death experience. That's what they call them, don't they? A near-death experience?"

How many times had she heard this before? It sometimes seemed to her impossible for one of her patients who had had an anaesthetic not to have dreamed while unconscious of that long tunnel and paradisal bower at the end of it. He seemed to expect an answer. "Perhaps," she said. "Go on."

"The surgeon told me afterwards. It was during the operation. I can tell you his words. He said, 'We nearly lost you. Of course we got you back, but it was a ticklish moment.'"

Ella's immediate reaction was to disbelieve this. If it was true, she was sure Joel's surgeon wouldn't have been so indiscreet as to say so. A nervous patient could be seriously frightened by something there was no need to disclose. But she said nothing beyond gently asking him to speak up. She knew what he would tell her, it would be the long tunnel again, the golden river, and the white city beyond meadows full of flowers. They always saw something like that. And he did tell her that, but not only that.

"Like I said, I went through the tunnel—I guess that was the bit where I was dead—and at the end I came out into these sort of fields with a river flowing through them. There was tall grass with tall flowers growing in it and the sun shining, and beyond that was this city, white marble it was but it looked very light, almost like it was made of very thin glass or even cloud. All the buildings had steps up to their doors and rows and rows of tall columns. Are you following all this?"

"Yes, of course."

He drank some water. "There were walls round the city with sort of battlements and angels were sitting on them. It was warm there but not hot. I could see people in white robes—I could see them through the gates in the walls—they were walking on lawns under trees, talking and singing. One of them came out through an archway and he came up to me. He took me by the hand and he said something to me about it not yet being my time. I was just to take a look at the city so that I'd know what to expect when my time came. So I looked at the city and up at the angels on the battlements. They had wings like great white birds. I looked at them but they didn't look at me. Then this man led me back across the fields and along the riverbank until we came to the tunnel. Going back through there was when I think the surgeon and the anaesthetist were bringing me back to life."

"It was like a rather nice dream, then?"

"It would have been." Joel was silent for a moment, clutching his glass of water so tightly that she thought he must break it. Then, shaking himself, he relaxed his fingers and set the glass down on the table. "It would have been, except that I brought him back with me."

In the dimly lit, stuffy room, she felt a kind of chill, the small shiver people used to say meant someone was walking over where one's grave would be. "I'm sorry. I don't understand."

"I said to you before I started please to believe me, not to say I'm making it up. Because to do that I'd have to want to do it and I don't. I hate it."

"I won't say you're making it up. But I do need you to explain."

"The man who came up to me out of the city and through the archway—well, I suppose it was heaven, or hell maybe if hell can be beautiful and

104

peaceful—that man came back with me, through the tunnel, into this life. Do you understand now, Dr. Cotswold? When I was conscious—well, not then, but later—he was sitting by my bed. He wasn't anyone I've ever seen in this world." Joel seemed to consider. "Maybe he was, though, maybe he was a sort of friend I had when I was a child now but grown-up, of course."

Guessing, Ella said, "By 'sort of' do you mean an imaginary friend?"

He nodded. "That's what I mean. But I don't know if this man is my friend grown-up. It's years and years, and he looks different. If he is, he's changed his name. My—well, imaginary—friend was called Jasper. This one is Mithras."

Tugged into this dream or nightmare, whatever it was, Ella had begun to feel disoriented. Naming the creature of Joel's fantasy and the fairly obvious transit of that name from a child's idea of what a boy might be called to a man's maturer concept of a denizen of heaven or hell brought her back to practicalities.

"Joel, you don't need me at all. Surely"—she must be tactful here—"you need someone you can tell all this to who would be sympathetic. I don't mean I'm not, but I'm a doctor of medicine, I'm really not qualified to help you over this."

"You mean a psychiatrist?"

"I meant a therapist, yes."

"You think I'm mad?"

"No, of course not. Of course I don't think you're mad because you have—well, a very active imagination." She took her phone directory out of her bag. "Look, why not let me phone this woman who's an excellent psychotherapist and make an appointment for you to see her?"

"She'll think I'm mad."

"No, she won't. She's the last person to think like that. Are you well enough to go out now if you go in a taxi?"

He said lifelessly, "Oh, yes, I've been out. I'm supposed to go out a bit, only I can't walk far. Mithras doesn't come with me."

"So I can phone Dr. Peacock?"

"Sure. Go ahead."

He kept his eyes fixed on her while she made her phone call. It seemed to her that it was darker in the room than it had been when first she came. Not much sun could penetrate this place, but what there had been had gone, the sky clouding over. She told Joel she had made an appointment for him two days ahead in the afternoon.

"I'd like to tell you about Jasper," he said.

"Perhaps it would be best to save that for Dr. Peacock."

"And my pa. I'd like to tell you about him and why he hates me. You will come back, won't you? Just because I'm going to this Dr. Peacock doesn't mean you won't be my doctor anymore?"

"Of course it doesn't, Joel. But I think you

106

should come to me now you're better." Anyone overhearing this would assume she was speaking to a boy of ten. "We'll fix a time for you to come after my usual surgery hours."

She got up and he got up. Out in the gloomy hall, he said, "Mithras is here. He didn't come in while you were with me. He's been waiting out here, over there in the corner by that thing, the thing like a tree where you hang coats."

Ella said calmly, "Would you please switch on a light?"

The sudden brightness made her blink. Joel covered his eyes with one hand. "Dr. Peacock will let me know how you get on. And you must let me know too." She held out her hand. "Good-bye for now, Joel."

"Good-bye." He wasn't looking at her but at the corner where the coatstand was.

He opened the front door for her, still looking away. The fresh air, the hazy sunshine, passing traffic, people, brought her back from something that was more than unease. Savouring her relief, she began the walk to Chepstow Villas. She had no patients this evening and Eugene had said he would be home early. It was a pity really that she couldn't tell him about her experience of the afternoon in that dreadful flat, hearing those dreadful things. But she couldn't, any more than a priest could disclose what was told him in the confessional.

SEVERAL REPLIES CAME to Uncle Gib's advertisement. Applicants were attracted by the low rent, but all but one of them were repelled by the condition of the house, the bare and dirty rooms, and, above all, the absence of a bathroom. The one who wasn't belonged in that class of people Uncle Gib described as beggars who couldn't be choosers. A young man from Eastern Europe, he had a job washing dishes in a tiny café in the Portobello Road, nearly as nasty as the house in Blagrove Road. At present, he told Uncle Gib, he was sleeping on the floor of his friend's bedsitter.

To him the top flat was a palace.

"I toilet in garden," he said, "and wash in kitchen."

"Scullery," said Uncle Gib, "and only when I'm out, mind."

9

EUGENE CONSIDERED THE items for sale in the health food shop unappetising, the fruit bruised and the vegetables looking as if a slug might crawl out between the leaves. As for quinoa, whatever that was, and kasha, did normal people eat those things? But Ella, who had put her flat on the market and more or less moved in with him, wanted ginger and garlic and something called fenugreek for what she planned to cook that evening, and this was the only place he knew for certain he could get them. Waiting to pay for his purchases, he was surprised to see stacked packs of Chocorange among the other sugar-free sweets on the counter. It was wonderful how he could look at them so casually, so lightly, almost as if they were mints or chewing gum he was seeing. Interesting, though, that here they were on sale in a health food shop yet while he was hooked on them, he had worried a bit that the chemicals in them might be harmful.

His mind went back to the time when he was running out of places where Chocorange could be found. How happy he would have been then, how overjoyed, to come upon a cache like this in such an unexpected place. But thinking about it, he realised that his favourites must also be used by diabetics, and here he could see chocolate and biscuits for those who had a problem with sugar. Shop assistants in the past must have thought he was diabetic. Strange that he wouldn't have minded that at all. Was this because being an addict implied weakness of mind whereas to be diabetic meant only a pancreatic deficiency beyond one's control? It was an interesting question.

He was almost inclined to put himself to the test. Buy a packet of Chocorange and airily suck one on the way home, knowing that he wouldn't require another all the evening. But, no. Better not. Not yet. He picked up a bar of diabetic chocolate instead and said he'd have that.

"A great improvement on what they used to be, these sweets and chocolate, aren't they?" the girl behind the counter said in a friendly way.

Eugene agreed. He even said that the Chocorange were delicious, as good as the "real thing," and he marvelled at himself for discussing his former addiction so openly. But of course what he was discussing was his mythical diabetes. The time might even come when he could talk freely about his habit, laugh ruefully about it, the way other people did about their past alcohol or drug dependency.

It had been a lovely day and was going to be a fine, warm evening. Warm enough for them to eat their dinner outside? Eating a square of diabetic chocolate, he went into the garden via the French windows, testing the air temperature. Ella would have to decide. In spite of their greater distribution of subcutaneous fat, Eugene had noticed that women seemed to feel the cold more than men. While he was reflecting on this anomaly, he glanced towards the side gate and saw that it wasn't bolted. Carli must have unbolted it to let the gardener in and out, then forgotten to bolt it again. But wasn't it rather absurd to keep a gate bolted when it was already locked? His neighbours were paranoid about the security of their homes. The couple with that crosspatch cat, Bathsheba, had bars on all the ground-floor and basement windows, and no fewer than three separate locks on their front door. That sort of thing fuelled people's fear of crime and did not, in fact, discourage burglars, who only looked on fortress mentality as a challenge.

The diabetic chocolate wasn't at all nice. It had a dry, dusty taste. He would eat no more of it.

THE BANK-HOLIDAY WEEKEND was coming up, and he was taking Ella away for two days on the Saturday to Amberley Castle in Sussex. It would be a short but luxurious holiday. He had booked a medieval but state-of-the-art-refurbished room with a four-poster bed. Spoiling Ella, he had decided, was to be an ongoing feature of his marriage, and he intended to get into practice. Carless himself, he was renting a car, and although this meant a horrible drive through south London, Ella could sit beside him, taking her ease and, at least for the second part of the journey, enjoying the view.

While they were putting suitcases into the boot, he told her about his newly formed decision to be less security-conscious. "Prudent but not too prudent," he said. "For instance, I shan't be bolting the side gate. All that would happen is that I'd forget to unbolt it and then the gardener can't get in. I shall lock and bolt the door into the area, of course, see all windows are shut and put on the alarm."

"Will you leave a couple of lights on?"

"I really think that only attracts their attention, darling. I mean, if you were a burglar—impossible, I know, but try to imagine—what would you think if on a bright, sunny day like this one you passed a house with lights on? You'd either think the householder was mad or they'd gone away, much more likely the latter."

Somewhere in Sussex, after the South Downs had come into view, he asked her if she had seen Joel Roseman again.

"He's become a patient, a private patient."

"Is there something wrong with him, then?"

"Well, he has had an operation on his heart," said Ella. "Isn't the sunshine lovely, darling? I really think this is the most beautiful time of year, don't you?"

"You mean you mustn't talk to me about your patients' ailments," said Eugene, laughing. "Darling, I entirely understand."

UNCLE GIB WAS as good as his word. He wasn't going to lend Lance a thousand pounds. "It wouldn't be a loan," he said, wreathed in smoke at the breakfast table. "You pass on cash to a bloke what's out of work and it's not a loan, it's a gift. And I don't feel like giving you no gifts."

Lance didn't argue. He doubted if Uncle Gib had a thousand pounds, though this wasn't the first time they had had this conversation. Lance fell back on it, opening the subject afresh, each time other people refused him. He had tried his parents and they didn't argue either. They laughed. He had to be joking. His mother already owed eight thousand on her Visa card. He tried his grandmother, his mother's mother, who was still several years under sixty, the women in his family giving birth while in their teens. She had a job, managing a launderette, and was looked on by her friends and descendants as practically an intellectual, but if she had a thousand pounds, she wasn't lending it to Lance. Nor were her other two daughters, Lance's aunts, or his uncle, the ex-husband of one of them, who had won ten thousand on the lottery. But Uncle Roy came in useful. When he had refused Lance's plea, he gave him the name and address of a receiver of stolen goods in a street just off the Holloway Road.

Robbing the bloke with the white hair was now Lance's last resort, and once more it seemed feasible. In spite of all his preliminary work in Chepstow Villas, he had almost given up the idea of actually breaking in because he had nowhere to take the stuff he nicked. Now he had Mr. Crown at 35 Poltimore Road, N7.

It was already Saturday, the day on which he

had to take the money to Fize. He had been unable to keep away from Gemma's flat and had been back there on two occasions. This would be the third, and his plan was to offer her and Fize all his week's benefit on account, accompanying it with the promise that the rest would be in their hands by, say, Tuesday. At any rate, he would get to see her, with luck actually be in the same room with her. But as he came up to the block where she lived, he spotted Fize on her balcony with the baby on his lap, apparently feeding him with something out of a bowl. Fize hadn't seen him, but Lance lost his nerve, crossed the street, and, putting his hood up and hunching his shoulders, hurriedly walked on down Leamington Road and into Denbigh Road.

Still in hoodie disguise, he saw in the distance White Hair putting stuff into the boot of a car. Lance recognised him with no difficulty. He had a woman with him that he had never before seen, in a trouser suit with dark, curly hair. It looked as if they were going away somewhere. More than likely, seeing it was the bank-holiday weekend. People like them, rich and comfortable and worry-free, people who'd never have a problem finding a thousand pounds, always went away at holiday weekends, while he was stuck forever in a dump full of smoke and rats.

He hung about on the corner, pretending to read yet another one of those lost-cat notices, the stripy one—apparently called William—having gone off somewhere on a jaunt. If they'd been offering a reward, he might have looked for the missing cat, but they weren't. And maybe not, he thought, remembering his scratched hand. Those two, White Hair and his woman, had disappeared into the house. Lance walked about a bit, sat on a wall, got off again when the person who owned the place came out, went back to the corner where the lost-cat notice was. They had come out again. White Hair opened the car door on the passenger side for the woman, then he got in and drove away. Lance let them get out of sight before moving slowly towards the house they had just left. Pity he couldn't go in there now, but it would be better to leave it until after dark. He wasn't going back to Blagrove Road and Uncle Gib. He'd go to his nan's in Kensal. Though she'd refused him a loan, she'd said she never saw him these days and how about coming round to her place, the launderette closing early on account of it was the bank-holiday weekend, and she'd cook him dinner or, more likely, take him down the Good King Billy for a beer and a ploughman's. He might get a shower too in her nice clean bathroom.

PITY IT GOT dark so late. Lance could tell his nan wanted rid of him round about six, but it was still broad daylight, the sun shining as bright as at midday. She'd told him twice her boyfriend was coming over, and they'd be going to the dogs at Walthamstow and he should be on his way. Lance felt uncomfortable. She'd given him fish and chips in the pub and two pints of Stella, and tea and crisps when they got back home, and he knew he was outstaying his welcome—but where to go until it got dark? It was the story of his life, nothing to do for most of the time and nowhere to go. At last, when his nan had got herself up in a miniskirt and white leather jacket and turquoise-blue shades, and Dave arrived, Lance got up and said he'd better be off. They saw him off the premises, all over him now he was on his way.

Though he'd come on the bus, he walked all the way back to Chepstow Villas to save the fare, making his usual detour to pass Gemma's flat. A light was on inside, the door opened a crack, and Gemma put her head out. Had Lance been given to that sort of thing, when he saw her come out he might have said to himself, Romeo-fashion though slightly paraphrasing, "But, soft, what light through yonder window breaks? It is the east and Gemma is the sun." However, she didn't appear to have seen him, for she leant against the railing gazing up the road in the opposite direction. He walked on, trying to think about the task ahead. Suppose those two, White Hair and his girlfriend, had only been out for the day? No, you don't take suitcases if you're only going to Richmond or Maidenhead. It was still light, but though he wasn't much for noticing what the sky was doing, he could see from the red glow when he looked behind him that the sun had set. Back to sitting on a wall, then. He'd walked so far he was exhausted, not to mention getting hungry again. A bit more time was used up by his buying a pie, a piece of fruitcake in a see-through pack, and a Mars bar, which he ate trailing along Westbourne Grove. Once, when he looked behind him, he saw in the distance a man who reminded him of Fize, but as far as he was concerned, one Asian looked much like another.

AT LAST IT was dark, and no streetlamp was directly outside White Hair's house. The dense trees in the pavements and the front gardens of Chepstow Villas helped to darken the place. Lance was so certain White Hair would have bolted his side gate after all this time that he was surprised when it yielded as he turned the key. Lights were on in a garden next door, the kind that glow green, half-hidden among the bushes, but none here. It was dark and there was no moon. Lance went up to the French windows and peered at the keyhole. As he had hoped, neither White Hair nor his girlfriend had taken the key out after they had locked the door. He could see the tip of its shaft inside the hole. Poking it through would be a skilful business, best taken slowly, because if it jumped out when he pushed at it with the screwdriver he had brought with him, it might easily jump away from the door and land inches away on the carpet. And that would be the end.

His eyes had become accustomed to the lack of light. He could see the keyhole quite clearly and no longer regretted not bringing a torch. Carefully he prodded at the end of the key, felt it move, then wobble, teeter on the edge of the keyhole, and, as he just tickled it with the screwdriver's tip, drop straight down surely no more than an inch in from the bottom of the door. Lance had brought a strip of thin card with him in his backpack. He slipped it under the door, which he could now see must have been a full centimetre above the carpet edge. Then, his difficulties began. He told himself he must be patient. If he got into a state, if he lost his cool, he would make a mess of it and perhaps only push the key away, farther into the room. At his fourth attempt, he felt the card slide under the key. By tilting the card slightly upwards, he began to move it towards the bottom of the door. He lost it and had to start again. Slowly he pulled the card backwards, praying it wouldn't catch on the base of the door and stick. It didn't. He couldn't remember a moment he'd been so happy since Gemma kicked him out as he was when he saw the brass shank of the key—to himself he called it a golden key—ease its way out and into his waiting hand.

Though he unlocked and opened the door quietly, the burglar alarm still went off. The chances were it wasn't the kind that summoned the police, only frightened the intruder. He was made of sterner stuff. He moved quickly round the room, scooping up stuff into his backpack, ornaments, statuettes, pretty things he couldn't identify, glass and silver, and from the top of a cabinet, evidently dropped there by the girl-friend, a gold necklace set with green stones. All this took about two minutes before he was back once more in the garden, the French window secured behind him and the key in his pocket. White Hair would change the lock, of course, but there was no harm in giving it a go.

He dared not go back through the gateway. Signs were that the neighbours were getting excited by the braying of the burglar alarm, which was just as audible outside as indoors. Voices were raised. A woman somewhere in the front said loudly that she was going to phone the police, and someone else said it was probably a false alarm. Lance began to feel trapped. He padded down the path towards the wall at the end of the garden where he detected a sturdy-looking trellis supporting the dense thickets of creeper. It was as good as a ladder. The lights were still on in the garden next door, but no one had come out. In the distance he could hear voices raised in an argument over what, if any, action to take. Gaining a foothold on the trellis, he began to climb up, his hands already scratched by the creepers, which were a lot more thorny than ivy. As he swung his right leg, then his left, over the top of the wall, the side gate opened and a man and a woman came into White Hair's garden. Lance swore. He should have locked that gate. But the people hadn't seen him. He hung on to the top of the wall on the Pembridge Villas side, watching them through the leaves, and he nearly laughed out loud when he saw them glance at the locked French windows, their glass intact, mutter something to each other, turn, and go back the way they had come.

His hands sore and bleeding, he let himself drop on to the soft ground below. The house whose garden he was in looked unoccupied. No lights were on. The people who lived there might have gone away for the holiday weekend too or just be asleep. He could still hear the rising and falling howl of White Hair's alarm, but now, quite suddenly, it stopped. The silence that followed was broken only by the sound of a big, expensive car purring its way towards Westbourne Grove. Lance found he could creep along towards the road at the back of the thickly planted border where the shrubs were tall and where, within a few yards of the house, a forest of bamboo took over. Its stalks were twice his height and they sheltered him until he reached these people's side gate, a wrought-iron door, easily climbed though hard on his sore hands. Within thirty seconds he was out in the street, all his difficulties behind him and surely a small fortune in his backpack. He was particularly pleased with the necklace, which he was already telling himself was gold with emeralds.

It was past eleven thirty. The streets here were silent and empty. He seemed to be alone, a solitary man in a hoodie with a heavy backpack, but when he looked over his shoulder, he saw someone far behind him. It was no one he recognised. All he could be sure of was that it was a man. The cafés and wine bars and pubs of Westbourne Grove were busy, brightly lit, and noisy. It had been a fine sunny day so there had been tables out on the pavements and people were still out there drinking and some eating a late supper. Then, he saw a man he thought was Fize, leaning against a pub wall talking to another Asian, but he showed no interest in Lance, seemed not to see him, though the deadline for bringing the thousand pounds would be up in ten minutes' time.

He passed the corner of Gemma's street, and after that, perhaps because there were no pubs and no cafés and the only place still open was an all-night Asian grocer's, quiet returned. A group of men about his own age were running along the opposite pavement, but they disappeared down a side turning. The Portobello Road lay ahead of him and a few hundred yards farther north, Raddington Road and Uncle Gib's place. But here there was no one and nothing, the place dark but for the occasional streetlamp. From a single forlorn, little all-night shop a feeble yellow glow spread out onto the pavement. He would have liked a bit of noise, he was used to it, even a radio playing softly, a human voice. But the only sounds were in the far distance, almost unheard, the murmur of London half a dozen streets away.

Quite suddenly, two men appeared from nowhere, walking abreast and coming towards him. They moved slowly, looking in his direction, looking at him, a black man and a white man. Somewhere, perhaps from a shop in the Portobello, a clock struck midnight, twelve sonorous strokes. Lance looked for a side street but there wasn't one, only an alley like a trap, and when he looked over his shoulder, thinking by then of turning and running, he saw Ian Pollitt approaching, his tread soft and measured as if he had all the time in the world.

Lance stood still. He didn't know what else to do. The black man was the first to close with him. He walked right up to him, the way no one ever does unless they mean something bad, and kneed him in the groin. When Lance doubled up with the pain of it and sank forwards onto his knees, Ian Pollitt pulled him up and punched him on the chin. Lance tried to cover his face with his left arm while he hit out with his right. They both attacked him then, along with Fize, who had appeared from somewhere, pulling the backpack off him and flinging it half across the roadway, punching his head and shoulders. When he was down, past getting up again, one of the white ones kicked him hard in the small of his back. The others followed suit, a heavy kick to the stomach from one of them, and the other's heavy boots struck what he felt might have been his kidneys. He was only dimly aware when they left him, all kneeling round his backpack, pulling it open, some objects flung out and others stuffed into pockets.

The Asian man emerged from the all-night grocer's when Lance's attackers had gone. He phoned for the police and an ambulance and, sitting beside him on the pavement, waiting till they came, stared in wonder at the shattered glass, the battered silver, and broken statuary scattered across the roadway.

10

ELLA HAD CONFESSED to leaving the necklace Eugene had given her for her thirty-ninth birthday on top of the cabinet in the drawing room. She had been wearing it with her trousers and sweater, decided it was too "dressed up" for a drive to Sussex, and taken it off, meaning to put it in her suitcase. Eugene was never cross. All he said was "Never mind, darling. These things happen. I'll buy you a nicer one for your fortieth."

He was more concerned about his netsuke animals, which the burglars had also taken, and the Nymphenburg porcelain the police had found smashed on the corner of the Portobello Road. All of it had been stolen, it seemed, by a bunch of thugs who had finished off their spree by beating up an innocent young man on his way home after a harmless evening out. The police had been rather severe with Eugene, scolding him for leaving his French-window key in the lock and not bolting his side gate. He had been so sweet to Ella that she didn't say she'd told him so.

The pleasures of the weekend were still with her when she walked into the medical centre on Tuesday morning, but she was brought down to earth by the news that Joel Roseman had made an appointment to see her at twelve noon after her morning surgery. He was physically much better. The receptionist said he laid stress on the word "better."

JOEL'S MOTHER VISITED him every day. He asked her if his father objected, if she was defying his father, spending so much time with him in this flat, but she said no, adding ingenuously that Morris didn't mind how often she saw their son so long as he didn't have to. Sometimes she suggested a walk in the park under the trees that stand in a long row parallel with the Bayswater Road, but Joel wouldn't unless it was after dark, so mostly she sat with him in one of the gloomy rooms and talked to him fretfully about his solitary life, his lack of a girlfriend or, indeed, any friend. One day he told her about his near-death experience, though leaving out the part about bringing Mithras back with him. When he said he had found not heaven, but hell, at the end of the tunnel, she began to cry.

He tried to reassure her. "Hell is beautiful, Ma. It's a bit like the park but without so many people."

After she had gone, driving the Bentley back to Hampstead Garden Suburb, he sat gazing at the endlessly reflected bronze heads. They made the flat appear enormous, Julius Caesar, Augustus, Tiberius, and all the rest. They were all the same man, all the same copy of an ancient ruler, dead two thousand years. As he stared at their hard mouths, aquiline noses, and sightless eyes, Mithras returned. Joel couldn't have said how he knew Mithras was present because most of the time he was invisible, yet Joel knew he was there as surely as he had known his mother had been. It was as if he had some extra sense, which no one had ever named.

He felt Mithras's presence rather like a perpetual touch, as if his visitor had laid a hand lightly on him and rested it there. At the same time he felt that if light could be admitted to the place, bright white light flooding the flat, Mithras would become truly visible, as clear as any human being, for he had come from a radiant, gleaming place. But Joel was too afraid of the light to take such a radical step. He felt it might blind him, literally destroy his sight. Besides, he was unsure whether he hated Mithras's presence or loved it. He sat somnolent in the living room or reclined on the brown velvet sofa for hours on end, not reading or listening to anything or watching television, sometimes falling into a doze. One afternoon he had decided to resume his infrequent habit of taking himself alone to the cinema. Wearing his blackest sunglasses, he set out to see *The Lives of Others*, but when he was halfway there, he felt a dizzying sensation he thought might be the start of a panic attack and he turned back towards home. Just heading for home, his dark sanctuary, calmed him.

The morning he was due to see Dr. Peacock, the psychotherapist, Mithras spoke to him. Joel couldn't see him, hadn't seen him for several days, though he had felt the touch of his hand, but he heard his voice. At first he wasn't sure who it was or where it came from. Sometimes, though the walls were thick and this dark, shadowy place well insulated, sounds could be heard from his neighbours. They were loud-voiced people who often moved their furniture about and once or twice had given noisy parties. But this voice was soft, persuasive, and almost seductive.

He knew this was human speech he was hearing, but for a while he couldn't make out the words, only that the rhythm of what was said was the rhythm of English. Then, quite clearly, he heard it say, "She will ask you if you hear voices."

Joel said nothing. He lay back and closed his eyes, wondering as he did so why human beings have the ability to shut off their vision but no mechanism for doing the same for hearing. On his way to Dr. Peacock he went into a pharmacy and bought himself some earplugs made of wax, though he was beginning to feel he would have no need to use them.

Dr. Peacock said nothing about hearing voices. She said little. She was a white-haired woman, the hair copious and long, with the face of a Russian ballet dancer and the barrel-shaped body of a bricklayer. The suit she wore was charcoal-coloured linen, the trousers tapering, and the jacket like a mandarin's. Joel expected a couch and there was one, but not for him. Dr. Peacock reclined on it while he sat in an armchair.

The psychotherapist had a high-pitched voice with the slight lisp of a camp vicar in a comedy show. Joel found it rather hard to believe she was a woman. She asked Joel to tell her why he had come, and Joel told her about his heart operation, his near-death experience, and Mithras. When he paused or hesitated, Dr. Peacock said, "Go on," and when he had told her everything in detail, Dr. Peacock said, "Tell me again." It reminded Joel of police interrogations he had seen on television when the investigating officer asks the suspect to repeat his story in order to catch him out in a lie.

At the end of the second recounting, the psychotherapist asked him who he thought Mithras was, but soon after Joel had begun talking about him, Dr. Peacock said time was up and she would see him next week. Joel had, perhaps naively, supposed that after even a single session he would begin to feel better about things, but he didn't. He put on his dark glasses and walked slowly to a bus stop, not knowing or much caring which buses stopped there. One came, but it was the kind where you have to have a ticket or a pass before you board, and the driver turned him off.

"You have to get off," the driver said. "It's no use arguing. I don't make the rules."

This unnerved Joel and he hailed a taxi.

The people in the streets all seemed to be staring at him, sitting alone in the back. They stared at him, he thought, with resentful eyes or, worse, with savage glares, and children made faces. One little boy stuck out his tongue, and Joel put his face in his hands. He hadn't enough money on him so he got the driver to take him to a cash dispenser. Three men were ahead of him. They all seemed to know each other and began to whisper together, one of them turning round to eye him before going back to their conversation. This was what happened when he exposed himself to the light. He felt uncomfortable, wondering if they meant to attack him. But nothing happened; he got his money and was soon at home.

His living room, which until then had always seemed rather too dark, nearly as dark as the rest of the place, was now too light for him. He settled that by pulling down the dark green blind to its fullest extent. The gray dimness of a wet afternoon now prevailed, and reclining on the sofa in much the same attitude as Dr. Peacock had taken up, he phoned Dr. Cotswold. Or tried to phone her. He got the receptionist, who said the doctor was with a patient but she would pass on his message and ask her to call him back. The call didn't come for almost an hour, the longest hour Joel thought he had spent for years. When she did phone, though Joel had supposed Dr. Peacock would have given her a careful report by now, she knew nothing about what had happened during his visit.

Would she come and see him? He had a lot to tell her.

"Today won't be possible," she said.

"Tomorrow, then." When she didn't answer immediately, he said, "Please."

"I think you should come to me, Joel. Shall we say twelve thirty when my last patient will have gone?"

"I will be your last patient, won't I?"

He could hear little in the flat; with the windows shut, not even more than a faint hum from the traffic. He fetched the earplugs he had bought, and working the wax with his fingers, moulding two cone shapes, he inserted them into his ears. The peculiar silence that descended was unlike normal quiet but made him feel rather as if he were being smothered. He had to make a conscious effort to breathe, but gradually the feeling went and he appreciated his new deafness. Now he was enclosed, sightless and without hearing, and he fell asleep. When he woke, two hours later, remaining in his dark cocoon, he found himself thinking about what he would say to Dr. Cotswold next day. He would tell her about Amy, about his father, and what had divided them so terribly and irrevocably.

THE NETSUKE LION and the monkey had turned up. Much to Eugene's gratification and gratitude, a shopkeeper in Westbourne Grove had found them in the gutter and handed them in at the police station. He wanted to reward Mr. Siddiqui but the shopkeeper refused his offers and said being able to return these valuable objects to their owner was reward enough. A Crime Protection officer had made an appointment to come round to Chepstow Villas and advise Eugene on sensible measures to take to make his house more secure.

"Keeping a light on in the garden, I expect they'll say," said Ella, "and putting bars on the French windows and making sure the side gate is bolted on the inside. Where's the side-gate key, by the way? I can't find it."

"Oh, God, I've no idea. That will be something else they'll bully me about, no doubt."

"They won't bully you, darling. They're only being helpful."

"If you say so, Ella. I shall hate having them poking about the place. Shall we talk about something else? Like our wedding?"

This had provisionally been fixed for October, and since neither of them had been married before, why not have a church wedding?

"I'd prefer something quiet," Ella said. "Church would be a big affair, wouldn't it?"

"But I'd love a big affair. With me in a morning coat and you looking beautiful in a white, frothy dress like a meringue and masses of flowers and all our friends and relations there. And a big lunch somewhere grand. Where shall we go for our honeymoon?"

"Italy?"

"Well, I was thinking of Sri Lanka," said Eugene.

The robbery had been a setback. If his life had proceeded in tranquillity, everything pleasant and anxiety kept to a minimum, he was sure he could have kept up his abstinence. He had kept it up throughout their weekend, and if he had drunk rather more than usual, so had Ella, and there had been something sweet and companionable about saying, "I really mustn't have another one, darling," yet having one just the same, and she replying, but with a laugh, that they must watch it or they would both be on their way to Alcoholics Anonymous.

Then they had come home to discover the burglary. From the first moment of being aware of the loss of his netsuke, he had felt on his indrawn breath an urgent desire for a Chocorange. He needed it for comfort when he saw what was missing and, though he made light of it to Ella, remembered the large sum of money he had paid for the gold and peridot necklace. It was Sunday, nowhere was open—well, nowhere in the vicinity that sold the things. If Ella hadn't been there, he would have been off to a Tesco or a Superdrug. The temptation, the longing, would have been too compelling to resist. Instead, he had had to suffer a worse deprivation than he had known at any previous time of Chocorange shortage. He craved, he longed. Secretly—but how secret was it really?—he took sips of whiskey throughout the evening until he dared take no more.

The only way to handle it, he decided next morning, a hangover throbbing at his temples, was not to think. No thinking, just doing, and doing meant walking swiftly down to Elixir the moment they opened and stocking up with five packets of Chocorange. The relief was so great that he went on not thinking. No self-reproach, no recrimination, just abandonment to this wonderful solace. Next day he replenished his stocks in the kitchen drawer by a visit to the shop in Spring Street and the day after that up to Golborne Road. Packets inside plastic bags went into the bottom drawer of the cabinet in the guest bathroom and another lot in the drawing-room bookcase behind the novels of E. M. Forster. Far from its troubling him, he laughed with delight when he counted twenty-two packets carefully stowed away for the future.

Euphoria lasted four days. On the fifth day, after asking himself (while Ella slept) if he was going mad, he resolved that this couldn't go on. It was no use saying, as he had yesterday, that he would never be without them again. He must be without them. With the wedding set for October, he had four months and a bit to begin the phasing out. For phasing out was the way. His mistake had been this cold-turkey business. If he had been gradually giving up, when he came back from his weekend away, there would have been, say, half a packet in the house, and he could have allayed his stress by sucking one that evening and another perhaps in the night. That was the way. If worse came to the worst, he could just go away on his honeymoon with a single packet of Chocorange in his baggage to tide him over. Easy. Why, he might even have conquered his habit before that. Nothing, he told himself, sucking his twelfth of the day, could be more likely.

"HOW DID YOU get on with Dr. Peacock?"

"I don't know," Joel said. "She just made me tell her about Mithras coming back from hell with me, and when I'd done, she made me tell her all over again. I thought she'd ask me about my father. I thought they always asked people about their fathers."

They were in Ella's surgery. She had been hoping to meet Eugene for lunch, but this would have to be cancelled. Joel, who clearly had only a hazy idea of time, had been fifteen minutes late and evidently intended to spend a long time with her.

"Perhaps you should ask Dr. Peacock if you can talk about your relations with your father."

"I'd rather tell you."

"Let me just make a phone call."

Although it must have been plain to him that Ella was phoning her fiancé to tell him she couldn't keep their lunch date and plain too from Ella's responses that the fiancé was disappointed, Joel showed no sign of intending to curtail his story or even postpone its telling. When she put down the phone, he launched straight into it. "I want to tell you because you're sympathetic. You understand things. It happened like this, oh, years ago. I was sixteen."

"Just a minute, Joel. I have to tell you again, I'm not a psychiatrist. I'm a doctor of medicine. I'm not qualified to practise as a psychiatrist. You know that, don't you?"

"Yes, but someone told me that anyone can be a psychotherapist in the UK, anyone. You don't need qualifications. And you're a doctor and all those others aren't. Now, like I was saying, this happened when I was sixteen. . . . Are you listening?"

"I'm listening," Ella said, keeping her sigh silent.

He began, speaking rapidly, giving the impression that if he hadn't uttered it before—though maybe he had—he had rehearsed the telling over and over thoroughly. It had loomed large in his life, it was his life. Later, as she turned it all over in her mind, she wished more than anything that she could have told Eugene about it. But she couldn't. Joel was confiding in her as his doctor, and that was all there was to it.

He had had a sister, he told her, ten years younger than himself. Her name was Amy. They had just moved, his parents, Amy, and himself, from Southampton to a house in the Hampshire countryside with twelve acres of land and a lake. From being rich, his father had become a millionaire. When the move was taking place, Joel was away at school, and coming home for the summer holidays, he saw Mossbourne House and its grounds for the first time.

"It was beautiful. I loved it. I'd never seen anywhere like it. But I'll tell you something." Joel looked to right and left and then, rather diffidently, over his left shoulder. "I'll tell you something. That place at the end of the tunnel, that place I went to when I died, that was hell but that was Mossbourne too. Those white columns and the turrets, they were Mossbourne, and the river—but not the lake. There's no lake where I went when I died." He shook his head ruefully. "Hell is beautiful, you know. It's not all ugly and burning up like those old writers said."

Ella's office was light and bright and practical, but suddenly it seemed to have grown dark. She would have shivered if she hadn't controlled herself.

"Go on."

"You sound like Dr. Peacock. My sister wanted to show me all round the place. She had been there for three weeks by then. She thought she knew all about it."

Amy had taken him all over the grounds, sometimes holding him by the hand. It was fine hot weather, the sun shining every day. She led him into the wood and along the little stream. One evening they saw an otter, and there weren't so many otters about then as there were now. She liked best to take a picnic and eat it by the lake.

"I'm not supposed to go into the water unless Mummy or Daddy are with me. Or you. Mummy says it's all right with you because you can swim and she says you're a grown-up now. Are you a grown-up?"

"Of course I am," he had said.

"But you're not to keep me waiting because I'm longing to go in."

They put on swimming things and jeans and T-shirts on top, and took towels along with the picnic. The lake had fish and long green weeds trailing through the water like streaming hair, but it was clean and clear. You could see the round cream and golden pebbles on the bottom. Joel was teaching Amy to swim. But it wasn't the best place to learn. A swimming pool would have been better, with steps to go down into the water, a shallow end and a deep end and a bar all round its rim. He said he would take her to the pool in Salisbury next time their mother drove in there. Meanwhile, they bathed in the lake. The hot weather couldn't go on like this, perfect every day, it must change soon, but it did go on. It got even hotter.

One day they both went into the water in the morning, and at midday or a bit later they ate the picnic lunch they had brought with them, quite a big lunch, half a cold chicken from the fridge with bread rolls and butter and tomatoes, and a big piece of Brie and a chocolate cake and a box of shortbread biscuits.

"You can really remember all that?" Ella said.

"I remember everything about that day. Except the bit when I was asleep."

"You went to sleep? A sixteen-year-old?" She said it for something to say because she could tell now what was coming and she wanted to stop it or at least postpone it.

"I've always slept a lot. My mother says I was a very good baby. I slept the whole night through

138

from the time I was born. I can sleep now—I only have to lie down and close my eyes and I'm asleep."

This time she didn't say, "Go on."

He was full of food and it was warm. He lay down on a blanket, meaning just to lie there and stare up at the blue sky, and he told Amy not to go into the water. It was too soon anyway. It was bad for you to go swimming straight after you'd eaten. She was to wait for him—lie down and have a rest and wait for him. They should give it half an hour. When he woke up, she was gone. Her clothes were still there in a heap, but she was gone.

"I'd slept too long, you see, Ella." It was the first time he had called her by her given name. "She must have got tired of waiting. I was so frightened, Ella. I was in a panic. I ran up and down, calling her. I picked up her clothes and looked underneath them—mad, wasn't it? As if she could have been hiding underneath her clothes. I was afraid to go into the water—I don't mean I was afraid of the water—I was afraid of what I'd find. And I did find it. I went into the water, I looked for her, and I did find her. In the end I did. I found her dead body. It was bleached so white like she was made of bone, soft bone. And she was all caught up in the weed and the reeds. I couldn't pull her out, not on my own I couldn't. I went back to the house and told my parents. I had to, though it was terrible. At first my father wouldn't believe she was dead, he said I'd made a mistake, she couldn't be dead. We all went down to the lake, and he and my mother managed to pull her out. When Pa knew she was dead, I thought he was going to kill me. My mother had to hold him back. She put her arms round his waist and held on to him and told me to run away, to go into the house."

Ella was shaking her head, murmuring, "How dreadful, how dreadful."

"I'll tell you the rest of it next time. He never spoke to me again. I'll tell you about that next time I come here or you come to me. You will come to me, won't you? I want to tell you the rest of it. I can't tell you now. I'm so tired. There's nothing tires me so much as talking about it."

11

WHILE HE WAS in the hospital, Uncle Gib never came near him. Lance didn't expect it, he'd have been so surprised to see him he'd have thought he was having a nightmare. It was amazing enough when his mum came. He was all over bruises, he had something wrong with one of his elbows and two broken ribs. It was touch and go whether they would remove his spleen, or so he thought he'd overheard them saying, but this might have been something he remembered

140

from watching *ER*. He didn't know where his spleen was or what was the use of it, but he was relieved they weren't going to take it out.

The day before they discharged him, something wonderful happened. It was the last thing he'd have thought possible, but the only thing he really wanted. The ward was full of visitors except round his bed. He had no one, which was normal, and when Gemma came in, he thought he was seeing things because all that kicking and punching had done his head in. She was looking more beautiful than ever, like Paris Hilton, in a sleeveless yellow dress and silver sandals with four-inch cork wedges. He couldn't speak, he just stared.

"I left Abelard with Mum," she said. Abelard was the baby. "How're you doing?"

"I'm good. Going home tomorrow. You're the last person I thought I'd see, but it's great to see you. It's great."

"Yeah, well, they hadn't no call to do what they did. I mean, that Ian don't know his own strength. He gets carried away. I thought, you know, I'll go over there and see Lance, it's the least I can do, I mean, tell him I'm sorry and they'd no call to do that."

"He don't know you're here, that Fize?"

"Do me a favour. You was jealous, but Fize is an animal. He reckons I'm round at Michelle's place, and Mum won't say a word."

141

"Gemma?"

"What?"

"Did they—I mean, that lot, did they get enough dosh from all that stuff they took off me—I mean, the necklace and stuff—like to pay for your tooth?"

For answer, she inserted one long, white finger, the nail lacquered lemon yellow, into her mouth, pulled back a gleaming peach-coloured lip, and showed him her flawless incisors and molars. "It's a temporary for now, but Mr. Ahmed'll be putting the permanent one on soon as it's been made."

"That's good. I'm really glad. That's all I nicked that stuff for. It wasn't for myself."

Gemma smiled at him quite fondly. "Oh, you. You was my tooth fairy, Lance, only you don't want to be so free with your fists. Specially round women. Now I've got to get over to Mum's and pick up Abelard. Shall I come and see you when you're back in that dump with old what's-his-name?"

IT WAS A strange part of the world, the edge of Kensal, where the Portobello Road squeezed under the train line and the Westway and, wandering on, passed the Spanish convent before coming close to the suburban line and turning sharp right to become Wornington Road, a street of stalls and shops and stalls in front of shops, and especially on Saturdays, that space between was crammed full of people. American visitors, tourists from India and Japan, white-skinned, white-haired housewives who lived in the old council flats and had done so since they were girls and had always shopped down the Portobello, hippies from the sixties, old now but still wearing robes and strings of beads, their long gray hair tied back in a ponytail, and the young, hundreds and thousands of the young, wearing a different uniform from their flower-power grandparents but still a uniform, jeans and T-shirts and boots, unisex gear, distinguishable only because the girls had breasts and the boys carotid cartilages.

The shops sold meat and fish and cheese and bread and flowers, and junk of every possible provenance and description. The stalls sold junk too and plenty of things that weren't junk, prints and watercolours, good jewellery and bad, umbrellas, handbags, hats, leather jackets, lampshades, masks, fishnet tights and miniskirts, mirrors and fire screens and cigarette cases and long white gloves. The young ones could buy things unknown to their flower-power grandparents: star fruit and custard apples, amaranth flakes, wild rice, aubergines striped like dahlias, samphire, chorizo, and Chinese cabbage. The hallucinogenic fungi had been banned a couple of years before, but certain herbs in innocuous-looking cellophane packs did the job just as well.

Some of the stallholders kept up a running commentary on what they had for sale, kept it up for hours, the street cries of the twenty-first century, and their voices never grew hoarse. One of them was shouting the virtues of a cigarette substitute with a battery inside it which produced a red light and tasted of cloves but could be used—hardly smoked—in any pub or restaurant or enclosed space. As the Portobello climbed and dipped northwards and passed the old Electric Cinema, the decoration of shops and adornment of stalls became more colourful and bizarre, as if an army of graffitists or students of Banksy had been called in to make this the brightest market in London. One or two of them had painted whole sides of buildings with Caribbean festivals or medieval ladies with unicorns and knights on gold-caparisoned white chargers. Bright green and scarlet and acid yellow, orange and turquoise and, more than anything else, a rich violet.

When the houses were built around the top of the Portobello, *road* was a classier name than *street*. And the houses are becoming classy again, tall ones divided into flats, smaller ones, the size of Uncle Gib's, smartened in ways that would be unrecognisable to their early owners. New front doors, new windows, discreet cladding, window boxes, bay trees in tubs—anchored down because this place is rich in crime—driveways off the street for cars. Curtains are gone; these windows have blinds, and when these are raised, you can see right through the house to the rear garden beyond. All the front rooms and dining rooms have been knocked into one through-room and the garden revealed has gum trees and spiraea and fremontodendrons—for this is twenty-first-century Britain where everyone has luxury and no one has any money. They have spent it on their homes and their holidays as it comes in and keep on spending it. All except Uncle Gib. His house is almost in a state of nature, a unique original Victorian dwelling, circa 1880. If they had any sense, the Royal Borough of Kensington and Chelsea, on whose northern border this is, would buy it off him, titivate it a bit, and open it as a nineteenth-century museum.

But all they had done was send a Pest Control officer round to deal with the vermin. Far from all wanting a rat of their own, as Uncle Gib had suggested to Lance, the neighbours had complained. The Pest Control officer sniffed, poked about in the outside toilet, and shook his head at the state of the kitchen. "This place needs a spot of attention," he said, adding unwisely, "if you ask me."

Uncle Gib said what he always said to visitors who criticised: "I'm waiting for the builders to start next week," and then, because he wasn't going to have any rat catcher finding fault with his arrangements, "and I don't ask you. You want to mind your own business, which is clobbering vermin."

Uncle Gib felt so pleased with this put-down that he went about the house after the man had gone singing "Jesus Wants Me for a Sunbeam." He hummed it now, threading his way among the ambling tourists and the slouching young, past the shop that sold venison and guinea fowl, and the stall that sold Persian perfumes: "A sunbeam, a sunbeam, I'll be a sunbeam for Him." No one took any notice of him, this tall, emaciated old man with his Voltairean face and his fluffy white hair singing hymns as he bounded along. Eccentricity is the norm in the Portobello Road.

At one of the last stalls he stopped to buy eggs, and at almost the last shop, next to the one where, in the previous week, he had bought a second-hand single mattress for the new tenant, slices of mortadella and chorizo and a piece of Double Gloucester. Uncle Gib ate only eggs and sausage-style meats and cheese, and not much of that. With a scornful glance at the stall displaying cigarette substitutes, he put his purchases in the old pink plastic bag he carried everywhere with him and which had seen many such outings since it started life in Superdrug. Saving the environment suited Uncle Gib. He had lived frugally long before global warming became an issue.

So sharp right and then right again down to the

bottom of Blagrove Road. The Pest Control officer hadn't done much beyond poisoning the rats with warfarin (or so Uncle Gib supposed), but approaching his house, he seemed to see it as somehow refurbished and smartened up by this vermin-cleansing operation. Hygiene had been effected and, what interested him most, at absolutely no cost to himself, so he let himself into his house, right up against the Westway and the Hammersmith and City Line, in a cheerful frame of mind. This soon changed. Like an animal, which without seeing or hearing or even smelling the intruder, immediately knows when someone else has entered its home and is present there, Uncle Gib sensed that he wasn't alone. He lit a cigarette before he went upstairs.

Lance's bedroom door was shut. Knocking on doors was a courtesy unknown to Uncle Gib, who opened it wide and stood on the threshold.

"I'm back," said Lance.

"I can see that. I'm not blind."

Lance had a cast on his left arm, which was in a sling, and a wide strip of gauze held in place by plasters on the side of his head where the hair had been shaved away. Making no comment on his injuries, Uncle Gib stared searchingly at the cast and the plasters, then cast up his eyes as if expecting some heavenly visitation or judgment.

"Is there anything to eat?" asked Lance, coughing at the smoke.

"You can have an egg and a bit of sausage. If you want any more, you'll have to fetch it in yourself. Missed your slave, did you?"

Uncle Gib went downstairs and Lance shifted his position on the bed—his ribs ached—not too dismayed because he was thinking about Gemma and thinking too that, when all was said and done, he would have been a highly successful burglar but for the intervention of Fize and company. Perhaps, when he was better, he would try again.

Above his head he could hear Dorian Lupescu moving about. He hadn't yet encountered him and didn't want to. That top flat should have been his, not handed over to some immigrant or whatever he was. The man had moved in while he was in hospital, and Lance was sure this had been arranged on purpose so that he wouldn't be there to tell Dorian about the inadequacies of his flat, complain about the missing table, and give him an account of the sighting of the rat. Still, when Lance had accomplished a successful burglary, he'd be able to move out and leave Uncle Gib and the Romanian (as that, apparently, was what he was) together on their own. He'd shake the dust of this place off his feet forever.

The footsteps upstairs continued, followed by a swishing sound as if a mattress was being dragged about on a dusty wooden floor. Lance rolled over onto his front and went back to sleep.

12

EUGENE HAD SOLD a picture by a painter who worked in the style of Max Ernst, just a small drawing called *Dagon's Wife*, which Ella found rather frightening, a woman with a cat's head in a silver dress and holding a fan made of bones, but Eugene had got a large sum for it, his share of which, he said, would pay for their wedding. He was determined this must be lavish, her wedding dress not a bit like the one in the picture, but to be made by the designer who had made the Duchess of Cornwall's. Ella had got her own way only about the venue for the ceremony, not a church, not a register office, but a beautiful old house in Chiswick, licensed for marriages. The reception, which Eugene in his old-fashioned way called the "wedding breakfast," though it would be a late lunch, was to be at the Connaught.

They had had a not very acrimonious argument about Ella's insisting on visiting this private patient of hers, Joel Roseman.

"I don't want to go over there, darling, you must know that. I've put him off twice and now I must go. He wants to tell me something."

"Yes, I know. You said. But though you won't tell me what it's about, you say it's not a physical illness he has. Isn't this a matter for a psychiatrist?"

"He's seeing a psychiatrist, Gene, but he doesn't like her. I think he'll give up. And you know I can't tell you things he tells me in confidence. Well, I don't think I can, though if they're not about an illness . . . I honestly don't know. It's just better not."

With that Eugene had to be content. It wasn't that he was in the least jealous of Joel Roseman. Of Ella's love for himself he had no doubt. But at present he needed to be with her every moment neither he nor she was working. She had seemed, he'd noticed, rather surprised, if gratified, by his new attentiveness and, apart from this insistence on dancing attendance on Joel Roseman, accepted it delightedly. Of course Eugene loved her, there was no doubt of that, but while they were together, his consumption of Chocorange sweets was severely curtailed. He was obliged to pass hours without one. This withdrawal from his fix, whole evenings of abstinence, a Saturday and Sunday in Rye and another in Gloucestershire, whole weekends, he hoped would help him in his phasing out. Unfortunately, what always happened was that as soon as he and Ella parted, he was unable to resist gorging on the bloody things, one after another until half a pack was gone. He thought of them this way now, the classic addict's reaction, needing but hating, longing but loathing. The bloody things.

The sale of the quasi-Ernst, acknowledged decorously in the gallery with the purchaser and Dorinda in several glasses of champagne, he had personally and privately celebrated by dashing down to Elixir and tearing open a pack of Chocorange before he was even out of the store. Half the pack was eaten while he sat on a seat in Kensington Gardens, and when he closed it and put it in his pocket, he felt, for the first time, despair. In every respect his habit had become odious to him. He was a dignified man, and no dependency could be more undignified than a craving for the sort of sweets guzzled by children and old ladies. It might also be seriously bad for him. Could you ingest vast daily quantities of a chemical sugar substitute without doing yourself enduring harm? The secrecy too appalled him. He knew he was naturally secretive, but only to the extent of not wanting casual acquaintances and employees to know his private business. With regard to these wretched, horrible, bloody lumps of caramel gunge, he had constructed a whole covert, hidden, humiliating world of pretence and lies, sneaking around pharmacies and stores to find his fix, inventing a serious disease for himself to cover an addiction as compelling and overpowering as if it had been heroin that enslaved him. And the phasing out wasn't a success. Or, rather, it was only when his life was calm and stress-free. Give him an hour or so with a client who couldn't make up his mind to buy or not to buy, give him a disagreement with the Customs and Excise or his accountants, and once it was past he was down the road to the nearest pharmacy.

Sitting there on a seat under a spreading copper beech, Eugene bent over and put his head in his hands, for once not caring who saw him or what people thought.

SHE RANG THE bell and banged on the brass knocker, but it was a while before she could make Joel hear.

At last he came, trudging, bleary-eyed. "I was asleep." He peered at her as if he had never seen her before. "I sleep a lot. I don't have much to do, so I sleep."

It was brighter outside than the last time Ella had been to the flat but darker in here. *The dim halls of sleep and death* came into her mind, but she didn't know if this was a quotation or she had made it up. The darkness seemed to carry its own silence with it. She followed him into the living room, where the blinds were down and this time no lamp was on. On the brown velvet sofa the cushions were crushed where his head had rested.

"I went to the hospital to have my checkup. The doctor said I should start taking gentle exercise. I said what was gentle exercise and he said walking. But I get very tired when I walk. Mithras tells me not to walk, to rest."

"Have you told Dr. Peacock about Mithras?" Speaking the name nearly made her shudder but she persisted. "If you've started hearing his voice you ought to tell Dr. Peacock."

"I'm not going to Dr. Peacock anymore." He sat down, waved her to a chair. "I don't want someone like her. She doesn't tell me what to do. She doesn't tell me anything. I don't like the way she looks at her watch and tells me that's enough for today. It upsets me."

"Joel, you must see someone. Your condition needs to be assessed and a suitable—well, a regime of drugs prescribed for you. I should think," she added uncertainly. "I can't do that. I'm not that sort of doctor."

"But you're the doctor I want. You listen and you answer. You're not like Dr. Peacock."

"I shall refer you to someone else, Joel. I'll find someone you feel more comfortable with. Now, you were going to tell me about your father. Could we have the blinds up, do you think?"

He shook his head. "I like it better when it's dark." He made a little sound, which might have been a sigh or only a rather strong expulsion of breath. "I don't think I could talk about it in the light." He looked at her and turned sharply away, but it was a few seconds before he began to speak. "Pa never spoke to me again, I told you that. My mother tried to get him to speak to me but he wouldn't. He sent me messages by her. I mean messages about money and school and going to university, that sort of thing. You know who he is, don't you? He's Morris Stemmer, you'll have heard of him."

She had heard the name, she couldn't remember where. "But you're called Roseman."

"It was my mother's name. He made me take it. He told Ma he didn't want me called Stemmer anymore. You know who he is, don't you? They call him the king of the tycoons."

Some head of an insurance company or the chief executive of a huge syndicate? She never knew about things like that but she would ask Eugene. He would know.

"He was punishing me because he said I'd killed Amy. He never seemed to see that it was as bad for me as for him. I loved Amy too and I had guilt as well. I told Ma that over and over and she told him, but it never made any difference. I left school but my A Levels weren't very good. I got into one of those universities with a name no one had ever heard of, and I stuck it for nearly two years. Then I dropped out. I don't know what he thought. Ma never said and I didn't ask."

"Were you living at home?"

"I wasn't allowed to. He took a flat for me near my college and he gave me an allowance, a big

154

allowance, bigger than I wanted. I told Ma but he just went on paying it into my bank account. I had some jobs, unskilled stuff, the sort of thing illegal immigrants take these days, cleaners and working in cafés, that sort of thing. I worked in a sandwich factory for a while. All the other people were Italians and we never spoke. I couldn't stand it so I left."

"If your father was giving you money, why did you need to take that sort of work? Couldn't you have trained for something? Done a course?"

He said simply, "I hadn't the heart." And then, "I never felt very well, I was always tired. Ma said it was my imagination but it wasn't, it was my heart. I literally hadn't the heart, you see, Ella.

"Pa had bought this flat for me. Like I said, he bought it with all this furniture and curtains and everything. I didn't have any choice about it. By then I couldn't have worked if I'd wanted to. I got so tired, especially in the evenings. I'd do nothing all day except sometimes go to the shops, but still I'd be wiped out by seven. I'd fall asleep on that sofa. Ma wanted me to go to the doctor, but I didn't. Then I had that heart attack, which was how I came to meet you."

And have a near-death experience, she thought, or what he thought was a near-death experience. The question she wanted to ask was a therapist's question, not a doctor of medicine's, but she asked it. "That place you went to that was beau-

tiful but you thought was hell, was that somewhere you knew? Was it familiar to you?"

He said nothing for a moment or two, then, "I
don't know. It was a bit like Mossbourne, it had
the white columns and a turret, but it wasn't
really very like. I tried to make it like that in my
mind, but I couldn't, it wouldn't work. The place
I went to was a river with grassy banks and at the
end of it a city. The view was of a city with
domes and palaces and towers. It wasn't the
house at Mossbourne. That would be too conven-
ient, wouldn't it? Hell as the lake at Mossbourne,
where you could say everything began—or
maybe where everything ended."

She gave him the name of another therapist and
said she would phone this woman and tell her
about Joel. The dimness was beginning to
oppress her, the unnatural dark, which almost
anyone else would have altered by pulling up the
blind or switching on a light. It was almost as if
this contrived dusk were making it hard for her
to breathe. She found herself drawing in deep
gulps of night-in-daytime air. Writing a letter for
him to give Miss Crane, she had to peer closely
at the paper. The therapist's phone number,
which she could usually remember, she had to
look up in her address book.

Joel seemed to be listening. "Can you hear the
people next door? I can hear they're talking but
not what they say."

She could hear nothing but she thought it might be best to say she could. "Maybe just a murmur."

"I bought earplugs so that I couldn't hear it, but they didn't make any difference." He stared at her through the gloom, leaning forward across the space between them. "You see, Ella, I'm not mad, I know it's not the neighbours I hear. It's Mithras. He makes a noise like two people talking when he's trying to get through. But he always does get through. He will in a minute."

For the first time since she was a child and her father had accidentally driven into the back of the car in front (with no injury to anyone), she wanted to scream aloud. She'd screamed then and sobbed while her mother tried to comfort her. Now, thirty-five years later and a responsible person, a doctor, she controlled herself and no sound came till she said in a hoarse voice, "You must see Miss Crane and as soon as possible. You will, won't you, Joel?"

He nodded. "I want to get better," he said like the child he still seemed to be.

WHILE MITHRAS WAS talking to him, Joel found it impossible to sleep. The voice, otherworldly, very low, to some extent like an automaton's, droned quite softly, and sometimes another voice, which he fancied was his own when he was a boy, answered Mithras or asked him questions. Because there were occasionally two speakers, Joel had been able to tell himself it was the neighbours he heard. An argument or discussion went on in his head, but afterwards he couldn't say what it was they had been talking about. He had absorbed enough pop psychology to expect Mithras and his companion, his own other self, to tell him that certain people he knew were his enemies and perhaps that they would kill him if he didn't kill them first. This didn't happen or hadn't happened yet.

The strangest aspect of all this was that he could hear Mithras and the other Joel talking and know they were speaking English. He knew too that they hadn't, either of them, that kind of foreign accent that would make sorting out what they said difficult. This unknowing was the worst of it. Having hated Mithras's voice, tried to explain it away, and taken steps to block up his ears, he now wanted very much to understand what was said. He felt excluded, isolated, and lonely. How could he teach himself to decipher their conversation or simply interpret Mithras when he spoke on his own? And how did he know his visitant was called Mithras?

The discussion ended and there was absolute silence. Those who live in the country, come to London only seldom, and view all its doings with suspicion, believe everywhere is noisy, night and day. There is no peace, no quiet, and stress reigns. They have no idea of the utter silence that prevails inside some of London's mansion flats in the afternoon. Joel knew well that his neighbours made no noise. If they had, it would scarcely have penetrated those walls. But for Mithras and the other one (himself?) not a sound would reach the interior of this flat, and when a neighbour came home from work, Joel would hear no more, and then only if his front door was open, than the whisper of the lift rising and the turning of a key in a lock. The earplugs were useless and he threw them away.

He lay down on the brown sofa to sleep again. The slats on the dark green blind were not entirely closed and thin strips of sunlight gleamed in the gaps. He got up and remedied this by pulling the cords as tightly as they would go. In the deepened darkness he lay down again, savouring the silence and the gloom. It occurred to him that this was likely what death would be with the added bonus of unconsciousness.

13

THE PAELLA STALL was almost too much for Lance. He couldn't afford to buy anything from it, any more than he could afford to buy one of the sugar-dusted pancakes he had seen on offer outside Magic City, the amusement arcade. But the circular pans of steaming and bubbling prawns in golden sauce, green peas and onions and chicken pieces, and another of gleaming saffron-coloured rice as beautiful as one of Gemma's quilted and beaded cushions, made him sick with longing. He forced himself to turn away and concentrate on the true purpose of his visit.

The woman in the red jacket and the floral skirt spent a long time looking at Lilla's window. Her companion, a man as thin and weedy as she was fat, seemed to be urging her to go into the shop, where he would buy her jewellery. Their voices were loud, and Lance, in the middle of the roadway, could hear every word they said. He moved closer. Few cars or vans come up or down the Portobello Road, though plenty cross it, but here pedestrians wander unthreatened, chatting, pointing, laughing in amazement. The couple he had his eye on passed him, crossing the road, and homed in on the stall where rings and brooches and long strings of beads were on offer, at half Lilla's prices. The woman was carrying a red shoulder bag, its flap, which fastened with a stud, left open. Lance, who knew something about such things, reflected that this kind of handbag was rubbish, as was the type with a zip. The only reasonably safe kind was the old-fashioned sort like that his nan had the sense to carry, which closed with a clip over which a kind of belt came down and locked into a buckle. There was no way a bag snatcher could get into that.

Before his encounter with Fize and his friends, he had experimented with cutting into a bag with a kitchen knife. The knife had been Auntie Ivy's and was one of several lying among forks and sharpeners, and what Uncle Gib called a fish slice, in a kitchen drawer. You had to work it in a crowded place. Lance had picked the tube—not the tube here really, the underground, for the trains from Edgware Road via Paddington to Hammersmith run along the oldest line in London, passing Uncle Gib's house almost too close for comfort. Ladbroke Grove was the nearest station to the Portobello Road, but Lance got on at Westbourne Park and in the rush hour. The train was loaded with commuters at five thirty in the afternoon, hundreds of them standing and crushed together. He picked on girls with large bags slung over their shoulders on short straps. These were the most accessible. Aiming for the side of the bag and from the back as the train moved out of Ladbroke Grove, he cut a slit in it about six inches long. The girl didn't feel a thing and no one noticed. The passengers were all too tired and jaded after a day's work.

Lance wasn't tired. He'd done nothing all day except buy junk food and eat it and watch the telly. He slipped his hand inside the bag and brought out a leather something that felt like a wallet and another leather something, the kind of case people keep credit cards in. It took nerve to remain inside the train after that, but he only had to stay until it pulled into Latimer Road. The girl got out when he did, but she hadn't noticed anything wrong with her bag. It was an unpleasant anticlimax when, trudging back to the Portobello, he looked at his haul and found the thing he'd thought a wallet was a pouch containing sunglasses and the case he'd thought was for credit cards was a kind of makeup with a sponge inside its lid. He threw them away in disgust. Since then he hadn't tried the trick with the knife again. Truth to tell, he was a bit afraid of carrying a knife. Getting caught with a knife when you'd done nothing with it but split a handbag, when you didn't mean to do anything else with it, was a bit of a waste. His injured arm felt heavy and sore, although the plaster had come off, and his ribs ached.

The fat woman in red and her husband—Lance thought the thin guy must be her husband as no man would be seen dead with her unless he was chained too tightly to get away—were now seriously studying the wares on show at the jewellery stall. Lance knew the girl who ran it, although not her name, but he wasn't too pleased at her "Hi, Lance," uttered loudly and drawing attention to him.

Still no one seemed to take any notice. He muttered, "Cheers," the term that served equally as "hello" and a "thank you" with him, and edged closer to the woman in red. She was holding up a long string of black and white beads, which she suddenly put down, and began rummaging in her bag. Lance thought she was reaching for a purse or wallet, but, no, she evidently left paying for things to her husband. Out came a pack of Benson & Hedges and a lighter. The strain of shopping was too much for her without the stimulus or sedative effect of a cigarette. Another one smoking those stinking things! Just wait till July first when they ban it forever, he found himself muttering under his breath, you'll know what it's like to have the filth slap a hand on your shoulder then. But would she? Wasn't this an open space where they could kill themselves with the things as much as they liked?

She was putting the cigarettes and the lighter back in the bag now and, no-brain that she was, leaving the flap hanging open. She held up the black and white beads to the girl who'd spoken to him, said she'd have them. Lance slipped his hand inside the bag, drew out a large, heavy wallet, and shoved it into the pocket of his jeans. Just as he'd thought, the man was paying for the necklace, asking her if she'd like a pair of earrings to match. Lance stepped back, turned and stared into the window of the cheese shop, as if entranced by the Jarlsberg and Roquefort on offer. The heavy wallet made a grotesque bulge in his jeans as if he'd got a hernia. One of Uncle

Gib's religious pals had a hernia, which gave him a small belly on top of his large natural belly. Slowly, pausing to glance at stalls he'd seen a hundred times before, Lance walked up the Portobello until he could safely turn into Golborne Road away from spying eyes.

There, sitting on a wall in a street harmless now but once, long before his time, a notorious crime hot spot, he opened the wallet. No credit cards. She left that kind of thing to her husband. Three twenties and a fiver and, in the purse section where she'd almost broken the zip stuffing it with change, a lot of two-pound coins and one-pound coins and fifty and twenty pences. She'd got too much of it to bother with the smaller stuff. He counted. With the notes it came to eighty-eight pounds all told. Not bad, might have been worse.

He wandered down Bevington Road, pausing first to drop the wallet into a bin and then to buy himself a Mars bar and a packet of crisps, finally getting on a bus, from which he was immediately ejected because it was the kind you had to have a ticket for before you got on. Lance felt aggrieved. He had fully intended to pay his fare out of Mrs. Red Jacket's change, but they hadn't given him the chance. There was no justice.

Ever since his bag-snatching he had been moving away from Uncle Gib's with no apparent purpose. But of course he had a purpose. A moth drawn to a flame, he was making for Gemma's place, for the flats with their balconies and black railings, their gardens full now of red flowers and purple flowers, and the graffiti-scrawled yellow walls that bounded them. After her visit to the hospital he no longer had that hopeless feeling that she would utterly reject him, clutch Abelard to her bosom as if he were one of those paedos, turn from him and slam the balcony door. Was it possible she would have him back? Give that Fize his marching orders and have him back? He'd have to make her believe he'd never smack her again, which was true, he never would. He'd tie his hands behind him, sit on his hands, before he'd touch her.

He was outside the flat now, looking up at her balcony. She must have seen him for she came out. Overflowing with love, he gazed ardently at her. She put one finger to her lips, then mouthed silently, "I'll come and see you," and was gone. Back the way she had come, the door closed carefully behind her.

REUBEN PERKINS AND his wife, Maybelle, were paying a rare visit to Uncle Gib and being served tea in the front room. The two of them were the only people Uncle Gib ever made tea for. Even the Children of Zebulun, attending a prayer meeting, were given orange squash. Mr. and Mrs. Perkins were provided tea and Garibaldi biscuits—they had to bring their own cigarettes—because Reuben was Uncle Gib's best friend and now no longer the assistant shepherd but the head shepherd himself. He and Uncle Gib were remarkably alike and could have been taken for brothers. Both were tall and thin, although Uncle Gib was taller and thinner, both had skull-like faces and a hungry, deprived look, thin-lipped, their eyes suspicious and their noses sensitive. Perhaps they had started off looking quite different from each other, but prison, the prison diet, and each other's frequent company had brought about this similarity. Maybelle Perkins wasn't at all like Auntie Ivy, who had been a handsome woman, but squat and round with a square face and frizzy ginger hair.

Conversation, having exhausted the weather, house prices, and the general moral decline in society, centred on Uncle Gib's recent tract on teenage single parents and his latest homilies to his correspondents in the church magazine. Both Perkinses approved, both marvelled at his wise advice and his literary skills. Maybelle, on her fourth fag, was commending him for telling a sixteen-year-old girl that if she took the morning-after pill she'd be a murderer and go straight to hell when a key was heard in the lock and Lance came into the house. The front-room door was open and the fug pervaded the hall. Coughing ostentatiously, Lance stood in the doorway, intending to annoy because he felt so happy and at ease with the world. Neither of the Perkinses had ever met him.

"This your nephew, then, Gilbert?" said Maybelle.

"My late wife's great-nephew," Uncle Gib corrected her. "I'm giving him accommodation and his meals all found."

Maybelle didn't say "out of the goodness of your heart" but her sweet smile conveyed it.

"A poxy room and an outside toilet," said Lance, and he went upstairs, Uncle Gib's threats following him.

Lying on his bed, he gave himself up to thoughts of Gemma. She'd said she'd come and see him, but why hadn't she said he could come and see her? Because Fize was for a while at any rate staying there. Lance didn't like the idea of that, and a cloud moved slowly across his clear blue sky. Nor did he care for the thought of Gemma, who was so spotlessly clean and beautiful—she often had two showers a day— being entertained in this grotty room. He looked dispassionately around, taking it all in, the paintwork, fingermarked and filthy, the window so encrusted with grime that you wouldn't know it was something made to see out of. Gray net curtains with ragged hems hung limply against the dirty glass. The floor was covered in brown lino, curling at the edges where it met the

167

skirting board, and the walls papered—where the paper wasn't peeling off—in a pattern of flowers and birds, all faded to a grayish pink and barely distinguishable for what they were meant to be.

He needed money. With money you could do anything, and he thought vaguely how he could get someone to come in and paint the place, clean the window, find a woman to put up real curtains. Not for himself; for Gemma. Should he go back to Chepstow Villas and try his luck again? He still had the key to that side gate in his jacket pocket. But unless White Hair was a complete nutter, he'd have not only bolted it by now, but barred his French windows as well. But what about the other house, the one in Pembridge Villas he'd escaped through? The place with all that bamboo stuff in the garden. Maybe he should go over there and check up on a few things, such as who lived there and when they went out and got back, if there was a dog or a burglar alarm. He could go now and on the way make that detour that led him past her place and perhaps he'd see her again. . . .

ELIZABETH CHERRY WAS talking to her neighbours through a gap in the ivy and honeysuckle and *Clematis armandii*, which rambled thickly over the terrace at the ends of their gardens. She had known Eugene Wren for quite a long time now. Ella Cotswold was her doctor, and through

168

Elizabeth the two had first met. She was reminding them of this, how Ella had been paying her a home visit when Elizabeth had suspected pneumonia and Eugene had come in bearing a bottle of Bristol Cream sherry and some smoked wild salmon to tempt her appetite. The invitation to their wedding, which she had just received, had prompted this recollection.

"How kind, Gene," she was saying. "I'd love to come. Where will you be going for your honeymoon? Or is that a secret?"

"No secret," said Ella. "Italy."

"Sri Lanka," said Eugene.

"I see. Well, one's on the way to the other. I must go in. I'm going round to my sister's later for a drink. You see how my life has become one mad round of amusement."

They laughed in a polite, understanding way and Elizabeth went back into her house. She was just in time to answer the door to a young man with fair hair and an unmemorable sort of face who wanted to know if she needed a gardener, just for tidying up and mowing the lawn. Though eighty-one, Elizabeth performed these tasks herself quite adequately and wasn't too happy about the imputation that she needed help.

"No, thank you. Good afternoon," she said, disliking even more the way the young man seemed to be peering into her hall, looking this way and that, and taking in more than was good

169

for him. Or perhaps more than was good for her.

But when he had gone, she thought, as Eugene had thought before her, that it was silly and verging on the paranoid to suspect every stranger of nefarious behaviour. He was just a poor boy who needed to supplement his probably low income.

IT WAS SATURDAY evening when Gemma arrived, the very time of all times when Lance calculated she couldn't possibly come. But there she was on the doorstep, looking more beautiful than ever in a diaphanous maxidress with low neck and puff sleeves, her long blond hair piled on top of her head and a rose tucked among the curls.

Lance was struck dumb with joy and longing. He could only gaze.

"Aren't you going to ask me in?" She stepped briskly over the threshold without waiting for him to answer. "My God, what a pong. You've not taken up smoking, have you?"

Lance found his voice. "It's Uncle Gib. He gets through fags like there's no tomorrow."

"Probably isn't, for him. Where is he, anyway?"

"Gone to a senior citizens' social. They're mostly seniors at his church."

Gemma wasn't interested. "Where's your room, then?"

170

An hour later, sitting up in Lance's bed, they started on the bottle of Cava Gemma had brought. Not until this point had Lance come round sufficiently from his bliss to enquire who was minding the baby.

"Fize is. He's really taken to Abelard, says he's like his own son."

This, to Lance, was like a jet of cold water in his face and enough to wake him thoroughly from his euphoria. Sympathetically, Gemma poured him more wine. "You're going to give him the boot, though, aren't you?" said Lance. "Get rid of him and have me back?"

"Ooh, I don't know, lover. Maybe one day. It'd be like awkward right now."

"But you said . . ."

"My idea's much better. We'll have an affair, you and me. I'll come round here in secret. Won't that be great?" She looked around the room, curling her lip. "I'll get this place cleaned up a bit. It's disgusting."

"It'll have to be Sunday mornings when Uncle Gib's at church."

"What's wrong with that? Mum'll have Abelard. She don't work Sundays." Gemma brought her mouth to his in a long, deep kiss. "I've never had an affair," she whispered. "It's always been relationships everyone's like known about. Boring, really. This way'll be romantic."

Another hour later Lance heard Uncle Gib

come in. They'd have to be quiet getting Gemma down the stairs. Faintly he heard Uncle Gib singing "Jesus Wants Me for a Sunbeam" and then the television started. Gemma got up and slipped on her dress and shoes with remarkable speed. Her hair had come down and she left it to stream over her shoulders. It amazed Lance that a girl could get up to what they'd just got up to—three times too—and emerge looking as if she was ready for a photo shoot.

Footsteps sounded on the stairs as they put their heads out, but it was only Dorian Lupescu on his way to the top floor. He nodded to Lance and Lance nodded to him, but they didn't speak.

"Who's that?"

"Guy who lives upstairs."

"Hot," said Gemma, casting Lance back into the depths.

14

ELLA WAS LOOKING for the key to the side gate. She had checked the hooks in the garage where various keys hung and glanced into the shed at the end of the garden. Keys were also kept in a drawer in the kitchen, but it wasn't among them. She asked Eugene.

"In the lock on the gate."

"No, it isn't. And it's not in the garage or the shed, or with the other keys in the kitchen."

172

"It doesn't matter, does it? The gate's always bolted on the inside."

"Yes, but I don't like the idea of that burglar having it, and I'm sure that's who's got it."

She wasn't quite sure. For a man with so many valuable possessions, Eugene was careless about security. She hadn't been aware of this before she became engaged to him. This character trait didn't affect their relationship. In the future she would see to the safety side of their living arrangements, so that was all right, but meanwhile, where was that key? When she came to think of it, what was the point of the burglar keeping the key? He would know the gate would in future be kept bolted and expect bars to be put on the windows at the back of the house. Whatever Eugene might say, he had probably put the key in some unsuitable place in the house.

If she couldn't find it, she'd have the lock changed. That was only prudent. With no surgery that morning, she waited till Eugene went off to the gallery and began to search the kitchen. That was where it might likely be, dropped into one of the many drawers by an absentminded man who wouldn't think twice about getting it mixed up with cutlery or microwave operating instructions or tea cloths. But it wasn't among the knives and forks or lying on top of an oven glove. Ella did a good deal of tidying up as she searched, always conscious, and happy to be conscious, that in a few weeks this would be her home as much as it was Eugene's. She folded the cloths more neatly, put the cooking implements in a different section from the forks and spoons, and the knives in the empty knife block. Squatting down to search the unlikeliest of places, the area at the base of the oven where baking and roasting tins were kept, she took hold of a kind of flange to hoist herself—really, she would have to join a gym; being stiff in the joints at her age was a disgrace—but found herself pulling open a drawer. A secret drawer—who would have thought it?

It was empty but for two small orange-and-brown packets containing sugar-free sweets. Chocorange, they were called. Ella took a sweet out of the already opened packet and put it into her mouth. Rather nice. Probably left behind by Carli the cleaner, she thought. Carli was always on the lookout for things to satisfy her appetite but help her lose weight. Ella finished searching the kitchen but the key still eluded her. It looked as if changing the lock was inevitable.

EUGENE HAD SOLD two John Hugons bronzes, lovely things he was almost sorry to part with. They would have looked beautiful in his drawing room and Ella would have liked them. Leaving Dorinda in charge, he went off to have lunch with a woman artist, an exhibition of whose work, tiny paintings rich in gold, silver, and copper lacquer, he was going to mount in the gallery. Lunch was to be at a restaurant in Knightsbridge, and on his way he called in at Elixir and bought three packs of Chocorange.

His intention had been to resist temptation. His intention was always to resist temptation, although the phrase *phasing out* he had abandoned. Lately, he had been seriously cutting down, largely the result of having Ella with him most of the time. Saturday and Sunday had passed without a single sugar-free sweet, but on Monday he had eaten several on his way to the gallery and three more while Dorinda was out at lunch, almost returning to his usual pattern. Just one pack remained in the secret drawer, four in the spare bathroom cabinet, and two in the drawing room. The cache behind the E. M. Forsters must stay there untouched. He envisaged a time when he was over this, when it was all behind him and he could, with ritualistic pleasure, take that bagful and drop it in the waste bin on the corner of Pembridge Road.

But that time wasn't yet. The craving had been sharp this morning. He was also hungry. The breakfast he had eaten was inadequate to satisfy him until lunchtime, but if he ate twice as much, which he would have liked, he'd start putting on weight again. Chocoranges were a substitute for real food. He had brought a full pack out with him, eaten two sweets on the way, two more surreptitiously, telling Dorinda he had a sore throat, and now three more on his walk to Elixir. He knew that if he didn't replenish his by now meagre kitchen, bathroom, and drawing-room stocks he wouldn't be able to resist breaking into the store in the plastic bag behind the books. And somehow, doing this seemed to him to signify the beginning of the end. What he meant by *the end* he wouldn't have been able to say, but it included such concepts as "downfall," "crack-up," and total abandonment to a loved, yet hated, habit. The Chocorange sweets in that bag were sacrosanct, never to be touched. So he could persuade himself that buying three more packs in Elixir was a prudent measure, postponing or avoiding altogether the final weakness. Now he had the three in his briefcase, he need not be careful to restrain his consumption of the sweets in the pack he had brought with him. In spite of the one he had put into his mouth before entering Elixir, still remaining there as a sliver between the side of his tongue and his back teeth, he helped himself to another, whose rich, creamy taste was so much stronger and more delectable than the fragment that had once been as delicious as the newcomer. Philosophising as he often did on the nature and constituents of his addiction, Eugene considered what makes a habit and what a dependency and, concluding that in his case the former had finally become the latter, entered the restaurant where he ordered a sherry to take away the taste and the smell of chocolate. It was a reversal of the accepted order of things. Instead of chewing a sweet to disguise the smell of alcohol when he opened his mouth, he was drinking alcohol to hide the smell of a sweet on his breath.

THE HOUSE OPPOSITE the one with the bamboo was up for sale. The owners had moved out, removing curtains and blinds from the windows. Lance sneaked round to the back, where he tried the handles of the back door and a glass door, which opened out of a living room. Both were locked, but he had known they would be. Telling himself that no one cares much if you break a window in an empty house that's going to be sold, he picked up a large flint which, with a hundred like it, formed the border of a circular flowerbed. He took off his jacket, wrapped it round the flint, and slung the wrapped stone against a glass pane in the back door. After that, he pushed his hand through the gap he had made, unlocked the door, and let himself in. He made little noise and what he had made had apparently gone unheard by neighbours.

Inside, all was empty and forlorn. A large wooden crate served him as a seat by the front-room window. From there he could watch the house opposite. Only then did he ask himself precisely what he was looking for. The old

177

woman to go out? Suppose she was out already? The house had no garage, and no car was on the short driveway. But she was about a hundred years old and people of that age often didn't have cars. Lance had been on the watch for no more than five minutes when the rain began. It started as a drizzle, then became torrential, creating a sort of fog through which nothing on the other side of the street was discernible.

Like most summer rain—of which there had been a great deal lately—the shower lasted no more than ten minutes. It cleared and the sun came out, blazing on the wet pavements. That made him think of Gemma, who'd been complaining that with this weather she couldn't get her washing dry. Fize had promised to buy her a tumble dryer, but so far he hadn't done anything about it, and meanwhile it was always bloody raining. She had come round twice more to visit Lance in Blagrove Road, though the first time there had been little time for the affair aspect of things as she'd spent two hours cleaning his room, taking down the curtains to get them washed, and changing the sheets. But the second time . . . The only alloy in Lance's happiness had been another encounter with Dorian Lupescu on the stairs. Gemma had made no comment on his appearance, but Lance hadn't liked the look on the Romanian's face, his eyes rolling and his lips pursed up as if for a silent whistle.

While Lance was thinking of ways to get rid of, or make Uncle Gib get rid of, the upstairs tenant, but keeping his eyes on the house opposite, the old woman came out of her front door, carrying an umbrella and pushing a shopping trolley. Heading for the Portobello probably, Lance thought. You wouldn't go up to Westbourne Grove unless you wanted to buy clothes or CDs or makeup, and this woman was too old for any of that. He watched her go off in the direction he had predicted. For someone of her age she walked fast.

That meant she wouldn't be long. Still, he wasn't planning on anything major today. All he wanted was to get a good look at the place; from the back, in daylight. No one would do anything about the window he'd broken for days, maybe weeks. Lance locked the back door on the inside and let himself out of the front door, pulling it closed behind him. The old woman's side gate wasn't locked, couldn't be locked, he saw when he was on the other side of it. No keyhole, no bolts. The back door, however, was locked, but a window was open. She must be losing her marbles if she thought there was any point in locking that door when she was leaving other easy means of access. He soon saw that she wasn't all that foolish, had calculated that no human being was thin enough to squeeze between the casement and its frame.

Lance was thin, had a narrow, concave chest

and no hips worth speaking of. He took off his jacket and then his T-shirt. Still, his shoulders got stuck and he had a moment of panic when he thought she might come back and find him trapped there, she might have to send for para- medics or, worse, the police. But by wriggling and contracting his upper arms, folding them across his still tender ribs, he got himself through, his shoulders scraped and burning. His poor hand wasn't right yet and now it had begun to ache—but no pain, no gain, he said to himself, quoting Gemma in another context. He found himself in a sort of laundry room from which a doorway led into the kitchen, a large place equipped with all sorts of ultramodern stuff, quite surprising in a woman of that age.

What wasn't surprising was the glass jar full of money he found in a cabinet. That was the kind of thing these geriatrics did, kept the house- keeping in a jar or tin. Knowing that she was behaving, in one aspect at least, the way old people should behave brought him comfort. The money wasn't all small change. Fivers and ten- ners were mixed up with the coins. Lance stuffed most of it into his jeans pockets, leaving only two- and five-pence pieces. With that and what he'd been saving out of his takings from the fat woman's handbag, he might have nearly enough to buy Gemma a tumble dryer himself. That would be one in the eye for Fize. . . .

Nearly a quarter of an hour had passed since he had seen the old woman go out and ten minutes since he got through the window. He ought to be out of there within half an hour of her departure. Old people didn't eat much, and she might only be buying a chop for her supper and a packet of biscuits. Thinking of food made him realise he was ravenous. Saving up for Gemma's present had made him cut his rations, and he'd been relying on the meagre pickings provided by Uncle Gib. He opened the fridge. A large frosted chocolate cake had pride of place in the front of the middle shelf. Saliva flowing, Lance cut himself a slice with one of her kitchen knives, stuffed it into his mouth with both hands, and cut another. Uncle Gib had once told him that it was usual for burglars on breaking and entering to eat the food they found. He found himself wanting to be like other burglars, to be a professional and do it right.

He cut a third piece, carrying it with him into a huge, lavishly furnished living room and leaving a trail of sticky brown crumbs. He made for a desk, lifted up the rolltop, and contemplated the contents. No money was to be seen, but two credit cards were right in the front and a chequebook. Better not touch them now. Twenty minutes had gone by and Lance thought that if he turned the cake round so that the side he'd cut slices off faced the other way, she might not know he'd been there. After all, he had entered but not broken in. Half-starved for the past week, he felt a little sick. Put the small change back into the jar and just keep the notes. A change of plan with regard to the cake would be to take what remained of it with him. He found a carrier bag and dropped it in. She wouldn't notice now. Old people had terrible memories, lots of them halfway to Alzheimer's, and she'd think she'd eaten the cake or, more likely, never made it.

From the living-room window, peering out between the festoons of lace and velvet curtains, he looked up and down the empty street. No reason why he shouldn't let himself out the front door. When he came to think of it, nothing else was possible; if he went by way of the back door, he couldn't lock it and leave the key in place on the inside. Cautiously, he emerged into the front garden, toting his carrier bag full of cake. His nausea was passing. At first he had thought of dumping the cake in the nearest bin, but a little foresight told him that next day he would be hungry again and a slice of it would be welcome as dessert after one of Uncle Gib's first courses of black pudding and fried egg.

He sat on a wall and counted the money, just as he had done when he plundered the American woman's handbag. Not so much from today, only forty-five pounds. He'd take the credit cards next time.

· · ·

THE SHARPES FROM next door and Elizabeth Cherry were being entertained to drinks at Eugene's house. They had all talked about the weather, how it was unbelievable, rain pouring down day after day, and so cold that Marilyn Sharpe had had her central heating on for two days. In July!

Ella thought talking about rain as boring as anything one could think of, and she was relieved when Elizabeth began telling everyone about her extraordinary experience of the previous day. Eugene went round filling glasses from the second Veuve Clicquot bottle. Everyone in this smart area of Notting Hill served champagne on such occasions, wine being considered rather mean and spirits unhealthy.

"I waited till the rain stopped," Elizabeth was saying, "and then I went out shopping. I'd absolutely nothing in the house except this enormous cake I'd made for my granddaughter's birthday. Or let me say I think I'd made. Really, I'm telling this story against myself because it'll make you all think I'm senile. And, oh, dear, perhaps I am."

She paused until the cries of "But you're wonderful" and "Absurd, you're like someone twenty years younger" had died down. "Well, anyway, I came back after about three-quarters of an hour—it was raining again, needless to say—and everything was just as I left it except that the house had an odd feel about it. That's the only way I can describe it. I think a child had been in there."

Ella asked why a child.

"I'd left the laundry-room window open to let out the steam. But only a little way. I mean, no adult could have squeezed through. A child could have. The next thing was, I found crumbs going into my living room, quite a trail of them, brown crumbs like my chocolate cake. Of course I went straight to the fridge and the cake was gone. Honestly, you'll think I'm senile, but if it hadn't been for those crumbs, I'd have wondered if I'd actually made the cake or if I'd dreamed of making it."

"Was there anything missing?" Eugene asked.

"Only the cake, as far as I know. I haven't searched the house. It's just what a child would do, isn't it? Eat cake and then steal the rest of it."

Eugene was trying to think up something witty to say about having one's cake and eating it when Ella's phone rang. "Leave it," he said to Ella. "Let them leave a message."

"It may be a patient. I'd better take it."

It was Joel Roseman. "I'm not well," he said. "Can you come?"

Inexperienced in the handling of private patients, Ella nevertheless thought she must have some rights. She could take a stand. It was seven

184

o'clock, a cool, wet evening. "What's wrong, Joel?" She kept her voice gentle and quiet, conscious too of listeners, fascinated as people always are by "doctor" conversations. She heard Eugene murmur to the others, "A private patient." "Are you in pain? Breathless?" After all, the man had a heart condition.

"Not in pain, not breathless. I'm just under the weather."

It seemed appropriate, she thought, watching the rain lash the French windows. "Would you like to come to me in the morning? I could fit you in after surgery. Shall we say twelve noon? Come in a taxi."

"I thought you'd come here."

"I'll tell you what." She glanced at her watch. "I'll give you a call at nine to see how you are or you can call me." She gave him Eugene's number.

He said nothing and the receiver was replaced. Ella worried for the next two hours. The Sharpes departed. Elizabeth Cherry went home and spent the rest of the evening puzzling over the mystery of the chocolate cake. The rain stopped while Ella and Eugene were eating the black-olive pasta Eugene had prepared earlier in the day.

"I won't be able to sleep if I just leave it," Ella said.

Eugene knew she meant visiting Joel Roseman.

"It's a pity you took him on, but it's too late to say that now."

She tried to phone Joel but there was no reply and the phone wasn't on message. "I'll have to go over there."

"You must do as you think best, darling," said Eugene.

The first thing he did after she had gone, even before he had cleared the table, was go to his Chocorange cache and break open a new pack. Oh, the relief after three hours of denial! The most wonderful taste in the world . . .

THE FLAT WAS in total darkness. Not even a feeble gleam showed through the small stained-glass panes in the top of the door. At first Ella thought he must be out. No, worse, he might be unable to reach the door when she had rung the bell. He was really ill after all. Her heart began beating rather fast. She rang the bell again, lifted up the metal flap, and called to him through the letter box, "Joel, Joel, are you there? It's Ella."

A moment or two passed. She heard footsteps, like an old man shuffling in slippers. He opened the door and stood there, blinking at the light, his dressing gown loosely tied and a blanket over his head like a cowl.

"I didn't expect you," he said, his tone accusing.

She walked into the hallway. "I was worried. I didn't want to leave you alone overnight."

He closed the front door. The light from the corridor outside made two faintly glowing patches, greenish, reddish brown, on the panelled wood. Apart from that the place was absolutely dark. She was aware of something she had felt once or twice before in his presence, a frisson of fear. "Please let us have some light, Joel."

She wouldn't have believed bulbs of such low wattage were available. But, yes, perhaps the one he reluctantly switched on was the kind for putting in the bedrooms of children afraid of the dark. They left the partial light behind to stumble once more into blackness as he led her into the living room. Rain roared against the window behind the muffling blinds. Without waiting for his permission she pressed the switch on one table lamp, then another.

He glowered at her as if she had committed some serious social solecism and took a pair of sunglasses out of the table drawer. She put down her bag on the brown sofa and seated herself beside it. The long procession of identical emperors seemed to come alive with the light. She made herself not look at them. "Now, what do you think is wrong with you? How do you feel?"

His head bowed, he stood in front of her. "I don't know."

"All right. Why did you want me to come?"

He lifted his shoulders and the enwrapping blanket with them.

She persevered. "Have you been breathless? Have you any pain?"

"No. Not either."

Asked to take off the blanket and remove his pyjama jacket, he obeyed with maddening slowness. Her stethoscope held against his chest and then his back, she listened to his heart, his lungs. "I don't think there's much wrong with you, Joel."

"It's not my body, it's my mind."

"That's for Miss Crane, not me. You are seeing Miss Crane?"

"I've been once. I told her about Mithras. I told her I wanted him to go away. It's strange, really, I liked him at first but I hate him now." Joel seemed to read the doubt in her eyes, the fear. "I tell myself he's not real, he's in my mind. I told him that. But when I'm alone with him, I don't know. How can he only be in my mind when he talks to me in a language I can't understand? I can't have made that up."

She said faintly, "Is he here now?"

"He's here but he's not speaking. He won't speak till you've gone."

"And when he does, will he speak—well, English or his own language?"

"It's hard to say."

She must stop asking him about this imaginary creature. It wasn't her province, that was for the therapist. "When is your next checkup at the hospital?"

"Friday."

It was a relief. She wanted him to be in other hands than her own. "I don't think you should be alone here, Joel. Would your mother come and stay with you?"

"Pa wouldn't let her."

"Is there no one else? No friend or relative you could ask to stay for a few days?" A few days wasn't enough but it was better than nothing. "There must be someone."

"No one who'd come unless I paid them. I mean, Pa paid them."

She came to a quick decision. "I will find someone for you."

"I don't want a nurse!"

"Not a nurse, a carer. Someone just to be in the flat overnight."

He put his head in his hands but he made no objection. "You can go now," he said, looking up. "It gets better when I talk to you. I feel a bit better."

When she was out in the street, heavy rain was falling from a leaden sky and it was as dark as winter midnight, the streetlamps dimmed by the yellowish fog the rain made. She drove back to Eugene's, thinking of the man she had left behind in that sepulchral place and wondering if, with her departure, the mind-created thing he called Mithras was muttering to him once more. She had meant to ask him how he passed his long, lonely days in that dark place. She would do so next time they met, perhaps after his checkup on Friday. The reason she hadn't asked might have been because she knew the answer. Nothing. Nothing at all. No exercise, no reading, no watching television, listening to music, no talking to friends, nothing but sitting dozing in the dark.

HALF THE COUNTRY was under floodwater. Uncle Gib saw the pictures of Tewkesbury and Gloucester on his computer and in a newspaper he found on a wall in Raddington Road. "We shall be all right up here," he said. "It's not called Notting Hill for nothing, is it? Haitch, *I*, double *L*, geddit?"

Dorian Lupescu didn't get it. He hadn't understood a word but he nodded in agreement. Uncle Gib had exited from the Internet and was replying to a few selected letters. One of them had come from a man in Marlow, a member of the Children of Zebulun's Cookham church, who was watching the Thames rise and who hadn't insured his house. The Agony Uncle had no intention of answering it, privately or in print. Questions of morality, usually sexual, were all he bothered with. He turned his attention to the letter from a woman in Kenton whose partner couldn't maintain an erection. Disgusting, thought Uncle Gib. He wouldn't sully the pages of *The Zebulun* with that word. A reply only would suffice.

Distraught, Kenton, he wrote. *Your letter is unsuitable for family reading. The man you call your partner must ask God's forgiveness for sinful living. Marriage to you will cure his problem. It is a well-known fact that guilt, justified guilt in his case, makes a man uncapable.* Uncle Gib wasn't sure about that final word. It didn't look right. He checked in the dictionary and corrected it. Then, although he wasn't going to reply to it, he looked again at the letter from the Marlow reader. In spite of what he had said to Dorian Lupescu, it had made him rather uneasy.

He had remembered the Brent reservoir that they called the Welsh Harp. It was quite a long way away but water travelled fast. Look how it had travelled all over Gloucestershire from rivers on the border of Wales. He switched on the television for the one-o'clock news just to check where that water had got to now. Fifteen flood alerts issued, the newscaster told him. Tewkesbury cut off, Oxford in danger, Bedford threatened. That Welsh Harp was a great lake and it was high up, a lot higher than here, he thought vaguely, geography not being his strong suit. He imagined it bursting its banks the way they said the Severn had and the Great Ouse. Water would pour down through Willesden and Kensal into North Kensington.

Uncle Gib looked up insurance companies in the yellow pages, but the abundance of them confused him. Turning down the volume on the television, he picked up the phone and dialled Reuben Perkins's number. Maybelle answered, which was just as well as it was she who saw to what she called "business matters" in their household. Within minutes she had given him the phone number of their insurance company.

The way they made him hold on before anyone was available to answer his call started to put Uncle Gib in a bad temper. Music played—if you could call that droning and throbbing music—interrupted every few seconds by a woman thanking him for his patience and inexplicably telling him his call was important to her. Uncle Gib had shouted loudly and threatened the speaker with dire punishments before he realised he was berating a recorded voice. After ten minutes of this, Lance came into the room, hovering on the threshold, looking apprehensive. "Get out!" Uncle Gib yelled, and threw the yellow pages at him.

But he got his answer at last, and by the time the weatherman had appeared on the screen and was forecasting more torrential rain, he had arranged for the insuring of his house. Against water damage, fire, tornadoes, and other acts of God, which Uncle Gib naturally thought less likely to be directed at his property than at that of the rest of the population. Forms would arrive, a cheque must be sent, but substantially the deed was done.

HE COULD HAVE the whole day in the old woman's house, the whole night if he wanted it. He could stay in the place. The thought of it made Lance feel quite dizzy. Before Uncle Gib got religion he'd told Lance how he and a pal had cleared someone's flat while the person was away on holiday. Just turned up in the pal's van and walked in with a key Uncle Gib had got from somewhere and taken everything, two TVs, a new computer, a CD player, a microwave, and most of the furniture. The pal was a good dad, devoted to his daughter, and he'd wanted the tables and chairs and whatever for her flat. She'd just got married. Lance decided that it wasn't likely the old woman had a computer, but she'd got a state-of-the-art TV with flat screen and built-in DVD player. He'd need a van, but now he and Gemma were having their affair, he and her brother were best mates again.

"You can only ask him," Gemma said when she and Lance were lying in his bed, having a post-coital glass of Soave. Uncle Gib was attending the baptism (total immersion in a disused storage tank) of two new members. "When d'you reckon on doing it?"

"The old woman goes away on August eight and she's not back till the twenty-first, but I don't want to leave it too long. How about the fourteenth? It's a Tuesday."

"What's with Tuesdays, then?"

"It's a weekday," said Lance incomprehensibly.

"I'll ask him, shall I? He may be doing his community service. It's cleaning graffiti off tube trains. But I'll ask him, see what he says."

"You know what you are? You're an angel, you are." This show of emotion soon led to renewed lovemaking, and it was another hour before Gemma left, making her way down the Portobello Road just as Uncle Gib turned out of it into Raddington Road.

15

BELIEVING THAT HER visit to Joel Roseman would cancel the appointment she had made to see him at twelve noon, after her morning surgery, Ella was preparing to leave. She had a fitting for her wedding dress at one thirty, and she hoped to have lunch with Eugene first.

Clare, the receptionist, put her head round the door: "Mr. Roseman is here, Ella."

Ella sighed. Her instinct was to say she couldn't see him, but of course she must. She sat down again behind her desk.

He was once more wearing sunglasses. "I

walked. I walked all the way. And in broad daylight. Aren't you proud of me?"

Those were the words a mother might be gratified to hear from her small son. She smiled. "It's a long way, Joel. You mustn't overdo it, you know."

"It's very bright today. The light hurts my eyes."

She stopped herself from saying the obvious. If he sat and lay all day in the dark, what did he expect? "Still, it seems you're feeling better. I've been in touch with the care agency. They can find someone for you. She'll come in the early evening and stay overnight. Get your breakfast for you if that's what you'd like."

"I don't like."

She lifted her head and looked at him for the first time for a long while, looked properly. She saw how long his hair had grown since he returned home. It hung down on his jacket collar, unwashed, unkempt. He looked as if he had stopped washing altogether and stopped changing his clothes. "Joel, you shouldn't be alone. You need someone to look after you. Not a carer, more than that. Will you let me speak to your mother? Explain to her how much you need looking after?"

"She hates coming. She's afraid of Mithras."

"What do you mean?"

"People are afraid of mad people and she

thinks I'm mad. Maybe I am. I'd be better if Mithras would go away. I can't sleep anymore. Not at night I can't. Will you give me sleeping pills?"

I'll give you the sort you can't overdose on, she thought but didn't say aloud, and took out her prescription pad. "I'd still like to speak to your mother."

"Pa might answer."

"That doesn't matter. I'll talk to him."

Joel shook his head, not to deny what she said, but apparently in doubt that she knew what she was talking about. "You want the phone number?"

"Please."

She wrote it down, she passed him the prescription. "That's enough for one week. I shall speak to your parents. Meanwhile, you must tell Miss Crane everything you've told me. Tell her on Friday, and you should tell her I've recommended a carer."

He stared at her, pushed one hand through his greasy hair. "I don't want a carer, I said. I want you."

"Well, you've got me. I'm your doctor."

"I want you to come and live in my flat."

She flinched, recoiling back into her chair. It was disconcerting, not being able to see his eyes.

Perhaps he read her thoughts for he took off his glasses and sat there blinking at her. "I'm not talking about sex. I don't do sex." He twisted the glasses in his fingers and looked down. "If you don't like my place, Pa would buy us a house. There's lots of money. We could live anywhere you like."

She was silent, feeling despair combined with a terrible desire to laugh, a desire she suppressed. She said in a cool, quiet voice, "That's not possible, Joel." She held out her left hand, showing him the diamond on the third finger. "I'm engaged, you know that. I'm getting married in October."

"Engagements can be broken."

"Not mine." Amusement was turning to anger. She controlled it, spoke in a brisk voice. "Now, you'd better go home in a taxi. You shouldn't walk any more. I'll speak to your mother or your father, and I'll talk to Miss Crane too."

It wasn't her job but she called the taxi company Eugene sometimes used. It would be there in ten minutes. She was longing to escape. As it was, she had no time to do more than meet Eugene and tell him—well, that she couldn't meet him for lunch. Joel could very well wait for his taxi in reception, but bringing herself to tell him so was too much for her. They sat in silence while she went through a stack of papers on her desk, papers she had been through before. Just when she thought she ought to say something to him, he said, "I saw a newspaper this morning. I don't often see a newspaper. There was a bit in it about how they've found how to breed schizophrenic mice."

"Really?"

"If they have delusions, these mice, what do you think they hear? Strange squeaks telling them to do bad things? Telling them to kill other mice? What about hallucinations? Do you think they see sabre-toothed cats, big as tigers?"

He began to laugh. She thought she had never heard him laugh before. The receptionist put her head round the door and said Mr. Roseman's cab had come.

EUGENE HAD LOST the argument and lost it with good grace. It's too early to go to Sri Lanka in October, Dorinda told him. You go to India and neighbouring countries in January. Surely he remembered when the tsunami was. Why did he think all those holidaymakers were in Southeast Asia in midwinter? So Eugene gave in and they fixed on Lake Como.

It was two months away. He had more or less resigned himself to the impossibility of giving up his habit in those seven or eight weeks. Like a smoker, like an alcoholic, he had cut down. This was achieved, as cutting down usually is, by making sure that he carried none of his fix about with him, kept none at the gallery—it too had once contained caches in secret drawers—

avoided streets with purveyors of Chocorange, and responded to his craving by having a glass of water. But he had never passed a whole day without a sugar-free sweet, and he still kept eight packs in their plastic bag behind the Forster novels in his bookshelves, and three more in a drawer in the spare bathroom cabinet. These were not to be touched, certainly not ever to be looked at or checked on. They were his emergency supplies for use if, for instance, he broke his leg and was housebound or got the flu. It was a measure of how Chocorange was driving him mad that he thought seriously of such eventualities as a smoker might lay in four or five packs of cigarettes and a drinker his bottles of vodka. But how much more dignified than his were their addictions!

They were recognised and in their way accepted. Alcoholism might be something to be a bit ashamed of, but people with a forty-a-day habit regularly talked to journalists about their indulgence and, with a laugh, conceded they "must give up one day." He imagined being interviewed as a gallery owner about to hold an exhibition of a promising young artist's work (as indeed he was to do next month) and saying in answer to the (no doubt impertinent) questions about his private life that he was fifty-one years old, lived in Notting Hill, was about to marry a beautiful and charming general practitioner . . .

and was hopelessly addicted to a particular-flavour sugar-free sweet. He couldn't pass a day without sucking the sweets. The whole thing was impossible. It was beyond measure ridiculous. To coin a doubly appropriate phrase he would never use, it sucked.

Of course he would never say such a thing to a journalist or anyone else. As with the secret alcoholic and his covert drink pushed to the back of the fridge shelf when his wife walked in, his gin which looked like water when no ice or lemon was added, he could never allow anyone else to know. If he encountered Elizabeth Cherry in the street or saw George Sharpe over the garden wall, the Chocorange he was sucking was surreptitiously slipped into the tissue he kept in his pocket solely for that purpose. And even that prudent move distressed him. It was such a waste. He still had to decide how to handle his addiction while on his honeymoon. Total denial was impossible. You were supposed to enjoy your honeymoon. But he and Ella would be away for two weeks, and the idea of being deprived of his fix for a whole fortnight didn't bear thinking of. He hated the idea of those Customs people, or whoever it was x-rayed and searched one's checked baggage, finding eight chocolate-brown-and-orange packs, say, inside one of his suitcases. He couldn't imagine denying himself his sugar-free sweets, but he could well picture the faces of those officials staring at their screen, shaking their heads, laughing at the chav who wanted his sweeties in a luxury Italian hotel.

But he would have to take them if he was not to suffer deprivation. Only vaguely aware of what withdrawal symptoms might be, he nevertheless thought he had them. He had his own kind. Finishing the modest lunch he was eating in a bistro in the Haymarket—Ella had phoned to say she couldn't make it—he had begun to feel the craving that came to him most acutely when he had been eating something savoury. His mouth went dry. Drinking water only brought him another manifestation of his longing—a need for some sweet but sharp flavour on his tongue. The waitress had brought him two small biscotti with his coffee. He ate them disconsolately.

BEGINNING ONE'S PACKING at least a week before one went on holiday was a habit Elizabeth Cherry's mother had instilled in her some seventy years before. You spread a sheet on the bed in one of the spare rooms, laid your suitcase on the sheet, and began. Her mother hadn't used suitcases but a cabin trunk made of thick, polished brown hide, lined in silk and with cedarwood hangers. It was immensely heavy even before anything was in it, but that didn't matter as you never carried it yourself. Porters did that, it was their job. Elizabeth used one modest case and a carry-on bag, but she still spread out the sheet and laid her luggage on it. Whenever she bought something wrapped in tissue paper, she saved the paper for her packing. A sweater or blouse was laid flat on one sheet, another laid on it before it was folded, and a third on top. Then all was placed inside the case. Shoes were put inside plastic bags. She prided herself on not taking too much. If what she took with her turned out to be inadequate, she reasoned, she could always buy something. She never did.

The packing done, she opened the drawer where, in envelopes, she kept foreign currency. Since the widespread use of the euro, the number of envelopes had much decreased. She would need euros and, as she would be passing through Switzerland, Swiss francs. This drawer was visited no more than twice a year, and it always surprised her. How had she collected so many U.S. dollars? Nearly five hundred? She couldn't remember how it had come about that such a lot had been accumulated. And there were far more euros than she wanted to carry on her. Better take one of the credit cards from the desk downstairs for use in a cash machine. It was years since she had been to Canada, yet here were more than three hundred Canadian dollars. They could stay where they were, as could the American money.

Remember to close all the windows, she told

herself. Not that she had opened any with all this rain falling daily. The child who had got in and eaten the cake might come back. Window locks might be a good idea, but arranging for these to be fitted would have to wait until after she came back. How about her jewellery? She only thought about her jewellery when she was about to go away on holiday. The rest of the time the two bracelets and the eternity ring her dead husband had given her, her mother's rings and heavy gold chain, remained in the jewel box and were never looked at. But the evening before going away for two weeks she worried about them. They were insured, after all. Every time she went away she considered taking them all with her. But considering was all she did. Imagine the nuisance going through security, that arch thing you walked through beeping so that some grim-faced woman in uniform searched you. Imagine putting them all in one of those plastic trays so that everyone could see exactly what you'd got. No, best leave them where they were. They had always been all right and they would be this time.

No mention was made of the jewellery when Elizabeth went next door at six o'clock to remind her neighbour to water her houseplants and take in any parcels that might arrive at number 25 in her absence. As she always did when Elizabeth called, at any rate after four, Susan said she was just about to have a small sherry and would Elizabeth join her? Elizabeth was fond of sherry, a civilised drink that seemed to be fast disappearing from all but the drinks cabinets of those over seventy, and she sat down.

When told that Elizabeth was going to Salzburg and Budapest, Susan asked if she would be meeting her "friend" en route. Elizabeth said she would, but at St. Pancras for the Eurostar, not at an airport. Like everyone else, Susan assumed that Elizabeth's friend was a woman, and she never enlightened them nor did she say that holidaying with a woman would hardly be her idea of fun. She merely nodded and smiled when Susan referred to the friend as "she."

"It's very kind of you to do this. I doubt if there will be any parcels. The most important thing is to water the maidenhair fern every day. But I know you won't forget," which was a nicer way of putting it than "Please don't forget."

"Have a lovely time," said Susan after a second small sherry had been drunk by each of them.

Elizabeth was due to leave the house early to get to St. Pancras at eight, and she slept badly, as she always did the night before starting her holiday. The alarm was set (unnecessarily) for five, and at ten to she dreamed that the child came into the house as he did last time. No, not quite as he did last time. She was standing at the window in the half dark and she saw his thin, little body squeeze itself out of the mouth of the drainpipe and pull itself up onto all fours. A child of seven or eight. He scuttled across the area of flat roof and skylight and slipped in through the casement she had left open in her bedroom. Except that she had no casements and no flat roof. This realisation woke her. She switched off the alarm and went into the bathroom to have her shower.

THE BLONDE IN a rather too short beige jersey dress introduced herself as Joel's mother—"Call me Wendy." The dress was plain but decorated with a good deal of gold jewellery, diamonds on her fingers and on her earlobes. She was polite to Ella and pleasant. It was hard to tell whose side she was on in the family quarrel. She spoke of it as if a father refusing to see his son for years on end but paying for him to live in comfort was quite normal behaviour. Joel, she said, must pull himself together. There was no reason why he should remain in his flat. If he wanted company and attention, he could go into a hotel for a while. His father would be content with that. As for her, she couldn't possibly move in with her son. "No, Doctor, it's out of the question. I can't leave my husband because my son needs a servant."

Wendy Stemmer had come to the medical centre. Ella had expected her to refuse her request to come and had been surprised at her acquiescence, reluctant though it was. She looked wonderingly at her surroundings as if she were in some far country she was surprised to be visiting, then said, "I lived in Notting Hill as a girl, but not around here of course."

Ella could think of no answer to that and said, "I could find a carer for Joel."

"Yes, that seems a good idea. I don't know how much these people charge, but you could have the bills sent to my husband."

"Is there a possibility of him coming to see me?"

"Oh, goodness, no. He's at the office."

Ella had long ago learnt that women of Wendy Stemmer's kind, when speaking of a husband's absence at work, always say he is at the office. As if, Ella thought, there were only one office in the world or only one of importance.

"I see. Leave it with me. I'll see what I can do and get back to you."

Later, she phoned an agency. It called itself Caregivers Inc. in the American way and could offer Ella either Noreen or Linda, both thoroughly reliable, kindly women. Whichever one came would stay in the flat from 8 p.m. to 8 a.m. The cost staggered Ella, but she wasn't paying. Joel's father was and he never seemed to mind what things cost so long as he was paying for his son's absence from his life. She phoned Mrs. Stemmer, and then Joel and told him, half expecting him to say he didn't want anyone staying overnight so that she would have to cancel the whole thing and think again, but he agreed to the presence of Noreen or Linda, his tone limp and indifferent.

"I won't have to make up beds or anything like that, will I, Ella?"

"She'll do that."

"I wish it was you coming."

It was her afternoon off, no calls to make, no evening surgery. She went to Knightsbridge, clothes shopping for Como, telling herself that she was walking there because at last after all the rain it was a fine sunny day, not to help her lose weight. Too many of her patients moaned continually about the pounds they had put on and their increasing waist measurement. If she really meant to reduce her ten stone to nine, she should have done something about it months ago, not when her wedding dress was half-made. The sun made her feel cheerful. Eugene liked her the way she was, and that was what mattered. She bought a long dress in dark blue lace to wear in the warm Italian evenings.

16

THE CHURCH OF the Children of Zebulun was in a poky little mews off the Portobello Road and nearly as far north along that long, serpentine street as you could get without coming up against the Great Western main line. A shop in the mews sold Central African artefacts, and another offered natural remedies in purple glass jars and bottles. The church had once been a garage with a flat over it. Its founder, now dead, had converted it into a single, high-ceilinged room, attached a plasterwork gable to its front, and painted the whole edifice a shade of burnt orange. A sign executed in black lettering said O, COME, ALL YE FAITHFUL.

A regular attender on Sunday mornings, Uncle Gib dressed himself in his best, a black pin-striped suit that had been new when he got married some forty-six years earlier, one of the shirts picked up in a Portobello Road sale, and a blue tie, also new for that distant wedding. The suit had in its long lifetime been cleaned once. That was in the days when Auntie Ivy was alive and able to take it to the dry cleaner's. Since then it had been kept in Uncle Gib's wardrobe, its pockets stuffed with mothballs. It reeked of camphor. He had been thin when he married and he was thin now. The mystery (to him) was that the trousers seemed longer than they had been, for Uncle Gib, if no heavier, had suffered one of the drawbacks of old age and shrunk an inch or two.

He enjoyed the services of the Children of Zebulun, usually had something to say when the spirit moved him, and sang the hymns lustily while Maybelle Perkins's sister played the piano. Afterwards there was tea and orange squash and Garibaldi biscuits, though Uncle Gib never ate any. He consumed no food outside his own home. But no food or drink was served this Sunday, and the service was ended after only fifteen minutes. The shepherd—the Children had no appointed priest or preacher—had no sooner moved to the lectern and uttered the opening words "Chosen people!" when he swayed, stumbled, and collapsed. His head had scarcely touched the floor before a woman in the front row was on her mobile, calling emergency services. Of that other kind of service there would be no more that day.

Maybelle Perkins assured Uncle Gib she would keep him posted as to the prognosis for the sick man, though he was more concerned at missing the hymn singing than for the elder's fate. He set off for home, feeling disgruntled, his mood intensifying at every outrage he encountered along the way: shops open on the Portobello Road on a Sunday, pubs open on a Sunday, and those foolish enough to go into them driven out to smoke their cigarettes on the pavement. Uncle Gib lit one of his own but he didn't linger. Turning into Golborne Road, he remembered it as it had once been. Not with nostalgia, still less with longing, but with a kind of practical assessing faculty directed at estimating how much the street had "come up." He did this most days and with mounting satisfaction. Doing it now went a long way towards dispelling his bad mood.

Continuous heavy rain had brought a rich green to the trees, sycamores and planes, which grew in the pavements. Trees were good. Their presence enhanced properties. The blocks of flats were a desirable replacement for the rows of little slum houses, while those that remained, including his own, were of superior size and in most cases, excluding his own, tarted up and painted with new windows and bright front doors. Of course he wasn't going to sell, or not yet, not for a while, but it was good to know one had an investment that made a steady profit. . . . A Sunday newspaper, much handled, which someone had left on top of a wall, he picked up and tucked under his arm. Save him buying one, though he had had no intention of wasting his money on such rubbish.

A man was standing outside his house, looking up at the first floor. He moved off towards the corner when he saw who was coming, though not before Uncle Gib had recognised him as Feisal Smith. This was the man who had come round to his place with another thug, wanting money. Uncle Gib had forgotten why he had wanted money, but he was a pal of Lance's, he was sure of that, and as such unwelcome in his vicinity.

Uncle Gib strode after him and, when he turned, shouted, "Godless layabout!"

A qualified electrician with a steady job, Fize might have taken umbrage at the imputation he was idle, but it was rather the adjective *godless* that riled him. Along with the rest of the males in his family, he had been to the Kensal mosque on Friday as he always did. He might have had a white father, the blond and blue-eyed Smith, but his Assam-born mother knew her duty and had brought him up a good Moslem.

"Fuck off, you useless old git," he said, and added the latest up-to-the-minute insult: "Smoker!"

Like two male cats who hiss and spit at each other while each keeping his distance, a few yards dividing them, Fize and Uncle Gib remained for a moment exchanging glares, then turned away simultaneously. Uncle Gib let himself into his house, lighting a fresh cigarette from the stub of the last. The place was utterly silent. In the kitchen the envelope containing the insurance company's form and his cheque for the premium lay already stamped on the table. It was

211

ready to be sent, but he had failed to take it with him because of doubts he had as to whether it was sinful to post letters on a Sunday. He had meant to ask Reuben Perkins's advice on this matter, but the collapse of the shepherd had put an end to that.

Lance might be upstairs. If so, he was keeping quiet. Uncle Gib concluded that he and Feisal Smith had been out somewhere together and had parted at his gate. Out all night drinking probably. He sat down on the sofa and opened the *Mail on Sunday.* Foot-and-mouth disease dominated the pages. The floods, now largely subsided, were being blamed for carrying the virus. There was no end to the damage floods could do, Uncle Gib thought, stop trains, cut off electricity, spread disease, and wreck your house. A picture on an inside page, accompanied by a scary article, showed how London might look were the floods to come here next time.

Uncle Gib's eye fell upon the letter on the table. How could it be a sin to post it when the contents of the pillar-box wouldn't be collected till tomorrow? There could be nothing wrong in a letter going out on a Monday. If it went by the first post on Monday, it would get to the insurance company on Tuesday, and then if the floods returned, his house might be engulfed but the insurance would pay up. Better take the letter now, and then, when he got back, read about

Noah and the flood in Genesis. That would be a good and appropriate way to spend the rest of Sunday morning.

UPSTAIRS, IN LANCE'S bed, Lance and Gemma lay in silence, afraid to move. Because his room was in the back, they had heard nothing of Uncle Gib's altercation with Fize. As far as Gemma knew, Fize was working overtime, rewiring a house in Shepherd's Bush, but they had heard Uncle Gib come in, a good hour earlier than he should have been. And twenty minutes afterwards they heard him go out again.

"Oh, my God, Lance, that was scary," said Gemma. "How long d'you reckon he'll be?"

"Don't know, do I? I don't know where he's at, coming back like that, spying on me."

Gemma got up, began putting her clothes on. "I'm outta here, that I do know."

He crept downstairs with her, opened the front door a crack. The street was empty but for a man hosing down his car. They kissed, a short but passionate clinch. "Give me a bell," said Gemma, and tottered off on her four-inch heels.

She had been gone no more than two minutes when Uncle Gib was back. Lance was upstairs, listening behind his half-open bedroom door. He wouldn't have been surprised to hear Gemma screaming as Uncle Gib dragged her back into the house, bent on punishing them both, but he was evidently alone. Lance retreated into his bedroom, sat down on the rumpled bed, and swallowed, straight from the bottle, the rest of the wine he and Gemma had been too frightened to drink.

Lighting a cigarette and pouring himself a glass of grapefruit squash, Uncle Gib sat down and read Genesis, chapters 7 to 9. One verse particularly caught his attention: "And I will establish my covenant with you; neither shall all flesh be cut off any more by the waters of a flood; neither shall there any more be a flood to destroy the earth."

That was all right then. Except that there were floods all the time, especially in foreign places such as India. Uncle Gib wasn't worried about the destruction of the earth, only about his house. Genesis and Noah and all that were a mystery. He must make a point of asking Reuben to explain when he was better, but meanwhile it might be just as well that he posted that letter when he did.

EUGENE AND ELLA were having a prenuptial party. Ella's sister and her husband were there, two of her friends from medical school, and two of her partners in the practice. Eugene's actor friend, Marcus, and his civil partnership partner, Lawrence, had come; as well as Priscilla Hart, the painter who painted the gold, silver, and copper miniatures and whose exhibition was due, and of course Dorinda; the Sharpes and the owner of William the Bengal cat; but not Elizabeth Cherry, who was away on holiday. The conversation, which instead of concentrating itself on the kind of intellectual plane Eugene would have preferred, had turned—at least among the Chepstow Villas contingent and Ella's practice partners—on Elizabeth and the interesting revelation made by Marilyn Sharpe that the friend she had gone to Budapest with was a man.

"It makes one understand that sex is never really over, doesn't it?" said Susan Cox, the oldest person present. "I find that very encouraging."

Ella's sister, Hilary, told a story about a woman who had come up to her husband and herself when they were entering their Edinburgh hotel and asked for a light. She had an unlit cigarette in her hand. "'I don't suppose you smoke,' she said. Don't you find that amazing, someone actually saying that? I mean, you wouldn't have believed it possible even ten years ago, would you? Of course we said we didn't. Had we any matches? Or a lighter? Well, of course we hadn't. Jim said we weren't arsonists either. I don't think she knew what he meant. She went into the hotel and I could see her going up to one person after another asking for a light and no one had one.

Not even at reception. I heard someone say, 'Well, I wouldn't light it for you in here if I did have a match.' Isn't that an amazing phenomenon? Matches will simply disappear, won't they? Book matches will vanish. . . ."

Eugene, who was going round with the champagne, filling people's glasses, passed on without hearing the end of her sentence. The reference—the oblique reference—to someone else's addiction brought his powerfully to mind. Not that it was ever far away. He had abstained for five days, and on the sixth day he had yielded. It was hunger rather than a specific desire for a Chocorange that had broken him. He had eaten his lunch, a sandwich and a cappuccino, in one of the rooms at the back of the gallery. It was a busy day. For some reason, although it was August and the silly season, the gallery had been crowded with American tourists, one of whom told him he and his wife had come over "because it's so cold here," a relief from Colorado summer temperatures. As he talked to visitors, explaining the provenance of certain pictures and the history of a group of figurines, Eugene was overcome with hunger pangs. The sandwich had been small and dry, the cappuccino watery. What he needed now and could surreptitiously have sucked, talking of a sore throat or some laryngeal problem, what would have staved off hunger, was one of his beloved sugar-free sweets. He could almost taste it, the sweet creaminess, the tangy orange, the blissful chocolate—but of course he couldn't taste it at all. His mouth was empty and dry. He heard himself utter a low moan and turned it quickly into a cough.

When all the glasses were refilled and two more bottles of champagne put into the fridge, he went out into the hall, opened the cupboard, and took a Chocorange from the pocket of one of his coats. He felt for it blindly inside the dark cupboard. It wouldn't have mattered which jacket; the day before, he had stocked up with the things, calling in at Superdrug, Elixir, Tesco, and the shop kept by the woman in Spring Street, putting one or two into the pockets of every coat he had. In all he had bought fifteen packets. For he had given up resisting temptation. He could go on no longer deprived. All last evening and most of today he had sought to reassure himself. Why had he got into such a state? Instead of telling himself his habit was ridiculous and demeaning, he should have contrasted it with addictions to crystal meth or brandy or even nicotine. What harm did it do? They sold it in health food shops, for God's sake. It said on the packet it was "tooth-friendly." It stopped him eating real food, so helped to keep his weight off. Why, it was well-known that Marcus's partner— even now happily drinking champagne in the drawing room—had been addicted to heroin for ten years. Did he castigate himself, lose sleep, agonise over his addiction? Did he, hell. Eugene savoured the Chocorange he was sucking, there in the half dark of the hall, until Ella called out, wondering where he was.

The one he had helped himself to would last him for a good hour. The Moët tasted even better than usual after the bland chocolaty sweetness. He would take, he decided, six packs away with him to Como. Why on earth should he care what those who scrutinised checked baggage thought of him? He wouldn't be standing by to hear them or see their faces. Six would give him three a week, more than seven a day. That was nowhere like the number he had consumed since he had taken up his habit again, but it would do. It would get him through the fortnight. It would prevent those two important weeks, the start of his marriage, from being wrecked by enforced abstinence. He smiled at Marcus and asked him about his new play, for which rehearsals had just begun.

LANCE HAD GIVEN a lot of thought as to how he was going to get into Elizabeth Cherry's house. This time she would have failed to leave the laundry-room window open. He had no hope in that direction. He had decided to cut out a pane of glass, preferably from a larger window than the one he had squeezed through before. To this end he had bought the requisite implement and been taking lessons in glass cutting from Gemma's brother, Dwayne. This operation was a lot more difficult than Lance had supposed, but once you got the knack it became quite easy, and by Monday he had no doubt he could remove a pane, without cutting himself or making too much noise, in ten minutes.

Dwayne was now on bad terms with Feisal Smith and Feisal's best mate, Ian Pollitt. Dwayne fancied Fize's sister Soraya, whose beauty was striking in spite of its being largely covered up in a hijab and long black gown, but Fize had taken exception to his even speaking to her and got Ian to demonstrate with the knife he carried exactly what he would do to Gemma's brother if any advances were made. Dwayne had transferred his friendship to Lance and offered to lend him the van, but driving wasn't among Lance's talents, and there was no chance of Dwayne's affection extending so far as to drive a getaway vehicle.

On the morning of Tuesday, August 14, Uncle Gib announced that this was the day of the Children of Zebulun's annual outing. They were going to Clacton in what he called a "chara-banc." It would be the first time since Lance arrived in Blagrove Road that Uncle Gib had left him alone in the house for a whole day.

"You mind your p's and q's," Uncle Gib said. "I don't want no drinking and no women fetched round here. You see you shut the front door when you go out. Hard, mind. Give it a push to see it's properly shut. And keep an eye on that Romanian. He's not to have a bunch of East Europeans round. Right?"

"Right," said Lance, not really listening.

Uncle Gib left for the coach. His worst fears were justified when the driver told him there was to be no smoking on the journey. But a singsong was permitted, and they started off with a favourite hymn, "If I Were a Butterfly." When they got to the line "If I were a kangaroo, you know I'd hop right up to you," Uncle Gib was asleep. He had passed the night worrying about going away from home for a whole day, not being able to have a cigarette and eating strange food.

When he woke up, the coach was sluggishly moving into a car park. It was raining and the place was already spotted with puddles. Putting up umbrellas or rainhoods, the Children of Zebulun made their way towards a gray and glassy sea.

17

ALL THAT ELLA knew of the two carers from the agency who were looking after Joel was that they were called Linda and Noreen. She supposed that they would be middle-aged or older, so when one of them arrived at the medical centre just as Ella's surgery was over, she was surprised to see a small, waiflike girl in her twenties. No appointment had been made. Linda had come on the "off-chance," as she called it, not sure that Dr. Cotswold would see her.

Ella told the receptionist that she could spare her visitor ten minutes. She had not heard from Joel in some time, and she had been thinking she must soon do something about him, if only to check that having a carer with him overnight had been beneficial.

"He told me you were his doctor, Doctor," Linda began. "It was no good telling the agency. It had to be you."

"But what's wrong?"

"It's no good beating about the bush, is it, Doctor? I'm scared. It's very scary being in that place, let alone being with him."

"You mean Mr. Roseman?"

"Joel, yes. I mean, no one told me he was mental. Mentally ill, I should say. But he is. And that's scary, Doctor. Not to you maybe. You're used to it. But for the likes of me, caring for the disabled is one thing. I've been with people so disabled you wouldn't believe they could be alive, let alone move themselves about in a wheelchair. But this is different. It's scary. If he just said funny things, I could take it. I mean, I'd ignore it. But he's got a person he talks to. Not a real person, a sort of thing he imagines, and he talks to it, he shouts sometimes."

"Mithras. Yes, I know," said Ella, then wondered if she'd said too much.

"That's the name." For the fourth time Linda said it was scary. "I try to let some light into the place. I mean, it's getting dark when I get there, so I turn on lights. That's the first thing I do. But Joel won't have it. He gets in a state. I can have the light on in my bedroom, but if there's too much of it showing under the door, he knocks on the door and tells me to turn it off. I can't sleep, not with him prowling about and talking to that Mith-creature."

"I'm sorry," said Ella, not knowing what else to say.

"He's supposed to be on tablets. I know he is, I've seen them. But he doesn't take them. Well, they don't, do they, mental patients?"

"I'll go and see him. I'll go today."

"Because, to be perfectly honest with you, Doctor, I don't think I can carry on. I'm too scared. To tell you the truth, I get so's I don't know whether that Mith-person is real or not, and as for sleep, well, it's out of the question."

THE FLAT WAS no longer in darkness. It was the first thing she noticed when the door was opened. She was aware of the unfamiliar light before she saw it was Joel's mother who had let her in.

"Come along in, Dr. Cotswold. It's good of you to come."

Outdoors it had been raining as usual, so the light was the faint grayish kind, but to Ella it looked bright in here, showing up the thin film of dust that lay on all the dark polished surfaces. Joel was where he always seemed to be, on the lushly upholstered sofa, but huddled up in one corner. He was wearing sunglasses and had a dark-coloured scarf wrapped round his head. The blinds were halfway up, the curtains half-drawn.

"How are you feeling?" Ella asked.

She expected his mother to answer for him, perhaps briskly or with impatience, but Wendy Stemmer only shook her head. She had once, Ella could see, been a pretty woman—pretty rather than beautiful—the kind of trophy wife rich men like Stemmer marry, with toothpaste-advertisement teeth and long fingernails on unused hands. Time and perhaps the tragedy of her daughter's death had faded her so that she was like a rose that has been worn all day in a buttonhole, limp, starting to wither.

Joel turned his head towards her. "My mother let the light in. She always does. She doesn't believe it hurts my eyes."

Nor do I, Ella thought, but still I wouldn't deny you the darkness you want. She had begun to wonder what she was doing here. It would have helped if Wendy Stemmer had offered her coffee or even a cold drink, but she had sat down beside her son, half smiling at Ella as if she expected her to take charge, say something to fetch Joel out of his apathy, perhaps take his temperature or listen to his heart.

"I understand you're not too happy with Linda," Ella said at last.

"Who's Linda?"

Was he indifferent or had he forgotten? "One of your carers."

"I don't mind her. It's her. She doesn't like it here. She wants it to be light all the time. You know I can't stand the light." He got up, moving more quickly than Ella had ever seen before, pulled down the blind in one swift gesture and pulled the curtains across. Mrs. Stemmer shook her head and pulled down her short skirt over bony knees. "When it's light, I can see Mithras."

"Now, Joel," said his mother in an almost jocular tone.

Joel took no notice of her. "When I can only hear him, I think he's a figment of my imagination, but in the light I see him and he's real." Joel spoke in a low voice. "I can't stand it when he's real."

"He isn't real, Joel," said Mrs. Stemmer.

"I've spoken to Miss Crane," Ella said. "She says it would help you a lot if you would take your medication. If you got into a routine of taking a pill every morning."

Joel made no reply. He got up and went out into the hall, trailing the scarf behind him like an infant with his comfort blanket. His purpose was evidently to pull down all the blinds his mother had raised and draw all the curtains his mother had opened, for darkness began to close in. Wendy Stemmer peered at Ella through the dimness and cast up her eyes and said, "He's not having any heart problems, you know." She switched on one of the low-wattage lamps. "The results of his scan were absolutely fine. There's actually nothing wrong with him anymore."

But Ella thought how much worse Joel was now than when she had first seen him in the hospital. Then he had been just another more or less normal man recovering from heart surgery, while now . . . Joel came back, ignored his mother, gave Ella such a sweet and tender smile as to cause a tremor in the region of her heart. She remembered how he had asked her to come and live with him.

"I've said it before, Joel," she said. "I don't think you should be alone here. Here or anywhere else. Linda won't come again. Noreen will, and we can get you another carer." She glanced at Wendy Stemmer, who sat with her hands moving slightly in her lap, the gesture of someone growing impatient. "But I don't think that's good enough. It should be someone close to you. It should be family."

"You," said Joel. "You come and live here."

That was too much for his mother. She almost screamed the words. "You're mad, you really are, expecting your doctor to move in with you! What next? You've got a beautiful home with everything provided for you and no expense spared, I'm sure. You're perfectly well. You need work, you need something to occupy you and take your mind off your so-called troubles."

He nodded sadly, unperturbed. "Yes, they are troubles. I call them troubles and that's what they are." He sat down beside his mother. "You see, Ma, I've got someone living with me. He's here now only I can't see him in the dark. If he would go away, I should be all right, wouldn't I, Ella?"

It was the first time he had called her by her given name in his mother's presence. Ella saw Wendy Stemmer's slight frown, the sharp glance she gave her son. "I must go. Good-bye, Mrs. Stemmer." Not for anything would she say it had been nice to see this woman again. "Joel, I'll see you very soon."

LANCE HAD SPENT a lot of time in the past weeks speculating about what treasures he might find in Elizabeth Cherry's house. Credit cards or one credit card, a chequebook maybe, though what use a chequebook was these days to someone like him he didn't know. Maybe you could order something on mail order and send a cheque.

He would have to find out. There would be jewellery and probably more money. Perhaps a strongbox under the bed. He had heard tales of old folk who didn't trust banks and who never had bank accounts but kept all their money in cash, thousands and thousands, stuffed into socks or even pillowcases.

If there was jewellery, he'd flog it to the man called Mr. Crown in Poltimore Road his uncle Roy had recommended. Would it be best to get along to the man before he did the job and see how the land lay? Ask him, for instance, if it would be all right to go over there with his haul the next day? He'd ask his aunt's ex-husband only he'd gone on his holidays to Lanzarote. There was a lot to learn when you got yourself into this kind of thing. If told of the proposed job in advance, what was to stop the man in Poltimore Road from alerting the police? It would be a way of getting in good with them. Lance decided against it. If only he had a vehicle, he could remove a few bits of furniture, but if Dwayne wouldn't drive a getaway car, he certainly wasn't going to come in with him on a job like this. Gemma's brother was already doing God knows how many days' community service for breaking into a car and stealing from it a computer and a leather coat.

A long day lay ahead of Lance and nothing to do with it but think about the job ahead. He would have slept half the morning away but Uncle Gib's departure on the coach for Clacton woke him at seven, an hour Lance barely acknowledged as existing, one of the small hours, more or less the middle of the night. And Uncle Gib didn't leave quietly as any normal person would but yelled, "I'm off. Don't you get up to no tricks, mind," and slammed the front door behind him so that the house shook.

The diesel throb of the coach's engine made a noise like half a dozen taxis. Lance tried to get back to sleep but couldn't. He understood, perhaps for the first time in his life, how an event planned for the evening ahead can send tentacles of anxiety creeping up through the day to clutch the mind at dawn. It was a revelation to him, and when it became clear, at about eight, that the octopus grip wasn't going away, he got up. These August mornings should have been warm, the sun up but not yet strong, not the way they were this year, chilly and dark. Shivering, he mooched outside to what Uncle Gib called the privy and he the "bog." One thing to be thankful for, the rats had taken themselves off or, full of warfarin, died underground. He washed himself at the scullery sink, something he wouldn't have bothered about a couple of months back. Fastidious Gemma insisted on cleanliness, even providing him with a bar of Dove soap. He thought of her fondly as he dried himself on a thin, gray towel.

The house in Blagrove Road was the only dwelling place Lance had ever been in where there was no fridge. His nan had told him that when she was a child, they didn't have one in their house, but, apart from that, he had no experience until he came here of the fridgeless state and had never before seen a larder. That, apparently, was what this dark and damp-smelling cupboard was called. It was empty but for a shrivelled knob of black pudding and a cracked egg on a plate. Lance would have liked to break the place up, smash everything, the useless telly that got only four channels, the laptop, which was so old it took ten minutes before a picture came on the screen, the glass in the painting of Jesus holding a lantern and standing among a lot of weeds, the clock in its dark wooden case that didn't go, which had never gone as far as he knew, the dead plant, growing out of dust in a cracked china pot. He would have liked to smash it all but he didn't. He feared finding the place locked against him when he came back from the job at two in the morning.

But leaving the house with all the money he possessed in his pocket, just under four pounds, he met on the doorstep the woman next door on hers. Knowing her slightly—she was the one who had complained about the rats—he couldn't resist giving speech to his feelings. "This place is a fucking disgrace, a shithole. It wants pulling down. Destroying is what it wants till there's fucking nothing left."

Probably not knowing what answer to give, the woman said, "Oh, dear."

Shaking his head, Lance went out into Aclam Road and made his way through the secondhand-clothes stalls down to the Portobello to buy the cheapest breakfast he could find.

"SUMMER SUNS ARE glowing over land and sea," sang the Children of Zebulun. "Happy light is flowing, bountiful and free."

It had been raining ever since they left Clacton, and for some time, sporadically, before that. Uncle Gib hadn't enjoyed himself. But he had known he wouldn't. He didn't like being away from home, he had had too much of it in the past and had gone only because it was his duty as an elder. The food was the trouble, for one thing. Fish and chips in a café, and he had always hated fish. At least he'd been able to have a fag out on the pavement.

Dodging the showers, they had walked along the front. More or less recovered from what the doctors had told him was a TIA or transient ischaemic attack, Reuben Perkins stumbled along, talking monotonously about the crime that had come to the Essex coast, something called "gang culture," binge drinking, and crystal meth, whatever that might be, for sale on every street corner. There was no evidence of any of that during the daylight hours. The only people about were old, sitting in shelters with sticks and Zimmer frames beside them, and young girls wearing clothes that showed everything they'd got, tripping along arm in arm and falling over their high heels. One or two of the old people waved their hands, fanning the air, when Uncle Gib's cigarette smoke wafted over to them. He fixed them with his steely eye and they turned away, defeated.

Tea was baked beans, more chips, and green leaves that looked like the weeds growing in the flowerbeds at Portobello Green. Uncle Gib asked for a fried egg but they said they'd no eggs. That was the sort of dump it was. Now, returning, all but he singing lustily, they were coming into Ilford and he was longing to be home. He'd get the coach to drop him at the corner shop where Golborne Road turned out of the Portobello and buy himself half a dozen eggs and some slices of Polish salami. Then he'd smoke all the way on the walk home. The rain had stopped and the evening was clear, cool, and damp.

LANCE WAS SITTING in the kitchen, watching Pierce Brosnan in *Die Another Day* on the television, when Uncle Gib came in. Lance hadn't expected him so early. Only just gone eight. Lance's idea of a day out was one that started about three in the afternoon and came to an end around two the following morning. Uncle Gib put a carrier bag full of food down on the table.

Lance asked hopefully if he could have an egg.

"I left one for you on a plate. And a bit of pudding."

"It was cracked, that egg, and it was off. A horrible pong it made. A person could get fucking salmonella from that."

"Don't you use that language here," Uncle Gib said, but absently. He was watching James Bond and lighting what was only his tenth cigarette of the day.

Lance went upstairs. He had counted on spending the evening in front of the television, but that was out of the question with all that smoke and Uncle Gib doing a running commentary on things he disapproved of such as sex and dirty words and girls' figures. Lance was hungry and began to wonder if the old woman would have left any food behind in her house when she went away. Tins maybe and something in the freezer, which he could defrost in the microwave. No chocolate cake this time, though. Even thinking of it brought the saliva into Lance's mouth.

He checked on his equipment, taking everything he had put in there out of his backpack to make sure. A see-through black stocking he'd found in the Scope clothes bank—it had a ladder in it—to put over his head in case anyone saw him, the glass cutter, a pair of black cotton gloves nicked off a stall in the Portobello, and a torch, which must be Uncle Gib's, that he'd found under the scullery sink. It actually lit up, which was a miracle. He would wear his hoodie and he'd have to wear his trainers. They were the only shoes he had.

When he had assembled everything and put it all back in the bag, he lay down on the bed, preparing himself for a long wait. He must have dozed off for when he woke up it was dark and he heard Uncle Gib climbing the stairs on his way to bed. It was just after eleven. No longer hungry, the tension stifling appetite, he crept down the stairs. The hall of Uncle Gib's house was unfurnished but for a wooden chair, long ago painted pea green, on which reposed the lid of a tin once containing Auntie Ivy's favourite mint humbugs. In it, for it was in use as an ashtray, lay, still smouldering, Uncle Gib's last cigarette of the day. Lance stubbed it out, cursing under his breath.

Then he let himself out the front door, closing it behind him as quietly as he could.

18

THEY HAD BEEN to the theatre to see *St. Joan* at the National. It ended rather late and it was after eleven when the taxi brought them home. The driver passed Elizabeth Cherry's house, and Eugene, knowing she was away, glanced at its windows. "Just to see that everything is all right," he said to Ella.

Looking at her house wouldn't tell us, she thought. She didn't say it aloud but he guessed. "All right," he said, laughing. "Burglars aren't going to hang out a sign saying Occupied. We'll go home and then I'll just walk round there. She gave you a key, didn't she?"

"She gave her key to Susan. She always does."

He knew very well that Ella hadn't a key. After all, Elizabeth had been away a week. He wanted ten minutes on his own so that he could eat a Chocorange. The craving had come on him just as they were leaving the theatre.

His habit made him lie to her all the time. "It's remembering our own burglary that makes me anxious."

"I know, darling."

It was hateful to him that she trusted him while he deceived her, but that didn't stop him from picking a Chocorange out of the packet as soon as he turned the corner. Oh, the blessed relief of it after those hours of abstinence in the theatre! Lights were on in most houses, including Elizabeth Cherry's, but it went out as he approached and Susan came out of the front door. They both laughed at the small coincidence.

"Everything all right?" Eugene pushed the Chocorange behind his back teeth with his tongue.

"Everything's fine."

"No emaciated children eating chocolate cake?"

"Nothing like that. Good night."

"Good night, Susan."

Back in Chepstow Villas, Ella had opened a bottle of wine. She poured herself a glass and gave him one. She showed him the bill she had prepared to send to Joel.

"I've never done one before. As you know, I don't charge the other private patients."

"No, perhaps you should. But it's excellent, darling."

"His father will pay it, but I think it would be more polite and—well, kinder, to send it to Joel, don't you?"

"Yes, of course. What does Father do?"

"He's a hedge-fund manager, whatever that is. He's very rich and grand."

It was the eve of her fortieth birthday. Ella wondered if Eugene would remember. But of course he would. He always remembered her birthday and the anniversary of the day they had first met, as he would in the future remember the date of their engagement and then their wedding.

LANCE AVOIDED PASSING Gemma's flat at night. It was great seeing her on her balcony in the daylight, but by night he couldn't help imagining her in there in bed with Fize, and that made him jealous and angry. In the Portobello Road and Westbourne Park Road environs plenty of people were still about, many of them drunk, most of them young, a lot of teenagers among them. It had been raining heavily in the early evening but had stopped. The dark air was damp and still, the sky thickly overcast.

At the crossroads he went on down Ledbury Road, branching off into that quiet, rich, and select neighbourhood where he had carried out his first burglary and planned to achieve his second. No one was about. Dogs had been walked hours before, cats slept in their baskets, cars on the residents' parking were locked up, after being emptied of everything young men like himself might steal. Lights, dimmed by heavy, lushly lined curtains or slatted blinds of rare rain-forest woods, showed in one or two bedroom windows, and absent holidaymakers, prompted by a misplaced prudence, left their hall lights on in a vain effort to deceive people like

236

him into believing them at home and on the watch.

The old woman's house and those next to it were in total darkness. He studied the houses opposite, including the empty one from which he had kept watch. It was still empty, but not a light or a glimmer of light was to be seen from its neighbours. The owners were asleep, he thought, or away at their country homes. Without attempting to sneak into the old woman's house, he walked boldly up to the side gate, found it unlocked, and let himself into the back garden. There seemed no reason now not to use his torch, and he took it out of his backpack.

Not the same window he had squeezed through before. He had nearly cracked an already cracked rib doing that, thank you very much. Farther along he found a larger sash window, which was more suitable, and putting on his gloves, he got to work straightaway with his glass cutter. The job took longer, far longer, than when he had operated on builders' junkyard windows under Dwayne's tutelage. And all the time the little wheel made its slow progress round the frame, his hunger increased. So near his goal—he almost had to remind himself that he was here for money and jewellery, not food—he felt sick and his stomach rumbled, making trickling and squelching sounds.

The torch, which he had balanced on the sill of

the next window along, he jogged with his elbow and it fell to the ground. He picked it up and put it back on the sill, but it seemed to him that its light had grown dimmer. As he reached the point on the frame where he had begun cutting and eased the glass out into his hands, the torch went out. It hadn't occurred to him to bring a replacement battery. But he was in the house. He was standing up inside a room he hadn't previously entered, a dining room with a long marble table and high-backed chairs made of black wood. It didn't interest him. He made for the kitchen, feeling his way in the dark. Once there, although rather late in the day for precautions, he pulled the black stocking over his head.

IN SPITE OF his age, Uncle Gib didn't usually wake up in the night. He had slept in such uncomfortable circumstances during the prison years that to lie down now in a real bed in solitude and peace and quiet was a treat he hadn't yet got over. The bliss of it sent him to sleep at once, and his strong, old bladder seldom disturbed him. So it was a disconcerting surprise when he woke up at what he thought—he had no watch or clock in his bedroom—must be well after midnight. It was pitch-dark and silent. Of course he had no bed lamp. He lay in the dark, feeling what had wakened him, the stirrings, squeezings, and sharp, recurrent pains of indigestion.

Uncle Gib never had indigestion. But then he never went out anywhere to eat unaccustomed food as he had done the day before. With growing distaste and increased pain, he reflected on what he had been obliged to eat: fish, chips, multigrain bread, baked beans, green leaves, more chips. Thinking of it made its consequences worse. He levered himself out of bed and switched on the light, a central light that hung from the ceiling in a parchment shade. The panacea for all ills was at hand. Uncle Gib reached for the packet and the matches and lit a cigarette.

Perhaps the contractions caused by that first inhalation led to the sharp, stabbing spasm in the depths of his gut. Something must be done and now, immediately. Barefoot, wearing pyjama bottoms and an ancient cardigan of Auntie Ivy's, he raced down the stairs, dropped his cigarette in the tin lid on the green chair, and ran for the scullery. Getting the back door unlocked nearly finished him, but he made it to the privy just in time.

OUTSIDE UNCLE GIB'S front door, Feisal Smith, in a hooded jacket, and Ian Pollitt, in defiance of the weather wearing a red T-shirt on which PORN STAR was printed in white, stood on the step, doing their best to raise the letter-box flap without making a noise. They had made careful preparations for this undertaking. First a couple of litres of petrol had been siphoned off from the tank of the van Fize drove for his employers, into a bottle once containing sparkling water. Ian Pollitt had helped himself to two squibs from his teenage brother's stock for the forthcoming Guy Fawkes Day. The bottle was in a cloth bag, one of the environmentally friendly kind issued by shops to save customers from using plastic carriers, and with it a box of matches.

The porn star was calm and truculent as usual. Fize, on the other hand, was scared stiff or, rather, scared to the point of trembling. Through his head wandered thoughts of losing his job and losing Gemma, not to mention incurring the wrath of his mother and grandfather. But it was too late to back out now. He was more afraid of Ian's contempt than of any other possible retribution. His hand shook as he tried to raise the letter-box flap. It caused a good deal of noise, a creak and a clatter, making Ian swear at him and shove him aside with his elbow. They listened, but all was still and silent inside the house.

Fize fished the bottle out of the bag and passed it to Ian, its cap starting to come unscrewed. The bottle, and now both men and the bag, reeked of petrol. Ian took off the cap and thrust the bottle as hard as he could through the letter box with a mighty shove. It had been Fize's intention to follow this up with a lighted squib, which would ricochet into the fountain of petrol, but there was no need to use it. They heard the bottle smash, and something inside the house, seemingly already prepared, ignited it with a roar. Suddenly the whole house seemed to explode into light, every window brilliantly lit. A fierce flame streamed out towards them through the open letter box.

They jumped back, staring at each other, then they ran, pounding down the street, through the covered market and out into the Portobello Road.

SLICED BREAD FROM her freezer he put directly into her toaster and, while he waited, pulled the black stocking off his head. He ate the toast layered with strips of butter he shaved off a block of Lurpak. The Brie was ripe but nothing wrong with that. He ate half a pound of it with Branston Pickle. Then, spooning peach halves from a can, he made his way upstairs. All the jewellery he could find he scooped into his backpack. In a couple of her handbags he found a five-pound note and another five pounds in change. Getting down on his hands and knees, he scrutinised the floor under her bed, the floor under the beds in the spare room, and the next spare room, and the next. No strongboxes and no stockings crammed full of notes.

Back in her living room, opening the desk, he saw that one of the credit cards was still there.

He helped himself to it along with her cheque-book, though he had doubts how this would ever be of use to him. Three plastic bags contained foreign money. Lance couldn't remember ever before seeing U.S. dollars, Canadian dollars, and euros but they were money, weren't they? They could be changed into real money at those places outside Paddington Station he'd passed by without much noticing them. He'd notice them now. The best of the haul was undoubtedly the jewellery, destined next day for Poltimore Road.

He no longer needed the torch. His eyes were used to the dark. He rather liked the darkness, the way it hid him. Why not have some more to eat while he had the chance? No one had seen him. No one had a clue he was in here. The roads were empty, the neighbours asleep. He had taken the peaches from a cupboard where a shelf was full of tins: more fruit, beans of various kinds, soup, and fancy rubbish such as artichoke hearts and asparagus. Lance helped himself to a can of tomato soup, heated it up in a saucepan, made more toast, and settled down at the kitchen table to have a second supper. Strawberry ice cream, also from the freezer, would do for afters. A clock on the kitchen wall told him it was five past two.

WHEN THE SOUND of it reached him, the huge bursting roar, Uncle Gib knew at once what it was. A bomb or some such thing had been pushed through his letter box and the cigarette he had left in the tin on the green chair had set it off. Immediately he thought of Lance and Lance's pals. Barefoot and wrapped in the brown cable-knit cardigan, he padded out of the privy to look through the kitchen window, which gave onto this narrow strip of concrete. As he did so, the flames were just licking the doorway from the hall, and within seconds they streamed through, intense yellow flames, which roared through the kitchen and poured into the scullery. He turned his gaze upwards and saw behind the window of Lance's room dense eddies of black smoke. The window was open at the top, and the smoke billowed out as currents of fresh air fed the fire.

It was a little to Uncle Gib's credit that he told himself Lance couldn't be in there as he must be responsible for this conflagration. He had no doubt what was the better part of valour, and with one backward glance at the flames engulfing his home, he ran down the garden through the rain-soaked bushes and stinging nettles, to the shed in the corner where his garden met that of his neighbours. On the other side loomed the flyover with its cargo, even at this hour, of traffic tearing east and west. There, side by side, inside the shed, the door of which had long fallen off its hinges and got lost, stood the two chairs, one missing a leg, the other intact.

Uncle Gib sat down in the chair that had all its legs and found he was trembling all over. It had been a shock.

But the spectacle before him was worth looking at. By this time Lance's window had split open and flames and smoke were spilling out, curved flames like waves in an orange sea, but waves that hissed and roared, licking the windowsills of the room above. The fire itself had reached there before them or the smoke had. Inside the closed window he could see dark clouds of it, still and thick.

It didn't occur to him to call anyone or attempt to phone the emergency services. Someone else would do that. In the midst of his wonder and astonishment he remembered that he had insured his house, had filled in the form, sent the cheque, and received confirmation of his cover. It was wonderful, it was much better than trying to sell the place. With relish he stared at the window frames, the woodwork, the bricks and stone facing of his house beginning to glow red from the heat generated within.

"It's a goner," he said aloud, and then he heard the braying sirens of fire engines coming down from Great Western Road.

It would be best, when they came, to find him a broken, defeated old man, feeble and helpless, shocked almost to death by the destruction of his home. Carefully he lowered himself to the ground and lay facedown, his bare feet on concrete, his head and upper body among the shaggy grass and weeds. He heard them come into the garden. Not through the house, that would have been impossible, but by climbing over the wall that divided his property from that of the people who had complained about the rats.

Someone said, "We'll want an ambulance for the old chap."

A woman's voice next, her next door, he thought. "How dreadful for him. Losing his home like this. They can come in this way and get a stretcher over the wall."

The rats were forgotten, she was all sympathy and concern. Uncle Gib stirred a little, aware after a few minutes that a paramedic was kneeling beside him. The heat from the burning house was far from unpleasant, just what was needed on a night in this unseasonable August.

"Can you tell me your name?"

They always said that, he'd seen it on the telly. It happened in nearly every installment of *Casualty*. "Gilbert," he said in a quavering voice.

Hoisted onto a stretcher, wrapped in nice clean blankets, he took a look at his house or what remained of it as he was floated expertly over the wall. It was as well to make sure the place was a write-off, not that he could have done anything about it if it hadn't been. To maintain the pathos and the drama, he whispered to the kind paramedic, "My whole life was in there, all my worldly goods."

"Never you mind, Gilbert. You're all right and that's the main thing."

He was driven away at high speed to St. Mary's Hospital, the siren bellowing.

AN HOUR AFTER falling asleep Eugene woke up. The nearest packets of Chocorange were in the guest bathroom on the same floor. First dropping a light kiss on Ella's upturned cheek, he tiptoed out of the bedroom and across the landing. Still inviolate, the carefully hoarded packets sat inside their pink plastic Superdrug bag in the bottom drawer of the cabinet in the spare bathroom. He took momentary pleasure from looking at them, a glossy orange and chocolate brown, each sheathed in clear cellophane. So, he supposed, it must be for the druggie who contemplates a carefully hoarded jar of ecstasy tablets or a slab of hashish. The advantage to his habit was that it was harmless, whereas theirs was destructive, damaging, and often deadly. On the other hand, theirs was also glamourous, sexy, and raffish while his was—what? There was no use in thinking along those lines, especially in the middle of the night. He put a sweet in his mouth, restored the rest to the cabinet, and wandered into one of the spare bedrooms.

From there he could see across the gardens to

the rear of Elizabeth Cherry's house. It was as he had left it earlier, still, silent, unlit. Streetlamps gave enough light to see quite clearly at the front, and here at the back, a wall lantern, permanently kept on by the Sharpes as a security measure, shed a green radiance, half-masked as it was by fronds of jasmine and ivy leaves. There was nothing to be done about it, one must indulge one's neighbours, but Eugene disliked that lantern burning there all night almost as much as he disliked Bathsheba. He could see her sitting on the shelf that ran along the wall, her deep furry blueness turned to emerald by the light, her cold eyes open and staring, themselves like lamps. Why not have another Chocorange? He took a second one out of the bathroom bag and walked softly into the bedroom next to his own.

Chepstow Villas, the finest houses of this part of elegant Notting Hill, slept behind their pillared walls, their exotic shrubs, and their trimmed hedges. White stucco, most of them, Georgian, which really meant mid-Victorian, Italianate, and the rare example from the Arts and Crafts era, all bathed in faint moonlight. The street was empty but for one incongruous figure. Plodding down towards Denbigh Road was a young man with a backpack. Even in the lamplit and moonlit dark, Eugene recognised that potato face and shock of straw-coloured hair. He could actually remember his name from the time he had sat in this house, nervous, not knowing what to do with his hands, as he tried to make his potential benefactor believe that he had lost ninety-five pounds.

What could he be doing here at this hour? He was walking in the Denbigh Road direction, heading perhaps for Westbourne Park Road and, ultimately, for the council housing in Wornington Road or Golborne Road. It's nothing to me, Eugene thought. He's not doing any harm. It's a bad way to live, searching for crime where none exists, suspecting innocent people. What did he know to make him think Lance Platt was anything but a harmless and somewhat gormless youth?

He was out of sight now, and something more interesting to look at was on the horizon. A red glow like a sunset—but the sun going down in a black sky? It was a fire. And a big one, someone's house on fire. As he gazed, he heard the sirens of fire engines braying in the distance. He listened to the bray changing to a wail, then, finishing his sweet and rinsing his mouth under the tap, he went back into his bedroom.

Ella was sitting up in bed. "Are you all right, Gene?"

"I'm fine. I was looking out of the window and who d'you think I saw go by? That pudding-faced boy who came here after that money I found in the street."

"Well, the streets are free to all."

"And there's a fire at the top of the Portobello Road."

"Come back to bed."

"You look so lovely sitting there." Eugene took her in his arms. "It's half past two so it's your birthday now. Many happy returns of the day, darling."

19

IT WAS ALMOST dawn. The streetlights had gone out and the sky was no longer quite dark. The woman from next door and her husband were standing outside in Blagrove Road. If they hadn't been there and hadn't spoken to him, if the street had been empty and stripped of everything familiar, Lance would have thought this was a dream. The nightmare unreality of the sight broke over him the moment he turned the corner; something that should have been there, was always there, as unchanging as the Westway, as the Earl of Lonsdale, was no longer there, was gone. Or half-gone, unalterably destroyed. It was like those pictures you saw on the telly of places in Baghdad or Afghanistan where a bomb had fallen. All that remained was a blackened ruin, a wall standing here, half a wall there, glassless windows like potholes, and on those walls the old paper still clinging, half-burned pink roses and faded butterflies peeling off. He stared, silent and aghast.

The woman looked at him as if he were a ghost, taking a step backwards, putting her hands up to her face.

Then, "Thank God, you're all right," she said, her tone heartfelt, her smile wide. It was rare for anyone to show so much joyful relief at the sight of him. For a moment he thought she was going to throw her arms round his neck.

His voice came out weak and thin. "I've been out. I've been out for hours." Now he wondered why he'd stopped for so long at an all-night pub to spend the old woman's money on vodka and beer chasers.

The husband looked at him, looked at what remained of the house, and back at him. "If it wasn't you, who was it they took away? The one they found dead up at the top?"

Mistaking Lance's expression, his eyes staring, his mouth hanging open, for the beginnings of grief, the woman said, "Not your uncle, dear. He's all right. Just gone to the hospital for a checkup. There was a young chap. We thought it was you."

Oh, my God, Lance thought. Oh, my God. His sense of the unreality of it all deepened. The air smelt of burning. At his feet lay pools of black water and yellowish foam, and in the foam floated the picture of Jesus holding a lantern.

Inside the shell of the house he could see his own bed, a black skeleton laden with black rags, stark against the dirty floral wallpaper. Higher up, what had once been a mattress hung over the edge of the charred and broken floor.

"He wasn't burnt," the husband said, evidently trying to dispense comfort. "He died from inhaling smoke. That's what they said."

"You don't look well yourself. You've gone white as a sheet. You'd better come into our place for a bit. I'll make us a cup of tea."

Lance couldn't speak. This must be what they meant when they talked about shock. Whatever he may have said about shock in the past, he had never really known it till now, never known its power to numb and deaden. He looked blankly at this couple, these neighbours, as if he had never seen them before, as if their words were no more than the twittering of birds. He looked at the concrete supports of the flyover. Perhaps nothing so overawed him as the sight up there of police notices and the absence of a single moving vehicle. They had closed the carriageway because of the fire.

Dawn was breaking. The eastern sky over Kilburn and Maida Vale had turned a pale and gleaming gray. Without a word to the woman and her husband, he turned and walked away. His feet seemed to move mechanically without his taking thought or even moving them himself. It

251

was automatic, this slow trudging, his mind empty, his steps taking him down the Portobello Road, past the closed shops. His backpack bumped against his spine. At an all-night café, a couple of men were inside drinking tea. Another one stood outside smoking. Lance went on, past the Electric Cinema, past the houses painted ice-cream colours, down into Notting Hill Gate. There in a shop doorway, resting his head on a black plastic bag of rubbish, he curled up and fell instantly asleep.

HELPING THE POLICE with their enquiries brought Uncle Gib a lot of pleasure. It was a new experience for him to find himself, so to speak, on the right side of the law. Neither the detective sergeant nor the detective constable who spoke to him seemed to know anything of his past history. To them he was simply an elderly house-holder, respectable, innocent, hard done-by, who had suffered the misfortune of having his home destroyed by an arsonist and murderer. By the time they came to interview him at the Perkinses', it was known that the fire had been started deliberately and that its victim was Uncle Gib's Romanian lodger.

The hospital had kept him in only until the afternoon following the fire. They had asked him if there was anyone they should notify, and he had told them to phone Reuben and Maybelle

Perkins. Within the hour both were at his bedside, overflowing with sympathy while not
making any direct offer of accommodation. The
first thing Uncle Gib did was borrow Maybelle's
mobile, get the nurse to bring him the phone
book (Business and Services edition), and call
his insurance company. That out of the way and
the assessor due to come next morning, he
informed the Perkinses that he would be staying
with them for the foreseeable future. They had
brought him a copy of the *Evening Standard* in
which the fire was the lead story, and the rest of
their visit passed in speculation as to how the
newspaper had got hold of a head-and-shoulders
photograph of Dorian Lupescu. No one mentioned Lance until the police did. Or, rather, until
Uncle Gib did when the police talked to him.

"My late wife's great-nephew," he said in
answer to their question about the occupants of
the house. "Lance Platt's his name. There's no
knowing where he was. Keeps very late hours, he
does."

"Have you any idea where he is now, Mr.
Gibson?"

"Not a clue." Uncle Gib held out his cigarette
packet to the two policemen and, when his offer
was refused, lit one himself. The worst part of
his few hours in hospital had been nicotine deprivation. "He never tells me where he goes. I
took him in out of the kindness of my heart when

his mum and dad wouldn't have him no more. That was after he'd broke a woman's jaw he was living in sin with."

"Can you tell us where he works?"

Uncle Gib laughed, then told them not to make him laugh. "He's on the benefit, isn't he? What else?"

He gave them Lance's parents' address. They weren't his relatives but Auntie Ivy's. Not knowing Gemma's address or, come to that, her name, he described to them where she lived. They couldn't miss it. All they had to do was follow the graffiti. "He's got aunts and uncles all over the place," Uncle Gib said with relish. "Mates too, the same sort as he is."

If Maybelle Perkins was dismayed at finding herself saddled with Gilbert Gibson as a non-paying guest, she gave no sign of it. It was many years since he had slept in such a clean, well-appointed bedroom, if he ever had, or eaten at such a neat, well-laden table. Maybelle made a special journey to the Portobello Road and the Spanish grocer's to buy his favourite chorizo.

The police came back and told him that as a result of "information received" (from the woman next door, but they weren't divulging that) they knew that Lance Platt had said that Uncle Gib's house was "a disgrace" and "a shit-hole" that needed destroying. Did Uncle Gib know anything about that? He disliked his former home being referred to in these terms. It reflected badly on himself and might damage the rosy picture the police had of him. Angrily, he said that Lance was a liar and he personally had heard him say he resented Dorian Lupescu having the top flat because it was superior to his own accommodation.

ONLY WHEN HE had moved in with Gemma, now more than a year ago, had any householders actually welcomed Lance into their home. His parents had turned him out, eventually Gemma had shown him the door, Uncle Gib had taken him in only because having him there was lucrative. So when he had presented himself at his nan's, dirty, unkempt, exhausted, instead of putting her arms round him and promising him supper at the Good King Billy, she unlocked her front door in silence and pushed him in ahead of her. Like most members of a large extended family, particularly those who are employed and in possession of a home, she lived in mild dread of her relatives wanting to move in with her.

A Community Support officer had moved Lance off the Notting Hill Gate shop doorstep at nine in the morning. Five hours' fitful sleep had gone some way to healing the shock he had suffered, though it partially returned as he trudged up Ladbroke Grove, barely noticing the rather grand and elegant police station as he passed it.

Who had set fire to the house? Where was Uncle Gib? He shook his head violently in answer to these questions, and passersby thought he was drunk. It took him a while to remember he had money, enough certainly to buy himself break-fast and take transport somewhere.

Working for one's living was so rare in Lance's family that he had forgotten his nan had a job. He waited for her, sitting on the floor out-side her flat until she came home. Gaining experience by then of spending time on door-steps, he ate the coronation chicken sandwich he had bought on the way, drank from the can of Cobra, and fell asleep again. It was nearly five when his nan arrived, and he had only been inside ten minutes when she sent him out to buy takeaway for their supper. She put a note into his hand. "Don't lose the receipt," she said. "I'll be wanting the change."

Talking of change, it was funny how people you thought you could rely on became quite dif-ferent people almost overnight. His nan had been lovely to him that day she'd bought him fish and chips, and it was only a couple of weeks ago. But she'd changed in those ten minutes he was in the flat. She'd changed when he'd told her about Uncle Gib's house and that he'd nowhere to go. It would serve her right if he didn't go back with the Thai green curry but went off and threw him-self on the mercy of his mum and dad. Only it wouldn't be a punishment, she'd be pleased. He began to feel low, sinking down to rock bottom.

The only bedroom was hers. He had to sleep on the sofa. That would have been all right if it had been a soft sofa with proper cushions, but hers was covered in shiny and slippery red leather. At some point in the night he slid off onto the floor. His fall woke him and he could hear his nan and her boyfriend laughing in the bedroom and some old country music from the seventies keening through the wall. In the morning she gave him what she called an ultimatum. He had never heard the word before but he soon knew what it meant.

"You'll have to go, Lance. Dave's thinking of moving in and there's not room for three. You can stay one more night and then you'll have to be on your way."

As it happened, Lance never had another night slithering on those red cushions. He hardly anticipated it because by this time he confidently expected that the sale of Elizabeth Cherry's jewellery would make him a rich man. It was all there, safe in the backpack he had carted from one end of Notting Hill to the other and up to College Park. Once more he intended to carry it, this time across north London to Holloway and Poltimore Road. Then he remembered the foreign money. There was a place down the Portobello, for some reason called *cambio*, someone had told him exchanged money. Did that mean they'd change this stuff into real pounds? It did. He was amazed, as much as anything because he had guessed right. They gave him just under three hundred pounds for the notes in the three plastic bags.

Now, at the tube station, there was no need to lower himself to the ground and wriggle, snake-like, under those two gray padded doors which only opened when a ticket was inserted in the slot or touched to the circular pad. He had money and felt quite virtuous when he spoke to the man behind the ticket window. The machine was too complicated for him. The house in Poltimore Road was found without trouble. It was in a street a lot like Uncle Gib's but not smartened up so much, and like Uncle Gib's it had no door-bell, only a knocker. Lance knocked. A thin, dark girl answered, and when Lance asked for Mr. Crown, said, "Oh, you must mean Lew," and that he was away on his holidays. He'd gone to Corsica and wouldn't be back till Sunday week. Lance had no choice but to return to College Park and his nan's flat. It was a blow, but things weren't as bad as they might have been.

BY THE TIME his nan came home he had packed up the jewellery in newspaper and two plastic bags, securing the lot with elastic bands. The postmen dropped elastic bands all over the streets when they'd delivered their letters, so finding a couple of them wasn't a problem. Worse than chewing gum, his nan said it was. He handed her the package he'd made and asked her to look after it for him while he found somewhere to stay. This request seemed to touch her heart for she smiled for almost the first time since he'd arrived and said she was sorry to turn him out. She might be sorry but she didn't say he could stop on. The package would be safe with her, she promised, and she didn't ask what it was.

The two of them were watching "World Athletics Highlights" from Osaka when the police came. His nan didn't want to switch off but they told her to in no uncertain terms. "In case you're wondering how your uncle is," the detective sergeant said, "in case you've been worrying, he suffered a serious trauma but he's on the mend. He's staying with some very caring friends of his who know how to look after him."

"There's no need to be sarcastic," said his nan.

They ignored her.

"Poor old boy," said the detective constable unnecessarily. "Now maybe you'd like to tell us where you were between eleven p.m. and one thirty a.m. on Tuesday night. Tuesday, fourteen August, that is, through to Wednesday, fifteen August."

"Out," said Lance, his mouth drying and his throat constricting.

"Pardon? Would you repeat that?"

"I was out."

"Out where?"

"I was walking around." He said it slowly and carefully.

"Around where?" said the detective sergeant.

Lance said he couldn't remember. He'd been into a pub. When they asked which pub, he said he couldn't remember that either. Pressed to remember, he said he thought it might have been in Westbourne Park Road. He still couldn't guess what they were getting at, and the most important thing to him was to keep them from finding out that he'd been breaking into a house in Pembridge Villas. Suppose they searched his nan's place and found that jewellery? Any minute now he expected them to say they'd like to search, they'd get a warrant, and all that stuff you heard on the telly. But they didn't. They asked him why he had said Uncle Gib's house wanted destroying.

"It's a shithole, innit?" he said. "It's a tip."

"So you did say it? You wanted to destroy it?"

"I never said that." Lance was getting seriously alarmed.

"Maybe you didn't say you resented Mr. Lupescu having the top flat."

"Well, it wasn't fair, was it? Him coming over here from some foreign place and getting the best bit of the house."

His nan was looking more and more uneasy.

"I don't reckon you want to say any more off your own bat, Lance." An inveterate viewer of *The Bill* and *Kavanagh QC*, "You want to ask for a lawyer," she said.

"Good idea," said the detective sergeant nastily. "He can do that when we get him down the station. Which is like now."

Lance was so relieved that they didn't mention the old woman in Pembridge Villas or ask his nan to show them the package of jewellery, which he had been convinced they must suspect her of having, that he settled quite happily into the back of the car in which he was driven to Notting Hill police station. The lawyer they found for him was a nice young lady who didn't look old enough to be a qualified solicitor.

The questioning began again. It went on for hours, and Lance expected to hear those fateful words, so often lightheartedly listened to on TV, about anything he said being repeated in court. But in the middle of the night they released him on police bail.

20

KEEPING AN EYE on Elizabeth Cherry's house, Susan Cox let herself in on Thursday morning and went dutifully from room to room. But her mind wasn't on what she was doing. She was thinking about the Notting Hill Carnival, due to begin on the coming Saturday and continue until the Monday evening. Its route this year was down Great Western Road from Westbourne Park Station, along Westbourne Grove and up Ladbroke Grove, a U-shape which would take in the Portobello Road but not enter it. The nearest it would pass to Pembridge Villas was when it sang and danced and rocked and rapped down Chepstow Road, but stragglers from it often strayed into these quiet, sequestered streets, and Susan feared for the small pieces of statuary in her front garden and the flowers in Elizabeth's. At one previous carnival a dancer in white satin with feathered angel's wings and a man dressed like Captain Hook had picked all the dahlias and sat on the wall and rapped some lines of a current hit. Susan felt it incumbent upon her to stop that happening again, especially while Elizabeth was away.

It was a cool, pale gray day, dry and windless. With no wind the curtains hung straight in their regular pleats, and she failed to see that the glass was missing in one of the dining-room windows. Lance had been an apt pupil of Dwayne's and had cut cleanly. She saw the buddleia and bamboo in Elizabeth's garden, as she always did, without noticing the lack of an intervening pane. The kitchen seemed just as she had found it two days before apart from an odour of not very fresh tomato. It was unlike Elizabeth to have thrown into the bin a soup can without first rinsing it, but perhaps she had been in a hurry. After more than a week it would, of course, smell unpleasant. Wrinkling her nose, Susan removed it, still inside its bin liner, and took it home with her to be washed and put conscientiously in the recycling.

MAKING HIS PREPARATIONS for the end, Joel now lived in as near to total darkness as is possible in a flat in the middle of London. No longer did light come through the glass pane in his front door. He had covered it up with a sheet of cardboard fixed to the frame with drawing pins. But the lamps outside in the street never went out. After the wettest, dullest, cloudiest summer since records began, the sun had begun to shine by day and the moon by night. Absolute darkness was impossible, but his eyes had grown accustomed to the dark. Like a cat, he could find his way from room to room almost as easily as if the place had been brightly lit.

Noreen too had grown used to the way he lived. She came only three nights a week now and, to please him, brought with her a padded draught excluder in the shape of a snake, green and yellow with a forked tongue, which she laid along the bottom of her bedroom door. As well as draughts, it excluded the light from her bedside lamp. Linda no longer came. He couldn't understand why she was afraid of him and his home, but she was. He had said nothing about her absence to Ella or his mother or Miss Crane. As for his father, no doubt he paid the bills without noticing or caring.

Joel had accumulated a quantity of sleeping pills. The hospital dispensary had provided him with a supply, some of which he had never taken. Linda had told him she needed pills if she was to get any sleep under his roof, and on her last visit she had been so nervous that she had left hers behind. When she came round for them next day, he said he knew nothing about her Mogadon, and that she had to accept. The best sleeping pills, the strongest and most numerous, came from his mother. Her doctor gave her as many sedatives as she wanted, and she had just asked for double her usual prescription on the grounds that worry about her son kept her awake. Joel investigated her handbag under cover of the habitual darkness and added these to his cache.

Noreen shopped for him on her way to Ludlow Mansions. The list he gave her always included meat and eggs and ready meals, and sometimes a bottle of wine. She wasn't surprised when he added gin and whiskey to the list, and she took it as a sign he was getting better. Cunningly, he wrote down mixed nuts as well and rice crackers. Starting to enjoy life, she told herself. Inviting friends round. Soon he'd be switching on lights and pulling up the blinds.

But he wasn't enjoying life. Nor was he doing or planning to do what Ella or Miss Crane might have suspected had they known about the pills and the spirits. Ella hadn't come lately. His fault. He could have called her, sent for her, but that he was postponing until the right time came, the absolutely precise right time. He had given up walking. Miss Crane he continued to visit once a week, wearing sunglasses, going to her consulting room in a taxi and returning home in one. He talked to her about Mithras, making up most of what he said, quite enjoying his inventions. Perhaps the psychotherapist knew this, but if she did, she gave no sign.

"He's started telling me to kill people with red hair," he said. Miss Crane had red hair. "When demons are incarnated, their hair turns red." She made no answer, not even nodding. "I don't want to obey him because then he'll know he controls me."

Mithras—the real Mithras—was visible more often to him now. In every beam of light that managed to infiltrate its way into the flat, he saw him. He told Miss Crane he never saw Mithras, only heard his voice. He told her Mithras said Ella and his mother and Noreen were demons, and he would have to kill them if he wanted peace of mind and happiness. They weren't red-headed but they were women, and that was enough. Miss Crane said nothing. A thin, birdlike woman, her hair a mass of tight curls, she sat quite still, sometimes writing words on a sheet of paper. Joel only said those things because he had read that this is how schizophrenics behave. They hear voices and the voices tell them to commit crimes. It would be quite interesting to act the part of a schizophrenic, like a kind of hobby. Joel had never had a hobby of any sort. All Miss Crane said was that he should continue with his medication and she'd see him next week. On his way home, his hood up and wearing his strongest sunglasses, Joel went into a bookshop and bought a book about schizophrenia.

Noreen admitted a brief flood of light when she let herself out in the morning. Even after she had closed the door behind her, he saw Mithras across the hall. He had grown beautiful, like the Michelangelo statue of David he had once seen in Florence and many times since in pictures. But now Joel longed to be rid of him. Later in the day Mithras talked, never telling Joel to harm people, but speaking mostly about the place he came from, that glorious city where angels walked on the glowing battlements. Sometimes he said he wanted to be back there, in that light, that sunshine which shone on the walls and roofs and minarets. He wanted to be back there but he didn't know how to find his way.

"I will find you a way," Joel said to him. "I know how to get you there and I'll do it soon."

When he made this promise, and he was starting to make it every day, Mithras was silent and Joel knew he was grateful. Once he had been wary of addressing Mithras in Noreen's presence, but now he spoke to him loudly in front of her so that she would think him schizophrenic.

LANCE APPEARED IN the magistrate's court and was once more released on police bail. Not many years before, in Uncle Gib's day for instance, they would have remanded him in custody. But there was no vacant cell in the police station and no room in the prisons, so Lance came home and made his way to his parents' flat in Acton, for he knew the well-tried dictum that home is all that is left for you to go to and where they have to take you in.

They weren't pleased. Another rule in these homecomings is that Dad is hard-hearted and will do his best to show you the door, while Mum remembers how she carried you for nine months and what a lovely baby you were, only son et cetera, and dissuades him. They had a spare room, which had once been Lance's room and was now full of defunct kitchen equipment, old motorcycling magazines, a broken bicycle, and a stack of car tyres of unknown provenance. But a space was cleared for Lance to sleep there.

More than anything, he missed Gemma. He lay awake in that horrible bedroom trying to think of ways to reach her. Traffic thundered past the block where his parents lived. A pothole was in the roadway just outside, and every time a heavy lorry passed over it, the place shook as if an earthquake were happening, and Lance was afraid the broken bike and the stacked tyres would topple onto him. One of the neighbours had written to the council that it was time they mended the road, but nothing was done. He tried to phone Gemma when he calculated Fize would be at work, but he never got a reply.

The police were determined to victimise him. The *perpetrator* they called him, a word Lance hadn't previously heard. *Alleged* was another word he didn't understand. Of course he could have told them he couldn't have set fire to Uncle Gib's house because he was breaking into Elizabeth Cherry's at the time, but he dismissed that solution out of hand. The chances were they'd never be able to prove arson, and therefore murder, and he'd get off scot-free, whereas being found guilty of burglary would land him in prison. Uncle Gib always used to say that the British never cared much about what you did to other people, it was property they thought more of. Lance hadn't taken much notice at the time, but those words came back to him while he was in a police cell and now in his parents' flat.

Lying in his uncomfortable bed at night, shaken and buffeted by the lorries going past, he thought of Gemma and repeated that word *perpetrator* to himself, trying to decide whether it sounded worse than *burglar* or better.

THE NOTTING HILL Carnival starts on Saturday, but Sunday and Monday (a bank holiday) are always the big days. Its route this year, much the same as last year, eventually wound its way up Ladbroke Grove, and there Uncle Gib stationed himself. In years gone by, when he hadn't been inside, he regularly attended the Notting Hill Carnival, and he didn't see why he should miss this year just because his house had burnt down. He was a thief, or rather had been a thief, so he knew that pickpockets and bag snatchers infested the carnival route, mingling with the crowd. For this reason he took no money with him. If he had possessed credit cards, a watch, and jewellery, he wouldn't have taken those things with him either. He was an unaccoutred man but for his second-hand trousers bought off a stall in the Portobello Road and one of Reuben's collarless shirts. If anyone had stolen from his person, he would, as a former thief himself, have been deeply ashamed, so he gave them no opportunity.

Among the crowds watching the floats, the bands, and the dancers, the blazing colours under a freak sunny sky, he spotted first Lance, and later Fize with a black guy and a white one. To some extent Uncle Gib had what the average person (but not psychiatrists) call a split personality. A born-again religious man, he of course deplored stealing as in direct defiance of a commandment, but as a reformed thief, he watched with enjoyment the antics of such as Ian Pollitt, the black one, and the white one as they sized up the hundreds who lined the route and calculated which pocket or handbag might be rifled with impunity. Uncle Gib actually saw the white one remove what looked like a credit card from a woman's jacket pocket and Pollitt attempt, but fail, to extract a purse from a handbag.

Distracted by all this as he was, Lance caught him off guard. There was no escape. Uncle Gib rounded on him before he could speak. "If I wasn't against bad language like I am, I wouldn't call you an arsonist but an arsehole."

"I haven't done nothing," said Lance.

"Why aren't you banged up? That's what I want to know."

"I don't know. They never said. I'm on bail. Can I come and live at your place?"

Uncle Gib almost spat. "I haven't got a place. I'm homeless. Some dear friends took me in out of the goodness of their hearts and there's no room for the likes of you."

Next day came Dorian Lupescu's funeral, a grand, extravagant affair at the Russian Orthodox church in Moscow Road. Uncle Gib was invited. How Dorian's parents and wife and

270

aunts and uncles and cousins knew of Uncle Gib's existence and where to find him he didn't know, but they did find him and sent an invitation on beautiful cream-laid paper with a black border and a black silk ribbon bow. His striped suit having perished in the fire, he borrowed one from Reuben along with another shirt and black tie. Poor Dorian's body was transported in a mahogany coffin with brass fittings in a black-and-gold carriage drawn by four black horses with black feathers on their heads. The service was in Russian or Greek or something, but Uncle Gib sang along with the hymns in English, though he didn't really know the tunes.

Afterwards, they all stood out in the street smoking strong Russian cigarettes, and Dorian's mother thanked Uncle Gib in the best English she could manage for being kind to her son, and Gib was so moved that he had tears in his eyes for the first time since he was an infant. Back at home with the Perkinses a piece of good news awaited him. The Children of Zebulun had clubbed together and bought him a new computer. Maybelle was giving him the box room for a study to use for answering his Agony Uncle letters.

AUGUST WENT OUT like a lion, a wet and bedraggled lion, and September came in like a lamb, skipping in the sunshine. But before that, in late August, in the middle of the afternoon, Elizabeth Cherry came back from her holiday. Almost the first thing she noticed was the glassless window frame. Rain had soaked the curtains, which had dried again with unsightly stains, and left a damp patch on the carpet. She phoned Susan, who knew nothing about it and who began abject apologies for not noticing. You can't castigate your neighbour who has been keeping an eye on your property without payment even though that eye has failed to spot the only thing it was kept there for. Would Elizabeth like Susan to come over? Elizabeth said not now, tomorrow perhaps, and carried her case upstairs. Nothing appeared to have been disturbed. She unpacked her clothes and tipped the contents of the small jewel case she had carried with her—a spare watch in case the battery in hers gave out and a ring to wear for a dress-up evening—into the large jewel box on her dressing table.

In the kitchen, she looked through the freezer for a packet of strawberry ice cream. No sign of it. She supposed she was getting forgetful and had eaten it herself. The toaster was full of crumbs. She was sure she hadn't left it that way. Elizabeth went back upstairs to scrutinise the jewel box. The difficulty was that she couldn't now remember what had been in the box when first she opened it half an hour before and what she had added to it from the contents of her carry-on case. Still, there could be no doubt about what was missing: a diamond ring and a diamond eternity ring, a gold chain, and a gold bracelet. Elizabeth phoned the police.

The policeman who came was sympathetic and pleasant. He was happy to tell her where she could find a glazier to mend the window. There would be no fingerprints, he was sure of that, but an officer would come and check. No doubt the jewellery was insured? Elizabeth nodded. The house was, the contents were, and the jewellery. They asked her to describe what was missing. By the time she was halfway through the list, both of them could see that her description fitted thousands of pieces of jewellery.

"I wouldn't be doing you any favours," the policeman said, "if I told you there was much chance of our finding the villain. In fact, the chances are practically nil."

Only after he had gone did she miss the credit card, the euros, and the transatlantic dollars.

LEW CROWN WOULD be back from his holidays by now, as the old woman in Pembridge Villas must also be. When another day went by and another and no police officers presented themselves at his parents' door, Lance began to feel a little more secure. She was old, her brain would be going, and she hadn't noticed anyone had been in there. She must have seen the window, though. Lance refused to let himself worry about that. He'd got enough on his plate. That package must be fetched from his nan's place and taken over to Holloway.

Lance forgot he was out on bail on a charge of murder and arson and began dreaming of the untold wealth that would accrue to him from the sale of the jewellery. Perhaps he'd get enough, not to buy a place—even he wasn't so naive as that—but to rent somewhere nice enough to make Gemma leave Fize and come live with him. He tore the old woman's chequebook in two and cut her credit card in half.

21

IT WAS JUST midday and the last patient was leaving Ella's morning surgery. Mrs. Khan had brought one of the twins with her this time, her seven-year-old son Hakim. Ella told her it was wrong to keep her child away from school now the autumn term had begun, and the boy translated. Or maybe didn't translate but told his mother whatever suited him. How was she to know? Mrs. Khan got her usual prescription for tranquillisers, Ella having refused the sleeping pills she was asked for. Hakim was reading the prescription with an important air, nodding his head precociously, when Ella's phone rang. The practice receptionist said, "He says he's called Joel, Ella."

Ella sighed. She had been hoping to go home for a quiet lunchtime and afternoon with Eugene. "Joel? What can I do for you?"

His voice, cracked, weak, gasping, was almost unrecognisable. "Can you come? Now?"

"What's wrong?"

"I haven't taken too much. Should be all right. I only—want to—get—to . . ."

The last words were inaudible.

She ran, leaving Mrs. Khan and Hakim staring. At the office door she called out Joel's address and told the receptionist to call 999. Within two minutes she was in her car. Miraculously, there wasn't much traffic and she was there before the ambulance. She hammered on Joel's door, yelled his name into the darkness through the letter box. She was downstairs again, begging a porter to break the door down when the paramedics came in, two tall men carrying their first-aid bags. Between them they kicked the heavy door in.

"Why's it so dark?" one of them asked her.

"He likes it that way."

They switched lights on, the feeble bulbs of low wattage, which were all Joel had, and one of them flung back the curtains. Joel was lying on the brown velvet sofa, sprawled on his back, dressed as he always was in jeans and old, faded T-shirt, his long, shaggy hair spread across his forehead and eyes as if he had pulled it down to hide his face. A dribble of frothy saliva trickled

275

out of parted lips. On the low table were two containers half-full of pills, a half bottle of vodka, and a pop-psychology book about schizophrenia.

Ella said, "Help me get him on his feet."

"We'll do that," one of them said.

They began to walk him up and down, half dragging him. Ella raised the blind and opened windows. She read the labels on the pill containers, both made out to other people. Joel shuddered and twitched. His eyes stayed closed.

She thought of his heart and the operation from which he wasn't yet fully recovered and dared not give him Adrenalin. She took hold of one of his arms and the paramedic stepped back. "Joel, Joel, can you hear me? Speak to me, Joel." She turned to the waiting man. "Make coffee, would you?"

He was quick. The coffee was too hot and they added cold water. Ella held it to Joel's lips. He shuddered and the cup rattled against his teeth, but he sipped some of it, choked, and moaned. His body sagged and without their support he would have fallen.

"You must drink it. Come on now. You must."

This time he swallowed a mouthful and then another. His pale face took on a greenish tinge, and at last a voice came out of his mouth, a voice that barely sounded human. "Going to be sick."

The older paramedic fetched a basin from the

kitchen sink but he was too late. Joel threw up on the reddish brown Turkey carpet, his vomit much the same colour. Still kept on his feet, he began shaking and trembling, but he drank the water she brought him and at last uttered a long sigh.

"Shall we move him out of here now, Doctor?"

"I'll come with him," she said.

DAVE AND LANCE'S nan Kath had been sitting out on her balcony, sharing a bottle of wine and contemplating the traffic in the Harrow Road, which dawdled sluggishly below them. It was a fine warm evening, sunny and pleasant but for the foul air, foggy with pollution. Dave got up when the doorbell rang and let Lance in. Lance kissed his nan and looked longingly at the wine bottle.

"Oh, give him a glass, Dave, and open another bottle, why don't you."

Sitting out there with a glass of chardonnay in his hand reminded Lance painfully of such evenings spent with Gemma on her balcony. Would he ever see her again? He took a swig of his wine.

"I've got a bone to pick with you, my lad," his nan said. "That bag of stuff you left with me, it's made me nervous. What with you setting fire to old Gib's house and that East European getting killed, though I'll be the first to say that was no fault of yours, but all that's made me think maybe you're one of them terrorists. And what's in that bag is what I want to know."

Lance said it wasn't true, he'd never set fire to Uncle Gib's house.

"Never mind that. You tell me what's in that bag. No, you show me."

Dave came back with another bottle of chardonnay, which he opened with a corkscrew that looked to Lance more like a Black & Decker.

"I've said it twice and I'll say it again. I want to know what's in that bag. And what's more, it's not going out of here till you've opened it and let me see. Isn't that right, Dave?"

"It is, Kath."

Lance was starting to wish he hadn't come. But he had to retrieve the bag to take it to Mr. Crown.

"You've got no choice," said Dave. "You open it or else your nan'll put it out with the trash. Or drop it in the canal, more like. She will, you know," he went on admiringly, giving her a fond look. "You know what she is, a real Iron Lady."

"Where is it?" said Lance.

The package was produced. Lance took off the elastic bands and lifted out the pieces of jew-ellery, two diamond rings, a gold bracelet, and a gold chain. Neither Kath nor Dave made a sound.

"It's mine," said Lance, knowing he wouldn't be believed.

"Pull the other one," said his nan, recovering her voice. "Where d'you get it?"

"Posh place in Notting Hill."

"Breaking and entering," said Dave in a conversational tone. "Was it after dark?"

"What if it was?"

"Then it's burglary."

Kath reached for the bottle. "Let's have another drink." Two silent minutes were taken up with refilling the glasses. "Traffic's easing off a bit."

"Till it starts again in the morning," said Dave.

"You can look after that stuff for him, can't you?"

"Well, I can."

"I was going to take it to a bloke in Holloway."

"You don't want to do that," Dave said quickly. "You never know who you can trust in this game. Let me handle it. You won't be the loser."

"OK, if you say so." Lance was feeling quite relieved.

"Getting a bit chilly out here," said his nan. "The nights are drawing in. What say we all go down the Good King Billy for a quick one?"

"Or a slow one," said Dave, suddenly in a cheerful mood.

WHAT ELLA CALLED simply "an emergency," phoning him in the late afternoon, threatened to deprive Eugene of her company until late. He sat watching television and eating sweets, something he hadn't done since he was a child, and he found that he was enjoying himself. Was it true, then, that he was happier without Ella than with her? He tried telling himself that he had been single too long, an ageing bachelor with the occasional girlfriend. It was simply that he wasn't yet really used to living with a woman. But underlying these feelings all the time was the habit that had taken over his life. Even thinking about it brought him to reach for the pack—in Ella's absence it lay openly and open on the table in front of him—and help himself to a sweet. Giving up, phasing out, was now a distant memory.

It was September already and he was getting married in October. A few weeks of freedom to indulge himself in more or less unlimited amounts of Chocorange remained. He switched off the television, castigating himself for watching a mindless game show, and picked up with great care a small bowl of Sung celadon porcelain that stood on the table beside the Chocorange pack. Once, he thought, he would have talked to himself of the Chocorange being beside the Sung bowl, not the other way about. He palpated the bowl delicately in his hands while he sucked the last sliver of his sweet.

If Ella were here, he would even now be making excuses to her. He had to go upstairs to fetch something, he would make a phone call in his study so as not to disturb her, he must go outside and check that the tiresome Bathsheba wasn't once more using his rose bed as a feline convenience. Those few minutes away from her would give him the opportunity to suck a sweet. Though he knew it sounded like insanity, he had actually timed himself doing this and found that eating one lasted four minutes at most. When he came back to her, he always craved another. Consuming one set off the longing again. No more than half an hour ever went by before he gave in to desire, made another excuse to escape, and almost ran out to find one of his secret hoards.

She was beginning to notice. His sensitivity and percipience hadn't been blunted by his addiction. Once or twice lately she had asked him if he wasn't feeling well and, when he said he was fine, asked if he was worried about something. Of course he was worried, perpetually troubled by this craving, and seeing no way—he had tried—to change. "'Tis one thing to be tempted, Escalus, another thing to fall," says Angelo. He and Ella had seen *Measure for Measure* in the summer, and that line remained with him. But what if you tried desperately to resist and failed?

If you still fell, over and over? Angelo, of course, was principally referring to sexual indulgence. If he was honest, Eugene said to himself, alone in his house among his objets d'art, he was afraid of reaching a point where he preferred eating a sugar-free, orange-flavoured chocolate sweet to making love.

That confession frightened him. He had never put it into words before, had never been aware of it for long. Perhaps it was new. It must mean that his habit was gaining increased power over him. But he was getting married in a few weeks' time. He was getting married so that he might live for the rest of his life with the woman he loved and so that he might make love to her as often as he and she chose. He looked at the pale green bowl he held in his hands, looked into its depths as if, crystal-ball-like, it could foretell his future. When he set it down, his now free left hand reached out to pick up the brown-and-orange pack; his now free right-hand index finger and thumb picked out a sweet and put it into his mouth.

What he had realised ought to be the jolt that shocked him out of this, shocked him into throwing all those packs away and beginning abstinence. Other people resisted temptation. They stopped smoking simply by ceasing to buy cigarettes. But they had nicotine patches, he thought. If only there were a Chocorange patch! The idea made him smile, then laugh. It was easy to laugh when he was sucking one of those delicious sweets.

He couldn't give up cold turkey, he knew he couldn't. He had tried. What would happen was an enforced deprivation, starting with the last days of their honeymoon when, sneaking into the bathroom in Como or going off for a solitary walk while Ella shopped somewhere, he finished up all the sweets he had brought with him. No more would be available in Italy. He would have to exist without them until they got home, and then, even if he bought more—and he knew he would—because Ella would be living with him, not simply staying here four nights out of seven, the number he ate must necessarily be restricted. Gradually that number would grow less and less until the day came when it hardly seemed worth buying more. He must try to look on his marriage as the sure and certain cure for his habit. His marriage was his lifeline.

THEY WERE KEEPING Joel overnight. He was weak and utterly enervated but consciousness had fully returned. Ella had sat with him for most of the afternoon and was there when he tried to sit up. Without asking him she had phoned his mother and told her what had happened, not saying it was a suicide attempt, which was what she suspected, but that her son had mistakenly taken an overdose. Wendy Stemmer had arrived at five o'clock, anxious and exasperated, hair newly done, dressed in white broderie anglaise, and Ella had then left the room and phoned Eugene.

Returning, she found Joel with his eyes tightly shut and his mother holding one of his long, white hands.

"What will he do next?" Mrs. Stemmer asked her in a despairing tone.

Ella felt like saying that the remarkable thing about Joel was that he did almost nothing, but she only smiled.

"Is he going to be all right? He won't tell me anything."

"I'm sure he is. But you must ask the doctor who is looking after him here."

Wendy Stemmer tottered off in narrow-strap, stilt-heeled sandals to do that and Ella took her place but without holding Joel's hand.

He opened his eyes. "Has she gone?"

"She's coming back. She's very anxious about you, Joel."

"I know you think I meant to kill myself, but I didn't."

"All right. If you didn't, I'm very glad."

"I want to tell you what I was really doing."

"That's fine, but here's your mother coming back. Do you want to tell her?"

"No!" If he had been stronger, it would have been a shout. As things were, it came out as a strangled gasp.

His mother had been told he ought not to be left alone in his flat. Not even during the day. Ella went to speak to the doctor. Discreetly, he refused to say what he evidently thought, that this was a failed suicide attempt, and when she told him about the midday phone call, that rescuing Joel hadn't been due to any great intuition or acuity on her part, he agreed with obvious relief that his brush with death had probably been an accident.

"I think he wants to tell me about it, but it must be in his own time."

"Oh, I fully agree."

Wendy Stemmer had slipped off her punishing sandals and they lay on their sides under the bed. "He seems very fond of you," she said accusingly at Joel's bedside but with her back turned to him. "Tell me something. Are you his girlfriend?"

"Of course not. I'm his doctor."

"I asked because I've never known him so keen on a woman before. I always thought he must be gay, though he didn't give any signs of that either."

Ella was so angry she took a few seconds before she could trust herself to speak. "Mrs. Stemmer, don't you think you could persuade your husband to be reconciled with Joel? If you tell him how lonely Joel is, how he lives in the dark and now he's—accidentally, of course— taken an overdose of—well, pills that weren't prescribed for him?"

Ella watched the woman's face as a deep flush

spread over it under the thick makeup. Saying that she knew some of the sedatives came from his mother would do neither Joel nor her any good. It was useless. "Couldn't you try, Mrs. Stemmer?"

"It won't be any good." Wendy Stemmer bent over, perhaps to hide her face, and eased her sandals on again. She looked up and Ella thought she spoke for the first time with sincerity and maybe from her heart. "I've tried. I'm always trying. Last time I told him he ought to see Joel, he hit me." She drew in her breath. "Right across my face."

Ella had nothing to say.

22

LANCE THOUGHT HE had heard the last of Lupescu's death and the destruction of Uncle Gib's house. If the police were serious, they would have done something about it by now. The only condition of his bail was that he stay a certain distance away from witnesses' houses, such as Uncle Gib's new place and the people next door. He didn't want to go near them so that wasn't a problem. It wasn't enough to keep him awake at night, not even in that uncomfortable bed in proximity to the car tyres and the broken bike. Last night a defunct electric mixer had fallen off a shelf onto his head. Besides, he had the prospect of an influx of money when Dave sold the rings, the bracelet, and the gold chain. He spent a lot of his waking hours thinking what he would do with the money, spending most of it on Gemma but some on new clothes for himself as well as an iPod, and a really good mobile that would play radio, show TV, and take photos.

Like callous landlords who require their paying guests to vacate their rooms and indeed the whole building in daylight hours, Lance's parents wanted him out of the flat for most of the day. If they had had jobs themselves it might have been different, but they were always at home, watching television and exploring the Internet. Their son wasn't welcome.

His father put it to him plainly: "If you had work, it'd be another story. But you don't and no prospect so far as I can see."

Lance thought this a bit OTT considering neither of them had jobs, but when he said so, his mother ignored the gibe and said, "I don't know how that poor old Gilbert put up with you under his feet all day."

The one advantage of being there was that he had plenty to eat before he left in the morning and when he got home at night. His mother's family's tradition was that if you missed a meal or failed to finish everything on your plate or ask for seconds, you were likely to collapse from inanition. A story told by her grandmother and religiously passed down the generations was of their cousin Lil, who had missed breakfast and as a result fainted in a train going to Ramsgate and never fully recovered. So Lance was stuffed with eggs and bacon and sausages in the morning and plied with burgers or Indian takeaway in the evening, while his mother made lunch for him to sustain him in the interval. She might taunt him with having no paid employment though jobless herself, for in her estimation there was no disgrace in a woman being without a job, but to Lance, carrying a thick package of ham-and-cheese sandwiches and half a dozen Jaffa cakes in his backpack, then forcing himself to walk the streets and sit on park benches, staring at passersby and dozing, was what having work must be like.

He was leaving the flat at nine in the morning, the witching hour at which he was banished, his backpack laden with food, when two men got out of the police car parked outside and invited him to accompany them to the station. One of them he recognised. It was the detective sergeant who had asked most of the questions last time. Lance said OK because it was useless to argue, and besides that, it would be a change sitting at a table in an interview room instead of trudging up and down Ladbroke Grove and hanging about in Holland Park.

The young lady lawyer came back again, and

cups of tea were brought. They asked him all the same questions all over again, and the other man, the one he hadn't seen before, said the DNA sample they'd taken matched the DNA on various objects that had survived the fire.

"Mr. Platt lived in the house for six months," the solicitor said. "Naturally, he touched things. What did you expect?"

Some guy in a petrol station told them that Lance had paid for fifteen litres of premium unleaded several weeks before. At first he didn't know what they meant, then he remembered paying for Dwayne's petrol when he fetched Gemma's stuff over to Blagrove Road in his van.

"I never put it in no bottle, I never touched it," he said. "My mate put it straight in his tank."

They looked as if they didn't believe him. They asked more questions. Then the one he recognised started asking him about Dorian Lupescu. Wasn't it a fact that he was jealous of Lupescu? His girlfriend had said she fancied Lupescu—was that true?

"She's not my girlfriend," Lance said sadly.

A shaft of pain threatened to bend him double when it occurred to him that it might be Gemma who had told them this. But, no, she wouldn't. Not his Gemma, his love, his sweetheart. Fize would. Fize's pal what's-his-name would. Uncle Gib certainly would. Some bastard had betrayed him. He was sorely in need of comfort.

289

"Can I eat my sandwiches now?"

"I don't see why not," said the detective sergeant. "We'll take a break." He looked at his watch and muttered something into the machine recording all this. "Back in half an hour."

It went on for a few more hours, but they let him go on bail again without a charge and without any explanation, only to tell him he must attend court when required and not interfere with the process of justice. He could easily guarantee that; he didn't know how to.

ELLA HAD ACCEPTED an offer for her flat. It wasn't the first, but it was the best she had yet had and she was satisfied. Eugene had kept telling her that it was of no great importance whether she sold it now or in a year's time. They were not in need of the money from the sale. But, without saying a word of this to him, she wanted to have a substantial sum of her own to bring with her to the marriage and that she would have. The flat had been hers for fifteen years and had been free of mortgage for two. It brought her some gratification to know that she would sign the contract for the sale well before her wedding.

She had arranged to visit Joel next day, but first, on her afternoon off, she was going to drive over to the flat—she hadn't been near it for the past fortnight—and bring away various items that might as well be moved before the removers fetched the rest on completion day. That would be after she returned from her honeymoon. The place looked rather drab and dusty. But someone had liked it enough to pay a considerable sum for it, and after the furniture had been taken out, she would employ a team to clean it up for the incoming residents. First she packed into cardboard crates all the remaining books and, into suitcases, all her clothes. In the bathroom cabinet were a lot of toiletries she would probably never use, but there was no point in leaving them where they were. She loaded them into plastic carriers and, making several journeys, put the lot into the boot and back of the car.

Eugene said he was going to buy her a new car for a wedding present. Like many women, she couldn't get excited at the prospect. She was rather fond of her five-year-old car, but giving her things and choosing presents for her brought Eugene so much pleasure she disliked stopping him. He was at the gallery but would be home by six. Ella carried her boxes and bags indoors.

She was aware that Eugene had a greater appreciation of beauty and elegance than she had. She might like organising her life and tidying up details, but neatness in the home wasn't as important to her as it was to him. She had determined sometime before that she would conform to him in these things. He did so much for her, and she, she sometimes thought, so little for him. This stuff she had brought back from her flat she would put away neatly before he came home, starting perhaps with the clothes and all these bottles and jars.

The house had plenty of wardrobe space, including a walk-in cupboard opening off their bedroom. Ella hung up the dresses and the suits she had brought with her, folded sweaters and laid them on the shelves. Then she went into the second bathroom, well aware that all the half-used cosmetics and half-empty bottles of shampoo and bath essence would never be finished up. No doubt some people would have thrown these things out without wasting time, just as some took a garment to the charity shop when it hadn't been worn for six months. She wasn't among them. Foolishly, she admitted, she revolted against the waste of it even when she knew keeping stuff you would never use was mere hoarding for hoarding's sake.

This cabinet, seldom used except by the occasional guest, was probably empty. She wasn't much surprised to find a safety razor, a tube of arnica, and some wads of cotton wool in the top drawer. These were the things visitors left behind. All the other drawers were empty but for the bottom one, in which was a pack of some sort of sweets. Sugar-free sweets apparently. The packaging was brown and orange with a badly executed design on it of liquid chocolate being poured into a half orange. Ella put it into the top drawer with the razor and the arnica and tipped her bottles and jars into the bottom one. Carli again? She had just remembered finding a similar pack of sweets in the secret drawer in the kitchen. Carli was absentminded for someone so young, leaving these sweets of hers all over the house. She would ask her about it next time they encountered each other.

The books next. Ella loved Eugene's bookshelves. They had all been made for him from golden gray walnut and fitted to the walls in the study and the drawing room. There had apparently been a dilemma as to whether these should be plain shelves or cabinets with glass doors. Ella was glad Eugene had decided against the glazing because she much preferred open bookcases, where everything could clearly be seen, to cupboards with keys in their locks through whose windows spines were obscured or lost behind wood uprights. Tidy, precise Eugene had arranged all his books in alphabetical order if they were novels, and according to subject and then alphabetically for nonfiction.

Ella enjoyed just standing in front of the books and giving herself up to exulting in their beauty and the pristine state in which Eugene kept them.

She had intended to fit the books she had brought with her in among those already there. There were no more than twenty of them, some kept from her school days or received as presents, for Ella usually bought paperbacks and passed them on to her sister or a friend. But, like most people who love reading, she found it impossible simply to shuffle the novels around on the shelf and push the newcomers in among them. Each book she unpacked she had to study, recall how she had enjoyed it or otherwise, read its first line, and, before she set it down, congratulate herself on keeping it so well. These classics from the nineteenth and early twentieth century in their dark blue or mulberry red binding wouldn't disgrace Eugene's shelves.

E. M. Forster's *The Longest Journey* had better go next to the existing copy. They seemed to be identical editions. She was about to move Eugene's own copies, one of them necessarily onto the shelf below, when she heard his key in the lock. The time had flown past.

He walked into the room. His expression, quite unlike his usual pleasant composure, the look of a considerate and civilised man, was frowning and aghast. He shouted at her, "What are you doing?"

She flinched. Before she could reply—she was on her feet now—a transformation seemed to come over him, as if a hand had passed over his features, wiping away the cruel mask and leaving a gentle sweetness behind.

"I'm sorry, darling. I don't know what came over me. I've had a hard day."

"Who did you think I was?"

It was an opening and he took it. "It's rather dark in here. A strange person kneeling by the bookcase gave me a shock. Very silly, I know. Still, we have once been burgled. Look, let me do those books, will you?"

"If you like," she said, still a little stunned.

"We'll go and have a drink first." They went into the study. "Why don't we have a bottle of champagne?"

She smiled, took his arm. "You can't be going to propose to me again?"

"I will if you like."

"What are we celebrating, then?"

A lucky escape, he thought. An amazing stroke of good fortune. If I had been five minutes—no, half a minute—later . . . "The new exhibition, Priscilla Hart's show. It's going well. I sold three of her miniatures this afternoon."

"Good. Let's celebrate for ourselves too. Not long to our wedding now."

He kissed her. Because he had been saved from humiliation at her hands, had vindicated himself perfectly by pretending he had seen a burglar, he felt a surge of love for her. It was going to be all right. They were going to be happy.

THE SHORTENING DAYS of September seemed each one more beautiful than the last, the sky a clear blue, the air as warm as on a July day. Only

295

it hadn't been like this in July but gray and cold and constantly raining. Now, although the sun was strong, in the shade you felt the chill of autumn. It was too late for true heat. The time for hot days and mild evenings had gone by, and the nights were cold. Ella noticed how tired the trees were beginning to look, their leaves worn-out by onslaughts of wind and rain and now by belated sunshine.

The gardens in front of Joel's block were littered with fallen leaves, not those of the final shedding, which would come in November, but the September drop, which relieves trees of their weight. They crunched under her feet as she walked up the steps. The lift seemed to rise especially slowly, and when she rang Joel's bell, a woman she had never before seen opened the door to her. She introduced herself as the day carer, and although she didn't say so, Ella thought she might be responsible for letting more light into the flat.

In the grim and gloomy living room the blind had been raised and the curtains half drawn apart. The increased light revealed how shabby the furnishings were, the only bright and fresh object an amber glass vase on the table full of orange chrysanthemums. Had the day carer brought them or even Wendy Stemmer?

Joel lay on the sofa. He wore dark glasses but had also spread a black scarf over his face. He gave no sign of having seen or heard Ella. She sat down in one of the chairs drawn up to the table and asked him how he was feeling. To her surprise, after a long while he took the scarf off his face and sat up. Because he hadn't replied, she said again, "How are you?"

"Well enough." His voice was low and lifeless.

"When you were in the hospital, did they give you any tests? Did they check your heart?"

"You think maybe I damaged it taking all those pills? They did a lot of tests," he said indifferently. "They wouldn't have let me out if there was anything wrong, would they?"

"I will check with them. Did your parents find the carer for you?"

"Ma did. He's paying, I suppose. I don't want her. She opens the curtains. She brings me food and drink and whatever." He gave a small, unamused laugh. "I think she's frightened of me— well, I know she is. It's the shades and the scarf. Do I look frightening, Ella?"

"Not to me." She wondered as she said it if that was quite true.

Still wearing the glasses, he turned his gaze towards the corner where hung the long mirror in a carved mahogany frame in which the bronze face was reflected. And would have been reflected again in the mirror behind it and again and again infinitely. Today the room was too dim for anything to be seen in the glass but patches of shine and dull shadows. Joel's face contorted as he seemed to peer. He stretched his neck and concentrated, subsided with a sigh.

"I think he's gone. I really think so. Sometimes I hear a whisper, but I think that may be me imagining things. I haven't seen him, not since I came round—after what I did, I mean. Do you want to know why I did what I did?"

Ella could see nothing, but she knew the reflections were there, the faces half-turned, the neverending faces. . . . Was Mithras also there, though neither of them could see him? "I don't think you meant to kill yourself," she said.

"No. No, I didn't. I'll tell you about it. I haven't told anyone, not Ma or any of the people at the hospital." He took off the glasses and blinked as if, instead of a grayish dimness, the room were flooded with brilliant light. "Would you like something to eat or drink? I've never asked you that before, have I? I don't think I've ever asked anyone that before." He had, once, and Ella remembered the glass of water, but she didn't correct him. "Rita's here and she'll do it. She likes doing it."

"I don't want anything, thanks, Joel."

"I collected up those pills. It doesn't matter how. I don't go out much but I went out and bought myself a half bottle of vodka. I liked the taste. They say it hasn't a taste, but it has and I like it. I could take to drink—shall I?"

She ignored this. As she had thought before, in any sustained conversation he might begin by sounding adult but he gradually became more and more like a child. "Tell me, are you taking your medication? The pills you get from Miss Crane, I mean."

He nodded, turning his eyes once more to the mirror.

"Sure?"

"I promise, Ella. Shall I tell you why I did what I did?" It was the second time of asking.

"If you want to."

"Do you remember what I told you about having a near-death experience? When something went wrong under the anaesthetic?"

She nodded, feeling suddenly cold in the warm, close room. She felt fear as shivers touched her skin, moving across her shoulders and down her arms. Don't be silly, she told herself, get yourself together. You're a doctor, you've been a doctor for fifteen years.

He seemed not to notice her slight shrinking. His eyes were turned away from her, his gaze far away on some other plane. "Mithras, I wanted him to go. I brought him back with me from that white city at the end of the river. I think maybe he was one of the angels on the battlements. But, no, that's not right. They had wings and he didn't. I wanted him to go. He was getting bigger, you see. No, I don't quite mean that. He was getting clearer and his voice was too. He never said anything terrible like I was to harm someone, but I kept thinking he'd start. I thought that if he—well, went on getting bigger and louder and stronger, he'd take me over, he'd take this place over.

"I once saw a picture. It was an illustration for *Alice in Wonderland.* I was only about eight or nine. Alice had drunk something and it made her grow big. She grew huge till she filled the house, she had to lie down, her arms and legs couldn't get through the doors. I don't know why but that picture frightened me terribly. I screamed when I first saw it and I couldn't get it out of my head. That was how I was starting to feel about Mithras, that he'd get so big he'd never be able to get out. He'd take me over, kind of absorb me. I knew I'd have to do something."

"What did you do?" she asked, although she guessed.

"I thought that if I had another near-death experience, I'd go back to that place, the river and the meadows and the city at the end of it, I mean. I'd see all those white walls like castle walls and see the angels walking there. And Mithras would come with me, he would, he'd want to because it was the only way for him to get back there. And he'd stay. He'd be happy and I'd be free."

"So you took the pills and the vodka to get

yourself near death?"

"That's what I did. I told Mithras to come with me and he came, I think he did, and when I started to leave again, I think I left him behind, but I don't know. I didn't see the city or the river or the sunshine, Ella. It was all dark with kind of moving shapes, vague dark shapes moving in the dark. I talked to you out of the dark, and then I— then I sort of passed out. Now I keep looking for Mithras, but I can't see him and it's only in the nighttime that I hear his voice. It's coming from a long, long way off so I know he's talking to me from the city."

She sat quite still, feeling a kind of despair. There was nothing to say.

"I went to all that trouble to take him back, but now he's gone, I half want him back. I miss him." Joel lifted to her an abject little boy's face and met her eyes for the first time since she'd arrived. "I'm so lonely, Ella."

She reached for his hand but, thinking this inadequate for his great need, got up, sat beside him, and took him in her arms. Holding him, she felt his heart beating against her as if he was more afraid than she was.

23

ONCE MORE THEY were out on the balcony, watching the roadway. A crowd of gesticulating men ran about shouting at the driver of an articulated truck, which had wedged itself between a bendy bus and a concrete mixer. Lance's nan had let him in before rushing back to her ringside seat, anxious not to miss more than a minute of the sitcom currently being enacted in the Harrow Road. Lance followed her out there. His hospitable grandmother had already poured him a large glass of pinot grigio. Enthralled by the sight of the lorry driver landing a mighty punch on the bus driver's jaw, Dave passed Lance the crisps without turning round.

His nan leant over the railing and began yelling at the lorry driver, "Give him another, mate! Them bendy buses are a menace! They think they own the bloody road." Spectators in the street turned their faces upwards as one. "Who d'you think you're looking at?"

"Cool it now, Kath," said Dave as police sirens sounded, coming closer. "You calm down. We don't want no trouble."

Lance looked at him admiringly. Dave seemed to be the only one Lance had ever come across, within the family or outside it, able to exert any control over his nan. Two officers had got out of their car and strolled over to the men, who had moved into a standoff. Things quickly quieted down as the concrete mixer was expertly reversed through a narrow gap, and the crowd began to dissolve.

Lance's nan, deprived of entertainment, sighed resignedly and turned to him. "So how's the world treating you, lovely?"

"I'm good," said Lance with a hopeful glance at Dave.

Dave refilled their glasses. He shook the last of the crisp crumbs into the palm of his hand, dropped the bag over the railing, and watched it float gently down into the street below. Then he turned to Lance and smiled in an avuncular sort of way. "You'll be wanting to know what them bits and bobs fetched."

"Rings and things and buttons and bows," said Lance's nan unexpectedly.

"The market's very dodgy." Dave might have been talking about the current state of the euro. "There's like a world recession. Still, I've done my best for you." He pulled out of his pocket two dirty and crumpled notes, a twenty and a ten. The twenty had a rent in it mended with Sellotape.

Deeply disappointed, Lance stared. "That all you got?"

"Didn't I say the market's dodgy? After I took my ten percent that's the best I could do. It's not like they was diamonds."

Diamonds were exactly what Lance believed they were. In those few moments, sitting on his nan's balcony, the light fast fading and the air taking on an autumnal cooling, a metamorphosis came over him. Uncle Gib, in one of his biblical phrases, would have said that the scales fell from his eyes. His father might have said that he began to grow up. He saw that the trust he habitually had in people, in almost anyone, was misplaced. No one was going to do anything much for him. They never had and they never would. He was out on his own.

When his nan said the nights were drawing in and it was time for them all to go down to the Good King Billy, Lance got up and walked through the doorway into the living room. But instead of waiting to accompany them meekly to the pub—where he would have been expected to spend a good half of his thirty pounds—he said, not "Cheers," but like someone three times his age, "Good night," failing to add, as he would normally have done, the obligatory "See you later." They were silent, apparently aware that all was not well. He let himself out, went quickly down the stairs and out into the street, turning in the opposite direction to the one that led to the pub.

OF THE HUNDRED people who had been invited, eighty-three had accepted their invitations. The hotel on the river, licensed for wedding ceremonies, was booked, the lunch menu scrutinised (and frequently subjected to alterations) by Eugene, the flowers lavishly ordered, the cars organised, and, of course, every detail of departure for the honeymoon and the honeymoon itself arranged in advance. Ella had collected her wedding dress and her "going-away" suit. Her own two suitcases were packed, as was Eugene's.

"You want me to come over in case anyone comes back here?" asked Carli. "I mean, serve tea or drinks or whatever?" She was plainly anxious to feast her eyes on the guests and get a sight of Ella in her wedding dress.

"No one will come back here, Carli. Not even ourselves. We shall go straight from the hotel on our honeymoon." Ella could see no particular reason to tell Carli where that honeymoon destination was or when they would be leaving from Heathrow. "While we're away, perhaps you'd like to check up on your—er, sweets you've left in the drawers. There seem to be rather a lot of them, even some in one of the bathrooms."

The woman stared. "My what?" Her tone was belligerent.

Ella felt she had herself perhaps been too abrupt. "I'm sorry, Carli. There's absolutely no reason why you shouldn't keep your sweets in this house. Forget it."

"I never eat sweets. Never. You're mixing me up with someone else."

Ella started to say there was no one else, but she stopped herself. Carli had been vacuuming their bedroom, and Ella left her to it, going back into the guest bathroom. The brown-and-orange pack of Chocorange—for that, she saw, was its name—was still there. Down in the drawing room, Eugene had put all her books away as he had promised, neatly, precisely, according to author and each one alphabetically. She had been kneeling there, in front of the row of Forsters, when he had come in and shouted at, as he thought, an intruder. But had he really believed the person on her knees there in the fading light was a burglar? A bookish burglar with a fondness for literature? It was extremely unlikely. And why had he undertaken to finish the task she had begun?

She squatted down on the floor again and removed from the shelf *A Passage to India*, *Howards End*, two copies of *The Longest Journey*, *Maurice*, and *A Room with a View*. She put her hand inside, feeling behind the remaining books, first to the right and encountering more space, then to the left, her fingers coming in contact with a plastic bag full of something. She pulled it out. The something was a number of packets of Chocorange. She counted ten of them. The bag in her hand, she began walking about the drawing room, opening a tallboy, lifting the lid of a Chinese chest, pulling out a drawer in a console table. A carved flange, which Eugene perhaps believed concealed a secret drawer, yielded four packs of Chocorange. Under some folded linen in the chest she found six more. The house was full of the things. At the handsome late-eighteenth-century wardrobe, which stood in the hall where they hung their coats, she hesitated. The idea of going through a man's pockets was repugnant to her—but surely that distaste would only apply when the search was for letters or photographs? She opened the wardrobe door and felt in the pocket of Eugene's raincoat, which he hadn't worn much since the relentlessly wet summer seemed to come to an end in the last days of August. No Chocorange, but a mass of the cellophane covers with their distinctive red taping, which had to be stripped off to reach the contents. The pockets of a light linen jacket contained much the same discarded wrappings.

After that, Ella went all over the house, causing Carli, who encountered her in one of the spare bedrooms, to ask her what she was looking for. Ella simply smiled and shook her head. By that time she had found twenty-three packets of the things, but she had left them where they were, concealed inside drawers and cupboards, some hidden in a sponge bag. Those, she thought, he probably intended to take to Como with him. This find made her look inside his big suitcase, where she found another six in an inside zip pocket.

That must mean he couldn't exist without them, not even on his honeymoon.

SELDOM DID LANCE have occasion to go into a pharmacy or what Uncle Gib would have called a chemist's shop. He was doing so this time at the request of his mother. She herself was too busy watching repeats of *Cagney & Lacey* on ITV3 to go out and buy the aspirins of which she regularly ate fourteen or fifteen a day but had run out of, for she too was an addict in her own way. Lance chose this particular pharmacy because he passed its window on his way to visit Uncle Gib and it was the first one he had come to since walking down from his parents' flat. His walk necessarily took him down the Portobello Road, and the sight of the stalls and small shops full of delectable goods made him feel even more acutely the lack of the means to buy them. Copies of designers' handbags, but so much like the real things as to be indistinguishable from them, were everywhere this morning. A new shop had opened selling homemade soaps whose strong, nostril-burning scents dominated all the usual smells of bacon and cheese and döner kebab. They made Lance sneeze, but Gemma liked that sort of soap and the "natural" bath essences the shop also sold. He'd like to buy them for her even if they did give him an allergy. And he'd like to buy that green lace tunic with the sequins and those black velvet harem pants and that . . . It was no use. He was once more approaching skint status, Elizabeth Cherry's three hundred pounds and the thirty pounds Dave had produced nearly gone.

He hadn't seen Gemma for a long time. But he had heard from her. The postcard she sent him was the first missive that might be called a letter he had ever had. It came to his parents' address, which she must have remembered from when he first met her. The postcard was a picture of the late Princess Diana with the infant Prince William. It said, *How are you? I hope OK. I miss you. Abelard says to say hi. Lots of love, G.*

He turned into Golborne Road and there was the pharmacy on his left. The man standing at the counter he recognised at once as White Hair, the rich git who was the owner of all that stuff he'd nicked and lost when Fize and his mates attacked him. Lance would have expected White Hair, if he had been in that shop at all, to have been buying expensive perfume for his girlfriend or maybe a new electric shaver. Instead, he was paying for three packs of sweets the assistant was just putting in a paper bag. Lance didn't expect to be recognised, and he got a shock when White Hair turned round, gave him a curt nod, and said good afternoon. For a moment Lance thought he must know him in his burglar's identity. Then he remembered trying and failing to claim the money found in the street. He muttered a "Cheers" in return but by that time White Hair had gone, taking his sweets with him.

Lance bought his mother's aspirins and began the walk back to Kensal Road where his parents lived. But before he reached it, he recalled his mother telling him that Uncle Gib had moved in with those god-botherers, the Perkinses, in Fermoy Road. Lance didn't know the number but he had no difficulty in finding the house. Where its neighbours each had a laurel bush in their front garden, the Perkinses had a sign proclaiming JESUS LIVES! Lance rang the bell.

There was no response. He rang again. This time he was aware of a flicker across the corner of his eye on the left side. Someone had twitched a curtain in the bay window. Then he noticed a narrow gap between the front door and its frame. The door wasn't shut but slightly ajar. Expecting some kind of trap, he gave it a cautious push. It swung open silently, and stepping over the threshold, he found himself in a narrow hallway.

Framed texts on the walls told him that the better the day the better the deed, and that if he honoured his father and mother, his days would be long in the land. No one was about but an ashtray on the windowsill full of stubs of a familiar brand was evidence of Uncle Gib's presence in the house. The silence was disconcerting. Lance belonged to a generation that feels uneasy without a perpetual murmuring of voices or throb of pop in the background. But having come here and made his way in, he wanted to see Uncle Gib. He wanted to tell him the truth about where he had been that night, for Uncle Gib had once been a burglar himself. He might be angry, he would call him a no-good sinner, but he would understand and would know Lance couldn't have been responsible for burning his house down.

Someone must be at home. They wouldn't have gone out and left the place open like that. Lance put his hand to the knob on the door on his left and turned it slowly clockwise. The door opened silently and he crept in. Afterwards he hardly knew why he hadn't screamed but he hadn't. Perhaps he'd been fascinated as well as horrified by what lay on the table. He'd clapped his hand over his mouth and advanced—tiptoeing for some reason—up to the body of Reuben Perkins.

The former shepherd of the Children of Zebulun lay in state, the lower part of his body covered by a white sheet, his head resting on a white pillow. His hands were folded across his chest. The third stroke he had suffered had killed him, but the second had twisted his mouth, pulling down one corner. Death had erased this distortion, and Lance saw a noble face, more like that of a Roman emperor than an old lag. This was his first corpse, the first he had ever seen. So this was what it was like when you were dead.

The eyes were closed, the eyelids white as the rest of the face. Tentatively he put out one finger and touched Reuben Perkins's forehead. It felt cold, more marble than skin, the texture like touching the translucent surface of one of Gemma's candles.

A footfall in the hallway brought him back to reality. Then four people came into the room, elderly men and women he had never before seen. Uncle Gib and Mrs. Perkins and another woman followed them. They crowded round the corpse, too absorbed in staring, head-shaking, and muttering what a saint the dead man had been, what a loss his death was, to notice Lance. But now was no time to speak to Uncle Gib. Lance slipped quietly out of the room as another group of mourners arrived, come to view the body.

He felt rather shaken. A nasty idea had come to him that he might dream about that dead man lying on a table, his slack, cold hands folded, his eyelids unnaturally white. When he closed his eyes, he seemed to see that sight again, it was so different from the dead people he'd seen on telly almost every day of his life.

He walked across the railway bridge and along Golborne Road to the canal, its waters ruffled by the cold wind into a thousand little ripples. Leaves were falling, the wind blowing them into flurries and settling them in quivering heaps. If he had kept to the towpath it would have taken him on to the southern edge of Kensal Green Cemetery, between it and the great gasworks, but he left it for Kensal Road, heading for his parents' home. He had put the dead Reuben Perkins out of his mind and was thinking about the aspirins he had bought for his mother and how, when he handed them over, she might let him stay indoors for the rest of the day when an unmarked police car stopped and two men in plainclothes got out.

Most members of the public would have failed to recognise them as police officers, but Lance knew. He identified them for what they were as surely as if their car had been painted in red and yellow squares and they dressed in dark uniforms and chequered caps. He muttered something about having to go home and see his mum, and though they didn't exactly laugh, the older one's lips twitched as if he'd got some sort of tic. They got him into the car exactly the way police did on the telly, one of them holding his head down with one hand and pushing him into the backseat with the other.

Uncle Gib was always telling him how ignorant he was, but he wasn't so ignorant he didn't know they couldn't question him any more once he'd been charged. So he didn't mind being questioned yet again. It was warm in the interview room and he got cups of tea. At one point he said could he ask them something, and when they didn't answer but just looked, he asked if Uncle Gib, Mr. Gilbert Gibson, had told them he'd been round at his place and where to find him.

"We ask the questions," said the one who twitched.

He went on denying that he'd been anywhere near Uncle Gib's house at the time of the fire. The young lady lawyer arrived and kept asking if they were going to charge Mr. Platt. Because, if not, they should let him go. Lance wished she wouldn't. It only gave them ideas, and that was exactly what it must have done. He knew there would be no escape and this time it was for real when he heard the words of the caution and all that stuff about things he might want to rely on in court. *In court* made his blood run cold. It was going to be next morning, and murder and arson were the charges.

24

EVERYONE WHO READ the *Evening Standard* and those who picked up a freebie in the street read the paragraph about Lance Kevin Platt, twenty-one, of Kensal, west London, who had been charged that day with the murder of Dorian Lupescu and with setting fire to a house in Blagrove Road, West Ten. Ella read it but, because the name of the man who had applied to Eugene for his cash find had never registered with her, immediately forgot about it. Perhaps because he had seen him the day before in the Golborne Road pharmacy, Eugene remembered him and his name very well. When telling Ella that he had only seen Lance Platt twice, Eugene recalled that there had been a third sighting. Looking out of his bedroom window in the small hours of a morning, he had seen the youth (as he had thought of him) with his characteristic backpack walking along the street in the direction of Denbigh Road. It was the night after he and Ella had been to the theatre to see *St. Joan*. He had gone round to Elizabeth Cherry's to check that the house was secure, come back, and got up later to eat a Chocorange—what else?

Now he had a vivid memory of thinking that Lance Platt must be up to no good, then, immediately afterwards, telling himself that it was bad to be suspicious of someone just because he was out in the street at the time when people he thought of as law-abiding were in bed asleep. It looked as if he had been right that first time. Still, whatever Platt had been doing walking along outside his house, it was obviously unconnected with murder and arson half a mile or more away on the Kensal borders.

Uncle Gib also read about it. His source was a giveaway newspaper called *Metro*, and the news item brought him considerable satisfaction. It wasn't that he thought the police must be right or even that Lance had indisputably done the deed, but rather that someone he had always disliked and disapproved of was getting his comeuppance at last. Gemma read it when she bought the *Sun*. She was out shopping in the Portobello Road Tesco with Abelard in the buggy, and in her own words to her mother, it gave her quite a shock. It was a crying shame, it must be a mistake. Lance hadn't been with her that night, but maybe she should go along to the police station and say he had been.

"Oh, no, you don't," said her mother. "You want to keep a low profile. Suppose they've got proof it was him and you've stuck your neck out. You could go inside, and then what about your boy? Come and give Nana a cuddle, my lambkin."

Fize was refitting a transformer at a house in East Acton. As he put it himself, he broke the rule of a lifetime and went down to the pub in his lunch break, to Ian Pollitt's local. Fize knew Ian, being without a job or having the prospect of getting one, would likely be passing his empty midday hours in the Duchess of Teck. Fize had a lager and lime, which Ian said was a woman's drink, as bad as "lady juice," which was what they called white wine.

"Maybe," said Fize, "and maybe I don't want

to do my head in when we're talking about a couple of thousand volts. What d'you reckon to Lance Platt?"

Ian tilted his head back and poured down getting on for half a pint of stout. "Best thing that's happened to me for years."

"Yeah, but you know what I mean."

"It's not like they're going to top him. Not like they used to. What with eighty thousand banged up, there's no space for him. He won't go down for no more than five or six years."

"He never done it." Now that Fize had bought it, he no longer felt like his lager and lime and pushed it away across the table. "You know he never done it."

"I don't know nothing. My mind's a blank. Don't even know when it was."

"August fourteen."

"Is that right? Now that's funny. I was away on my holidays in Tenerife August fourteen." Ian laughed uproariously at his joke and was still laughing when Fize left and went back to work.

There was no bail for Lance this time. He was remanded in custody for however long it took. In his cell at the police station, stranded there until they decided where they could possibly put him until his appearance in a higher court, he took a philosophical view. Things could be worse. He'd get free meals with no effort on his part, he would no longer have to sleep in company with

317

the bike and the car tyres. As for freedom, there wasn't much you could do with it if you'd no money.

THEY HAD ALTERED the design on the pack. Instead of the bold chocolate-brown-and-orange lettering and the (hideous, Eugene the connoisseur had to admit) drawing of a kind of beige-coloured lozenge with a stream of something pouring onto it, the new colours were muted, the illustration more abstract and the name changed. Chocorange was now called Oranchoco. Accumulating enough of them to keep him going on his honeymoon, Eugene thought at first, with a sinking heart, that Elixir had run out of his favourite sugar-free sweets. An assistant passing by while Eugene was scouring the shelf both embarrassed and gratified him by telling him this was simply a name change.

"A lot of our customers have remarked on it. But don't you worry, they're just the same. Same taste, different pack, that's all it is."

Eugene got out of there as fast as he could, having first bought four packs of Oranchoco and the last remaining Chocorange in the shop. Hoping, but not very confidently, that this innovation might be confined to Elixir, he visited two branches of Superdrug and the lady in the sari in Spring Street. She alone still had Chocorange. Superdrug had changed everything in the store around, putting shampoos where skin creams used to be and switching vitamins with baby-care products. Eventually he found a single packet of Oranchoco in the sweets-and-chocolate section, which was now where perfumes used to be. No more than six months ago he would have considered knowing the layout of a pharmacy so that he could find items in the dark beneath his dignity. How are the mighty fallen! Perhaps to be brought so low was good for his character.

On his way back to Eugene Wren, Fine Art, he split open one of the new packets, took a sweet, and tasted it. Whatever that shop assistant had said, it wasn't the same. A subtle difference was not for the better. The essence of Chocorange had been its smooth creaminess, but this new one had a rough edge to the flavour, an undertaste of slight—very slight—bitterness.

His disappointment was profound. He would get used to it, he told himself. The difference was too subtle to affect him that much. But the change made him angry for the rest of the afternoon and even angrier that something so stupid, so banal and petty, could disturb his equilibrium to this extent. A woman who had arrived in a chauffeur-driven Bentley would certainly have bought Priscilla Hart's *Study in Precious Metals* if his brusqueness hadn't driven her out of the gallery. Walking home, he tried to dismiss the whole thing from his mind, but as he struggled to do this, bitter resentment kept coming to the surface. How could they do this to him, causing him to endanger his business? How could they spoil a flavour and a texture that had been close to perfect?

What did I think about six months ago, he asked himself, before this thing took hold of me? When I look back, it seems to me that I was free, and that freedom I voluntarily gave up just for a taste, for something to put in my mouth. All the time he was thinking this way he was sucking an Oranchoco, unwilling to waste a precious Chocorange on something so mundane as a walk home.

He chewed up the last of it, no better pleased with its flavour than he had been four hours before when he tasted the first one.

Ella called out to him as he let himself into the house, "Is that you, darling? You're nice and early."

His pockets were stuffed full of sweet packets. He hung up his coat, leaving the sweets where they were. She poured him a dry sherry and one for herself, taking them into the study. The warmth he so often felt when they met again after a separation, even if that parting was no more than a matter of hours, filled him with the kind of pleasure that made him smile. She was so nice, so sweet, and she looked just the way he wanted a woman to look, pretty rather than beautiful, not thin but not plump either, a lovable woman and wonderfully intelligent.

"What are you thinking?"

"That I'm lucky to have you."

She smiled, took a sip of her sherry, passed him a dish of olives. "There's something I want to ask you, but it can wait till we've eaten."

"That's quite terrible," he said, laughing. "It makes me think you've postponed your question, whatever it is, because if you ask it, I shall be put off my dinner."

"Oh, no, it's nothing like that. It's quite trivial, really. Let's say it's a question of our—well, our medical care after we're married. I mean, I shall go on going to Malina in the practice, but you might think you could leave Dr. Irving and I could look after you. Only I don't really think that's a good idea. Of course I'll still be a doctor and I'll still tell you when I think you ought to go to Dr. Irving because you've got something that needs attention. Am I being too fussy, do you think?"

"Not at all, my darling, you're absolutely right as usual." He felt obscurely relieved, he didn't know why. "Was that the question you're no longer putting off till after dinner? What is for dinner, by the way?"

"Only a Thai takeaway, I'm afraid. He'll be here with it any minute."

He was. They ate, but when Ella passed

Eugene the fruit bowl for dessert, although he took a small bunch of grapes, he was aware that what he really wanted, and wanted now, was a Chocorange or even an Oranchoco. As he helped Ella clear the table—showing himself to be at least halfway to the househusband all women seemed to want these days—he began to think of reasons for escaping from the house for ten minutes or even getting himself alone upstairs for ten minutes. That is, he tried to think of reasons but failed. Once he could have gone out to post a letter, but no one sent letters anymore. Replies to their wedding invitations had been the first post and the last (apart from junk mail) he and Ella had had for months. It had begun to rain, a thin drizzle misting the windowpanes.

Dry-mouthed, a sour taste on his tongue, he went into the drawing room and put on a CD. It was a harpsichord suite by Scarlatti, and it began to lull his craving, even making him wonder if, were he to play this kind of sweet baroque music as a constant background, his addiction would gradually depart. He listened and relaxed, but when Ella came in, his whole body tautened and tensed. And he was back to thinking, I must give it up. Now is the time, when the taste has changed, when it's no longer exactly what I want and, when I'm getting married and if I give in to this craving, face a life of subterfuge and concealment and, yes, lying.

He looked up at her and saw what she was carrying. Through the glassy transparency of the plastic bag, one of those ziplock bags that could be resealed after opening, he could see the orange-and-brown lettering and the illustrations on half a dozen packs of Chocorange. The feeling he had was that which most people feel when threatened with violence. His heart began beating hard and rapidly, and his mouth dried.

"Darling," she said, smiling, "how many more of these things are there in the house? I've found twenty-nine but I'm sure I haven't looked everywhere."

He couldn't remember when he had last blushed. Perhaps not since he was a small child. He felt the hot blood rush into his face and he touched one burning cheek with the palm of his hand.

"You mustn't be embarrassed about it, and above all you mustn't think of it as an addiction. It isn't. Believe me, I do know. It's a habit and it can quite quickly be got over. I once had a patient who was the same, only with her it was mint imperials. She was eating twenty of the things every day, but she was over it practically as soon as she'd told me." Ella put the bag down on the table in front of him and went to sit beside him on the arm of the sofa. "I must say you've done a very good job of hiding it. I've thought for weeks it must have been Carli who was hooked on the things. I never dreamed it might be you."

Still he said nothing. She leant over him and laid her cheek against his hair. "I haven't upset you, have I? I'm not going to try and stop you eating them. I did taste one and I thought it was rather nice. I said a habit like this can be quite quickly got over, but it doesn't have to be. Of course I don't know how many you're eating, but if it's a lot, like ten a day or something like that, it might be sensible to cut down. After all they are 'sugar-free' and that means aspartame or one of those sweeteners, so it's not a good idea to overload your system with the stuff." She moved away from him, stood back. "Gene? Are you all right?"

"Yes, of course," he said, his voice thin and shocked. He tried to clear his throat. "I think I'll go out for a bit."

"Gene, look at me. What's wrong? Is it what I said?"

"I'm just going out for a walk."

"It's pouring with rain!"

She moved a little towards him again. Her face was contorted with concern and dismay. "You can't go out now. We have to talk. We can't just leave it. I'd no idea when I spoke to you that you were going to take it like this."

"I haven't taken it like anything. I'm tired and I need fresh air."

"Well, when you come back, we'll talk about how you got into this and how you're going to handle it, it'll be a lot easier for you now I know. Remember it's not crack cocaine, it's not even cigarettes. You'll be over it in a week."

A lot easier now she knows . . . This was in such conflict with what was actually the case that he could almost have laughed. Except that he felt he would never laugh again. Without saying any more to her, he went out into the hall and put on his coat. The pockets were weighed down with Chocorange and Oranchoco packs. For the first time in his life Eugene experienced the emotion that is a combination of desire and loathing and is usually called a love-hate relationship. He pulled all the packs but one out of his pockets and threw them onto the floor of the cupboard. It no longer mattered if she saw them. It was too late.

But he waited until he was outside the door before splitting open the pack. With a Chocorange in his mouth, its flavour not at all diminished by the scene just past in the drawing room, he put up his umbrella and began to walk along Chepstow Villas towards the Pembridge Villas turnoff. The sweet was soon finished and he immediately craved another.

What was he going to do? Not go home again. He turned round, walked back the way he had come and towards the Portobello Road, passing his own house but keeping his head turned away.

The rain had dwindled to a drizzle and stopped. He put down his umbrella. The Portobello was just the same, only rather more crowded, ablaze with lights, alive with music and laughter and shouting. He went into the Earl of Lonsdale and bought himself a glass of white wine. A Chocorange substitute. Pubs had never really been his thing, and since knowing Ella, he had only once been in one. The wine was sour and sharp but he drank it, unable to find a seat and standing up at the bar. This was how it felt when a carefully guarded secret was discovered. It had been the same with the drink when a friend caught him in the men's room, swigging covertly from a hip flask. The same? No, this was far, far worse.

Going home was impossible. He considered finding a hotel. But Londoners know nothing about hotels in their own city, and besides, he had no change of clothes with him. He put another Chocorange into his mouth and wandered across the street among the crowds to the Electric Cinema. There he went up to buy a ticket and astonished the woman who asked which number theatre he wanted by saying he didn't care, it didn't matter, and he would take whatever she chose to give him.

It really didn't matter; he fell asleep as soon as he was in one of the red leather armchairs that had replaced the old seating. Someone farther along the row woke him by pushing past his knees when the lights came up. It was close on midnight but the streets were still crowded. Not when he reached Denbigh Road, though. He thought, I am a homeless person now, obliged to be a street sleeper, and then he thought how Ella would have reproved him for his callous insensitivity when he was healthy and rich and successful with a home in one of the most sought-after districts of any city in the world. Fool, he told himself, and he went home at last to a dark and silent house.

25

TWICE IN THE past weeks she had tried to phone him but got no reply. Eventually, his mother had phoned her, speaking in a bright gushing voice, to tell her that her son was "enormously better," thanks to taking Miss Crane's pills "religiously," and really there was no reason for her to see him again. The implication was that the therapist had succeeded where Ella had failed. Ella wondered if she was being paranoid in thinking this way or if she was simply feeling rather low. No wonder if she was, after what had happened with Eugene.

She had lain awake for much of the night, waiting for him to come to bed, unsure whether he had come home. She had gone downstairs to look for him but, when she tried the study door, found it locked against her. It must have been against her—who else? That door was still locked in the morning, and calling to him to let her in had no effect. She went to work but phoned him before seeing her first patient. Her relief when he answered was enormous.

"I'm fine," he said. "Just off to the gallery."

"Gene, where were you? What happened last night?"

"I'll tell you later."

She had never before, not even when they first knew each other, heard that remote tone addressed to her. It was the way he spoke to someone delivering a package—no, cooler than that, less polite than he would be to the postman. Halfway through the morning she phoned the gallery, to be told by Dorinda that Eugene was with a client but would call her back. No call came. She had no appetite for lunch. It was her afternoon for calls, three of them to be made to elderly bedbound patients, the fourth to Joel. But this one she made for something to do, for a way of passing the time, such a new departure for her that she couldn't recall experiencing the feeling before. His mother had told her she wasn't needed. Wendy Stemmer wasn't his guardian. However strange he might be, however ill he had been, he was in charge of his own life.

It was a view she quickly had to modify. As soon as Rita let her into the flat, she could see radical changes. It was a sunny day and the place was flooded with light. Whoever had done this must have seen that taking down the blinds and replacing the heavy velvet drapes with thin curtains revealed the shabbiness of the furnishings, so much of these had been replaced with IKEA tables, while the sombre upholstery of the chairs was hidden under stretch covers. The Caesars were gone and the ornate mirrors that reflected them.

Rejuvenation had been done on the cheap. A lot of houseplants stood about, the kind that come from supermarkets rather than garden centres. Ella found Joel in a room she had never been in before, only seen dimly from its doorway. He sat at the old dining table on one of the old dining chairs, holding a ballpoint pen above a sheet of paper resting on a table mat.

"Hello," he said, looking up, and she could tell at once from the tone of his voice that the drug he was taking had deadened his personality.

"How are you, Joel?"

"I'm fine."

"Is Rita with you all the time now?"

"Only in the day," he said in the same monotonous voice. "Bridget comes at night. They don't leave me alone." That last phrase could be interpreted in two ways: they don't let me be isolated, or they never stop harassing me. "Ma comes. She doesn't like it but she comes."

"Did your mother get the new furniture?"

A profound boredom dulled his features. "I suppose. Someone did. They took away those men's faces, said they were bad for me, made me brood." He gave a little staccato laugh. "I'm not in the dark anymore." It was impossible to tell if he meant that literally or metaphorically. She expected him to mention Mithras but he didn't. "I'm writing my memoirs." The sheet of paper was blank. "It's hard to start. I get an idea for a way to start, but then I get tired and I have to sleep." An empty smile stretched his mouth. "It doesn't matter, does it?"

She thought she should do something, but what? He was well, he was calm, he seemed content. Wasn't this better than when he was haunted by an imaginary phantom, the voice of a god? She watched him lower his head, put the pen to the paper, but on the right-hand side of the sheet. With real horror she saw his hand move the pen in linked circles and loops towards the left, a pattern rather than writing, as his lips moved with a fishlike opening and closing.

"I'll see you soon, Joel."

She got up. The woman called Rita was hovering in the hall, waiting for her to leave. As Joel's doctor, she thought she could ask about his situation. Out of his earshot, she asked, low-low-voiced, if Mr. Stemmer came to see his son.

"Only her," Rita said. "Only his mum."

On her way home Ella tried to think of how she had first met Joel. It had been when he was in hospital having his heart surgery and she had brought him the money Eugene had found in the street. He was a sick man then, or at least a recovering man, but his ills seemed all physical. In those five months his mind had grown sick and strange, and now it was as if he had been hollowed out and only a shell of that man in the hospital remained. There was nothing she could do, there had never been much. Her attention now must be given to Eugene, whom she was due to marry in ten days.

She expected him to be at home by now. The house was empty. She realised she had eaten nothing since breakfast, and breakfast had been only a slice of toast. The fridge was full of food, the fruit bowl laden with oranges, bananas, and the ripe figs that were just appearing in the shops. Carli had left a new spelt loaf on the bread board and beside it, in the cheese dish, a slice of fresh cheddar. Ella turned away from it all, went into the drawing room, where she stood at the window, gazing down the street in the direction from which he would come. The phone rang and she ran to answer it, but the caller's was an ingratiating voice enquiring if she wanted a new kitchen fitted. As she put the receiver down, she heard Eugene's key in the lock, the door close, and his footsteps move along the hall in a slow, reluctant way quite unlike his usual brisk pace.

GEMMA WAS THE loveliest thing ever to have been seen in that grim room with its ranked tables, each with a chair on either side of it, each chair occupied by a woman Lance set down as deeply unattractive. A bunch of dogs, he described them to Gemma, who reproved him for his cruelty. She, he told her with unusual flights of imagination, looked like a flower on a landfill site. Had they dared, the other men would have whistled at her as she came to take her seat opposite him in her pale pink miniskirt, high black boots, and white fur jacket.

"It's not real," she confided in him. "I wouldn't wear real fur, not when you know what they do to them poor little animals. How've you been, lover?"

"I'm good," said Lance, not because he felt well or happy but because this was what he always said when asked this question. "That Fize know you're here?"

"You must be joking. He'd kill me or get that Ian to do it."

"Like that, is it? Now, listen, Gemma. I never done that fire."

"I know that, sweetheart."

Lance lowered his voice to a whisper. "I was over in Pembridge Villas in a house." Now it

332

came to confessing it, he found himself increasingly reluctant to state baldly what he had been doing. "I was—well, I mean, you know, I broke a window and I, you know, got in. I'd been in before, had a look around and ate a chocolate cake."

Gemma started laughing. "You what?"

"I ate a chocolate cake and some soup. The old woman what lives there was away on her holidays, I mean the second time. I took some stuff, jewels and stuff, you know, whatever. I come back with the stuff in my backpack, and there'd been that fire, only it was all over and her next door and him too was outside, and they said about Uncle Gib was OK and Dorian being dead and they thought it was me—"

"Wait a minute, Lance. You've lost me. You mean, you was breaking into this old lady's place on Pembridge, so you wasn't burning Uncle Gib's house down? Is that what you're saying?"

"Yes," said Lance simply.

"You'd better tell the fuzz, then."

"They won't believe me."

"They will. The lady'll have told them there'd been someone in there and said what was missing and all. Look, lover, you have to tell them. You want to get sent down for murder?"

"I don't know."

"I do. You could go inside for life and that's fifteen years. Maybe the judge'd say"—Gemma put

333

on an accent she would have defined as "posh"—
"I recommend this evil person serve at least
twenty-five years on account of he burnt a house
down as well as murdered a poor harmless visitor
to our shores. He could, Lance, I'm not kidding."

"You reckon?"

"Look, if you won't tell them, I will. OK? I'll
write them a letter. Now you tell me the number
of this house you broke into and the lady's name
and the time, right? Maybe I'll tell them about
the chocolate cake too. It'll sort of prove it was
you."

SHE WENT UP to him, holding out her hands. He
took a step backwards, shaking his head. His face
seemed to have accumulated enough lines to age
him ten years.

"What is it, Gene? What's the matter? Are you
ill?"

Again he shook his head. He made a movement
with his hand, indicating that she should sit
down, the kind of gesture a man might make to a
female stranger, courteous, remote. She hesitated, then sat down rather heavily. They faced
each other but his gaze faltered and he lowered
his head.

"Please say something, Gene."

"There's only one thing I can say." An under-
current of despair was in his voice. "I wish things
were different, but they're not." He seemed to be

334

searching for words. "We can't be married," he said at last. "I can't marry you, Ella."

She stared at him, slowly clenching her hands. Her voice came at last, as hoarse as his had been. "I'm not hearing this."

He shrugged, his expression hopeless. "I can't marry you."

"I said, I can't believe I'm hearing this."

"I mean it. I can't marry you."

"But why?" The two words came out like a cry from the heart.

He avoided answering. "You can stay here. I mean, you can stay indefinitely, forever if you like. I'll go to a hotel. I'll do the cancelling of all the—the arrangements. I'll tell everyone what's happened. I'll try to make it as easy for you as I can."

"You'll try to make the breaking of our engagement easy for me?"

"What else can I say, Ella? I can't marry you, that's all."

"Don't you love me? You loved me yesterday, you loved me last week." She put her head in her hands but almost immediately looked up, staring at him. "Why? Why?" Events of the evening before came back to her. "It isn't—it can't be— it's not because of those—those things I found?"

The deep flush had returned to his face. He lowered his eyes. She saw a tremor start in his hands.

"It is. It's because I found those sweets. No, this is mad. It's not possible. Is it possible?" His attitude of humility, of a meek yielding to the inevitable, told her that it was. She jumped up, cried out, "But it doesn't matter, darling. It doesn't matter. I can forget all about it. I'll never mention them again. You can eat the wretched things to your heart's content. I don't care."

"But I do." He spoke with quiet finality.

"You can't destroy both our lives because I found out you'd got a harmless habit. For God's sake, it's not as if it was looking at pornography online or stalking women or—oh, I don't know. You can't split us up for that. We love each other."

"I'm leaving now, Ella. As I said, I'll see to everything."

He was shaking so much she thought he would fall. She went up to him, trying to touch him.

"Ella, please don't. I have to go."

She followed him out into the hall. It was as if she felt that so long as she stayed with him, shadowed him, kept close, he would be unable to carry out his threat. Yet she was afraid to touch him. He kept his back turned to her. She walked round to face him again, but he turned away once more, took his overcoat out of the cupboard, felt in the pockets, put the coat on.

He picked up his briefcase. She put out both hands and clung to his arm, but he loosened her grip with his free hand, finger by finger.

"You are making things worse for yourself and for me," he said in a remote voice.

Opening the front door, he stepped outside without looking back. She followed him down the path but, when he let himself out the gate, stopped and turned away. The front door was swinging in the wind and she had no key with her. She ran back, grabbed her bag with her key in it, and without attempting to find a coat ran down once more to the gate and the pavement outside. Eugene had disappeared from view.

26

UNTIL NOW, HIS journalistic experience had been confined to answering readers' letters; and when no letters from people with emotional and sexual problems came, to inventing suitably lurid substitutes. But now Uncle Gib was confronting a new challenge, the composition of Reuben Perkins's obituary. He sat in Maybelle's former dining room, now allotted him as a study, at work on the computer the Children of Zebulun had bought him. Its ivory-white keys were already dyed pale yellow from his cigarette smoke, and stubs mounted in the pottery fruit dish Maybelle had provided as an ashtray. *A life of selfless service and generosity to the community,* he had typed, *unparalelled single-minded devotion to one and all, regardless of age, sex, or creed,* when Maybelle came into the room with a cup of tea for him and a black-pudding-and-cheese sandwich.

"How d'you spell *unparalleled?*" he asked her.

"I don't know, Gilbert. I'm not intellectual like you." She scrutinised the screen. "Like you've done it. That looks right."

Uncle Gib thought it looked wrong. The trouble was he didn't know how. Maybe he'd put *unrivalled* instead. "You going out?"

"I can do," said Maybelle eagerly.

"Get me forty fags, then, will you?"

Maybelle said she would, smiling at him fondly. Uncle Gib lit a cigarette and set down a few episodes in Reuben Perkins's life that bore no likeness to reality. He ended with words he calculated would get him into even greater favour with Reuben's wife: *Cut off in his prime, he leaves a widow, the lovely Maybelle, some twenty years younger than himself.*

Now to attend to the final arrangements for the funeral.

THE FIRST THING Ella had done after he went was take off his ring. She took it off and immediately put it on again. This was ridiculous. He would come back, if not that night, next day; he would come back and say what a fool he had been and could she forgive him? Perhaps she believed this and perhaps not, for she couldn't

338

sleep. In the sad, mad hours between two and four, panic struck her and she sat up in bed sobbing, with tears running down her face. The ring had come off again in the morning and she had gone to work bare-fingered, weak with crying and lack of sleep. If any of the others in the practice noticed, they said nothing.

In between patients she asked herself what she should do. Get in touch with him? Go to the gallery? Leave him to come to his senses?

Mrs. Khan arrived with a different child to interpret for her. This time it was a girl wearing a hijab, though she was no more than nine, her small, pale face looking as if the black veil pinched it. Ella thought it unsuitable that this little child should have to talk about her mother's heavy periods and agonising cramps, but she said nothing. In normal circumstances she might have commented, but these circumstances weren't normal. But, no, she wouldn't run after Eugene. It would be useless. He would come back, she was sure of it, or told herself robustly that she was sure of it. Mrs. Perkins was next, inviting her to come along and view her late husband's body and please not to fail to attend his funeral.

There were no calls to make in the afternoon. She went home, that is, to Eugene's house. She hardly felt she could continue to call it home. This reminded her that on the following day she was due at her solicitor's to sign the contract for the sale of her flat. But was this the time to sell? Suppose Eugene had meant it and wouldn't change his mind? Whatever he may have said, she couldn't live in his house, occupy his home, if they were not to be together, not to be married. For the first time she put it plainly into words: we are not to be married. It seemed utterly unreal, yet the only real thing in her world at the moment. She went upstairs, and in their bedroom—she still thought of it as their bedroom—she saw that he had been back in her absence. He had taken some of his clothes. He had also, apparently, taken a good many packets of those ridiculous things, that sugar-free rubbish. With a spurt of energy she went round the house, hunting for them. Some remained in drawers and on shelves and in pockets. Breathing as if she had just run a race, she gathered them all into a plastic carrier bag, twenty, thirty, forty of them, took them outside into the garden and, almost ritualistically, set fire to them.

Searching for means of doing this, she remembered her sister's story about being asked for matches by the girl with the cigarette in the hotel foyer. She and Eugene had been so happy then. A sob caught at her throat, but anger came back. A book of matches was in that secret drawer in the kitchen, and alongside it another packet of those things, those bloody things. She found some paraffin too, an ancient bottle of the stuff, untouched for years. It worked, though, and the matches worked. Regardless of the ban on bonfires, in place for decades, she started the fire and it blazed up, consuming his stupid sweets, the garden stinking of—well, it couldn't be burnt sugar. Burnt chemicals, saccharin, aspartame. She stood, looking at the little blackened patch left behind on the grass until the phone's ringing fetched her indoors.

It must be him, it must be. To say he was sorry, he had lost his mind, he didn't know what had come over him. She stumbled and almost fell in her haste to get to the phone.

It was her sister.

"Oh, Hilary," she cried, "I don't know what to do. I think Eugene's gone mad. Would you come or can I come to you? I'm going mad too."

FIZE DIDN'T BELIEVE in letting women in on men's business. Besides, confiding in Gemma would mean confessing that he and Ian had set fire to that house. Or Ian had. But he had been there, he had helped, and Fize knew enough about the law to be pretty sure that in a case of murder and arson, when two people were there, even if only one of them struck the match, both were considered to blame. He wouldn't have cared about any of this if they hadn't arrested Lance, if they hadn't charged him and banged him up. He might not have cared too much if the man on remand had been someone he didn't know. At the time, or just before the time, when he and Ian had been on their way to Blagrove Road, armed with a bottle of petrol and a bag of fireworks, burning up Lance in his bed had seemed an entirely just and reasonable thing to do. Any man would feel the same towards the bloke who's been messing about with his girlfriend.

But there were objections to that. For one thing, he didn't really know that Lance and Gemma had been doing any more than she said they had when he asked her, that is, having a cup of tea with Uncle Gib and talking about old times. Backing up her story was that he had seen the old man go into the house while they were in there. Surely that meant they couldn't have been doing anything they shouldn't. Of course he hadn't felt like that when Ian was shoving the bottle of petrol through the letter box. As for Ian Pollitt, he didn't feel anything at all about Lance or Gemma, or Fize, for that matter, Fize was sure of that. Ian just enjoyed a bit of trouble and was always on the lookout for it.

But Fize had started to feel bad about things when first he heard that they'd killed a man who was living in the house that he'd never even heard of. Killing someone you didn't hate or want revenge on, someone you didn't know existed, seemed worse than anything. Fize didn't want to lose his job and Gemma or upset his mother, he didn't want to go to prison, but he had a vague idea, picked up from Hollywood films, that you could make something with the police called a plea bargain. You could in America, so presumably you could here too. If you confessed and told them the name of the bloke who had done it with you, he might go down, but you'd get off—or get a suspended sentence or something. Fize thought it was worth trying.

He tried it on Ian.

They were in the amusement arcade in the Portobello Road at the time, playing the fruit machines. Ian had just had a big win, but whereas anyone else would have ploughed the lot back, he pocketed his winnings. He always did. He didn't seem to hear what Fize was trying to tell him about Lance—not surprising considering the racket in there—but said he needed a drink. They went into the Portobello Arms.

Fize could never express himself well. Gemma could. She was what they called articulate. He tried to explain to Ian what he meant, but the way it came out, Fize stumbling over words and saying "you know" every five seconds, it sounded as if all he was doing was trying to drop Ian in the shit. And perhaps he was.

"Can you tell me why it is," said Ian in an aggressive way, "every time we go into a fucking pub you go ballsing on about bleeding Lance Platt. Can you tell me that?"

"It's on account of I don't reckon it's right him being banged up when he didn't do nothing."

"Oh, no," said Ian with heavy sarcasm, "he didn't do nothing. He's not a thief, he don't break into places and nick old ladies' jewellery. He never smacked your girlfriend so her tooth come out. He don't mug folks for their mobiles."

"Yeah, maybe, but he's not going down for that, is he? He's going down for something he never done."

"Oh, give me a break." Ian finished his drink and asked for another—for himself. No second one for Fize. "I'm going to say just two words to you"—Ian laughed at his own wit—"and the second one is *off*."

Fize saw Ian's big, calloused hand go to his jeans pocket, go into it and close over something. He said no more.

At home Fize and Gemma never said much to each other. His parents had never said much to each other. This was partly due to his mother speaking only a few words of English and his father no Hindi at all. Gemma liked talking, she was hours on the phone to girlfriends, and round at her mother's the two of them chattered away nonstop, but the things they talked about, kids and clothes and makeup and celebrities and music, interested Fize not at all, and he knew nothing about them. He liked Abelard but he had nothing to say to him. They watched telly together, and Fize and Gemma watched telly. Gemma talked about the actors in soaps and the things they did and said, but all he said was "Yes" and "Right" and "Don't know." He didn't know what to say, so he left all the talking to her.

She talked to everyone about everyone they knew, the people in the other flats, the other mums with little kids, his mum even though she could hardly understand a word, and, if he was there, he listened without saying anything much. But she didn't expect replies from him. And the one subject she never talked about was Lance Platt. It seemed as if she'd forgotten him. Fize would have liked more than anything to find out what she thought about his dilemma, but he was scared to mention it, even to touch on it. She might get up out of her chair, grab Abelard, and go straight down the cop shop. She was capable of that.

It was getting so that he lay awake in the night, thinking about what he and Ian had done, lay awake beside the soundly sleeping Gemma, often with Abelard snuggled up between them because the little boy had got into bad habits Fize's own mother would never have allowed. Gemma wouldn't leave any windows open in case Abelard fell out of them. It was stuffy and hot in that bedroom, and Fize sweated as he thought about Lance Platt in a much smaller room some-where, a cell with bunks in it and another bloke maybe. Not a lovely girl like Gemma. And the chances were Lance would stay in that room or somewhere like it for years. Fize knew he had to have another go at Ian, but not in a pub this time.

Here, maybe. Ask him round when Gemma was out of the way. Perhaps when he was babysitting Abelard, and she'd gone over to Michelle's or her mum's. If this fine weather went on, he could leave the door to the balcony open and there'd be people on all the other balconies. And Abelard would be around, running in and out. He'd have to persuade Ian to see things his way. If he couldn't, if there was no moving him—and Fize was afraid there wouldn't be— would he have the bottle to go to the police on his own?

27

ON HIS INSTRUCTIONS, Jackie printed off a hundred slips of headed paper inscribed *The marriage arranged between Dr. Ella Cotswold and Eugene Wren for 20 October 2007 will not now take place.* Eugene thought of adding a few words of apology to all those guests who wouldn't now have the pleasure of seeing him and Ella joined in matrimony, eating a splendid lunch, and drinking his Dom Pérignon, but somehow he hadn't the heart. He hadn't the heart for much anymore.

He had taken a room in a hotel in George Street, comfortable, expensive, but he doubted if, since he had arrived there several days before, he had slept for more than two or three hours a night. If he went to sleep at midnight, he was awake again at two, sitting up in bed eating an Oranchoco for comfort. Then another and another. They were just as nice as Chocorange. He wondered now why he had found their taste bitter at first.

Falling into a doze at the gallery wasn't unusual. Dorinda had sometimes found him at his desk, his arms spread out and his head resting on them. "Dead to the world," as she put it. She told him he should go home, he couldn't go on like this.

"I have no home," Eugene said.

There was no answer to this. She and Jackie exchanged glances. Neither of them knew the reason for the engagement's being broken, only that it was broken. No one knew. It would have been easier to tell people of the infidelity of either party or some recently discovered incompatibility than of his addiction to something so absurd and degrading. He was consuming more of the things now than ever, at least two packets a day. Because those two women were there, he was afraid to put one of them in his mouth while in the gallery, so he dragged himself outside to walk the pretty streets of Kensington, sucking as many as five in the half hour outside he allowed himself. Sometimes he simply stood in a doorway or under a tree like a smoker excluded from the workplace.

The original reason to buy Chocorange, as it was then called, that of keeping him from snacking between meals or eating too much at meals, at last seemed to fulfil its purpose. He had lost interest in real food. Without the heart to weigh himself—his bathroom at the hotel had no scale—he could see and feel he was losing weight. His clothes started to hang on him and his waistband was loose. The thought had begun to come to him that if he went on like this, he could die. He could kill himself. People did. He remembered reading somewhere of a man who had put an end to his life by eating nothing but carrots until he died of an overdose of vitamin A. Probably Oranchoco had no vitamins at all, but plenty of chemicals and no fat or protein and precious little carbohydrate. Thinking of that, he ate another and another and skipped going out to the restaurant in Crawford Place for his dinner.

A letter came for him at the gallery from Ella. Not an e-mail or a text message but a proper letter, which seemed to have been delayed for several days by the postal strike. *Eugene,* it said, *I have moved out of your house and back to my flat. Obviously, I couldn't stay there. You can go back now. I have taken all my things with me and left the key on the hall table. Ella.*

It upset him terribly. He was nearer to tears than he had been when he was eight and old Albert Gibson had shouted at him for knocking a lemon off his stall. But he checked out of the hotel and went home in the vain hope that he would feel better. He had believed that by being surrounded by his treasured things he would be comforted. He wasn't. The one single thing that would have comforted him wasn't a thing at all. Bitterly, he thought that he loved and needed Ella more than ever now she was gone. He opened his suitcase in the bedroom he had shared with her and tipped its contents onto the floor, clothes, shoes, and twenty or more packets of Oranchoco. One of these he ripped open, though he had two already open in the pockets of his jacket, and put two pieces into his mouth at once.

Lying on the bed, he thought that the best thing that could happen to him would be for Oranchoco to be withdrawn from sale. He remembered reading of certain foodstuffs that contained too much of a substance found to be carcinogenic when eaten by mice at the rate of a kilo a day for fifty years. Immediately they vanished from the shops. It was the result of the current mania for health and safety. If only it would happen to Oranchoco! If only he could walk into the sari lady's shop and when he asked her where the things had gone (only he never would) be told they had been taken off the shelves owing to their newfound toxicity. Come to that, if only the new taste of Oranchoco had put him off the things, as he had hoped it might.

When he had put all this stuff away, should he go out for dinner? Cook himself something at home? He was aware that he had begun to feel sick. Better not eat, then. He had his consolation here in his bedroom, twenty packets of it.

ON HER WAY back from seeing another patient, Ella found herself driving past the block where Joel Roseman lived. It was weeks since she had heard from him, even longer since she had seen him. Her life had become a mechanical routine: get up, go to work, resist with a forced smile the sympathetic glances of colleagues, see patients, visit patients, go home to the flat, eat something she need not bother to cook, have a whiskey, and go to bed. Joel had not been one of those patients she visited. She had come near to forgetting him. Now, as she parked the car, she glanced up to the windows of his flat.

The blinds were gone, the curtains too, as far as she could see. Had he gone as well? Not much could distract her from her own troubles, but this could. She was remembering how Joel had tried to take Mithras back to the river and the meadows and the city with the white towers but had only partially succeeded. Could he have tried again and this time it had worked? It had worked because it killed him?

Ella went up the steps and into the hallway. A porter sitting behind his desk asked if he could help her. Mr. Roseman?

"Gone, madam. He moved out a week ago."

It was a forlorn hope that they might have a forwarding address for him, but, remarkably, they did. The porter wrote it down. Ella recognised the street in Hampstead Garden Suburb. This was his parents' house, his father's, of course, as well as his mother's.

IF LIFE HAD been good to her, Ella would never have gone up there. Life was bad to her, so she went to take her mind off things, off Eugene and the madness of it all, and off her humiliation.

The Stemmers' house was a palace, a single-storey bungalow covering about an acre (Ella thought exaggeratedly) and surrounded by several more acres with palm trees and monkey puzzles and laid out geometrically as a tennis court, a bowling green, and a mini-golf-course with artificial hills and ponds. Eugene would have called it vulgar, a word few people still used. She could see all this from behind closed wrought-iron gates, which apparently only opened electronically. She pressed the bell and a voice asked her who she was.

"Dr. Cotswold. To see Mr. Roseman."

"One moment."

A growling sound was followed by the gates slowly parting. She drove in across a huge bare expanse of paving. Parked on that stony plateau, her car looked small. It slightly alarmed her that the right-hand half of the double front doors was opened before she had set her foot on the first of four steps. Standing inside was a woman in a dark blue dress, which would have been a uniform if there had been an apron over it or a label on the breast pocket. She might have been a mute for all she spoke to Ella, leading her across marble and polished wood and perilous scattered rugs.

This house appeared to have no doors and no means of excluding daylight. It was one of those brilliant October days, which would be all over by five in the afternoon, but now sunlight streamed in through walls of glass and a domed skylight. Rooms were separated from other rooms only by a cunning arrangement of walls and half walls serving as screens. On one of these hung a painting, a large oil of a mermaid inside a goldfish bowl but apparently struggling to get out through its narrow neck. The woman led Ella behind the wall with the painting on it, and there, in a silver leather chair behind a desk, sat a fat, white-haired man holding a silver phone receiver in his right hand.

He acknowledged Ella with a small dip of his head. The woman waved one hand at a chair and she sat down. For about a minute Joel's father, for this was surely who it was, continued to talk on the phone. Then he said a rapid "All right, that's enough. I get the picture" and put the receiver into a rest. He came over to Ella with hand outstretched, said, "Morris Stemmer. I believe you were my son's medical attendant?"

Ella had never before been called a medical attendant, and she wondered why he had used the past tense, but she shook the hand that was offered and asked if she could see Joel.

He smiled slightly, a smile that turned his fat cheeks into bulging cushions. "You may see Mithras if you like."

"I don't understand."

"This whole business is hard to understand, Dr. Cotswold. Perhaps it is best to accept that Joel has become a different person and one who may be easier for the rest of us to live with."

She could think of nothing to say.

"If there are any fees owing to you, perhaps you will send me an invoice and I will, of course, gladly reimburse you."

"You owe me nothing, but I would very much like to see Joel. Even if he is ill. Especially if he is ill."

"Mithras. He only answers to that name. It's best to remember that."

Now he was on his feet, she could see how extremely fat Morris Stemmer was. That overused word *obese* might have been coined for him. His girth had reached the stage where an apron of fat hung down against the taut cloth covering his swollen thighs. His breathing was laboured and he sighed when he sat down. Ella wondered how a man whose much loved little daughter had drowned could bear to have that picture of the desperate mermaid in his house.

A bell was pressed and the woman reappeared. She stood in front of Ella, waiting for her to rise to her feet. Ella followed her. The woman opened the only interior door in this central hall of the house. This room was the antithesis of the flat in Ludlow Mansions, with its velvet curtains and drawn blinds, and if not as light as the rest of the house, more than dimly lit. It was furnished pleasantly in soft colours, a deep pile carpet covering the floor, a trough of houseplants under the thinly curtained window.

The man who sat on a green velvet chair against leafy wallpaper was Joel, yet was not. His dark hair was a bright blond and wavy, his normally doleful face wearing a slight smile. For surely the first time since she had met him, he was without sunglasses. The smile widened when he saw who had come in, yet she had the impression he didn't recognise her. He would have smiled like that at any newcomer.

"Hello," he said in a tone unlike his usual Joel voice. "I'm Mithras."

"Ella," she said, her voice shaking. "I'm Ella."

The voice was higher-pitched, the vowels flatter, and he had a slight lisp. "I think we've met before. In another life maybe. When I had a heart. Before they took it out. You can't be a human being without a heart, you see. You're a spirit or a god."

A movement behind her made Ella turn round. Wendy Stemmer had come into the room. She made a little low sound, a soft whimper, and, walking over to stand beside her son, began stroking his newly blond head as one might stroke that of a cat or dog. But she looked sad, more real than Ella had ever seen her, all the meretriciousness, the desperate girlishness, gone.

Joel suffered the stroking, yet he managed to behave as if no one were there. He picked up a book and began to read it.

His mother withdrew her hand. "There is no point in staying here. He'll read that book for hours. It's always the same book, he reads it over and over."

Ella saw that the title was that of a currently popular work on schizophrenia, the picture on its cover a brain pierced by a lightning flash. This was the book that had been beside him along with the vodka and the pills when he tried to revisit "death's door." She turned, gave him a last look. They left the room and Ella found herself once more facing, across gleaming emptiness, the struggling mermaid in the bowl of water.

Wendy Stemmer closed the door behind her. "I'll come out to your car with you."

For the first time since Ella had met her she was wearing a skirt that covered her knees. She pulled it down when she was in the passenger seat.

"He bleached his hair himself. He must have used kitchen bleach because he never went to the shops. The carer said he didn't go out at all. I don't know why he did it."

I do, Ella thought. Mithras had fair hair and he wanted to become like Mithras, to become Mithras.

"I found him like that, the way he is now, talking nonsense, saying he had come back with Joel—he talked about Joel as if he were someone else. He said Joel had fetched him from a city made of cloud, but when he tried to take him back again, he couldn't. Joel stayed there, and he—this Mithras—had to stay here."

"But your husband," Ella said, "what happened to change his attitude to Joel?"

"I don't really understand." To Ella's surprise, Wendy Stemmer clutched at Ella's hand and held it. "It frightens me. It makes me feel I've two mad people to deal with, not one."

"But what happened?"

"I'd tried to tell him Joel was having this—this delusion. That he was someone else, I mean. That he was this Mithras and that he'd dyed his hair and talked in a different voice and all of it. Morris listened—he doesn't usually listen to me—and he said quite suddenly, "I'll come with you." I could hardly believe what I was hearing.

"I thought nothing would change my husband's mind, but hearing the state Joel was in did change him. He came with me to Joel's flat and—well, I don't know." Wendy Stemmer looked at Ella and looked away. Her voice was so low Ella could hardly hear her. "He said—my husband, I mean—he said, 'This isn't my son, this is someone else. We'll take him home with us.' It was as if he could never have forgiven Joel, but this man, this Mithras, he could accept him. He has accepted him. He came here with us quite willingly."

Ella said stiffly, "Has Joel"—she couldn't call him Mithras—"has he seen anyone? A doctor, I mean?"

"The psychiatrist, Miss Crane. She came here."

"So someone's looking after him?"

"Oh, yes. He's in her care. She's prescribing his drugs and she says he can stay here. There's no need for him to—well, go away, if you see what I mean. He has two psychiatric nurses, one for day and one for night. My husband says to spare no expense. Money is no object. You know how Joel wanted to be in the dark all the time? Well, this Mithras—I call him what he calls himself—he prefers twilight. Dusk, he calls it. He says it's always light, day and night, where he comes from, but he doesn't want that yet. He's not my son anymore, Doctor." Tears came into Wendy Stemmer's eyes and she caught her breath in a sob. "It's like we've got a spirit or an angel living with us. I must go in now. But that's what my husband wants, not Joel, but a different person."

She got out of the car and Ella watched her go. Ella was sure, without knowing how she knew, that she would never see any of them again.

28

THE DOOR TO the balcony was open and two chairs set out to catch what remained of the evening sun. Gemma's washing was dry. She had long ago taken it in, and by now it had all been ironed and put away. Though it wasn't yet seven, Abelard was bathed and ready for bed, sitting on Fize's lap being read to. Any observer would have called it a cosy domestic scene.

"You got anyone coming round while I'm out?" Gemma asked. She was going to her mum's for a meal, and her dad had also been invited, a rare event but one she looked forward to. He was a jovial guy, her dad, and when she saw him, he usually gave her a handsome money present for Abelard. "Who's that, then?"

"A friend," said Fize.

"Oh, really? It wouldn't be an enemy now, would it?"

"It's Ian."

Gemma always looked particularly beautiful when she was angry, her pretty face flushed and her large blue eyes sparkling. She flicked back her hair. "I thought I'd said I don't want that shit in my flat."

"Don't be like that, Gemma. He's OK. He'll only be here an hour. We can have a drink, that's all."

"If he's coming here, Feisal Smith, I'm taking Abelard to my mum's with me. I don't want him round my son."

Fize objected but it was really argument for argument's sake. Left with him, Abelard would expect the TV to be on, another story to be read, chocolate milk and a banana. He would demand to stay up till his mum came back. Fize wanted to be alone with Ian, so he gave in as ungraciously as he could manage while quite happy with the new arrangement. For most of the day he had been rehearsing in his mind what he would say to his friend, and for most of the day it had seemed quite easy as well as right. Now things looked different. Ian would undoubtedly refuse, and then what was Fize to do? Was there perhaps some other way of getting over this difficulty? Go it alone? He grew cold all over at the thought. Fize needed a drink. He hated feeling this way because it wasn't many years since he had given up the abstemiousness he was brought up to and taken to alcohol. Drinking still made him feel guilty. Favourite expressions on the lips of his mother and his maternal grand-father were "morally wrong" and "against Islam." Sometimes it seemed to him that these days these words applied to him most of the time. He broke one of their favourite commandments and, going out to the kitchen to fetch himself a beer, sat down with it to wait for Ian.

FOR MOST OF Eugene's day he had been feeling what Dorinda called "under the weather," a foolish expression, he thought, because the day had been what it often was in the middle of October, brilliantly sunny and clear-skied. Eugene knew that the only connection his malaise had with any sort of weather was that he was in a deep depression. He was enslaved to a stupid habit and he had lost the woman he loved. No wonder he felt weak and shivery. Probably he had a raised temperature, only he was too despondent to take it.

But by the evening, his appetite gone, disin-clined even to pour himself a glass of wine, he knew this was more than being depressed. He must be physically ill. If Ella were with him, she would know what was wrong. He searched the house in vain for a thermometer. If there had ever been such a thing in one of the bathrooms, Ella had no doubt taken it with her. Walking, even just standing up, he found himself swaying and dizzy. The only way to go upstairs was on his hands and knees, and they ached, as did most of the bones in his body.

He couldn't even find any Chocorange or Oranchoco, although he was sure he had left behind at least twenty packets when he moved out. Perhaps they were there and visible, though invisible to him because he was delirious. Sweat had begun to pour off him, he could feel it breaking through the pores of his skin. It trickled coldly down his spine. No longer hot, he wrapped himself in a blanket, then a duvet, and phoned Dr. Irving. As a private patient, he had the doctor's mobile number and he caught him at a dinner party.

"Sounds like a virus." They never said *flu* anymore unless it was preceded by *avian*. "There's a lot of it about." They always said that. "Go to bed, keep warm, and drink plenty." Dr. Irving added as an afterthought, "I mean dihydrogen monoxide. Water to you, ha-ha." It was a favourite joke, often repeated.

ELLA HAD BELIEVED it was impossible for anything to shock her. She had seen too much, witnessed too many sad or wretched situations, heard too many tales of pain and suffering and cruelty. But Joel Roseman's condition had shocked her. She had gone to that bungaloid mansion in Hampstead Garden Suburb certain she would find her patient kept under duress, perhaps even physically a prisoner, possibly maltreated, and she had been prepared to call the police and tell them here was someone detained against his will. But she had seen nothing of that, only a man who in any other period of history would have been described as mad, as stark raving mad, tended by his mother, the father with whom he was reconciled, and in the care of one of the most reputable psychiatrists in the country. She was shocked because she had been so wrong and because of Joel's pitiable state.

Their encounter had left her feeling nervous and vulnerable. Alone in the half-furnished flat from which all the books were gone and most of the ornaments, she longed for Eugene. Now that Joel was no longer her patient she could have talked to Eugene about him, described the horror she had felt when this poor man with his dyed yellow hair talked of himself as an angel or a god, and described too the pathetic mother, pared down now to a raw, skinless creature who had grown, in so short a time, from absurd girlishness into her true age. And the grotesque father whose own daughter had drowned yet who kept a picture of a drowning woman in his home. Eugene would have listened and comforted and suggested kind remedies, brought her drinks and kissed her and taken her out to somewhere lovely. None of which would have helped Joel but would have helped her.

She thought of those early evenings in his study when, over a glass of wine, they had talked about the day that had just passed. She thought of his cooking for her with greater skill than she possessed, of their quiet sitting side by side, each reading in companionable, tranquil silence, of their nights and his ardent lovemaking. It was gone and there was no one. Joel might be mad in the recognised sense of that term, but Eugene's was also a kind of madness, inexplicable, absurd, utterly destructive.

Ella buried her face in the only two cushions remaining in her living room and began to cry.

THEY HADN'T NAMED any specific time for Ian to come. They never made arrangements of that sort. But when it got to nine and he still hadn't arrived, Fize began to get worried that he wouldn't come at all, and at the same time he was relieved. He wanted to put off what he had to say, yet he knew he would have no peace of mind until he had said it. But most people are like that. They prefer the doubt to the fact. Fize knew he was weak while wishing he were brave and strong, he knew that women liked him because he was good-looking and nice and perhaps because they could kick him around. Sometimes he thought that the only bold and daring thing he had ever done in all his life was set fire to Gilbert Gibson's house, and while he was pondering along these lines, the doorbell rang.

Ian hadn't brought anything to drink. This was no surprise to Fize, who would have been amazed if he had. Because Ian was unemployed and living on the benefit, he thought people in work ought to pay for everything he consumed, drink, curry, fish and chips. The first thing he said was "You got anything to eat in this place?"

Gemma subsisted on a healthy diet. "There's bread. There's cheese and sardines and apples and stuff." Fize remembered another foodstuff. "Oh, and there's muesli."

"Christ."

"You can have a beer."

When Fize came back, Ian was sitting on the edge of Gemma's cream-coloured sofa as if it were made of thin ice. He had never before been there and was no doubt feeling the way Fize had when he first met Gemma and was invited back, that he had come into the showroom of a furniture shop. Everything was clean and brushed or polished, with flowers in a vase and magazines placed in a perfect stack on the coffee table. He had got used to it, but it was going to take Ian a while.

Ian took the can from him reluctantly. "Haven't you got nothing stronger?"

"No." Fize was beginning to feel so tense he could hardly breathe. Every muscle in his body was taut. "Listen to me, mate." He took a deep breath. "Listen to me. It's about Lance."

Ian took a bigger swig of lager than Fize would have thought possible. "What about him?"

"He's in jail." Fize hesitated.

"Surprise, surprise. I know that. So what's new?"

"Look, mate, will you just listen to me? He never done that. I mean burning down old Gibson's house. Burning that Romanian guy. He never done it. He wasn't there. You know that and I know it. They could put him inside—I mean, keep him inside—for like fifteen years, maybe more if he don't admit to doing it. And he can't admit it on account of he never done it." Unaccustomed articulate speech was taking its toll on Fize, exhausting him. "We done it, me and you. We got to go to the filth and tell them, mate. We got to."

Ian stared. "You're barking."

"How're we gonna feel when he's sent down for maybe years and years and we're whatever"—Fize searched for words—"free, we're free?"

"Me, I'm going to feel great."

"I'm not. If we don't tell them now, we'd have to then. We can't let the poor sod go down when he never done it. It's out of order."

"Is there any more of this gnat's piss?"

Fize fetched it, flipped the lid off the can. Beer foamed over Ian's jeans.

"Fuck you!" Ian shouted, jumping to his feet.

"It's only beer, for God's sake." Fize was getting angry now. "It'll dry. Listen, we gotta go to them and tell them. Like first thing tomorrow. Like tonight, if you want."

"If I want? Now you can do the listening." Ian approached Fize threateningly, the can in his hand held like a weapon. "You forget all that. Leave it out. It's bollocks, all of it. You better if you want to keep on the right side of me."

Courage came to Fize from somewhere. That which he had dreaded no longer seemed so undoable. "If we tell them, it'll be good for us. They'll do what they call 'take it into account.' We did do it, mate, we did set the place on fire." Fize was aware that Ian had set down his beer can and was standing with his hands closed into fists. "If you won't, I will. I'll go it alone."

"You what?"

Ian's voice was quieter and more menacing than Fize had ever heard it. For some reason he thought back to the evening he had braved Lance and Uncle Gib together, asking for the money for

Gemma's tooth. He had had courage then and it had worked. But of course Ian had been with him then, not against him . . .

"I'll go it alone. I gotta, mate. I gotta live with myself."

"Then I'll have to stop you, won't I?"

Fize saw the knife pulled out of Ian's jeans, the gleam of its blade, which he had thought might be a gun. It was just as lethal a weapon, a small knife with a long, thin blade. The blade glittered in the light from Gemma's table lamp. Fize backed away. They stood confronting each other, the way male animals do, quivering before one of them makes a move. Ian made the knife in his hand shift a little, a teasing movement, pointing at Fize, then letting it droop. He crouched slightly as if getting ready to spring. Fize made a gasping sound in the back of his throat. He snatched up Ian's beer can and flung the contents in his face.

Ian's scream couldn't have been louder if it had been acid Fize had thrown. He swore and scrubbed at his eyes, the knife still clutched in one fist, giving Fize a moment to escape. Fize sprang, kicked over a chair, and tried to open the front door, but his hand was shaking too much to move the latch. He felt the tip of the knife touch his back, right by his spine, and he felt it pulled away as Ian drew his arm back to strike. Twisting round, Fize kicked out, the knife glittering in the air between them. Then, somehow, he stumbled and Ian was upon him.

Fize clutched the upraised arm, forcing it back, and sank his strong, young teeth into the hand that held the knife. Ian yelled and dropped his weapon, giving Fize the chance to scramble to his feet. His mouth full of bitter, iron-tasting blood, he threw himself at the front door once more and this time got it open.

He was out of the flat, running down the concrete stairs, almost at the foot of the first flight when Ian caught up with him. Ian's breathing was terrible, like an engine or a crazed animal's. He grabbed Fize's shoulder, swinging him round, and as he hit out wildly to defend himself, Fize felt that thin blade sink slowly into his chest. Not like a wound but like a blow he felt it, a punch to where he thought his heart was, and then, as his legs buckled and he fell, nothing more.

ABELARD HAD FALLEN asleep on the couch in Gemma's mother's living room. Gemma picked him up and wrapped him in a blanket. It was only nine thirty, but her dad had said he'd take her home in his car if she'd come now. When she was in the backseat and Abelard on her lap— against the law but who would know?—her dad counted out a fifty-pound note, two twenties, and a ten and thrust them into her hand. "For the boy."

"Thanks, Dad, you're a star."

He dropped her at the kerb alongside the yellow concrete wall, and Gemma carried her son up the steps, through the swing doors, and onto the stairs. In later life she never ceased to be thankful that the little boy was fast asleep in her arms when she found what lay on the first landing in a pool of blood. For Abelard's sake, by a superhuman effort, she controlled her scream and it came out only as a gasp. Blood was no longer flowing, she noticed that, her legs trembling. She stepped over the body, let herself into her flat with a shaking hand, and once inside, the boy half-awake and grizzling, she dialled 999.

29

HIS NIGHT PASSED in a series of strange dreams, one following fast on the other, and each more bizarre than the last. Ghosts came into these dreams and reptiles, figurines from the gallery that came to life and walked about while Ella wandered among them, more beautiful and far less sweet and good than she was in life. Chocorange (or Oranchoco), laid mosaically, paved the floor like a cocoa-brown giant's causeway. The dream to wake him up, shivering under his piled blankets and two duvets, was the mermaid in the fishpond. This

369

was no goldfish bowl but water and weeds behind a glass wall as in an aquarium, and the mermaid, with her golden, scaly tail, beating against the glass, had Ella's breasts and Ella's face.

He sweated, soaking the bed. When Carli arrived in the morning, he asked her to change the sheets while he shivered in the next room, wearing a dressing gown with two blankets draped shawl-like over his shoulders. A jug of water and two bottles of the sparkling kind were brought up to him. He wanted a bath but was too weak to attempt it. Dr. Irving arrived at lunchtime, though he hadn't given advance warning of his coming, bringing with him the *Evening Standard.*

"Where's that lovely fiancée of yours? She not looking after you?"

Where anyone else would have said they'd split up, Eugene said, "We are no longer engaged."

"Oh, dear, I'm sorry to hear that. Very sorry. I may as well take your temperature now I'm here."

Eugene submitted to this. His temperature turned out to be 101. "Or something around thirty-eight, I suppose, if you go in for all this Celsius rubbish. I don't suppose you've got much appetite?"

"None."

"Won't do you any harm not to eat. You can do with losing a pound or two. I brought you the evening paper."

"Thanks."

Eugene buried his face in the pillows and the doctor went away, saying, as a parting shot, though Eugene hadn't asked, "No good me giving you antibiotics when it's a virus you've got. Keep drinking the old dihydrogen monoxide, ha-ha."

Later on Eugene picked up the paper, but only glanced at it, enough to see that yet another young man had died in London after being stabbed. Not far from here, maybe half a mile away. He dropped the *Standard* on the floor and gulped down another half a bottle of water. Carli would come back again in the morning.

He felt horribly alone. Tossing and turning, collapsing miserably into a sweaty heap, he dreamed again of Ella, but this time she was dancing in a club with a man Eugene had never seen but whom he somehow recognised as that Joel Something who was the real owner of the 115 pounds. They were dancing cheek to cheek and it was a slow waltz. He woke up groaning, but there was no one to hear him.

WHEN SHE CONTEMPLATED the empty shelves, Ella made up her mind that the books that had filled them were lost to her forever. In a strange way, she wondered if she ever wanted to see those particular books again. They would only remind her of that otherwise happy evening when Eugene had come home and found her about to discover his secret hoard of those wretched sweets. Now she asked herself why she had ever confronted him. She was a doctor— couldn't she recognise the signs of a habit such as his? Had she no understanding how deep such obsessions went with a person as secretive and sensitive as he? Apparently not, and now she was paying the price for it.

Almost for the first time since she became a GP she was wishing she had no need to go to work today. If only she could stay here in bed, turn over, and perhaps go back to sleep. Only just first thing in the morning did she really feel able to sleep soundly, and she recognised this as a sign of incipient depression. The female characters in those books she had left behind at Eugene's, how different they were from her and from most women today. They could stay in bed all day if they wanted to, daydreaming of their happiness or quietly nursing their sorrows. What else had they to do? Women now had to go back to work and carry on resolutely, soldier on, as if nothing had happened.

She got up, showered, dressed, picked up the newspaper off the doormat. Not so much in it about the Notting Hill murder as there had been in the *Standard* last night. The deaths of young men by violence had become almost commonplace. Talbot Road, Notting Hill. She had patients there but not this Feisal Smith. For once there was no eulogy from a relative, no bereaved parent saying he was the best son a mother or father ever had, the kindest, his future the brightest. Briefly, she wondered about Feisal Smith, knifed on a stone staircase, then she forgot him.

Mrs. Khan was her first patient, a highly articulate little girl with her this time. Her rapid translation of her mother's detailed symptoms made Ella think she had a future before her as an interpreter, especially when the child remarked as they were leaving that she spoke Bengali as well and was learning Chinese at school.

"Then make sure you don't miss too many days," Ella couldn't resist saying.

The next to come in was the most glamorous on her list. She always looked as if about to step onto a catwalk. This morning Gemma Wilson wore a black satin trouser suit, and she announced that she was in mourning for her partner. "I expect you've seen about him in the paper. The guy what got stabbed on the stairs. It was me as found him, me and Abelard, only he was asleep and he never saw a thing."

"Gemma, I'm so sorry. What a dreadful thing to happen. How is Abelard?"

"He's fine. He's with Mum. Like I say, he never saw a thing. The thing is, Ella"—it had never occurred to Gemma to call her Dr. Cotswold—"the thing is, I can't sleep and it's wearing me out. I close my eyes and all I see is pictures of my partner laying there in a pool of blood. Can you give me like sleeping pills?"

"Yes, of course I will, Gemma. I'll give you enough for two weeks. It's very easy to get into a habit of taking them and we don't want that."

Ella began writing the prescription. Gemma smoothed the sides of her new, piled-up coiffure with long, white fingers tipped with gleaming black nails, another feature of her mourning. "The fact is, I've been through a lot lately. I mean, there's Fize getting himself knifed, and then there's my lover—I mean, my real lover, Lance Platt—banged up for a crime he never done. It's all taken its toll."

"I'm sure it has," Ella said absently, unsurprised by Gemma's recherché love life. That name Lance Platt rang a bell. Wasn't that the man who had tried to get Eugene's 115-pound find for himself? The man who had been charged with arson and murder?

"That's him," said Gemma, "only he never done it. One in the morning it happened and he wasn't even there." It occurred to her just in time that she had better not say just why he couldn't have been there. "He couldn't sleep—like me—

so he went for a walk. He was like out for his walk up your way, Ella, when they was burning down that house. It's not fair, is it, if he gets sent down for years and years for something he never done?"

"Well, no, of course it isn't. It would be very wrong."

Ella said good-bye to Gemma and to come back if she was still having trouble sleeping after a fortnight. That had been her birthday, her fortieth, the night the house in Blagrove Road burnt down. She hadn't minded about being forty then because she had Eugene, she was going to marry Eugene, and he had been so lovely to her, coming back to bed and wishing her that delightfully old-fashioned "many happy returns of the day." They had made love and she had been so happy and . . . Her next patient came into the room, and Ella, with a silent sigh, asked him what the trouble was.

THE CROWD THAT streamed up the Portobello Road from Notting Hill Gate station and off the number 7 bus were mourners, not shoppers. They were on their way to the funeral of their shepherd. OH, COME, ALL YE FAITHFUL, the sign on the little church welcomed them. It was left to Gilbert Gibson to conduct the service, as the senior elder now Reuben Perkins was gone. Tall and emaciated, he presented a finer figure in the pulpit and while speaking the eulogy than poor Reuben would ever have done, for, as all models know, the thinner you are, the better you look when robed in a flowing gown. Uncle Gib spoke about the years when he and Reuben had "worked together" and emphasised the kindness he had personally received when Reuben and his wife had taken him in after his own house had burnt down.

The service was well attended, for Reuben had been popular, and a good turnout was gratifying to Maybelle, who invited thirty people back to her house for drinks and canapés. Uncle Gib played host, handing round the food and replenishing wineglasses while telling those guests who didn't already know it the tale of the wedding at Cana. When they had all gone and Maybelle was doing the washing up, he sat down at his computer to reply to the latest spate of letters from readers of *The Zebulun*. For almost the first time an e-mail had come to which he could give an approving and encouraging reply. *I see no objection,* he wrote, *to you being joined in Holy Matrimony with the lady of your choice. Second marriage is permitted to a widower and widow. Nor need age be a bar. Remember that eighty is the new fifty so eighty-four is only middle age these days. Why not propose to her today?*

The next one he replied to was from the usual

immoral applicant. Uncle Gib made short work of her, telling her that deceiving her husband into believing he was the father of her new baby would bring hellfire down on her and the innocent child. But his mind wasn't on it. He wasn't able to summon up his usual invective; his thoughts were still on his previous correspondence. Why shouldn't the advice he had given apply equally to himself?

CARLI CAME IN most days, and when she couldn't, she sent her sister Vicki. There was little for them to do beyond changing his sheets and replenishing his water jug, for Eugene had no appetite. His temperature went up every evening in spite of the aspirins he swallowed to maintain it at 98.4. After about a week, when he staggered into the bathroom to have a bath—he was too weak to stand up in the shower cabinet—he weighed himself and found he had lost five pounds. Once this would have pleased him hugely but now he was unable to summon up enthusiasm for anything.

But in the morning he managed to eat two small squares of Marmite toast, which Vicki brought him, and that evening found it possible to swallow a scrambled egg. Next day he had a needed telephone conversation with Dorinda, and later on Dr. Irving arrived, saying breezily that Eugene was obviously on the mend and becoming positively jovial when Carli appeared with two glasses of sherry on a tray. The taste of the amontillado no longer made Eugene feel sick when he sipped it, and after the doctor had gone he ate a slice of chicken breast and a small roast potato.

He came downstairs in his dressing gown. Both girls had gone and wouldn't return till next morning. Sitting in front of the mock but realistic-looking coal fire, he thought how miserable it was to be alone and how desperately he missed Ella, who should be sitting opposite him, telling him about her day and talking about their coming wedding and their future together. He could still only walk slowly but he had managed to come downstairs, so he could make it over to the bookshelves. He picked up one of her books and read on the flyleaf, *To Ella, on your sixteenth birthday, with love from Daddy.* With bowed head he closed it. He had never in his life felt quite so low and sad.

Two weeks after he had first succumbed to this flu or virus or whatever it was, he went back to work, taking a taxi rather than attempting to walk. The gallery had gone on perfectly well without him and Dorinda had sold two water-colours. He sat at his desk and Jackie brought him cups of tea. The great effort he made not to fall asleep failed, but still he made it until five. It was a start and next day was much better. On the

Friday evening he took Dorinda out to dinner, ate little, and wished all the time Ella were sitting opposite him. In the taxi taking him home he thought back to that day when he put off asking her to marry him, when he had actually asked himself if he wanted to get married at all. Had he been out of his mind?

Another empty, lonely weekend, made rather emptier and lonelier because his health had returned and he was beginning to feel well again. He poured himself a glass of wine before sitting down to eat the sandwich he had made for his lunch, but even in his semi-alcoholic days he had always disliked drinking alone. It passed the time, he thought, maybe it would send him to sleep for half the afternoon.

The dreams we have in the daytime are often more vivid and more lingering than those of the night. He was fitter and stronger in the dream than in life, marching along Westbourne Park Road towards the Portobello in search of a pharmacy. In search of Chocorange or Oranchoco. He remembered the pharmacy in Golborne Road and he headed for this, although as is the way of dreams, especially daylight ones, the place he was aiming for was no longer to be found where it should be. Golborne Road had vanished and a great lake had taken its place, its shores paved with the dark brown oval lozenges but magnified to the size of rugby balls. A mermaid surfaced and began to sing and beckon to him like the siren she was. He turned from her and ran, waking himself up.

Sitting up and rubbing his eyes, he thought of the quest in his dream and its purpose. He had been doing what had been a regular feature of his life before the virus struck him, shopping for sugar-free sweets. Not just a regular feature but the whole aim and purpose of life, his controlling obsession, the demon he was in thrall to. Now, as far as he knew, he had none in the house. It was November. The previous weekend the clocks had gone back and darkness had come by four. It was getting dark now but no matter, he must go out and find a shop that sold his fix. The one in Golborne Road itself, perhaps, or the sari lady's or Elixir in Kensington High Street or . . .

He stopped. He thought about what he was doing and realised something. He hadn't tasted or even thought about Chocorange or Oranchoco for more than two weeks. Now when he created one of the sweets in his imagination—once a surefire way of making him long to open a new packet—he felt a small quiver of nausea. He went out into the hall and felt through the pockets of those of his coats and jackets that hung in the cupboard there. He found one, just one, in the right-hand pocket of his leather jacket. The smell of it made his throat rise and he gagged. His reaction to the idea of actually putting it into his mouth, of the touch of it on his tongue, was much the same as it would have been to chewing something scraped off the pavement.

He opened one of the French windows to the garden. Icy air hit his face. A cold breeze had got up, making every branch and bough and twig dip and sway. But still he stood there, breathing deeply. He was over it. His addiction, habit, whatever you liked to call it, was gone. Seven months, excepting a few days' "phasing out," it had been with him, but it had gone. A virus had beaten it and without his knowing that the process was happening. Bathsheba, bathed in a greenish radiance from his neighbours' lights, her blue coat turned to emerald, stared at him from the shelf on the wall, and it seemed to him that her gaze had become mild and even benevolent. "It's gone," he said aloud to her. "It's over." He went back inside, closed the door, locked and bolted it. He should be rejoicing, overjoyed, congratulating himself that he was cured. But all he could think of now was that for this stupid fixation, which flu had had the power to destroy, he had lost Ella. For something so absurd, so base, so easily banished—and for good, forever, as he knew somehow that it would never come back—he had lost her. She was gone as irrevocably as if he had betrayed her with another woman or physically wounded her. For those offences she might have forgiven him, but not for this, not because he hadn't been able to give up sucking sweets for her sake. He had lost her forever.

30

HER FORTIETH BIRTHDAY hadn't been the depressing day she dreaded because Eugene had been with her. Then, in that early morning, when she woke up in the light from the street-lamps to see him coming back to bed, she confidently expected him to be with her for the rest of their lives. She could remember every detail of the brief conversation they had had. He told her what he had seen out of the window, then wished her a happy birthday in that funny old phrase she had last heard when her grandfather used it. "Many happy returns of the day, darling."

She was getting her returns of the day, though not in the way he had meant. That morning and their lovemaking kept coming back to her. His words repeatedly returned, those spoken in the middle of the night and those when he made her breakfast, brought her cards to her that the postman had left, told her about the new car he had bought her, which would be driven round to the house later in the day. Forty had no longer seemed anything to fear but rather the start of the first decade she would spend as Eugene's wife.

Why think of it? Why let it all run round in her head? Because she couldn't help it. Because whatever else she tried to think about, to concentrate on, their conversations, and, worse, their embraces and the real passion she had thought he felt for her as she did for him, kept coming back, and with a fierce intensity. How could he have said the things he had, repeatedly told her he loved her, then callously rejected her for a childish fixation? She didn't know how he could have, only that he had.

Gemma Wilson was back in the medical centre. A fortnight had gone by since Ella had prescribed sleeping tablets and now she wanted more. She had tried to do without them but her worries were keeping her awake. This time Gemma had brought Abelard with her, and Ella, who had known him since he was born, seemed to look at him with new eyes. Had he ever appeared quite so beautiful to her before? He was the perfect blond, blue-eyed infant, his skin pink and white, his body strong and neither plump nor thin. Ella, who had never before given much thought to him except to check on his health, now yearned for him.

Writing a second prescription, her head bent so that Gemma shouldn't see the tears that had come into her eyes, she said, "He's a lovely boy, Gemma, a credit to you."

"Yeah, I know. I love him to bits."

"You're not worrying about him, are you?"

"It's my bloke, it's Lance. They reckon he'll be coming up for trial next month. And he never done that fire, Ella, I know he couldn't have."

"No?"

A cautious look had come into Gemma's face, the kind of look that speaks defensiveness yet a need to confess reprehensible things at no matter what cost. "He wasn't near that house. He was in someone's place in the next street to yours, on the nick if you want to know the truth. It was August fourteen at one in the morning—well, August fifteen by then. Lance never hurt no one but he was on the nick in this lady's house that was away."

And then Ella knew too. Without her usual warning about not getting into pill-taking habits, she handed the prescription to Gemma. She knew what she had to do and she had to do it quickly.

THE FILMS ON offer were all on immoral themes. One was actually called *American Gangster.* All of them made a feature of gangsterdom and sexual licence. Instead of studying house prices in the free or discarded newspapers he picked up, Uncle Gib scanned the cinema pages for film ratings, the number of stars awarded each one by reviewers and what they said about dramatic content. Eventually he chose one showing at the

Electric Cinema in the coming week. It was called *Elizabeth: The Golden Age* and was historical and likely pretty to look at, which was something women liked. Its being set hundreds of years ago had nothing to do with its sexual content, but any excesses would give him the opportunity to air his feelings, comparing the depravity of that era and this one. And this might be no bad thing in his efforts to present himself as a paragon.

This outing was to mark the first stage in his courtship. That was what you did, he remembered from the first time round, you took her to the pictures. And he had chosen the Electric, not only because it was the nearest cinema—after all, there were buses and what his dad had called shank's pony—but because he used to take Ivy there when they were courting. This memory had nothing to do with sentiment. Uncle Gib was essentially a practical man with an eye to the main chance. He knew the Electric. If it had been given a makeover and now comprised three or four theatres instead of just one, if it had been newly decorated, it would still hold no major surprises for him. It stood where it always had, its façade was the same, though now painted turquoise, and he could have found his way to it blindfold. Of course, in the old days you could smoke there—everyone did and some, though not Uncle Gib, smoked marijuana—but for years now the smoking ban operated there, as was lamentably true of every cinema in the United Kingdom and Europe too, for all he knew. But never mind. He could smoke at home, as he was beginning to refer to Maybelle's house. She had even taken up cigarettes herself, a move he saw as a tribute to her guest as a man of discernment.

His invitation was accepted but only after a sign of doubt. "You don't think it's too soon after Reuben's passing, do you, Gilbert?"

"I wouldn't encourage you to do anything what was wrong, now would I?"

"No, that's true." Maybelle struggled with her cigarette, trying to learn the art of inhaling.

"The only thing that bothers me is us living here together under the same roof. A single man and a single woman, I mean. If someone was to write to me at *The Zebulun* that they was doing that, I'd have to advise against it. Maybe I should think of moving out."

"Oh, don't do that, Gilbert," said Maybelle, and coughed.

He said no more. The seed had been planted.

THERE WAS NOTHING to be done about it. Lance Platt must take his chance. Those were Ella's first thoughts. Besides, if she called Eugene, what was to stop him putting the phone down as soon as he knew who it was? She couldn't call him. So her pride was to get in the way of doing what she could to give a man back his freedom? It wasn't so simple. Eugene might have forgotten, he might have made himself forget. He might refuse to do anything about it. She could write to him. This seemed to present insurmountable difficulties. She asked herself how she would begin the letter and how end it, how to refer to the past without letting love creep in or resentment or recriminations, and what she would do if he didn't reply. Surely the chances were that he wouldn't reply. He would tear up the letter and throw away the pieces.

She went home to her depleted and no longer comfortable flat, took a ready meal out of the freezer, and poured herself a glass of wine. Every time she did this it reminded her of having wine with Eugene in the study, and any enjoyment she might have had was lost. How about a broken heart as a cure for alcoholism? Not that she was in danger of either condition, she told herself firmly.

Gemma's anxiety had been at the back of Ella's mind all day. She hardly needed reminding of it, but an item on the BBC six-o'clock news brought it back to the forefront. A man had appeared in court that day, charged with the murder of Feisal Smith, twenty-eight, of Notting Hill, west London. The accused was Ian Pollitt, twenty-seven, of Harlesden, west London, and he was committed for trial and remanded in custody. It had nothing to do with the detention of Lance Platt, she was sure, but it reminded her of Gemma.

Ella switched off the television. She poured her wine down the sink. She knew what she had to do, and it was best done without thinking about it. Hadn't someone in history or a play said that there was nothing good or bad but thinking made it so? She would walk. Even after only half a glass of wine she never drove. It was a mild, damp evening, dark as midnight but bright lights polishing every surface. Although Guy Fawkes Day was past, fireworks were still going off and would go off somewhere every evening for weeks to come. Rockets made their high-pitched whine as they mounted into the dark gray starless sky, bursting into a cascade of red and green sparks.

Most people would have advised her not to walk alone after dark through this part of London, but she knew it well, and the streets were full of people, dozens of them spilling out of the Fat Badger onto the pavement, drinking and laughing. I would like to drink and laugh, she thought, and not be alone.

NO WOMAN HAD ever held Gilbert Gibson's hand. There had never been the occasion to do so. In his day a man and a woman walked arm in arm or separate from each other. He and his friends never shook hands with each other. But they had been sitting in the Electric Cinema for no more than half an hour when he felt Maybelle's hand slipped into his. It was warm and soft and rather plump. His own had been lying on the seat arm between them, and when hers locked into it, quite tightly at first, he moved the two joined hands to rest, not on his thigh or knee, but on the edge of the plush seat.

He could never have said he had been touched or moved by this gesture of Maybelle's. It was a sign, that was all. The film seemed to be holding her interest entirely. She gazed at the colourful activities of Elizabeth's court with rapt attention, her mouth slightly open. It was possibly many years, Uncle Gib thought, since Reuben Perkins had taken her to the pictures. Most likely he, Gilbert Gibson, would never take her again once they were married.

The film held no attractions for him. Films hadn't in the days when he was courting Ivy. For him, reality was the thing, and the rest of the world could keep their stories, their fantasies, and their dreams. All he really wanted was a cigarette, but lighting one would lead to an argument, a row, and eventually his forcible removal. His mind moved purposefully on to a practicable future, free of speculation and baseless hopes. When his house in Blagrove Road was finished, he would let it out in flats. It would make three fine apartments. Uncle Gib grew almost dizzy at the prospect of the money he could make in rents, and when he let out a sort of gasp, Maybelle thought it signified his enjoyment of Cate Blanchett's performance and she squeezed his hand.

THE FIREWORKS REMINDED Eugene of his own childhood, when you had been able to buy rockets and Catherine wheels and Prince of Wales feathers without age restriction and no one tried to stop seven-year-olds from setting them off themselves. He had bought his off a stall in the Portobello Road between Cambridge Gardens and Chesterton Road a long way up from his father's shop. These seemed to be coming from somewhere up there, red and dazzling white sparks falling in showers over those streets, Talbot Road, Golborne Road, and Powis Square, which, in his youth, his mother told him to keep away from. They were infested (her word) with hippies and flower people and immigrants from goodness knew where. Now the hippies had grown old or died and the immigrants' children were respectable executives who owned smart houses in those same streets with fuchsia and taupe front doors and window boxes full of petunias.

He watched the fireworks from his bedroom window, wondering at himself for doing something so unlikely. But now almost everything he did was out of character from this harking back to the past to staying in every evening, mooning dismally about what might have been. He turned away. The pyrotechnics were over. Whoever had produced this display had run out of rockets. Eugene went downstairs wondering what nasty ready meal to take out of the freezer or if just not to eat at all might be the better option. It was strange, all of it, inexplicable, because when Ella had been here with him, he did most of the cooking. In his drinking days he would have got through a bottle of wine instead and in the Chocorange era consumed a packetful. He was standing in the kitchen thinking how pointless it was to eat if you were not hungry when the door-bell rang.

On Halloween, he had answered the door to three teenagers, who, when he refused them money and told them to go away, threatened to break his windows. Far from being intimidated, he had said he was calling the police and picked up his mobile. They had fled, he pursuing them to the gate. Since then he had made it a rule never to answer the door after dark unless he expected a caller, and the dark came early now. But there had been no callers. He went up to the drawing-room window from which he could see the front path, though not the porch and doorstep. The bell rang again.

He waited. Whoever it was had given up. Down the dark path a woman was walking away. She turned her head to look back and he saw it was Ella. He ran to the door and flung it open.

In a manner quite unlike him he shouted, "Ella!"

"Gene," she said, and took a few steps towards him.

He gasped, "Come in. Please do come in. Don't go away."

"All right. I won't."

They confronted each other in the hall and Eugene closed the door. Ella looked back at the door as if things were moving faster than she wanted.

"Take your coat off, please. Please let me take your coat."

"I didn't mean to stay."

"Oh, Ella, Ella," he said, his voice full of longing.

"I came to ask you to go to the police."

"To do what? Don't stand there, not here, come in. Please come in."

She walked ahead of him into the drawing room but hesitantly, as if she had never been there before. At a loss for words, he simply gazed at her. Like him, she had lost weight, and like him, she looked distraught, disoriented, shattered. He closed the door, opened it again, and ran out into the hall, where he bolted the front door, came back, his hands spread in a despairing gesture.

"What are you doing?"

"I don't know. Shutting you in, I think. Making you my prisoner."

She did the only thing which, at that moment, could have made him happy. She began to laugh. A moment of stillness passed, then his arms were round her and she was pressed closely against him.

"I have been the most monstrous fool," he said, "but I don't think I've done anything against the law, have I?"

"Against the law? Oh, I see. Me asking you to go to the police, you mean." She pulled him onto the sofa and, still holding him, told him about Lance Platt, and the fire and Gemma.

"Oh, yes, I saw him," Eugene said. "It was your birthday, it was two thirty in the morning. And what's more I saw the first flames go up from that burning house at the same time. I'll go to the police tomorrow."

"Let's go now, Gene."

"Oh, my darling, anything, anything you want, we'll go anywhere as long as you'll promise to come back here with me and never go away again."

Neither of them, then or later, said a word about sugar-free sweets, though next day when he had left for the gallery, Ella searched the house and satisfied herself that no more had been bought to replace those she had burnt in the garden. She went through the pockets of all his coats and jackets, finding nothing, but laughing at the thought of hunting for Chocorange where another woman might look for love letters.

But that evening Eugene unbolted the door, they put on coats it was too mild to need, and walked hand in hand across the Portobello Road past the Earl of Lonsdale, along Kensington Park Gardens and so to Ladbroke Grove where stands the imposing and rather grand police station.

31

THE PRESENCE OF Lance Platt in Chepstow Villas on the night of August 14 was never connected with the theft of Elizabeth Cherry's jewellery. No one told him why not and enquiring about it could lead to no good. It would only be sticking his neck out. Elizabeth's insurance company had paid up, and Ella, the only person to be told about it, had completely forgotten that aspect of Gemma's story.

As soon as his alibi was accepted and he was released from prison, Lance moved in with Gemma. She nagged him so much about his work-free state that this time, instead of hitting her, he got a job. At the next interview he was offered as a Jobseeker he behaved properly, answered politely, and said thank you very much when offered a position as assistant in a cut-price hardware shop in the Portobello Road. The owner pays less than the minimum wage, which is illegal, but he tells Lance that if he doesn't like it, there will be plenty of people from Romania and Bulgaria who will.

A new house has been built at the end of Blagrove Road, but Uncle Gib, as he had foreseen, has never moved into it. After waiting a decent interval of six months, he and Maybelle were married in the Church of the Children of Zebulun and held their reception in the Fat Badger. Uncle Gib has become the new shepherd of the Children of Zebulun and is deeply respected by his congregation. The pressure of work is heavy, and he has had to give up his Agony Uncle activities, but much of what he used to say he preaches about from the pulpit. The new house has a bathroom on each floor, and each floor is let as a separate flat. The area is prestigious and Uncle Gib charges accordingly. He tells prospective tenants demurring at exorbitant rents that if they don't like the heat to get out of the kitchen.

Instead of the elaborate affair Eugene once wanted, he and Ella were married quietly with her sister and his brother as witnesses, the bride wearing what the local paper called "a simple afternoon dress." Ella's baby is expected in

August, her due date is the fifteenth, her forty-first birthday, that historic date that gave Lance his freedom.

Joel Roseman has become Mithras and seems to be happier in his new identity than he ever was as himself. He lives with his parents in Hampstead Garden Suburb, where Morris Stemmer treats him with kindness and consideration, and Wendy with timorous love. Joel's father could perhaps never have been reconciled to the son who let his daughter drown, but Mithras is a different person, sunny-tempered, even playful. He loves the light and keeps his bed lamp on all night. His parents have got over the embarrassment they used to feel when he talks about the city from which he is a wistful exile, its towers glittering in the sun, its wide boulevards and its white walls on which angels sit and gaze at the broad, shining river.

Undine in a Goldfish Bowl has lost its attractions for Morris Stemmer since his son came back in his new avatar. Morris tried to sell it back to Eugene, but Ella's husband was unable to afford the exorbitant price he was asking and eventually got elsewhere. Anxious about the coming birth of his child, Eugene succumbed and bought a single packet of Oranchoco in the Golborne Road pharmacy. It lasted him a fortnight; he threw the last two sweets away and has had no compulsion to buy another.

• • •

THE PORTOBELLO ROAD changes little. There is talk of Woolworth disappearing and a tower block of flats with car park going up in its place, rumours too of arcades scheduled to be converted into mews to satisfy the demand for more houses. Some say the pubs are to be renamed because no one knows who the Earl of Lonsdale was, still less the Prince Bonaparte, and those wanting change favour that cliché name the Slug and Lettuce. But there are always rumours and mostly they come to nothing.

On Saturday mornings the young pour out of Notting Hill Gate tube station and off the number 7 bus and the number 23, on their way to spend their week's wages at the stalls and in the shops, on soap and beads and pashminas and herbs and all the perfumes of Arabia. To sit at the pavement tables drinking cappuccinos and lattes and chardonnay. The old people come with their shopping trolleys because they have always come, because, if you live around there, the Portobello Road is where you do your shopping. The graffitists come and the pickpockets and the serious thieves. Prudent shopkeepers pull down metal grilles over their windows before they go home for the night.

And in the deep of the night all is silent while the centipede street draws breath and prepares for another day.

About the Author

Ruth Rendell has won numerous awards, including three Edgars, the highest accolade from Mystery Writers of America, as well as three Gold Daggers, a Silver Dagger, and a Diamond Dagger for outstanding contribution to the genre from England's prestigious Crime Writers' Association. A member of the House of Lords, she lives in London.

Center Point Publishing

600 Brooks Road ● PO Box 1
Thorndike ME 04986-0001 USA

(207) 568-3717

US & Canada:
1 800 929-9108
www.centerpointlargeprint.com